dedication

I'm dedicating this book to true friends. Without them, our
souls would perish.

also by
B.B. REID

PART ONE

Secrets

prologue

The Pawn

THE COOL BREEZE FROM THE OCEAN SLAMMED INTO MY ACHING chest the moment I burst through the door. The wind carried with it the salt and water from the sea, blending in with my tears.

How could he?

There were murmurs and whispers and a few laughs as my former classmates looked on, and I could only guess what they were all thinking.

Had she *actually* believed him when he said he loved her?

Yes. I had.

I foolishly believed every word that passed through his lips from the moment he first pressed them against mine. How could someone who kissed so beautifully tell such ugly lies? I looked to the sky as if it had the answers. All I found was the full moon and its callous glow shining down on me like a spotlight. *Here she is*, it seemed to say, the fool who thought Vaughn Rees had a heart and wouldn't break hers.

"Tyra!"

Hearing my name shouted over the music, I rushed down the wooden stairs. I never realized before now how many there were. The stilts the blue beach house sat on were fourteen feet high to protect from flooding. Somehow, despite my blurry vision, I managed not to fall. A broken neck was all I needed to match my broken heart. The moment my sandaled feet touched the sand, I looked around in desperation. The parking lot would be the first place my friends would check.

Not ready to face my devastation, I slipped into the shadows underneath the house. I couldn't outrun them, so I'd hide until they gave up—*if* they gave up. I held my breath while my tears flowed freely. A moment later, the obscure figures of my friends darted past where I was hiding.

They'd witnessed everything.

Vaughn's betrayal.

My humiliation.

And the bitch who'd stolen everything from me.

My cheeks heated in shame as I recalled how I had turned and ran in defeat. I should have stayed and killed them both. Hindsight really was twenty-twenty.

Swallowing the sob that threatened to spill, I leaned into one of the stilts, wrapping my arms around the beam. With my forehead resting against the cold, damp wood, I closed my eyes. It was the only thing keeping my knees from buckling.

Vaughn had warned me. A year ago and almost every day since, he told me that we could never be, but my arrogance hadn't allowed me to believe him. That and the way his eyes defied the words his lips had spouted.

I'd chosen to listen to the teachings that a person's actions spoke louder than words. So, naïvely, I clung to hope. And tonight, Vaughn had shown me the truth.

Seeing him with her, touching her, giving her what only should have belonged to me was more proof than anyone could deny. And the look in his eyes when he finally noticed me witnessing it all… I hugged the sturdy wood tighter when I felt pieces of my heart tumble into the rage building in my gut. As much as it burned, it was still just an ember. Only time would tell when the fire would finally roar. My stomach was twisted in a knot so tight I feared, any moment now, I'd break in half. It was inevitable, wasn't it?

I was inhaling the salted air when behind me, I heard the

soft crunch of sand. I froze, humiliated again that he'd caught me like this—pathetically weeping and irreparably shattered. I didn't have to turn to know it was him. I hadn't made a sound. The darkness underneath the house cloaked me entirely. Yet it still didn't matter.

From the moment our gazes first connected, Vaughn and I became a siren's song. We would always be drawn.

"I'm sorry you had to see that."

With my eyes still closed, I pictured him with his hands tucked inside his jeans, his cold gaze assessing and calculating. Like everyone else, I'd mistaken that look for boredom, but Vaughn was never as disinterested as he was careful. Months of allowing me to hold him close, and I had yet to find out why. I realized then that as much as Vaughn had let me in, I'd only ever had one foot in the door.

"But you're not—" I squeezed my closed eyes tighter, hating the way my voice broke and how it barely carried over the sound of the waves crashing in the ocean or the music playing from the beach house above us. I still couldn't find the courage to turn around. "You're not sorry you did it?"

"No."

"And when you said you loved me…are you sorry for that, too?"

It took a long time for him to answer, long enough for hope to creep its way back in and long enough for Vaughn to crush it with a single word. "Yes."

"Why should I believe you?" I asked anyway. It was weird, wasn't it? Odd that I could argue his point after catching him with his pants down and his dick inside—I dug my fingernails into the wood, ignoring the pain. It was more than weird. It was pathetic.

Vaughn sighed, and my guess was because I wouldn't take the hint he was waving around on a sign the size of a billboard with flashing lights so bright they blinded. Maybe I was still too head over heels to see it. He might not have meant it when he said he loved me, but I had. Love didn't just fade the moment the other pushed the big red "abort" button. Instead, you're left standing alone in the place that had once been your Eden and was now your own personal hell.

"I'm bored, Tyra. I don't know how else to put it."

"So, you put it inside of that bitch instead?" My voice had become granite, and if I weren't clinging to this fucking beam as if it were a life raft, I would have patted myself on the back. I felt him closing in—felt his warmth, the strength of his muscles, and even the rhythm of his heart as if he'd taken me in his arms and made it all better.

If only he would.

I pressed my fists against the wood.

"Look at me," he demanded as if he had the right.

I shook my head, denying him. I was afraid that if I did look at him, I'd see that his heart was no longer mine. A moment later, I felt his hands on my shoulders, gently turning me to face him.

"I made a mistake," he said once he'd captured my gaze.

I knew he wasn't talking about tonight. Just as my heart, on its last desperate stitch, begin to splinter, I felt the telling tap of his finger on my shoulder. It was subtle, like a phantom touch, only it was very much real. Immediately, I started to melt into the comfort of his strong arms. The demand to know why he was doing this was poised on my lips when I felt the bite of his fingers keeping me at bay.

His rejection rippled through me, and I no longer cared about his reasons. I closed my eyes, hating him, and wondering how many times I'd have to disgrace myself. How many before I accepted that this was real?

Vaughn and I were over.

But then...how could something that never truly started end?

While Vaughn had been sure to remind me that we weren't exclusive, he'd often forgotten that fact himself. Once he'd sunk his teeth into me, it became a full-time job scaring off the guys at our school, and when he wasn't savagely defending his territory, he was attending to my every need. There'd been no time or desire for anyone else.

Until now.

Pushing him away, I forced my spine to straighten. "It took you a *year* to figure that out?"

Callously, he shrugged, and I realized the glow that usually shone from his green eyes was gone. The wind ruffled his light-brown hair as the ache to run my fingers through it—as I had many times before—was greater than the pain in my chest.

"I was looking for something different, and until now, you provided that."

"You mean up until I let you—" I choked on the words caught in my throat. God, why had I given him so much? I'd waited a year, and still, it wasn't enough. Swallowing past the lump, I tried again. "Until I let you fuck me."

His eyes quickly narrowed. "Let's not forget," he said slowly and with a touch of cruelty, "you begged me not to stop."

"I thought maybe—" I stopped, wondering if it was wise to admit just how stupid I'd been. Vaughn's eyebrow perked, daring me to continue. "I thought maybe you'd change your mind." Summer's end had been rapidly approaching, and I'd never been more desperate. I believed in the idea of soulmates, and from the moment Vaughn first kissed me, I knew he was mine. That kiss was the reason I stopped fighting his pursuit at the start of my senior year.

Vaughn obviously didn't feel the same, judging by the way his body stiffened and nostrils flared at my confession. "You mean you thought you could manipulate my feelings with sex?" If possible, his tone became even colder than before. "While you were a phenomenal fuck, Bradley, no pussy is that good."

I looked away, unable to meet his gaze, my tone despondent when I spoke. "I guess it doesn't matter now."

"Finally, something we can agree on," he immediately spat. "No, it doesn't matter now."

I never realized before how much power Vaughn had over me. For a moment, we listened to the waves crash. For a moment, I wanted to walk into the sea and let them drown me.

"Just tell me one thing," I urged as a lone tear slipped down my cheek. I vowed that it would be the last I shed over him. Vaughn said nothing while he waited. "Of all the girls you could have screwed, why did it have to be *her?*"

chapter one

The Pawn

One month ago

"**D**on't go."

Despite my shift starting in ten minutes, I pressed myself harder into Vaughn's lap. I could feel his hard dick through his gray sweatpants, and it was begging me to throw caution to the wind. It would be ten times harder to walk away from Vaughn right now than it would be to walk away from the job I've had since I was fifteen.

"Stay with me," he continued to plead between kisses.

It was his fault for insisting he drive me to work when I had my own car and then being bold enough to do it without a shirt. During the entire fifteen-minute drive, I kept stealing peeks at his bare chest, ripped arms, and that crazy six-pack of his until he caught me ogling and pulled the car over. We ended up making out on the side of the forest-lined road for twenty minutes.

"I can't," I whined even though I really wanted to stay. I recognized the look in his eyes. Vaughn wanted to play, and I was more than eager to be his mate. In the blink of an eye, we'd gone from strangers to friends to something we weren't allowed to put a label on. Still, it was a long way from him being a god among men—one that I had secretly pined for from a safe distance.

With a sigh, I returned to the quilted leather passenger seat of the Aventador. The car was worth over four-hundred grand,

and I wondered about the man brave enough to buy his teenage son a Lamborghini. With pursed lips, I realized the only thing the star quarterback loved more than football was this car, so there was little chance of anything happening to it. Deciding not to go down that road, I turned to face the green-eyed boy who kept my stomach in knots. Although—after raking my gaze over his broad shoulders—I realized using the term *boy* to describe Vaughn was a straight-up felony.

"I need to save as much money as I can," I reasoned when Vaughn gripped the steering wheel in frustration. "I don't know how long it will be before I find something in Cambridge."

I'd gotten accepted into Harvard, my life-long dream, yet, somehow, I couldn't muster the excitement that was expected. All I could think about was the distance it would put between Vaughn and me—however much. Everyone knew he'd gotten offers to play at several schools, but he'd been tight-lipped for some reason about the one he'd chosen.

Vaughn said nothing as he started the engine and steered the foreign car back onto the road. Just like a spoiled prince used to getting everything he wanted, Vaughn was pissed. I could feel the sweat we'd worked up drying as my skin suddenly cooled. How much longer could he go without? Overnight, Vaughn had gone from having a little too much sex to none at all. He'd been patient, but I wondered if he was reaching the end of his rope.

Five minutes later, we were pulling into the parking lot of the coffee shop where I worked, and he still hadn't said a word. Rather than continue this guessing game, I took a deep breath, knowing the risk I was taking. He'd always shut down whenever the subject came up.

"Speaking of school," I started and almost lost my nerve when I felt his gaze. How was it possible that, after nine and a half months, he could still send the butterflies in my stomach soaring? "Have you decided who you're going to play for?"

Vaughn didn't immediately look away. In fact, he stared at

me long and hard until I began to squirm in his passenger seat and not for any of the usual reasons. When he finally, mercifully looked away, I could see the muscle in his cheek ticking.

And just as I was about to give up and flee his car, he surprised me with a curt but quiet "Yes." Dread pooled in my gut because he didn't seem happy about it, which left only one possible reason.

"How far away is it?"

"Far."

The ringing in my ears could only have been caused by the deafening sound of my heart dropping to my feet.

"Oh."

The silence that fell over the car made it feel as if we were the last two people on earth. Vaughn would be hundreds, maybe thousands of miles away. How long before the feelings he wouldn't admit to having faded?

"Is that why you kept it a secret?"

Closing his eyes, he rested his head against the seat. "Yes," he answered easily, though his voice sounded strained.

My gaze dropped to his lap, where his right hand rested, in time to see his finger tap his thigh. It hadn't taken me long at all to learn his tells.

He's lying.

But about what? The distance or the reason he'd kept it a secret in the first place?

Checking my watch, I realized my shift had already started. Before Vaughn, I'd never been late or missed a day of work. Now I was skating on thin ice and one tardy away from being fired. What else was I risking for a boy who kept secrets and lied about the reasons?

"I have to go."

I quickly lifted open the scissor door, and my irritation skyrocketed when I realized I wouldn't be able to slam it behind me.

This day just keeps getting worse.

I felt Vaughn's gaze tracking me as I stormed inside, but I didn't dare look back. Macchicino, the owner's indulgent amalgamation of macchiato and cappuccino, was yet another over-priced pretentious coffee shop. Thanks to all the tables and booths doubling as comfortable workspaces, Macchicino stole a lot of business from Starbucks down the street. The only things not painted either black or gray were the lightbulbs, and that included the fake plants and the exposed beams in the ceiling. It made the millennials who frequented feel posh while the boomers thought of themselves as hip.

I made eye contact with Terry, who pointedly checked the clock on the wall before giving me a dirty look and disappearing in the back. Thankfully, his office, an old desk pushed against the wall near the supply shelves, was where he spent most of *his* shift. I was only four minutes late, but with my recent track record, I might as well have been forty. Relieved to see that we weren't too busy, I quickly waved to my coworkers before ducking inside the bathroom. Even though I was late, I needed a minute to clear my head, or else I'd be no good to anyone.

Why was Vaughn lying to me?

It had taken me nearly a year to get my head out of the clouds, and I almost wished I could shove it back up there. Impossible. No way could I ignore all the questions flooding my mind now. Questions such as why Vaughn hadn't introduced me to his parents. Could it be because of the rumors about his father being a crook? If they were true, then I guess I could understand why Vaughn wasn't eager to introduce us, but what about his mother? Where was she, and why does Vaughn never mention her? All I knew about her was that her ancestors founded Blackwood Keep.

Sighing, I closed the bathroom door behind me and started to flip the lock when the door was pushed open. Before I knew what was happening, Vaughn had forced his way in and had locked us both inside.

"What are you doing? If my boss sees you, he's—"

"What is the number one rule?" he inquired—as if I weren't in the middle of speaking.

"I—what?"

"What. Is. The. Rule?" With each word, he'd taken a step until I was trapped between his warm body and the cold porcelain of the bathroom's lone sink. Without warning, he lifted me onto the edge, bringing us eye level and leaving his hands on my hips. I bet he knew just how hard I found it to be annoyed with him when he touched me. I was already short of breath and wanting to run my hands down his chest and maybe find out if he was still hard underneath his sweats. As a scientist, I found Vaughn to be a most impressive specimen.

"You first," I shot back. His brows dipped in confusion, so I decided to help him out. "Tell me why you're lying to me when I specifically asked you not to."

I expected for him to storm out or maybe even deny it. I wasn't prepared for him to rest his sweaty forehead against mine and exhale. "You're too smart for your own good. You know that?"

That was debatable. At least when Vaughn was around. Needing to touch him, I gave in and rested my shaking hands against his warm chest and felt his heart pounding underneath the muscle there.

"You're just used to airheads."

If I were a genius, I would have started asking questions months ago.

He chuckled and then squeezed my hips before lifting his head. He suddenly looked serious again, which made me gulp. Vaughn could be so…dominant, and at times, a little more than I could handle. "What's my rule?"

I bit my lip with indecision. On the one hand, I wanted to remain defiant. On the other, I knew how important this was to him. Once again, I just didn't know why. "Always kiss you hello and goodbye," I eventually whispered.

He remained silent, keeping our gazes locked, waiting. After a beat too long, I gave in—as I always did when it came to him—and kissed his soft lips. Like an asshole, he didn't kiss me back, so I dug my nails into his shoulders, determined to win him over. After the third press of my lips, he gave in with a groan, deepening the kiss. I wasn't sure how long we remained locked, but it took several hard knocks on the door to break us apart. By then, I had my hand in his sweats, toying with the ring piercing his dick while Vaughn had slyly slipped his hand underneath my collared shirt, groping my boob.

That frustrated gleam in his eye was back, and my gaze dropped to the floor because I wasn't quite sure I was ready to give him what he wanted. Sure, we'd done stuff, but it was no longer enough… for both us.

So why couldn't I take the plunge?

Vaughn stepped from between my thighs and ripped open the bathroom door before glaring down at whoever had been brave enough to disturb us.

"What do you want?" he snapped.

"Excuse me, sir, but we can't serve you without a shirt. I'm going to have to ask you to leave."

Shit, shit, shit. I quickly hopped down from the sink at the sound of my boss's voice and pushed my way past Vaughn. As soon as my gaze connected with Terry's, I knew there was no way I could explain why I'd been held up in the bathroom with my shirtless friend-with-partial-benefits for the past…

My gaze darted to the clock on the wall.

Twenty minutes.

I was so fucking fired.

If looks could kill, Vaughn would be six feet under instead of fighting back a grin as he sped out the parking lot with me riding shotgun. Terry hadn't fired me, but he did send me home.

For *two whole weeks.*

Irritated, I bounced my legs as I mentally calculated how much money I'd miss out on while I sat at home twiddling my thumbs. The only upside was that now I wouldn't have to miss Four's race again. I'd only seen my best friend race once, which was six months ago, but it had been all I needed to become a fan for life. Now that we'd graduated and she was free of her mother's tyranny, she was on a mission to get her license and race professionally and, not to mention, *legally.* Unfortunately, I hadn't been able to attend her first pro-am race last weekend because Terry was on another one of his rampages and wouldn't let me have the weekend off.

Feeling strong fingers curl around my own, I abandoned my thoughts and found Vaughn staring at me while we waited at a red light. I frowned when I recognized the street. We were heading in the opposite direction of my house. "Where are you taking me?"

"The Manor."

My lips curved because it seemed Four's nickname for the McNamara's' mansion was catching on. I briefly pondered telling Vaughn that we've been calling the monstrosity he lived in "The Castle" because, well…it looked eerily similar to the palaces you'd find in medieval times.

Obviously, his family held themselves in pretty high regard. My stomach flipped, wondering about the day I'd eventually meet them. *If* that day ever came, that is.

The light turned green, and once he was busy focusing on the road, I freed my hand from his and slid it inside the pocket of his sweats. I rolled my eyes when his lips split into a dirty grin.

"Now you're talking, Ty-ty."

His smile fell when, instead of reaching for his dick, I grabbed his wallet before sitting back and flipping it open.

Thumbing through the fifties and hundreds, I counted out two weeks' worth of pay plus overtime before chucking his wallet, which was significantly lighter now, back into his lap.

With a smirk, he tossed the leather billfold onto the dash. Then he rested his hand on my thigh in ownership and sped all the way to our friends.

chapter two

The Prince

"So I guess you two made up," Tyra observed with her arms crossed. She was currently standing over Jamie and Bee, who were cuddled on the couch. It was so natural no one would suspect they'd spent four years with an ocean between them and the last year hating each other.

"Yeah, and I know you're disappointed because you and I can never fool around now, but I hope we can still be friends," Jamie implored. Feeling my glare, he glanced my way and winked.

Jackass.

"Actually, I thought she could do better."

Four and Lou rushed inside the family room before Jamie could retort, so he settled for flipping her off while Bee's attention was diverted.

"We're missing a couple of assholes," Jamie announced as he looked around. "Where's Wren and Ever?"

"Wren is…gone again," Lou supplied with a subtle lift of her chin designed to fool us into thinking she didn't care. "Ever was right behind us, but then his old man asked to speak to him in his office. Does anyone know what that's about? Moneybags did not seem like a happy camper."

In the blink of an eye, the playful expression on Jamie's face disappeared. Smooth as a button, he lifted his arm from around Bee's shoulder, stood, and slipped from the room. Yeah, he definitely knew something. And because I knew him so well, I didn't have to wonder for long if he was behind it.

The girls had already forgotten I was even in the room as they talked, so I took advantage of their distraction and followed Jamie into the hall. I saw him rushing through a set of double doors, and I started after him. Mr. McNamara's office was on the farthest end of the west wing, which meant we'd have to pass through the gallery, grand foyer, and library to reach it.

Jamie, who had his hand wrapped around one of the knobs, didn't seem at all surprised when he glanced over his shoulder and found me standing there. With a finger to his lips in warning, he pushed inside, leaving the door open enough for me to hear the voice of Evelyn McNamara—Ever's mom.

"Son, there's something you should know."

"Just a minute," Mr. McNamara interrupted. There was a pause, and then, "Jamie, we could use some privacy."

"I'd say you've had enough of it for eighteen years." Through the crack, I could see Jamie defiantly cross the room and then lean against the wall between two floor-to-ceiling windows. "Proceed," he said once he'd gotten comfortable.

I could just make out the resigned sigh of his uncle before Mrs. McNamara began speaking again. "It's about your father," she announced. The way her gentle voice shook, I knew whatever secret she was about to divulge wasn't going to be good and that Jamie knew exactly what that was. "I don't quite know how best to say this, but Thomas isn't…well, he isn't your real father, dear."

Unable to see the expression of anyone else in that room, I focused on Jamie after too much time had passed in a silence so complete, I swore I could hear the grandfather clock ticking down the hall. Judging by the dip in Jamie's brows, he felt as confused as I was, although for different reasons.

Ever still hadn't spoken.

Anyone else would have been sputtering in confusion, spouting questions, and making demands. I knew that had it been me standing in that room instead of Ever, there'd be at least one hole in the wall by now.

Say something! I silently urged my best friend.

As if hearing my internal plea, Ever's voice, dripping sarcasm and venom, finally filled the room. "It's bad enough you lied to me, but to believe I hadn't already figured that out is insulting to my intelligence. I took an elective in Human Anatomy and passed with flying colors."

"We should have told you sooner," his not-real-father admitted. The sorrow in his voice couldn't be mistaken. It couldn't have been easy to acknowledge that the son he raised since he was a baby wasn't truly his. "It was my idea to keep it a secret, and it was my ego that caused your mother to leave. I'm sorry, son. I take responsibility. For all of it."

"Should you be calling me that?" Ever shot back, causing Jamie and me to wince.

Damn.

"You are still my son." The sharp edge of Mr. McNamara's tone left no room for argument. Unfortunately, Ever had never been easily cowed.

"I was never your son. Isn't that why we're in this room?"

I started to push in to get my best friend the hell out of there before he said something he could never take back. Jamie seemed to read my mind, meeting my gaze through the crack of the door. The subtle shake of his head kept me at bay. Whatever was happening here needed to play out, and I could tell by the nervous look in Jamie's brown eyes that the McNamaras were far from done.

A small sound behind me had me spinning around, and I barely suppressed a groan when the girls filed into the library one by one. Quiet as a mouse, I quickly moved from the door to meet them in the middle of the room.

"What's going on?" Tyra whispered.

I was grateful that her instincts were sharp enough to sense that none of us were supposed to be here. I gave her a look, letting her know that it wasn't good, and I'd fill her in later. Over the months, we'd been able to establish a silent line of communication that apparently still had its kinks. Tyra had deftly stepped around me and made her way to the door, despite my dismissal, with Lou and Bee hot on her heels. Like Jamie, Four hadn't hesitated to slip inside the office.

At least she left the door cracked.

"Four, could you give us a minute?" Mr. McNamara requested.

Like Jamie, she refused to leave. "What's going on?"

This time, Evelyn was the one to speak, and her voice was surprisingly chilly. I'd only ever known Mrs. McNamara to be warm and kind. "We're speaking to our son about a *private family* matter. He'll be with you shortly," she assured Four dismissively.

I guess her propensity for kindness made an exception for the daughter of the woman her husband was sleeping with. I was sure that if circumstances had been different, Evelyn would have adored Four. We all did despite her being nothing but trouble since she came to Blackwood Keep.

"She stays," Ever dictated. "Or I go."

"Sweetheart," Mrs. McNamara attempted to gently reason, "this situation is more delicate than you realize. We're only thinking of you and what could happen if this information falls into the wrong hands."

I frowned at that because… *Dramatic much?*

"I also passed English with flying colors," Ever retorted slowly, "so I'm sure you understood me the first time. She stays, or I go."

Being the sickeningly sweet good girl that Tyra was, she released a squeal of shock at Ever's blatant defiance.

"What was that?" Mr. McNamara inquired.

"Nothing," Jamie quickly lied. "Just get on with it."

Coming to stand behind Tyra, I placed my hand over

her mouth before bending low to whisper in her ear. "Quiet, pip-squeak."

Eyes wide and apologetic, she nodded obediently, and I rewarded her with a kiss on her cheek. Lou and Bee pretended to gag at my display of affection, and I rolled my eyes to the ceiling, praying we weren't caught before the shit hit the fan.

"There's more," Mr. McNamara announced. I could hear the creak of leather and imagined him shifting awkwardly in his desk chair. "Your biological father is Sean Kelly, the man you were named after." If Ever was surprised by the news, he sure as shit didn't express it. Clearing his throat, Thomas started again. "As you know, we were best friends—"

Jamie snorted at that before his uncle could finish, and I wondered what he knew but wisely wouldn't divulge himself.

"But we drifted apart," Thomas continued as if Jamie hadn't rudely interrupted. "It was years before we saw each other again, and even then, it must have been written in the stars because…" He stopped, and I wished I could see the expression on Thomas McNamara's face that caused such a weighted silence.

"Because he saved me from…from being raped in an alley," Mrs. McNamara finished for him. "After Sean scared those guys away, he took me to the hospital and insisted on waiting with me. He was still there when your father"—she paused at that as if unsure before continuing in a firmer tone—"when your father showed up with your Aunt Dilwen and Uncle Douglas."

"It was the shock of my life," Mr. McNamara admitted much easier than he did telling his son that his mother had almost been raped. "I'd convinced myself that he was dead. No one had heard from him in over a decade. Not even his parents."

"I admit I was a little captivated by him," Mrs. McNamara said shyly. "After what Sean saved me from enduring, it was easy to think of him as a hero from a storybook. He was so dashing and brave. I thought I'd found my prince." No one said anything while Evelyn attempted to reign in her emotions enough to continue.

"These fantasies were the reason why I didn't listen to Thomas when he warned me away from Sean. I-I assumed he was jealous."

"Of who?" Jamie casually inquired. "You or him?"

Collectively, every heart within hearing distance, including mine, stopped.

"Jameson, not another word," his uncle warned in a low voice.

The demand went through one of Jamie's ears and out the other. "I said the truth, the whole truth, and nothing but the truth or else I'm walking," he shot back angrily. "Now tell your fucking son that you were fucking his father!"

At this juncture, I was sure even the jaws of the mice hiding in the walls dropped.

This was getting out of hand fast, and instinct told me it was about to get even uglier. Jamie always had a hard time controlling his emotions, which meant someone needed to intervene before the entire goddamn train derailed.

My gaze connected with Bee over Tyra's head and a silent war ensued that ended with her exhaling and pushing inside the office. She headed straight for Jamie and started tugging on his tatted arm. If the occupants of the room were surprised by her timing and presence, none of them felt the need to express it. They were all too grateful she'd been there to intervene. "Maybe you should come with me," Bee gently suggested.

"Yes, I think that's a good idea," his uncle readily agreed.

"I'm not going anywhere," Jamie denied while crossing his arms and ignoring Bee. "You were saying," he added as if he hadn't just outed his uncle while dropping an atomic bomb on his cousin.

"Maybe we should call his mother," his aunt suggested.

"Call my mother?" Jamie mocked. "What am I, five?"

"Right now, you're acting like it," Bee snapped.

Jamie glared down at her, but he should have known better than to think Bee would back down. "Fine, fuck it. I won't say another word." Each of us, including the mice, released a sigh of relief. "But no more bullshit," he warned his uncle. Relaxing against the wall with his girl by his side, he turned his head to broodily stare out the windows. If the situation weren't so serious, I would have laughed.

After a beat, Mr. McNamara was the one to break the tense silence. "If it's all right with you, Ever, the rest of your friends should come in rather than we pretend they aren't listening behind the door."

Startled, Tyra, Lou, and I made eye contact. A moment later, we were rushing inside the office without needing to be welcomed twice.

The first thing I noticed was my eerily silent best friend calmly sitting in one of the leather sofa chairs positioned in front of the massive oak desk. Ever's forearms were resting on the wide arms of the chair, and his feet were planted, legs spread wide as he remained facing forward. All I could see was the back of his head, but I knew his mask was in place. No one else could perfect a blank expression quite like Ever could when he was feeling too many emotions at once and holding them all back. Four sat on the edge of the matching chair next to him, and I could tell she was eager to offer him comfort.

Evelyn McNamara currently stood behind the desk where her husband was seated, and when the door shut firmly behind us, she huffed. "This is highly inappropriate," she scolded despite the tears glistening in her gold eyes. I wasn't sure if the reprimand was directed at her husband or us.

"They've already heard too much," he retorted with a dismissive wave of his hand. "Ever," he said, sounding somber when he addressed his son. "This is not how I wanted to tell you, but what Jamie says is true. Your father and I were lovers."

After finally admitting the truth, Thomas's shoulders slumped as if a weight had been lifted. I could tell he was still holding his breath, waiting for a reaction from his son.

Unfortunately, he got nothing in return.

"Shortly after you were born, Sean left," Mrs. McNamara informed her silent son. "He was involved with some really bad people, so he decided you'd be better off without him. Safer."

For the first time since Four entered the room, Ever finally spoke. "You said he died *before* I was born."

"I...well...that wasn't exactly true."

"Just say the words, Mother. They're simple to understand. *You lied. You fucking lied.*"

Thomas's face looked like a bruised tomato as he glared at his son. "I know you're upset, son, but you will not disrespect your mother in my home!"

I guess my best friend decided he'd rather leave than submit to either of his parents. Without a word of explanation, Ever rose from his seat and made a beeline for the exit.

Shooting to his feet as well, Mr. McNamara desperately shouted four words in hopes of stopping Ever from leaving. "You have a brother!"

It fucking worked like a charm.

My eyes squeezed shut as Ever paused in front of the doors. This was getting a little too hard to watch. And to think it had been my genius idea to drag Tyra here to hang out rather than to the beach house to make out as I should have done. The worst part was knowing that I could never fully be there for Ever. Hell, for any of my friends. Not unless I wanted to put them all in danger.

When I opened my eyes, my gaze landed on Lou, and I found it interesting that the usually smug pickpocket was suddenly shaking in her boots. In fact, she looked ready to bolt as her gaze met Four's, and something passed between them. Obviously, the people in this room knew more than they were letting on, which begged only one question. How much did Tyra know?

She slipped her hand inside mine, and when I turned away from the train wreck ahead, I found her looking just as baffled as I felt.

"What did you say?" Ever's hoarse demand was a telling sign that the tumultuous emotions he was trying to keep at bay were fighting to break free and *winning*.

"You have an older brother, and he knows about you. He's here in Blackwood Keep. He's *been* here and he—"

"Maybe we shouldn't do this right now. I think Ever's had enough."

The only people in the room who seemed surprised by Lou's interruption was Tyra and me. It was obvious she was protecting more than just Ever, but who? The only people in this town she gave a shit about were standing in this room. Everyone except—

Somehow, our gazes connected across the room, and the guilty shift of Lou's feet confirmed what I'd already pieced together.

Wren.

She was protecting Wren.

Holy shit.

"Who is he?" Ever demanded, ignoring Lou's protest. No one in the room spoke, and for the very first time, I witnessed my best friend lose control. Shoving his fist into the wall—*told ya*—he shouted at his parents. "*Tell me!*"

"It's Wren! Wren is your brother," Four blurted. Ignoring the dirty look Lou gave her, Four rushed across the room. She reached out for him, but the look Ever gave her stopped her in her tracks. It was one of blind hurt and utter betrayal as he took a step back, rejecting the comfort she offered.

"You knew?"

Those two words hit me like a punch to the gut. I could only imagine how Four was feeling.

"Only for a little while," Four swore. "I-I didn't know if I should tell you."

"How long is a little while?" he pressed through gritted teeth.

Four's gaze darted to the side, and I filled my lungs with as much air as I could. Whatever the answer, Ever wasn't going to like it, and knowing my best friend, two seconds was too long. Four never stood a chance at doing the right thing. The situation was too delicate. Too murky.

"Lou and I figured it out after Thanksgiving dinner," she mumbled. "I showed her the picture on the mantle of Thomas, Sean, and Douglas. Lou recognized Sean and told me he was Wren's father." Inching closer and closer toward him, Four continued. "The day you showed me that picture after telling me he was your namesake, I—" Four inhaled deeply before letting the air free with a frustrated whimper. "I suspected that he might have been your real father. I just wasn't sure until Jamie confirmed it a few weeks ago."

"She wanted to tell you then," Jamie said, breaking his vow of silence. "I made her promise not to. I wanted to give them," he added while nodding to Ever's parents, "the choice to tell you themselves."

"You didn't give me a choice," Mr. McNamara spat. "You gave me an ultimatum."

Jamie shot his uncle a cruel smile. "It worked, didn't it?"

Slamming his fist on the desk, Thomas's face turned purple as he pinned his nephew with his glare. "Get out of my office before I throw you out of my home!"

Jamie looked ready to bait his uncle some more, but then remembering Bee, who was also at his mercy thanks to her reptile of a father, wisely decided against it. Taking his girlfriend's hand, Jamie strolled from the room as casually as he'd arrived. As far as Jameson Buchanan was concerned, his job was done. And what destruction he'd left in his wake.

At least Ever knows the truth now.

Even if it had been a horrible shit show.

"Is there anything else I should know?" Ever inquired. And then with a heavy dose of sarcasm… "Perhaps you want to tell me next that Four is really my sister," he said, making everyone in the room cringe. With pursed lips, Four took his hand, and surprisingly, Ever didn't pull away. He did stare down at her long and hard, though, with a look that promised he'd make her pay dearly for keeping secrets. I knew I would.

"Yes," Thomas admitted sheepishly, making everyone in the room groan without thinking. How the hell could there possibly be more? "Your father is here in Blackwood Keep. He wants to meet you."

"Holy shit!" Tyra exclaimed the moment we were alone inside my ride. After Thomas sternly ordered everyone but Ever to leave his office, Tyra and I practically raced for my car. Lou had refused to leave when Four offered her a ride home and instead frantically attempted to get ahold of Wren and warn him. "That was *not* how I was expecting the afternoon to go. Did you know about any of this?" she asked me with a hint of accusation.

"Not a fucking clue," I mumbled as I started the car and got the hell out of there. As I drove toward the outskirts of town where Tyra resided alone with her father, I wondered about the mystery man who caused such an uproar. And all without even being present.

If you asked me, he fucking sounded like trouble.

chapter three

The Pawn

MMEDIATELY AFTER GRADUATING, I'D BEGGED TERRY FOR AS MANY full-time shifts as I could get this summer, which meant I hadn't made many plans for anything else. I spent the entire first day after I was suspended, twiddling my thumbs. By the end of day two, cabin fever had already set in. Vaughn was too focused on conditioning his body into shape for college ball to shower me with the attention I required. Four was still somewhere holed up with Ever, probably begging and working overtime for his forgiveness. Knowing how much Ever adored Four, I was willing to bet he'd forgiven her the second he found out. He was simply milking the situation to his advantage as any boy would do—the *one* time they weren't in the wrong.

Being in love never made anyone a saint. It just made us better, happier versions of ourselves.

The faint sound of my phone ringing pulled me out of my thoughts and recognizing the tone, I abandoned my food on the stove and rushed up the stairs to answer the call.

"Hey," I greeted, smiling at the image of a sweaty, shirtless Vaughn with a white towel wrapped around his neck. It was obvious he'd just finished what was probably another grueling workout. He'd barely stopped to catch his breath or wipe the sweat away before calling me. My crazy heart did cartwheels in my chest. That is until Vaughn's gaze narrowed, seeing me out of breath as well. "What the hell were you doing?"

"I ran up the stairs so I wouldn't miss your call." *Next time, I'll just let it go to voicemail, asshole.*

His lids lowered, and I rolled my eyes. Vaughn was definitely pleased and turned on by my eagerness. I watched him bite his lower lip as he seemed to contemplate something. "Is your father home?" His tone was suddenly sultry.

"No."

The warmth traveling up my neck couldn't be contained. My father had accepted a summer job coaching a youth football camp down in North Carolina and had left this morning. For some reason, though, I'd been a little hesitant to tell Vaughn that I'd be without parental supervision for the next four weeks. Sure, I was eighteen, but to my father, I would always be his little girl. At least now that we'd graduated, Vaughn was no longer one of his players. My father would have never condoned our relationship, as complicated as it were, otherwise. I'd had a hard enough time convincing him to let his quarterback take me to prom. Vaughn had told my father that he simply wanted to repay me for all the "tutoring sessions."

"I'll be there in twenty minutes."

"Make it ten, or I won't bother answering the door," I challenged before hanging up. I didn't want to make it too easy for him, after all. I rushed downstairs and turned off the dinner-for-one I'd been preparing before heading back up and straight for the bathroom. I knew exactly what was running through Vaughn's mind.

Goose bumps appeared on my skin as I filled our garden tub with hot water, Epsom salts, and my favorite lavender bubble bath. The tub was only half full when the doorbell rang minutes later. Checking my phone, I smirked when I saw that it had only taken him eight to reach me.

When I opened the front door, Vaughn swept me up in his big arms, pressed me against his naked chest, and kissed the hell out of me. Anyone else and I might have been grossed out by the sweat now soaking the front of my T-shirt, but with Vaughn, I couldn't get enough of the testosterone seeping from his pores.

He was just so damn *male*.

"Miss me, pip-squeak?"

Even though it had only been two days, I'd been anxious to see him again, and even though summer had only just begun, it was already starting to feel like the end. "What I *don't* miss is your new pet name. Can we please discuss you going back to Ty-ty?"

Grinning, he gripped my ass before wrapping my legs around his waist, and it was then that I remembered I only wore panties. He'd seen me in much less, but I couldn't help the blush that warmed my cheeks as he kicked the door closed and carried me up the stairs.

He went straight for the bathroom without having to be told.

Like all the other times, he quietly removed his clothes after setting me on my feet. All he wore were navy-blue basketball shorts and matching trainers, so he was naked in no time, and I was in danger of swallowing my tongue. Everything about Vaughn Rees set my body on fucking fire. Even, ridiculously, the hair on his legs. I loved feeling the roughness of them against my own whenever we became tangled underneath the sheets.

"Are you sore?" I asked when he grimaced while lowering himself into the hot water and lavender-scented suds.

Eyes closed and head tilted back, Vaughn replied as casually as if we were discussing the weather. "Not as sore as you're going to be when I fuck you."

My legs were suddenly too weak to hold me up, so I sank onto the wide ledge surrounding the bathtub, brought my knees to my chest, and hugged them for dear life. I believed him. "When will that be?"

It was a dangerous question, indeed, but the silence had become too thick with tension. I needed to break it somehow. It wasn't as if I was saving myself for marriage, but it turns out, I wasn't as open or eager for casual sex as I thought. I wanted—no,

I *needed* more, and ironically, it was Vaughn who made me see that.

In the beginning, he'd set out to make me just another notch on his belt and nothing more. But in a twist of fate that neither of us could see coming, during the weeks he spent chasing me, his dick had grown a conscience. And then Vaughn gave me what he hadn't given the others. Honesty.

He admitted to me that even by some snowball's chance in hell he'd want more, he couldn't and wouldn't give it to me. I never learned why. I'd been too afraid of driving him away to ask.

The most obvious reason was that he wanted to keep his options open for when he inevitably went pro. We were young. We still haven't met the people we'd become. There was an entire world out there waiting, and for Vaughn, it would be even bigger. What were the odds that the girl he was meant to give his heart to had been right here in Blackwood Keep all along?

The skeptical pessimist in me would say slim to none.

"When you can accept the fact that you deserve better, Tyra." His tone was grim, and the frown he wore was troubled. I'd say a little too much for a boy who was simply trying to keep his options open.

"Is there a reason why you think you're aren't what I deserve?"

"There are many."

I pondered that for a moment before deciding that I wouldn't back down. This was a battle worth fighting, and my gut told me the victory would be sweet. I just didn't know how forbidden the fruit. Not yet, anyway. "Then start with the biggest one."

His eyes opened slowly. I wasn't prepared for the pain I saw within them and his apology before the answer even left his lips. "My father."

I didn't need to see the stillness of his finger resting on the porcelain lip of the tub to know that Vaughn was telling the truth. The breathtaking green of his eyes had been darkened by shadows too thick to penetrate.

And then came the questions.

Why would his father not want us together? How could a man who'd never met me hate me enough to bar his son from true love? And most importantly, why did Vaughn obey?

Rather than a light bulb glowing over my head, helping me see the answer, I felt like I'd been shot through the eye with an arrow.

"Is it because—" Bile rose in my throat as my heart raced. "Is it because I'm...black?" I'd always been proud to be who I was, but I almost choked on the word that now seemed tarnished, tainted by the hatred of a stranger.

Vaughn didn't answer right away, but then something akin to regret flickered in his eyes before he responded. "Yes."

Out of the corner of my eye, I caught the subtle tap of his index finger before he gripped the edge of the tub as if he were trying to strangle it.

I was too stunned to call him out on it.

Vaughn hadn't lied when he said his father was the reason we couldn't be together, but why would he lie about his father being racist if he wasn't? What could be worse?

I considered the rumors floating around that his father made his money illegally, but I never truly gave them credence. There had never been any evidence to support them. To the naked eye, Franklin Rees had only ever been a shrewd businessman with a few friends in high places. Maybe he was corrupt, very few people with power aren't, but that hardly made him dangerous.

Before I could find the words to confront him, the doorbell rang. Vaughn's eyes were already closed once again, telling me he'd assumed the conversation was over. *Not even close.* Reluctantly, I stood with a frown that only deepened. Whoever was at that door was keeping me from getting the answers I needed once again, and they weren't going to feel very welcome.

Snatching open the front door—because let's face it, my mood had turned to shit—I wasn't prepared to see a stranger standing on the other side. And an insanely beautiful one no less. She was short like me, although taller by two inches or so, with full Kerry Washington lips that matched the heart shape of her face. She had blemish-free brown skin and hair, so lush that I almost slammed the door in her face out of envy. I could tell right away that she was older. Maybe by two or three years. Her almond-shaped, light-brown eyes, which eerily resembled my own, gave her away.

Clearly startled, she blinked a few times before greeting me. "Hi!" And of course, her voice was like silk. I almost rolled my eyes. "Did I catch you at a bad time?"

"That depends on who the hell you are and what you want." I immediately winced when I realized I sounded like Vaughn. He could be so damn rude sometimes. Apparently, it was starting to rub off.

"Oh, sorry! I'm so rude." The sound of her giggle, light and musical, grated on my goddamn patience. "My name is Selena Taylor. I was hoping to speak with Cedric Bradley. Is he home?"

"No, sorry. He's out of town for the next few weeks, but I can take a message." The entire time I spoke, forcing a pleasant tone, I wondered what the hell she had to talk to my father about. Glancing at her exposed midsection over the tight shorts she wore, I was relieved to see that she wasn't pregnant. Not visibly anyway.

Shaking off the ridiculous thoughts, because my father would never touch a girl so young, I met her gaze or at least tried to. She was busy gaping at something behind me. Looking over my shoulder, I saw Vaughn approaching, suds and water still dripping from his massive chest and only a towel wrapped around his waist.

"I guess I *did* catch you at a bad time," Selena teased before winking. I didn't miss the way her teeth sank into her bottom lip either—as if she were picturing licking him dry. I'd cut her tongue out if she tried and claw her eyes out while I was at it if she didn't stop gawking soon.

Moving to block her view, I remembered she was slightly taller—not to mention the fact that Vaughn, being well over six feet, dwarfed us both. There was no hiding him and all his deliciousness.

"What's going on?" he asked when he finally reached the door. His gaze bounced between Selena and me before settling on *moi*.

Good boy.

"Nothing," I quickly replied when I noticed her reaching out a hand for him to shake. I bet she'll try to grab his dick next. *Stop, stop, stop it!* "She was just leaving. Maybe you should go put on some clothes?"

I didn't give a damn how obvious I was being. Vaughn had marked his territory so many times. The double standard ends now.

Smirking at my possessiveness, Vaughn ignored me and shook Selena's hand. "Vaughn."

"Selena."

"Can we help you?" he graciously asked after dropping her hand and immediately wrapping his arm around my waist. His strong hand squeezed my hip in reassurance. Liking the fact that he said "we," I immediately felt myself relaxing into his embrace.

Oh, God...

I was acting nutty, wasn't I?

This girl hadn't done anything to me, and here I was acting like a jealous bitch.

"Oh, God," Selena groaned. "This is stupid, and I shouldn't have come here. It's just that..." She gazed down at me, her bright smile wavering as if reading my thoughts. I told myself to get a grip and offered her an apologetic one in return. It seemed to give her courage because she quickly reached inside the Gucci purse hanging from her shoulder and fumbled around before pulling out sheets of worn-out pale-pink paper. "I found this letter my mom wrote, and I was just curious about the man she wrote it for. She died a long time ago, and to be honest, I barely remember her. I-I guess I'm just grasping at straws. I'm so sorry," she said, already backing away from the door. "I didn't mean to disturb you."

"Wait," I said while untangling myself from Vaughn and stepping outside. There was a sadness in her brown eyes that called to me. Maybe it was because I lost my mom before I ever really got to know her, too. I couldn't turn her away. Not now. "What's your mom's name?"

My father had never spoken of any woman other than my mom, the love of his life. I had to know what was written in that letter. Nothing other than monumental would have brought Selena all of this way. I recognized that Texan accent.

Selena looked unsure for a moment, but it passed faster than a shooting star, and then she was squaring her shoulders. "Monica. Monica Taylor."

It felt like the air had been knocked out of me. I was no longer standing but rather flat on my back. Helplessly, I watched the world spin out of control and knew that when it finally stopped, it would no longer look the same. I wasn't sure how long it took me to find my voice, but when I did, I hated how small it sounded.

"But that's my mom's name."

chapter four

The Prince

THIS IS WHAT I GET FOR THINKING WITH MY DICK.

After my workout this morning, I had planned to crash, but in a moment of weakness, wanting to hear her voice, I'd called Tyra instead. The Twilight Zone was a fucking walk in the park compared to the shitstorm wreaking havoc on Blackwood Keep. Tyra's older sister showing up out of the blue, one she never knew existed, was pretty much like jumping from the frying pan and into a roaring fire. First, Ever and Wren being half brothers, and now *this*?

What were the odds?

What were the *fucking* odds?

I naïvely thought the next two months would be the easiest, most carefree time of my entire life, but it was apparent fate had other plans. The summer had gone to shit as far as I was concerned.

Both girls stood frozen, their gazes locked, with what I could only assume were a million questions begging to be answered. I wondered at the chances of Selena being mistaken. Still, after studying the possible sisters carefully, I realized that if not for the two-inch height difference, Tyra and Selena could have been carbon copies.

Feeling my dick slowly deflate and remembering that I only wore a towel, I pulled a stunned Tyra back inside. After a moment of hesitation, I awkwardly invited Selena into a house that didn't belong to me. Once I showed her into the living room, I took Tyra's small, trembling hand in mine and led her up the stairs.

Her small bedroom was a teenage girl's wonderland.

The lights Tyra had strung up on the wall above her bed illuminated the pictures of us covering the entire wall adjacent to it. Most of the time, I pretended not to see them or feel the sharp chord in my chest, knowing they were there. I gently placed her on the bed and shoved Mr. Bear, her favorite stuffed pig—I still scratched my head at that one—into her lap. Tyra immediately wrapped her arms around it before staring at her bedroom floor.

Turning away to dig out the duffel—one her father didn't know I kept in his daughter's closet—I dropped the towel, hurriedly pulled on a pair of sweats, and then shoved a loose-fitting muscle shirt over my head. I decided to keep some clothes here after the third or fourth bubble bath when it became clear that this was now a routine for us. Soaking in a tub hadn't been my thing until Tyra convinced me of the benefits. Let's just say it involved her getting wet that first time, too.

Just as I was pulling on a pair of socks, I heard the faint but unmistakable sound of sniffling. I looked up in time to see the first tear fall down Tyra's soft, supple cheek.

Fuck.

As much as I wanted to get the hell out of there, I knew I could never leave her like this.

Sounds an awful lot like you're starting to give a damn, Rees.

I gritted my teeth and shoved the possibility into the deepest, darkest recesses of my mind where my father could never hope to reach it. Not even if he made good on his many threats to torture me.

Pulling Tyra up, I took her place on the bed before planting her in my lap. She wasted no time curling into me for the comfort that I had no business giving. I wasn't her boyfriend. It wasn't my place to be the foundation that kept her from crumbling. I had every right to walk out that door.

I balled my hand into a fist in frustration as I kept my ass planted on her overcrowded bed.

"Just say the word, and I'll toss her out on her ass," I heard myself whispering in lieu of goodbye. The hole I'd been digging for the past year was getting deeper every day, and if I weren't careful, my father would throw both of our lifeless bodies inside.

"I don't understand," Tyra cried in response. "My mother and father were in love. How can she be my sister?"

"She's older," I gently pointed out. "Maybe they found each other after she was born."

"My father said he was with my mother for five years before she got pregnant with me. Selena can't be more than twenty-one years old."

I thought about that for a moment. Unfortunately for us both, Tyra was right. Selena barely looked old enough to be out of high school. No way could she be almost thirty. "It's possible you share the same father, too. Maybe they gave her up for adoption," I reasoned. "Maybe they weren't ready to be parents at the time." I dried her tears only for twice as many to fall in their place. *Fuck, fuck, fuck!* "Not until you came along."

Tyra went still, and instantly, the tears dropped as a cold look took over her normally warm gaze. "Then how did she get her hands on that letter? A letter that was meant *for my dad*?"

Before I could respond, Tyra was up and rushing from the room on a mission. I leaned forward, holding my head in my hands and considered calling Four. I was way out of my depth. Unfortunately, even though I knew she would come, Four already had her hands full with Ever.

Biting the bullet, I shot to my feet and rushed down the stairs in time to see Tyra facing off with a startled Selena. Her eyes were rimmed red, making it clear that she'd been crying, too.

"How did you get that letter?" Tyra demanded.

"Excuse me?"

"The letter our mom wrote to our dad, how did you get it if they gave you up for adoption?"

Selena's head jerked in genuine surprise. "I don't know what you're talking about," she said, nostrils flaring. "I was never given up for adoption. *My* dad raised me alone after *our* mom died giving birth to *you*."

You could hear a pin drop in the house next door.

The sudden hostility in Selena's tone when she uttered that final truth had my eyes narrowing. It was a far cry from the bright-eyed girl with the too-easy smile we'd met just minutes ago. Tyra sank onto the couch, too distraught to notice the resentment in the other girl's eyes. I watched Selena like a hawk as she sat next to pip-squeak, an apology ready at the lips. It was debatable whether it was genuine.

"I'm sorry. That was insensitive of me. This is not at all how I thought our first meeting would go."

Tyra's head shot up at that. "You mean you knew who I was when I answered the door?" Her suspicious tone had Selena rushing to answer, albeit nervously.

"I wasn't sure, but yes. I had a hunch you were my baby sister. My mom wrote this letter right before you were born. She said she wanted to name you *Tyra*. Tyra Morgan Bradley." Selena met my gaze, a look of uncertainty there, before continuing. "Even though it broke my father's heart to learn you weren't his daughter, he still honored her wishes."

Biting back a curse, I was ready to make good on my offer and toss this bitch out on her ass when Tyra shot to her feet. "What are you talking about?"

"M-m-my parents," Selena stammered, "were married for ten years. Your father was having an affair with our mom. It almost broke their marriage."

"You're *lying*," Tyra growled.

"I wish I were, but it's the truth!"

"Get out."

"Please, Tyra, listen to me." In a bold move, Selena reached out to pip-squeak, but I quickly stepped between them with a look that brooked no argument. She was lucky I hadn't clotheslined her instead.

"I don't care what lies brought you here," Tyra said in a tone I'd never heard from her before, "but I don't care. Our mom and my dad were soulmates, and nothing you say will ever change that. Now *leave*."

Wordlessly, Selena picked up her purse, and I made sure she was gone for good before lifting a broken Tyra off her feet and carrying her upstairs. She spent the entire night crying in my arms, and when she finally tired herself out enough to sleep, I wondered where the hell her father was.

The next morning, I awoke soaked in sweat in a bed that wasn't mine and my throwing arm completely numb. It took a few blinks to clear my vision and figure out where I was and why. My location explained the back pain. Tyra's mattress always made me feel like I was sleeping on a bed of nails. Groaning, I palmed my face and contemplated slipping quietly from Tyra's bed and going the hell home. Even Jamie would have been the better choice to deal with an emotionally distraught female.

I'd spent most of my formative years learning not to care about the people around me or at least pretending not to, and it almost worked. Until her.

I froze when Tyra suddenly shifted in her sleep, and I spent the next thirty seconds praying she didn't wake up yet. I needed time to think of a way out of this. I hadn't even gotten so much as a blow job from her after nine and a half months of wooing, and here I was dealing with this heavy shit like some sappy ass hero from a porny romance novel.

Jesus fucking Christ.

Carefully and quietly, I freed my arm from underneath Tyra. She immediately curled into her small frame as if warding off the demons that awaited her once she finally opened those whiskey eyes. Her long lashes fanned her cheek, and her lips were stuck in a pout as her frown grew deeper. It seemed her troubles had followed her into her dreams. It wasn't until my phone softly pinged from the nightstand that I realized I'd been watching her sleep like a goddamn creep.

Fuck it.

Leaning down, my hands planted on either side of her head, I asked myself if I was really willing to risk everything for one goddamn kiss. As if hearing my thoughts, she softly moaned in her sleep, and I decided the answer was a resounding yes. Pressing my lips against hers, I warred against deepening the kiss. When she rolled onto her back and spread her legs, I decided it was time to go. Snatching my phone and my shoes up, I shook my head in disgust.

This newfound chivalry could seriously bite me.

Any other girl and I would have taken what she freely offered. Keeping my steps light, I made for Tyra's bedroom door. Once in the hall, I listened for her father, already thinking up an explanation if I was caught.

The house was as quiet as a mouse.

Stepping out into the early morning sun and finding the driveway empty except for Tyra's little Honda, I considered throwing caution to the wind and calling Coach Bradley so that he could be here for his daughter.

That was until I reminded myself that none of this was my goddamn business.

Throwing myself into my Lamborghini, I sped all the way home. Even though I'd run from Tyra, my mind and heart were left behind, still in bed with her. Worry over the state she'd be in when she found me gone gnawed at me, but I forced myself to push it aside.

Not my problem. Not my fucking problem.

"Where have you been?" my father greeted the moment I walked through the heavy iron doors. Despite the gray peppering his thinning hair and mustache and the wrinkles lining his pale skin, Franklin Rees put on an imposing display in his tailored suit. Perhaps it was the cruel set of his mouth that matched his cold gaze or the fact that at least a dozen armed guards surrounded him. He was standing in the foyer when I arrived, but I doubt he was waiting for me. In fact, I was sure he'd only just realized that I never made it home last night. I could have been wrapped around a tree as long as his precious gang was okay. My father didn't give a damn about much else.

"I was out." *As you could see when I walked through the door.*

"Your frequent and lengthy absences are starting to alarm me. Do I need to put a detail on you again?"

"Why ask as if I have a choice? Why care as long as I come back?"

As head of Thirteen, the largest and most notorious gang on the east coast, my father didn't shy away from corporal punishment. To be honest, he reveled in it, which made my open defiance that much more stupid.

"Because I fear for the day when you dare not."

"I've never kept my plans a secret from you. I'm leaving to play ball, and there's nothing you can do about it."

"I could have one of my men break every bone in your body. What good would you be then to the head coach at the University of Southern California?" I could feel my blood draining from my skin as my father's cruel grin spread. "Oh, yes, son. I know all about you accepting their offer. I'm curious why you chose them over Ohio State even though they had the better offer. Is it because you foolishly believed California was far enough to run from me?"

"Bones heal," I said rather than answer his question. I didn't believe it, but the west coast seemed my best shot at escaping my father. After all, my mother had done it. Only she hadn't taken any chances and had left the goddamn country.

I hadn't heard from her in years. Not a single phone call, a letter written, or a birthday card sent. *Maybe she's dead.* The thought didn't make me feel any better. Especially knowing that my father would likely be responsible.

"Perhaps," he agreed in a way that left a lot of room for doubt.

"What good would I be to you if you caused permanent damage? Who'd follow me if I couldn't walk or even lift a spoon to feed myself?"

"Your cock would still work," he coldly replied, "and my dynasty would be ensured."

I felt ice in my veins where warm blood should have flowed. "You're fucked if you think I'm bringing a kid into this world knowing what you have planned for them." And if I thought there was a doctor out there who wouldn't turn me away, I would have had a vasectomy already.

"Not all of them. Just your sons."

"Not gonna happen."

"I guess we'll have to wait and see." My father waved his hand dismissively, the discussion over for now. "Thanks to that little fool you call a friend and her spineless father, I'm back at square one. Consider this a momentary reprieve." With that, he left me alone, his grim-faced security detail following him out the front doors.

Good fucking riddance. I said a silent prayer that he was gone for longer than a few days this time.

It had been hard enough looking Bee in the eye knowing that my father had made Elliot Montgomery an offer he couldn't refuse. Rather than a wife to make me whole, all my father required her to be was a fucking broodmare for me to mount. By some miracle, none of my friends had figured it out yet, but it was only a matter of time. Luckily, Elliot had got himself arrested before my father could fork over the money. If he had, Bee would never be safe, and what was worse, Jamie would die trying. Bee might have believed her father to be a monster, but she'd yet to look pure evil in the eye.

My phone rang, snatching me from my thoughts. Reading Tyra's name on the screen, I paused then pressed one of the buttons on the side, silencing the call before heading upstairs.

I'd meant it when I told her she deserved better.

chapter five

The Pawn

"I HONESTLY CAN'T DECIDE WHO'S THE BIGGER ASSHOLE—VAUGHN or that Selena bitch."

I'd just finished telling Lou about Selena's visit and waking up alone this morning. Oh, and the fact that it's been hours and Vaughn still hadn't returned my call. Not wanting to be alone with my thoughts, I'd called up Lou, who immediately invited me over.

I could have used one of Four's hugs right about now, but she already had her hands full with Ever. I was almost sorry that I'd been there that day. I couldn't imagine going through yesterday's drama in front of an audience as Ever had. He might not care on principle what anyone thought of him, but it had still been a pretty harsh blow.

I watched Lou pace the length of the living room, a troubled frown marring her pretty face. "Where's Wren?"

She paused, her nostrils flaring and lip curling. "Who the hell knows anymore? Who the hell cares?"

"I think you do," I teased her. She would have done the same to me because Lou was rarely merciful. She made a sound of denial and turned away, but not before I saw the sadness and worry in her eyes. "He loves you. You know that, right?" He even adored the brat. Wren had been dedicated to Lou's well-being long before they fell in love, and that determination had only intensified.

"I did."

"Lou..."

"I thought maybe I was enough for him, but he's gone more than he's here, and he's so secretive. He never talks to me anymore." Staring out the window with her arms wrapped protectively around her body, she whispered, "I think he misses it."

"Misses what?"

There was a heavy beat of silence before she finally answered. "Exiled."

I struggled to find the words to say. While I knew all about their hair-raising story, I couldn't claim to know Wren enough to be sure of anything beyond the obvious. He fucking *lived* for Lou. He'd die for her, too. If he was keeping secrets, I was sure he had a good reason. But how the hell do I convince someone who'd been his best friend and knew him better than anyone?

The simplest part of the problem was that Lou was spoiled, and Wren had only himself to blame. For years, he'd catered to her every whim and desire while somehow keeping her on a leash. And now, when what she wanted most of all was for Wren to give up his old life, he struggled for the first time to give her what she needed.

Or maybe not the first time.

No one had forgotten Lou's shameless seduction of Wren until he finally cracked and crossed the line he'd drawn himself. I doubt either one of them had regretted it for a single moment, not even when she found out that he'd been partially responsible for the death of her adoptive parents.

The front door opened and in walked Wren as smooth and silent as a panther. He was dressed in simple dark clothing that made me think Lou was on to something. His dark hair, blue eyes—although one was currently blackened—and powerful body were something to behold. Somehow, I found the will to leave the beholding to Lou, as any good friend should.

Besides, he had eyes only for Lou, the tension between them palpable.

"Did Ever give you that?" she smugly greeted after long moments of extended and meaningful eye contact. They'd both expressed more than either of them realized in that single look.

"Yeah."

"Good. You deserve it," she told him with zero sympathy.

Sighing, Wren moved deeper into the living room, purpose in every stride. That was until he noticed me curled up on their huge sofa.

Awkwardly, I waved. "Hey."

A frustrated gleam entered his eyes before he nodded politely, turned on his heel, and stalked toward the stairs. I watched Lou as she pretended to ignore him and barely hid my grin when she started bouncing her leg. I could tell she wanted to follow him, but her pride and stubbornness wouldn't allow it.

"You know, I can go and give you guys some privacy if you want."

"Don't bother," she muttered as she flopped onto the couch next to me. "He'll shower, get dressed, and be gone again within the hour."

"Do you really think he's gone back to work for Fox after everything that's happened?"

I released the air I'd been holding when she shook her head. "No. I think Wren wants to find Fox and kill him."

Stupidly, I blinked as I processed her words. That was a pretty dark revelation and way outside of my comfort zone. I felt like an accomplice, just knowing about it. I knew that Wren hadn't always been an upstanding citizen, but was he truly a killer?

"And that bothers you?" It was the only thing I could think to say or do. I wouldn't bolt when she'd listened to me whine about Vaughn for an hour. Suddenly, my problems seemed smaller, less complicated.

"Wren's only doing what he *thinks* he has to. Trust me, no one wants that animal put down more than I do, but I...I don't want it to be Wren. It took a long time for me to convince him that he deserved happiness. If Wren takes a life, even Fox's, it will haunt him forever."

I found myself speechless, and it seemed Lou was done sharing. We didn't speak for a long time, and after a while, the only sound came from the water running in the shower upstairs.

The sound of glass shattering jerked me out of my sleep. I sat up in a panic that only slightly dissipated when I looked around and realized I was still at Wren and Lou's. Feeling groggy and disoriented, I wondered how long I'd been asleep as I looked out the window and realized night had fallen. The only light was from the soft glow of the television. The romcom Lou and I had been watching before I fell asleep was paused halfway through. Checking my phone, I saw that it was a quarter past nine and still no text or call from Vaughn.

Ignoring my spinning head and shaking hands, I wondered at the last time I'd eaten as I slowly rose into a seated position. My appetite was nonexistent as I considered swallowing what was left of my pride and calling Vaughn again. The thought fled when I heard what sounded like a whimper.

I froze, hearing the sound more clearly a second time.

Remembering the glass, I shot to my feet. Was Lou hurt? Had someone broken in? Where was Wren? Tiptoeing into the small foyer—because if someone had broken in, the last thing I wanted to do was startle the burglar and get shot in the face—I came to a stop.

There were two figures cloaked in the darkness near the front door.

Oh, shit. I'm so toast.

I started to back away, hoping maybe the intruders hadn't seen me yet when I noticed the large vase that normally resided on the entry table lay shattered at their feet. Either they were the world's clumsiest burglars or… Just then, one of them mumbled something too low for me to hear. My lips parted to reply, but no words came. A moment later, the deep voice I recognized as Wren's beat me to it.

"I said, arch your fucking back."

My spine became a rod as I immediately straightened. The smaller figure, on the other hand, obeyed, and I could only assume it was Lou. She released a choked cry as Wren ruthlessly flexed his hips, driving himself deeper. My eyes nearly fell out of my head when I realized what I was seeing. I never thought I'd be grateful for the dark, which seemed to grow fainter as my eyes slowly adjusted. The skirt Lou had been wearing earlier was hiked around her waist while Wren's jeans were shoved around his powerful thighs, giving me an unobstructed view of his muscular buttocks. Nothing but the sound of their skin slapping filled the foyer, and then Wren began to fuck her even harder. The table he had her bent over slammed into the wall with each drive of his hips, neither caring about the damage.

And the worst part? They blocked my only exit.

Back door.

Spinning on my heel to make a hasty escape, I realized I must have moved too quickly. The lightheadedness from before hit me with greater force this time, and as my oblivious friends continued to fuck mere feet away, I reached out for the wall. Unfortunately, I grabbed nothing but air when I swayed on my feet. The bright spots dotting my vision became too much to bear, so finally, I gave in to the overwhelming feeling and collapsed.

The first thing I noticed when I came to was how soft my bed had gotten. Vaughn had complained so many times that it hurt his back, but right now, it felt like I was sleeping on a cloud.

"Hey, this is it. I think she's really waking up this time."

Recognizing the voice, I frowned as my eyes fluttered open. I desperately wanted to stay asleep for a little while longer, but my brain seemed to have had enough, even if my body disagreed. When my vision cleared, I found myself staring into a warm set of beautiful brown eyes—eyes that filled with relief when I didn't immediately close them again. The blinding grin that followed as Jamie hovered over me was equally breathtaking. Still, why was he in my bedroom?

"Seriously, Ty-baby, you could make a nun feel shame," Jamie teased. "I knew you were a virgin, but damn, fainting?"

"Wha—what are you talking about?" I demanded, my voice hoarse for some reason. "I fainted? Why?"

"You walked in on Wren raw-dogging Lou, that's why." After glancing over his shoulder, he turned back to me and smirked. "Judging by his scowl, I'm guessing it was before he blew his load."

"Seriously, Jamie?" Lou screeched while sounding scandalized.

Everything came flooding back after hearing her voice. My lips twisted at the irony. Lou didn't seem to have much shame when she was screwing her boyfriend out in the open—while I slept in the next room.

I got that this was their house, but jeez...they could have just asked me to leave. Sighing, I sat up with Jamie's hands around my arms, making sure I took it slowly. Once he stepped away to stand next to Bee, I looked around the crowded room and realized everyone was here.

Everyone except Vaughn.

Four stood from Ever's lap where they'd been waiting in the chair by the window and sat next to me. "How are you feeling?"

Stealing a peek at Wren and Lou, who were making an amusing effort not to stand too close to each other, I answered. "A little awkward."

"I am *so* sorry," Lou offered. "We shouldn't have done that."

"It's okay." I waved off her. "By the way, I did *not* faint because I walked in on you two."

Jamie smirked at that as if to say *sure*.

"Then why did you faint?" Four asked with a frown. Everyone seemed eager for the answer as they all leaned forward.

The slam of the front door downstairs made us all pause before I could answer. Always alert, Wren immediately left the room to check it out after turning his scowl on Lou. He was always getting on her about forgetting to lock the door. A few seconds later, he returned, but he wasn't alone. Vaughn was on his heels, carrying a brown paper bag from a local sandwich shop.

"Well, fuck, did you at least bring enough for everyone?" Jamie deadpanned.

Vaughn didn't bother acknowledging him as he moved deeper into the room. Our gazes connected, and I could see the concern in his green eyes before he cruelly blinked the feeling away. Four reluctantly stood, and he immediately took her place on the bed.

I didn't speak, and neither did Vaughn as he opened the paper bag and produced a small container of chicken noodle soup. My empty stomach growled in relief as he wordlessly handed it over along with a spoon.

"I know what you're going to say," I grumbled as I pulled the top off and dove in.

His jaw clenched as he pulled out a bottle of apple juice and a chocolate chip cookie. My mouth watered when I realized it had been more than twenty-four hours since I'd last eaten. "That's where you're wrong," he replied dryly. "I'm not a fan of repeating myself."

"I'm sorry for not having an appetite after finding out that my entire *existence* has been a lie, and I'm sorry for needing you to be there when it was an inconvenience to you."

"What about all the other times you forgot to fucking feed yourself?" he snapped. "Was that my fault, too?"

My gaze dropped to the bedspread as every set of eyes in the room zeroed in on me. Vaughn had callously put me on blast, but could I blame him? I wasn't used to having friends or a social life—much less a love life. Not knowing how best to balance it all, the number of hours I had in a day had been stretched thin. These past months, I'd been killing myself to make sure I not only got into Harvard but remained a top candidate for the Theodore Lidle Scholarship. It was a private fund offered to low-income minorities accepted into Ivy League universities, and they only awarded two per graduating class. That scholarship could pay for my entire four years at Harvard. I just had to keep my GPA once I got there above a sphincter-tightening 3.7.

My grade point average my entire four years at Brynwood Academy had never dropped below perfect, but college was designed to be more challenging. With me attending Harvard, let's just say it had been causing me to lose a bit of my appetite.

"I'm not blaming you," I whispered, feeling shame warm my cheeks.

"Maybe we should give them some privacy," Bee suggested. She'd been silent this entire time, but when our gazes connected, I could sense her understanding. It was a shock to discover that Brynwood's cold queen was actually one of the warmest, nicest people around.

"And maybe you should come up with better ideas," Jamie shot back. Folding his arms, he made himself comfortable against the wall. Clearly, he wasn't going anywhere.

"You're absolutely right. How about I start with sleeping alone tonight?" Not waiting for a response, Bee sauntered out of the room. Jamie quickly followed her with his tail tucked between his legs. The rest of our friends left, too. Wren was the last one out, closing the door behind him, but neither Vaughn nor I spoke again until our friends' footsteps faded. I wouldn't put it past any of them to listen behind the door.

"You didn't have to do that," I said, deciding to speak first. "Now they all think I have some sort of eating disorder."

"Do you?"

"No!" Feeling my shoulders slump, I stared into the now cold soup and once again felt my appetite wane. "I don't know. I guess I've been a little stressed out."

Taking my soup from me, he placed it on the nightstand and pulled me into his lap. "I know what's at stake," he claimed in a soft voice. "But none of it will matter if you don't take care of yourself."

"I know."

I felt his chest expand when he inhaled deeply, and then his minty-fresh breath caressed my cheek when he exhaled. "And I'm sorry for leaving you."

Nodding, I silently admitted to myself that it hadn't totally been his fault. I still hadn't told him that my father would be out of town for weeks, so it made sense that he hadn't stuck around. What didn't make sense was why he'd left without saying good-bye. If I'd done the same, there would have been hell to pay.

"You're here now," I said rather than give into my thoughts. He simply squeezed my hip in confirmation. "Thank you for the soup. I won't forget to eat again. I promise."

"I know you won't," he responded a little too confidently. "You're going to eat three meals a day, even if I have to spoon-feed you myself." Dumping me back on the bed next to him, he deftly plucked the soup from the nightstand. I watched him, my eyes wide as he spooned some of the soup before extending it toward my mouth.

"You can't be serious."

"As a fucking heart attack."

"I can feed myself."

"Recent evidence suggests otherwise."

"Vaughn, don't be ridiculous. I'm not letting you—"

He managed to shove the spoon between my parted lips before I could finish my sentence. Not all of it made it inside and spilled onto my shirt. I had no choice but to swallow it down, glaring at Vaughn as I did so.

"I can make airplane noises if it will help?"

My lips pressed even tighter together. I was not letting him win a second time.

"Train then?"

Silence.

Tsking, his hand shot out, quick as a rattlesnake, and he pinched my nose, cutting off my only airway until I had no choice but to part my lips to take a huge gulping breath. "Resistance is futile," he said, mimicking the Borg from *Star Trek*. I remembered the day he made me watch the movie with him. It was the day I realized that the hot jock was a closet Sci-Fi nerd.

I was fed a second bite of chicken noodle, and when he offered a third, I didn't fight him, not even when he made airplane noises on the fourth and yelled "Choo Choo" on the fifth.

God, I hated him.

I might have even loved him.

Only time would tell.

Before either of us knew it, the soup was gone, and the butterflies in my full tummy were fluttering out of control. Wisely, Vaughn let me eat the cookie he'd brought me on my own, but I noticed he kept a watchful eye, making sure I ate the entire thing. By the time I was finished, I was bursting, but I downed the entire bottle of apple juice anyway to avoid another argument.

The moment I took the final sip, he leaned over and kissed the lingering drops of juice from my lips. "Fuck, I missed you," he said with a groan even though it had been less than a day.

"You weren't acting like it," I retorted with a pout.

Vaughn didn't respond as his fingers unbuttoned my shorts and started pulling them over my hips and down my thighs.

"What are you doing?" My heart was racing because I already knew the answer though it baffled me. We were just fighting moments ago.

"Relieving some of your stress."

I bit my bottom lip, not knowing if I should let him despite really wanting him to do just that. Bringing me soup and then feeding it to me didn't change the fact that he'd been an asshole. Not to mention all the lies and secrets he was keeping. Suddenly, I understood Lou's anger and frustration toward Wren.

It was the ego of the alpha male. They couldn't fit it inside of Jupiter.

I shook off my thoughts just as my shorts cleared my ankles. Rising to his feet, Vaughn moved across the room and flipped the lock. He obviously wasn't expecting much argument from me.

"Maybe we should go back to my place? I'm sure Wren and Lou are eager for privacy after what happened."

On cue, our phones pinged with a text from Lou in the group chat Jamie had made.

Lou: Everyone took off. It's late, so feel free to stay in the guest room.

My phone pinged again, but this time, it was a private message.

Lou: Sorry you had to see Wren's butt.
Lou: It's okay if you liked it. It's pretty fucking cute. ;-)

I snorted, making Vaughn's eyes narrow. "What did she say?"

"Nothing," I quickly lied. Blacking the screen, I placed it face down on the nightstand just in case Lou felt the need to discuss Wren's butt some more.

Contrary to my fainting, it had been a pretty fantastic view.

"Looks like we're staying the night," Vaughn said with a smirk before tossing his phone on the bed. I lost my train of thought when he gripped the collar at his nape and pulled his shirt over his head.

Fuck me.

The look in Vaughn's eyes promised he'd do just that, and

he'd take all night if I'd only ask. I wasn't a saint, which meant I told the occasional white lie, usually to spare someone's feelings. However, promising Vaughn that I was okay with never having all of him in exchange for one night? That was one lie I couldn't tell because despite what Vaughn claimed, we were already in deep.

They say sex is what complicates a relationship, but what if you've already given the other person something much more valuable? Like your bleeding, beating heart?

Walking over to the bed, he pulled me from it until I was standing and relieved me of my shirt. It was now a heap on the floor.

"Do you trust me?" he asked after cupping my chin with his fingers.

"I'm starting to question if I should."

Vaughn's nostrils flared as his gaze searched mine. It lasted long enough to make my heart stop. "Yes or no, pip-squeak?"

"Yes," I admitted reluctantly. I just hoped the day never came that he made me regret it.

I shivered at the heat that rose in his eyes. His fingers left my chin, and I almost jumped out of my skin when I felt them unhooking my bra. In no time, it joined my shirt on the floor, and I fought against the urge to cover myself. Almost reverently, his thumb brushed back and forth over my nipple until it was a hard point. Pushing me back onto the bed, he lay beside me, resting his head on his hand.

"I'll never get used to this with you," he whispered while gazing into my eyes.

"I don't think I will either."

He kissed me then, and I forgot the fact that I wore nothing but my panties until the hand that had been caressing my belly dipped inside them. I moaned when his fingers found and softly teased my clit. He did that until my panties were soaked, and then he pushed his fingers between my lower lips.

"Why are you so wet?" he asked between kisses. He was

rubbing me soft enough to drive me insane but not enough to give me what I ached for. "Hmm?"

"Because you're touching me."

"Want me to stop?"

By now, I'd figured out that he was teasing me with more than just his fingers. And getting off at the same time by making me beg. "Please don't."

I held my breath when Vaughn began slowly filling me with his finger, but then reaching the first knuckle, he stopped. When I tried moving my hips to get him to go deeper, he pulled his finger out, only filling me once more when I lay there submissively. "I'm not a mind reader, Ty-ty. Tell me what you want." He cruelly added a second finger, making speech temporarily impossible.

"I want you to stop being an asshole," I finally answered breathlessly, "and make me come."

The sound of his deep, throaty chuckle had me tightening around his fingers. "Your wish is my command," he said before kissing me one final time. "But tonight, we do things my way."

I frowned, wondering what he meant as he stood and pulled his wallet from his jeans. My breath stalled a second later when he plucked a square, gold foil from inside before tossing his wallet on the nightstand.

I shot up into a sitting position before grabbing the sheet to cover myself. "Vaughn?"

"Relax," he said as he unbuttoned his jeans. "I won't be popping your cherry tonight." My heart thundered as he pulled his jeans and his boxers down before stepping out of them. Vaughn was already hard, and the small, titanium barbell piercing the head of his dick glistened with pre-cum.

"Then why do you need that?" I asked.

All I got was a smirk in return. As my arousal skyrocketed, I watched transfixed as Vaughn ripped the condom open with his teeth before slowly, *carefully* sheathing himself. Thanks to Prince Albert, the likelihood of the condom breaking was too high to think about, or I'd surely back out. If I thought my life was stressful now, I didn't want to imagine how it would be with a baby on my hip—at *eighteen*.

"You trust me, right?" he challenged once he was done. I'd told him so, and now he was making me prove it.

I inhaled as much air as I could before letting it all go. "I do."

Without further ado, he seized my ankles and dragged me down the mattress until my bottom half nearly hung off the bed. My lips parted because although I trusted him not to go too far, I didn't trust myself not to beg for it.

He ended up silencing me before I could speak with a kiss so desperate, I couldn't help but respond with complete submission. Once I was lying on my back again, Vaughn ripped the sheet covering me away and pushed my legs up and out. My chest heaved as I watched him grip his thick cock and stroke it slowly while meeting my gaze.

"You're beautiful, pip-squeak. So fucking beautiful that I can't go another day without being inside you."

I think my heart stopped when he rested his knee on the foot of the bed. Kneeling over me, he began teasing my clit with the head of his cock. Even with the latex between us, I could feel his piercing providing friction that only intensified with each pass of that monster between his legs. Mimicking his fingers from moments ago, he dipped his hips, parting my swollen pussy lips with the underside of his dick. He repeated the action over and over until my eyes began fluttering from the sweet sensation.

"Pretty fucking pussy," I heard him mumble. His voice sounded strained—like he was barely holding onto his control. Overwhelmed with the sudden surge of power and pleasure, my hips lifted of their own accord, bringing his cock to my entrance. "Jesus, Tyra."

Feeling my body shaking out of control, I closed my eyes and inhaled deeply before letting it all go.

I trust him.

My lips fell open from shock when a moment later, I felt him pushing inside. He was so thick, and despite my arousal soaking the sheets, my pussy immediately protested the invasion. And just when I thought he'd go deeper and take my virginity, he pulled out, only to repeat the action.

"Vaughn, you're…you're…"

He kissed me again, and I swear his lips were voodoo.

"Just the tip, pip-squeak. I promise." He entered me again, and my legs seemed to spread of their own accord. He immediately settled between them. "You feel so fucking good."

Gripping the sheets, I found myself biting back a moan. Even though this wasn't something that I ever saw myself doing, I had to admit that I was already eager to do it again. "You too."

Feeling overwhelmed with such raw fucking emotion, I shot up to my elbows at the same time he leaned down. When our lips met, nothing else mattered. Vaughn kept his word, never venturing past the ridge separating the head from his shaft. This was reckless sure, but somehow, special. Unconsciously, we'd both decided that the other was worth the risk. It was the closest we'd come to admitting our feelings to one another.

"I need you to come for me, okay?" he begged against my lips. "I'm not going to—"

His mouth fell open when I tightened and pulsed around him, coming on his dick as he commanded. Neither of us should have expected to last long. The sensations were too powerful. Before I was even done, his body stiffened mid-thrust, and then he was filling the condom with a groan.

I fell back onto the bed as he settled between my legs, and for a few long minutes, we held each other as we both tried to catch our breath. Vaughn, being the athlete, caught his much sooner. Rising onto his forearms, he stared into my eyes. Worry, but minimal regret filled his green gaze.

"Are you mad?"

Slowly shaking my head, I reached down and gripped his ass with both hands. Wren's was nice, but Vaughn's belonged on a statue. It was already as hard as a rock. Even his abs poking into my stomach could put Michelangelo's *David* to shame. "I want to do that again."

chapter six

The Prince

THIS TIME, WHEN I AWOKE NEXT TO TYRA, I DIDN'T LEAVE HER SIDE. And it had nothing to do with her threat—to get Four to cut my brake line—just before her tired eyes drifted shut. It was because trying as I might, I couldn't help but give a damn. I felt responsible for yesterday, even though I hadn't shown it. My frustration with myself had boiled over and spilled onto her. I might not be her boyfriend, but I was still her friend, and I'd bailed.

Fingers linked behind my head with Tyra softly snoring on my chest, I watched the ceiling fan spin and wondered if I could be hypnotized into caring a little…less.

My phone pinged, but I didn't bother reaching for it. I knew it was none other than Jamie texting his usual morning selfie of him and Bee waking up together. It had been less than a week since they made it official, and I was ready for them to break up.

Needing to take a piss, I carefully slipped from underneath Tyra. After pulling on my jeans, I left the guest room. The sun was barely up, so the house was quiet as I made my way down the hall. There was a faint glow underneath the bathroom door that made me frown. Wren and Lou had an ensuite, so I wasn't expecting to fight anyone for the toilet.

Thinking maybe one of our friends forgot to turn off the light before they left last night, I had my hand ready to knock just in case. I had no doubt Wren wouldn't hesitate to shoot me if I walked in on Lou while she had her pants down. Or worse. Naked.

Just as my fist came bearing down, the door flew open. With honed reflexes, the man himself used his forearm to block my fist from connecting with his cheek. Something fell out his hand, and when we both rushed to pick it up, we bumped our heads instead.

"Fuck!" he barked in a volume louder than I'd ever heard him speak. I guess my head was harder than his—in more ways than one.

"Shit, sorry, man." I grimaced as I rubbed my temple. This time, I was quicker and swooped up the blue, velvet box he'd been holding. I started to hand it over and paused when the lid popped open, revealing what rested inside. I gaped at it a few seconds, wondering if I was seeing things. The modest diamond curved on the sides, the ends too sharp to be a simple oval. I didn't know shit about rings, but I knew that it was beautiful and exactly what I pictured adorning Lou's finger.

"You're going to propose?" I choked out when my initial shock cleared. "When?"

I watched the gray of his irises turn a startling blue before he spoke. Lou hadn't been kidding. "Soon."

"Fuck, man..." I stood there for a moment, not knowing whether to hug him or not. He didn't seem like the type. "Congratulations," was all I ended up saying when it got awkward. And then I made it even more so. "I won't tell anyone, I promise."

There was relief in Wren's eyes when he dipped his chin in gratitude. "Thank you."

"So, are you nervous?" He had to be. My armpits were sweating just thinking about it, and I wasn't even the one proposing. "Do you know how you're going to ask her?" Wren simply shrugged in response, but I could see the wheels turning in his head. "You don't talk a lot, do you?"

Neither did I, but that was because I had a lot to hide, especially from the former Exiled lieutenant. Wren had yet to learn that my father was once his rival. Even though he was no longer Exiled, I wasn't quite sure if I could trust him with that information. He sure as shit wouldn't be safe with it. The only reason my father hadn't killed Ever for knowing was that he knew I'd never work for him if he did. The head of Thirteen also knew my desire to keep Ever alive wasn't enough to give him what he wanted. For the moment, I had him trapped at a crossroads. Unfortunately, my father was clever, which meant my time was running out.

For years, he'd been searching for the perfect incentive—someone or something worth selling my soul. Remembering Tyra asleep down the hall, I realized if I wasn't careful, he just might get it.

Smirking, Wren took the tiny blue box from my hand and slipped it into his pajama bottoms. "Lou talks enough for both of us."

I snorted as he stepped around me, letting me have the bathroom. When I stepped inside and looked around, I realized he must have stashed the ring in here and was now looking for another hiding spot. Shaking my head at Wren's naïveté, I stepped back into the hall, catching him before he made it to the stairs.

"Hey," I called out, making him whirl around. Coming to stand in front of him, I held out my hand. "Give it to me." Wren's expression was blank as he stared at me—to the point that I wondered if I'd imagined the whole thing. "Unless you're planning to propose tomorrow, she's going to find that ring if she hasn't already." Although, it didn't seem like Lou's style to pretend while patiently waiting for him to pop the question. "Give it to me," I insisted when he still hadn't moved or spoken. "I'll keep it safe, I promise."

I patiently looked on as Wren considered it before slowly, finally handing over the ring. I took the box from him before slipping it into my pocket. He didn't look happy about it, but at least he was smart.

"One last piece of unsolicited advice?" I took his silence as my cue to go on. "Don't even think about proposing to her without us there to watch."

His jaw tightened before he spun on his heel, grumbling all the way down the stairs. Grinning, I quickly relieved my bursting bladder before rushing back inside the guest bedroom. Tyra must have just awoken because she was sitting up, hair all array and drool drying on her chin as she blinked sleepily at me.

"What time is it?" she croaked.

"Hell if I know. Pip-squeak, you won't fucking believe what I just found out." Not waiting for her to respond, I pulled Wren's engagement ring from my pocket and watched the tired haze clear from her whiskey eyes.

"I still can't believe he's going to propose," Tyra said for the fifth time since I'd spilled the beans.

I know I promised Wren I'd keep it a secret, but girlfriends—um, dear, close, personal friends with whom one shared a complicated relationship with were naturally exempt from such promises, right?

Tyra would make good on all of her many death threats if she found out that I'd known all along and didn't tell her. A man's got a right to self-preservation. Besides, I made her promise not to tell anyone.

"Well, he is," I said as I stopped at a red light. I was taking Tyra home to shower and change. Wanting to keep my eyes on her, I'd made her leave her car at Wren and Lou's. Pretty soon, we'd be calling them the Harlans. "And remember, you can't tell anyone."

"Why should I keep it a secret?" she shot back. "You didn't."

I could only sigh because I knew she wouldn't listen and simply laugh at my threats. *So much for secrets.* "Just don't tell Lou. It should come from him."

"I would never do that," she said as she reached for the glove compartment where I stowed the ring for now.

"What are you doing?"

"I just want to see it again."

"Pip-squeak, I've shown you like eight times already."

"So?" she mumbled as she slowly opened the lid.

My palms became a little sweaty when she carefully lifted the ring from the box and slipped it on her ring finger. Lou was a small thing, but Tyra was one inch from having to shop for clothes in the kids' section. Needless to say, the ring fit a little loose on her finger. I didn't realize that I was staring until someone behind me beeped their horn. I'd been so busy wondering what it would be like to see her wearing my ring that I hadn't noticed the light turn green.

"Put it back," I barked a little harsher than necessary. It didn't fucking matter that marriage to *anyone* would never be possible; I was only eighteen for fuck's sake. Wren would be twenty-one in a couple of months, and even he was pushing it.

When you know, you know.

Just as quickly, I shoved the thought away.

Fuck that.

"Be a dick," Tyra mumbled as she obeyed. "That'll get you into my pants."

I snorted even as I strangled the wheel. My frustration was a direct contrast to the arrogant bullshit spilling from my mouth a moment later. "We both know I don't need to get in your pants to make you come."

I could practically hear the steam coming out of her ears as Tyra bristled in my passenger seat next to me. "Yeah?" she said, crossing her arms. "Well, I'd give you a six out ten in that department, which is above average but still average."

Feeling her burn below the belt, I tucked my lips to keep from laughing as I focused on the road. *Lying bitch.* She seemed pretty satisfied with my performance last night. In fact, I *knew* she was.

"How would you know, virgin? You have someone to compare me to?"

Turning to stare out the window, she responded, "Maybe not, but that can always change." Even from her profile, I could see her smirking. "We're just friends, remember?"

Yeah, okay. This time, I was the one pissed off, so I turned up the radio to drown out my thoughts. I wish she fucking would. That would be the day she'd find out how jealous an asshole I could be, and my father would finally have his way.

Wisely, we didn't speak to each other the rest of the way to Tigerwood Lane. When I pulled into Coach's driveway, the weighted silence became a stunned one as we both stared at the visitor waiting by the front door.

chapter seven

The Pawn

"WHAT THE HELL IS SHE DOING HERE?" I WAS THE FIRST to break the silence even though Vaughn had recovered quicker. I could feel him watching me as he waited to see what I would do.

"I don't know," he replied with a deep sigh. He ran his fingers through his gorgeous hair, and I could tell he was two seconds from tugging on the ends. "Maybe you should go talk to her."

"About what? She's said enough. She's *done* enough."

"I don't think that was her intention, pip. People fuck up more than usual in the heat of the moment. I'm sure she's just here to apologize."

I pursed my lips, hating the fact that Vaughn was being rational when I wanted to rage. I didn't want to talk to her. I wanted Selena gone so I could get on with pretending she'd never existed. I still hadn't gotten up the courage to confront my father, not even when he texted me this morning to make sure that I was okay. All I could manage at the time was a thumbs-up emoji. If I'd tried using words, there was no telling what might have come spilling out.

My father *lied* to me.

My entire life, I was led to believe he and my mom had something special when all along he'd been nothing more than her goddamn sidepiece. Did that mean what I felt for Vaughn weren't real, either? My parents had been the reason I believed in true love and soulmates. What if the feeling I'd gotten when Vaughn kissed me for the first time had only been...I don't know, gas?

I felt strong fingers curling around my own and that same feeling, like watching a flower bloom on a warm, spring day, returned. *It was real.*

"Come on," Vaughn gently urged. "We'll do it together."

"Fuck, you're sweet," I blurted, making the corner of his lips turn up in a crooked grin.

Leaning over, he slid his other hand between my thighs, and I gasped when he roughly cupped my pussy through my shorts. "Remember that when I want more of this later on," he whispered before kissing my cheek.

I was still sitting there, blinking stupidly and feeling my temperature rise when he came around to open my door. He ended up having to lift me out when I couldn't seem to move my legs. His hands stayed around my waist, making sure I was steady before taking my hand and leading me up the stairs where my long-lost sister waited.

"Is she okay?" Selena asked when I swayed on my feet.

I was sure it seemed like I was a bit dramatic, but only to those who'd never had themselves a Vaughn Franklin Rees.

"She's fine," Vaughn answered when I only stared.

Selena was the one who'd shown up unannounced. *Twice.* If she hadn't come here to apologize, I wasn't about to beg for one.

"Oh...okay." She started wringing her hands as she searched for words, but I wasn't falling for her shy act again. "I know you probably don't want to speak to me, but I'm heading back home today, and I was hoping we could talk." She glanced at Vaughn when she said the last part, and I heard the unspoken "alone."

I could tell by the way he smirked and made himself comfortable against the railing that he did, too, and made it clear he wasn't going anywhere. I'd never been so grateful for his arrogance before.

"I'm pretty sure I've learned all I need to," I told her. "Let's recap. My father was a home-wrecker, my mother didn't love him, and I ruined your life."

"But you didn't ruin anything!" she said. A moment later, she was rushing toward me and taking my hand. For some reason, I didn't push her away. Her skin was warm and soft instead of cold and scaly like I had imagined it would be. "How could you say that?"

"It's what I would think if the shoe were on the other foot."

She paused at that before nodding. "I'm sorry about the other day. I didn't mean to turn your life upside down like that. I just wanted to meet you. You're—" She turned away but not before I saw the tear that slipped as she swallowed hard. "You're all I have left."

I found myself squeezing her hand and moving to stand closer. I didn't want to believe her, but how could I not? The pain in her eyes... No one could act that good. "What do you mean?"

"My father, he...he died."

"Oh." Before I could consider if it was a good idea, I pulled Selena into my arms and held on for dear life. I couldn't imagine what I would do if I lost my father. It made me even more grateful for my friends. I wondered about Selena's friends and if she had any to come all this way in search of comfort. My back was to Vaughn so that I couldn't see his face, but I figured if he thought this was a mistake, he would have pulled me away by now. For someone who claimed I wasn't his girlfriend, Vaughn sure protected me like I was.

I ended up inviting Selena in and offering her a cup of tea. I didn't really drink it myself, but it was what you made someone when they were upset or sick, right? Vaughn followed me into the kitchen after she accepted, and I felt his gaze on me the entire time as I filled a kettle with water and set it on the stove to boil.

"You don't have to do this, you know? She's not your responsibility."

"You're the one who told me to talk to her, and if she really is my sister, I can't just turn her away." I finally looked up to meet his gaze and melted at the worry there. "She already told me the truth about our mom and my dad. What more harm can she do?"

Vaughn chewed on his lip as he stared into space, and I had the feeling he was actually trying to figure that out. Walking over to him, I wrapped my arms around his trim waist and listened to the steady rhythm of his heart beating—the heart that belonged to *me*. He just wouldn't admit it.

"It'll be okay," I whispered when I felt him run his hand down my back.

Tugging on my ponytail, he pulled my head back until our gazes met. "It fucking better be," he said after he'd kissed me. "Otherwise, sister or not, I'll make her ass disappear."

My heart squeezed, but it wasn't a lighthearted feeling. No, I was wondering where the hell that had come from, and why did it sound like he meant it?

"Vaughn?"

His phone pinged, and I watched, feeling dumbfounded, as he casually pulled his phone from his pocket as if he hadn't just threatened my sister. His lips flattened as he read the message, and I could see the battle waging in his green gaze.

"You don't have to stay," I said, realizing his dilemma. "I'm a big girl. I'll be fine."

He looked like he wanted to argue, but instead, he sighed before looking me over. His lips twisted in amusement, and I was relieved to see the Vaughn I was hopelessly falling in love with.

"You're tiny as shit, pip-squeak, but I get your point." Only after tonguing me while groping my butt like a horndog did he let me go and head for the door. "Call me if anything changes."

He was gone seconds later, and I pretended not to notice Selena watching him as he left. I guess I couldn't blame her. Sometimes I still found myself drooling even after all of this time. Taking a deep breath, we stared at each other awkwardly until I broke the silence. "So...how do you like your tea?"

"I still can't believe you're going to Harvard," Selena gushed as she slid on a pair of oversized sunglasses. She then lay back on a beach towel in my borrowed bikini, and I had to admit that it looked better on her than me. While I was mostly skin and bones, Selena was artfully toned. She'd obviously spent a lot of time perfecting her body. We were currently soaking up the sun on the crowded beach after staying up all night talking. Somehow, I ended up letting her crash on our couch instead of driving back to her hotel at the two in the morning. "That's amazing. My baby sister is going to be a surgeon."

"I hope so," I mumbled, humbly admitting my fears. "To be honest, I'm a little worried." Not only would the coursework prove more challenging, but the competition would also be stiffer. It would be ten times harder to stand out. And I didn't just need to get through undergrad. There was also medical school and then finding a good residency and fellowship.

"You have no reason to be." There was so much confidence in her tone when she spoke that I had no choice but to believe her. "I saw those trophies your father keeps displayed, girl. You're going to kick ass at that stuffy school." I snorted because most of those trophies were from spelling bees when I was in elementary school, but I appreciated her trying. "*And,*" she said in a sing-song voice, "you already have a man, and he's *to fucking die for.* At least you won't have to worry about those nerds at Harvard distracting you."

I frowned at her assuming everyone at Harvard was a nerd but pushed it aside for a subject more pressing. At least to me. "He's not my man," I whispered, my gaze fixed on the sand. Out of the corner of my eye, I could see Selena pause before she lifted her sunglasses enough to see me clearly.

"What do you mean?"

"We're just...friends." The word tasted like acid in my mouth, and it only seemed to be that way whenever I was referring to Vaughn.

"Friends? That's not how he acted when you were together." She lifted a brow skeptically. "Is he seeing anyone else?" I shook my head before hugging my legs and resting my chin on my knees. "So how long have you two been just *friends*?"

"Ten months next week."

"So, are you fucking him?"

My eyes widened at how quickly she'd gotten personal. I wasn't as prudish as Jamie accused me of being, but sister or not, I barely knew her. Suddenly, I wished for my friends. I'd invited them to the beach, but no one had been able to make it. Four and Ever had gone to visit her mom in psychiatric care, Wren and Lou were spending some much-needed alone time together, Jamie and Bee were still honeymooning their new relationship, and Vaughn was MIA. Once again, he hadn't answered any of my phone calls or text messages. Something was definitely up. Training had never kept him this busy before.

"I know what you're thinking, baby sis, but I'm not going anywhere, so you better get used to my bluntness. Besides, it's just between us girls." She nudged my shoulder with her own before offering me a conspiratorial smile.

I briefly considered her point before deciding not to be so uptight for once. "We've done stuff but...no. We haven't gone all the way."

There was a twinkle in her eye that I didn't know how to interpret as she sat up. "Well, it sounds like you're in a relationship to me. If he were just in it for sex, he wouldn't be waiting a year for you to give it up. Especially not a guy that looks like that."

I started to tell her that there was so much more to Vaughn than his Adonis looks, overwhelming popularity, or the fact that his parents were as well-connected as they were rich. For some reason, I held back. I guess I wanted to keep those hidden trea-sures, the parts he'd only shared with me, all to myself.

"He said we couldn't be together even if he wanted to," I told her instead.

She frowned at that but didn't seem surprised. I was start-ing to see the benefit of having an older sister. Obviously, Selena was wiser and had experienced more. Maybe I should pick her brain and figure out how to make Vaughn mine once and for all. "Why?"

I shrugged even though he'd told me why. I also knew he'd been lying, so I wasn't quite sure what to think. There wasn't much that could top a bigot on the despicable-human ladder— except a child molester or maybe a serial killer. I had a hard time picturing the man who could sire Vaughn Rees as either of those.

Sticking to my original theory, I said, "I think he wants to keep his options open for when he goes pro but doesn't want to hurt my feelings."

"Pro?"

"Yeah. He got a lot of offers to play college ball. It's only a matter of time before the NFL picks him up."

"Shut up!" Selena said, sounding even more excited than when I told her I'd been accepted into Harvard. "He's that good?"

"He's amazing," I said, meaning that in more ways than one. I never expected Vaughn to stick around when he realized I wouldn't be an easy conquest. I certainly hadn't expected him to be so patient with me. Even though it was looking like we'd never be a couple, I was lucky to have him as a friend.

"Well, then you *have* to show him what he'll be missing if he lets you get away. Vaughn might be the coveted football star, but *you* are the real prize."

I am the real prize.

I met Selena's gaze, and it was like looking in a mirror. "How do I do that?"

Her lips slowly spread in a smile that almost seemed triumphant. I blinked at that. "For starters, you said you two had done stuff before?"

"Yeah…"

"In the bedroom?" she clarified at my confused look. I had a hard time meeting her gaze as I nodded. "Then you can start by telling me what he likes. Down to every dirty detail."

chapter eight

The Prince

I STARED AT THREE DAYS' WORTH OF MISSED CALLS AND MESSAGES FROM Tyra and knew that she'd be pissed. I hadn't meant to ghost her, but my father had insisted on starting my training, despite me maintaining that I'd never work for him. Unfortunately, there hadn't been much I could do with a gun pointed at my head, so I sat dutifully by his side, pretending to soak it all in as he slowly opened the door to his world.

My father liked to kid himself, but he was nothing but a low-life thug dressed in a fancy suit. He stood for nothing except the motto under Thirteen's insignia, and that was only because it benefited him the most.

Honor thy Father.

Its meaning was clear. To obey him, and I wasn't talking about God, in all things. Essentially, to kill and bleed for my father whenever he commanded it. Thirteen was nearly seven decades old, formed in 1949 by the original thirteen members. From there, a round table began, like King Arthur and his trusted knights, except there was nothing heroic about the men around it, and Thirteen's table was more like a pit of snakes. Whenever the presiding Father died, because there was no such thing as stepping down, another took his place. The thing was, that person could be anyone—literally anyone willing to fake their death and give up their identity to become a myth.

Franklin Rees was an alias, a person who did not exist. I

didn't even know my own father's real name and wondered if I even cared.

My mother, realizing she'd given birth to a monster's child, fled to Paris when I was six years old. I barely remembered her. I couldn't recall what she sounded like, looked like, or if she ever loved me.

Shaking off the familiar anguish, I ignored the notifications and let "Wrong Side of Heaven" by Five Finger Death Punch burst through the speakers. Without my father's blessing or knowledge, I'd set up a private gym in one of the unfinished spaces in the basement. He hadn't bothered tearing it down, but I didn't kid myself. I knew it was because he had hopes of putting my brute strength to use one day.

Never gonna happen.

Lying down on the bench, I forced myself to focus on benching the two-hundred-pound weight. The players at USC were already lifting three-hundred pounds, maybe more, and if I were lucky, I'd be at two-eighty by the time camp started in August. I'd also be taking hits from much bigger guys and would need to pack on more muscle. The Trojan's head coach had already emailed me a training plan to prepare. Unfortunately, I'd been too busy sniffing after Tyra and the little scraps she threw my way to start. They tasted ten times better than the smorgasbord I'd grown accustomed to, and maybe it was knowing that no one else had eaten off my plate.

This analogy is getting weird.

I thought about my theory as I lifted the weight before bringing it back down and admitting that virgin or not, I'd still be obsessed. There was something so pure about Tyra that went beyond the physical. Something that made me wonder if I wasn't without hope, after all. Tyra didn't know it, but she could have had anyone. She'd chosen me instead.

As if on autopilot, I set down the weight, stood, and grabbed my phone and keys before rushing from the house. My sudden urge to be near her was almost unbearable. I dialed her number as soon as I got behind the wheel of my car, but it rang once before going straight to voicemail.

See? Pissed.

Ignoring Tyra's hint to steer clear, I sped all the way to the little house on Tigerwood Lane only to find her car gone. I wondered how she'd gotten it back from Wren and Lou's in the first place and assumed Selena must have given her a ride. Remembering the girl who'd shown up claiming to be her older sister, I understood why Tyra was pissed. I promised her I had her back only to ghost her when she needed me.

Snatching my phone from the dash, I tried calling her again only to get the same result. Ignoring Einstein's definition of insanity, doing the same thing over and over and expecting a different result, I tried three more times. I bet ole Albert never had himself a girl as stubborn as Tyra Morgan Bradley.

Gritting my teeth, I finally gave up calling and tapped the tracking app I installed on her phone on the sly. Yeah, it was an asshole move and a little creepy, but dare to ask me if I gave a fuck. Tyra had made it easy with all the apps on her phone that she never fucking used. After installing the tracker, I hid it in one of the folders she kept to organize them. It had been there a month now, and Tyra had yet to realize it.

I'd taken a page from Ever's book, but in his creepy defense, Four had almost gotten herself killed racing in that junkyard. Had Ever not been there, he would have lost her.

Still, up until a few weeks ago, I thought that installing the app was hilarious and a little much—something I sure as fuck would never do. Ever, the smug prick, had simply smirked when I asked him for the name of the app.

Desperate times…

I hit the refresh button and waited while the app searched. This was my first time putting it to use, so I had no idea how accurate it would be. After a few agonizing seconds of searching, it finally gave me her location, and I frowned, recognizing the road. What the hell was she doing in the middle of nowhere?

Assuming it was wrong, I hit refresh again only to get the same result. Confused, I sat there fuming for a few seconds before I realized what day it was. Tomorrow was the Fourth of July. The fair had come to town.

I was only a couple minutes out when I got a call from Jamie. "Dude!" he greeted over the sound of the fair in full swing. It was always a highlight in our sleepy, little town, so everyone came out. "Where the fuck are you? Gang's all here."

As it turned out, my friends had texted plans in the group chat this morning to meet at the fair, but I'd chosen to ignore them. I was even more annoyed at myself when I realized I'd had Tyra's location all along.

"I'm almost there," I responded. "Have you seen pip-squeak?"

"Nah, not yet. Oh, shit, wait. There she is. Who's the chick with her? She's hot." There was a pause and then, "Don't tell Bee I said that."

"He doesn't have to tell me. I'm standing right here," Bee snapped in the background. I pictured her standing with her arms crossed and her blue gaze cold as ice.

"Aww, don't be mad, baby. Your face is the only face I want to jerk off to," he flirted.

Bee said something I couldn't make out, and then they started kissing all loud and shit as if I weren't still on the fucking phone.

"Guys? *Guys?* Are you shitting me?" I whispered to myself when I couldn't capture Jamie's attention. "Yo!" I ended up yelling. Finally, the kissing ended. "I'm still on the fucking phone."

"Oh, my bad," he said while not sounding sorry at all.

How much longer until they broke up? "I'll be there in sixty seconds."

"K," he replied. He then hung up before I had the chance to ask where to meet them.

I sighed as I pulled into the makeshift lot and paid the parking attendant the ten-dollar fee. Just as I'd found an empty spot, my phone pinged. I looked down and frowned at the message from an unknown number.

555-666-6969: Meet me by the Ring-The-Bell. :-*

As I made my way into the fair, I considered ignoring the text, but there were only a handful of people who even knew I was coming. Obviously, it wasn't a stranger. Since the number wasn't saved in my contacts and the area code wasn't local, I decided against replying until I knew for sure. When I arrived at the Ring-The-Bell, I looked around, seeing no one familiar. I was just about ready to take off when I felt a soft tap on my shoulder. Whirling around, I looked down and found the last person I expected.

Selena's smile was radiant as she stood before me in an off-shoulder, white tube top that pretty much only covered her tits and jean cutoffs so tight and short that I just bet her ass was hanging out. Her body made the outfit provocative—maybe a little too provocative for the fair. I knew that had it not been for Tyra, I would have gamed and cornered Selena inside one of these secluded corners by now.

"*You* texted me? How did you get my number?"

"I have my ways," she replied.

Okay, but why? Not wanting to be rude to Tyra's sister, I kept my thoughts to myself while wondering if I'd imagined the flirtation in her tone. I'd fucked enough sisters to know how ugly this always ended, and none of them had ever been remotely close to being someone special to me.

Feeling weird, I immediately started searching the area for the only reason I was even here. "Where's Tyra?"

"She's in the bathroom," Selena said before nodding toward the crowded brick building twenty feet away. "Poor thing is still a little hungover. I had no idea she was such a wild, party animal."

I felt myself scowl even as confusion ripped through me. Wild? Hungover? *Tyra?*

I'd seen her drink but never enough to get drunk much less enough to have a hangover the next day. I narrowed my gaze on Selena. "What exactly happened last night?"

"Nothing much." I might have believed her if her gaze wasn't meeting everything and everyone except mine. "Some guys we met got a little head start on the holiday weekend and invited us to a party."

"*What* guys?"

"To be honest, I don't remember." She began twirling the ends of her hair. "One of them mentioned being home for the summer. I think he said something about being a Delta at NYU."

Just then, Tyra stepped from the bathroom, and we immediately made eye contact even across the huge crowd. She looked caught red-handed when her puffy eyes widened, and I couldn't help but notice her brown skin, which always glowed, appeared a little dull and gray. Selena hadn't embellished her story one goddamn bit. My first instinct was to march over there and wring Tyra's goddamn neck. Knowing I would never forgive myself if I hurt her, I decided to walk away instead.

Partying with frat guys? She must have lost her fucking mind.

I didn't leave the fairground, but I didn't bother seeking out my friends. There was no telling what I might do if I found myself within reaching distance of Tyra. Instead, I found myself at one of the food stands and then sitting alone while I mustered the stomach to eat.

"There he is!"

The sound of Jamie's voice had me tensing nearly an hour later. There weren't too many people in Blackwood Keep with a Boston accent, so I knew it had to be him. Ignoring my uneaten turkey leg, I looked over my shoulder and found my friends, along with Tyra and Selena, heading my way. The rest of the picnic table had been empty. I think bystanders could sense my foul mood, so my friends immediately crowded around me. Tyra wisely sat on the other end of the table, but I could feel her troubled gaze as I made a point to ignore her. Selena, on the other hand, was chatting with Four as if nothing had happened.

"Dude, you said sixty seconds, not sixty minutes," Jamie fussed before snatching my turkey leg from the plate and biting a large chunk out of it. Usually, I'd punch him in the throat for poaching, but my stomach was still in knots.

Had Tyra finally figured out that she was too good for me and was looking for someone to give her what I couldn't?

"We've been looking all over for you." Jamie became distracted when he caught Bee glaring at him for talking with his mouth full. Grinning, he offered her a bite of the turkey leg, which she responded to by rolling her eyes before turning her head to talk to Lou.

Wren, to no one's surprise, was absent again.

I just hoped he lived long enough to give Lou the ring I was currently keeping safe for him. At least then someone would get their happily ever after. Lou stood, her expression tight, before announcing she had to go to the bathroom. Bee, deciding to join her, stood too.

"Did you guys hear the news?" Jamie blabbed the moment they were out of earshot. "Wren and Lou are getting hitched." I shook my head. News traveled too damn fast in this group, but this time, I only had myself to blame.

"He hasn't asked her yet," Four deadpanned.

Ever snorted. "Like she's going to say no."

I was both surprised and relieved to hear that coming from him. Ever hadn't spoken two words to Wren since finding out they were half brothers. After blackening his eye first, of course. I could only imagine the tension whenever they were in the same room. Both were bullheaded and prideful, something they must have inherited from their father. Ironically, Wren and Ever started out hating each other, and it looked like they were back to square one. Although, I didn't think that Wren hated Ever. I think he was more frustrated than angry. Maybe he thought he'd been doing the right thing by keeping their familial ties a secret.

"I know why he wants to put a ring on it so soon," Jamie claimed even though no one asked.

"Um…" Of course, the sound of Tyra's voice drew my gaze as she crossed her arms defensively, "because he loves her and wants to spend the rest of his life with her?" I knew she felt me watching her when her gaze nervously flicked my way before shifting in her seat.

"That, and he's tired of wearing a rubber."

"He doesn't need to marry her for that," Tyra argued. Usually, I found it funny whenever the two of them had their little squabbles, but all I could still think about was choking the life from her. *Just wait until I get her alone.* "That's what birth control is for."

"But he'd still have to worry about diseases if she stepped out on him. He puts a ring on it, and I guarantee she'll have stars in her eyes for the next three to five years. She won't even look at another dude."

"And what happens after that?"

Jamie smirked. "She'll realize she should have married me when she had the chance."

"Wow. Your view on marriage is quite, um, deluded. By any chance, did you tell Bee any of this?"

Jamie suddenly looked down his nose at Tyra. "Bee and I are the exceptions, not the rule. Besides, my dick game is hypnotic. Just look at her walk when she comes back. She's *still* dizzy."

I snorted though it was too low for any of them to hear.

"You and Lou would have never worked," Tyra insisted. She'd wisely chosen to ignore Jamie's comment about his dick.

I probably would have flipped this fucking table over if she'd fixated. I was still questioning how Jamie hadn't gotten to Tyra before I did. It wasn't like he hadn't tried. Girls fell over themselves for him until he opened his mouth. "You and Lou are too similar. One of you would have ended up buried in the backyard."

Jamie gave a sad sigh, but he didn't look all that sorry as his gaze wandered, drawn to Bee just as she stepped from the bathroom nearby. Their gazes connected across the way before he responded to Tyra. "You're probably right," he conceded in a low tone. He sounded distracted when he added, "I'm glad we never got to find out." Standing, he took off after Bee when she and Lou hooked a right, stepping out of sight rather than coming back to the table.

Like a moth to a flame, my gaze returned to Tyra and found her already watching me. It was all I could do not to flip her ass off, so I reluctantly rose to my feet instead. "I'm going to take off," I mumbled.

I didn't wait for anyone to respond, least of all Tyra, before I got the fuck out of dodge.

chapter nine

The Pawn

"**D**ID YOU *SEE* THE LOOK ON HIS FACE WHEN I TOLD HIM WE'D been partying with frat guys all night long?" Selena squealed as she played with my makeup without a care in the world. I, on the other hand, was squeezing the life out of Mr. Bear as I sat on my bed with my knees to my chest. "He was so jealous."

"He seemed more than jealous, Selena. He looked really hurt. Are you sure this is going to work?" The truth was, Selena and I *had* been drinking but not with some frat guys. It had taken her plying me with alcohol until I was ready to puke before I could share with her the intimate details of my relationship with Vaughn. Even now, I felt like I'd made a huge mistake. I just didn't understand why.

"Like a charm," she responded confidently. "I know it seems bad, but listen, Vaughn is an alpha male who grew up an only child fed with a silver spoon. Those are not the characteristics of a man who likes to share. Trust me. He's going to be eating out of your palm before you know it."

"I don't know…"

"Well, I do." She proceeded to touch up her mascara. It was almost midnight, so I wasn't sure why she was even bothering. We'd blown the entire day at the fair despite Vaughn storming away and leaving everyone confused. I remember how they'd all turned their expectant gazes on me, waiting for me to chase after him. I almost did until I caught the subtle shake of Selena's head. "I'm your big sister, sweetie. I'd never steer you wrong."

"Maybe we should call my father and let him know you're here." Last night, while I was drunk out of my mind, Selena had invited herself to stay the summer. Wanting to be a good sister and get to know her, I ignored the queasy feeling in my gut and obliged.

"Why would you want to do that?" Her cheerful tone didn't match her question.

"Because you came here to speak to him?"

"And meet you," she reminded me. "Look, you said he's going to be back in a few weeks, right?" At my nod, she added, "Well then, I say we use the time to bond as sisters, and when your father gets back, I can meet him then, okay?" She stood and flounced out of my bedroom as if the discussion was already closed.

Sighing, I picked up my phone, and after taking a deep breath, I started to dial. I didn't care what Selena said. Vaughn Rees couldn't be manipulated so easily. If he could, we would never have gotten this far. For months, I'd endured the whispers and opinions of my peers whenever Vaughn walked proudly beside me, a nobody, in Brynwood's halls. And now it felt like I was turning him into someone he wasn't just to get what I wanted. I felt like I could throw up.

It all seemed so harmless when Selena laid out her plan. I thought that I was stealing his heart once and for all. What if I'd broken it instead?

My stomach was all in knots as the phone rang, and my bile rose. The wait for Vaughn to answer was pure agony. When the pause came, and I heard Vaughn's voice rather than the automated response of the voicemail, I almost cried tears of joy.

"What?"

Even though I expected it, I flinched at the coolness of his tone. "I-I was just calling to see how you were. You didn't talk to me at the fair."

"You didn't talk to me either, Tyra." I couldn't help but notice how he hadn't called me pip-squeak. I thought I hated his pet name, but now I wanted nothing more than to hear him whisper it to me. "Tell me why that is," he demanded. "Is it because you had something to hide?"

"What? No!" *Yes.* I squeezed Mr. Bear even tighter as my guilt grew. "What would I have to hide?"

"You tell me." And then he hung up.

I immediately yanked the phone from my ear, thinking I was mistaken and ended up staring at my home screen. It was a picture of us together as he stood in his bathroom mirror at the beach house, lifting me high over his head like a barbell or whatever.

He'd actually hung up on me.

I told myself that I understood, that it was all my fault, but seconds later, I was shoving on my shoes, grabbing my keys, and ignoring Selena's questioning look as I stormed out of the front door.

Vaughn knew I had a temper. He'd stumbled upon it by accident during the beginning of his courtship. Why he thought I'd take him hanging up on me lying down was a mystery. My meek little Honda couldn't quite get up to the speeds that his Aventador could, but I damn near topped out all the way to his castle looming on the hill.

It might as well have belonged to Vaughn since I doubted his father was ever around. Vaughn had way too much freedom to have any sort of regular parental supervision. It made me wonder more than ever what his father did for a living. Some jobs required parents to be absent often and for long periods, but not even pilots and flight attendants were gone as much as Franklin Rees. And where the hell was his mom? These thoughts continued to wreak havoc as I flew through the open gates and up the winding drive. I then slammed on the brakes, parking next to Vaughn's Lamborghini.

Questions that still needed answers.

If Vaughn wanted to touch me again, he had better well start answering some, and I meant it this time, unlike the forty times I vowed to leave Vaughn's ass alone. At least once a week for the last ten months, I'd convinced myself that I was done only for Vaughn to pull me back. Sometimes all it had taken was a smile. He might as well have just snapped his fingers.

Storming up to the big iron doors, I started pounding.

I pounded until my wrists were sore, my skin was red, and my fists throbbed. I was breathing fire minutes later when there was no answer. Even if there was a slim chance Vaughn had left with someone, he wouldn't have left the gates open, especially at this time of night. Trying my luck, I gave up being polite and twisted the knob. I blinked in surprise when the door opened. Taking advantage of my good luck, I stormed the threshold and closed the door behind me. I would have slammed it if it hadn't been so heavy. Looking around, I waited for a housekeeper or a gardener or someone to appear and kick me out. Then I remembered the holiday and the fact that it was midnight.

The house was dark and quiet, and if it hadn't been for the polished surfaces, elegant furniture, and the smell of fresh flowers, I would have thought the place was haunted. I'd only been here twice before, and even then, I hadn't ventured beyond the first floor. The last time was a few months ago when we'd staged an intervention for Ever, Four, Bee, and Jamie. Thinking about that morning, I shook my head. I was glad to see their little weird love square come to an end. The icing on the cake was that Jamie was almost bearable now. I'd never seen someone so obviously in love and yet so haunted by it.

The cherry on top had been witnessing one of Vaughn's rare fits of jealousy after Jamie alluded to sleeping with me to get under his skin. And when no one else was looking, the busybody had smugly winked as if he'd proved some great argument. I remembered feeling the butterflies fluttering in my stomach the rest of the day and grudgingly admitted that Jamie definitely had given me a rare peek inside Vaughn's mind.

My footsteps were quiet as I climbed the four marble steps leading up the two-story foyer. Even in the dark, the chandelier shimmered, highlighting the dining room's entrance on my right and the seriously impressive library to my left. I knew that if I crossed through the dining room, I'd find a narrow hallway on the other side that led into the kitchen.

I remembered being in awe and couldn't begin to imagine how the rest of this castle looked. The kitchen was state of the art and the shape of the room unique—like an octagon with fewer sides or whatever a square with round corners was called.

Maybe a squircle?

Laughing to myself, I pulled my phone from my back pocket, ready to patent my genius and googled:

A square with rounded corners is called a squircle.

You've got to be fucking kidding me.

I made a mental note to pen a letter to whoever had beaten me to it when I heard what sounded like metal clang in the distance. Returning my phone to my back pocket, I followed the sound until I reached two sets of stairs situated between the foyer and an even larger room that resembled a small ballroom. The double sweeping staircases on each side of the small gallery led up to the second floor and down to what I could only assume was the basement.

Crossing to the side where the stairs led down and the sound of music playing heightened, I stood on the first step and wondered if this was a good idea. What if Vaughn wasn't home after all, and it was his father I was disturbing? Suddenly, the rumors didn't seem so farfetched as I stared into the shadows waiting for me below.

Reasoning, I pulled out my phone again and dialed Vaughn.

A moment later, I heard the music stop, interrupted by the faint trill of a phone ringing down below. I heard the bang of metal again, a beat of silence, and then…

The ringing stopped.

The silence was broken a moment later by the automated prompt telling me to leave a message, and then the music played once again but much louder this time.

Releasing the air I'd been holding, I tightened my grip around my phone as I stormed down the stairs and into an even smaller gallery. Having no clue where I was going, I hooked a hesitant left through sliding doors. My jaw dropped when I saw the length of the indoor pool. It had to be maybe seventy or eighty feet long, and though narrow compared to the length, it was still a whopping twenty feet wide. It resembled the lap pools athletes used and even had a small jacuzzi at the end. Maybe this was how Vaughn's shoulders became so impressive. It seemed as if he literally had the world at his fingertips.

Remembering that I was on a mission and not a house tour, I crossed the enormous pool room to the other side and followed the sound of "Power Trip" by J. Cole featuring Miguel through an open door into yet another hallway.

At this point, I wasn't so sure I'd be able to find my way back alone.

There was an elevator and another set of stairs leading down, but to *where*?

Maybe it's an underground graveyard where his father hides dead bodies because he's a serial killer.

I snorted at my ludicrous thoughts and stepped through the door across from the stairs. There, I found a room, the walls and floors made of cement and the low ceiling revealing wooden beams. Taking up the area was every single type of gym equipment known to man, and it was all state of the art. There was even a punching bag hanging from one of the wooden beams. I had no doubt Vaughn put it to good use.

Speaking of the devil…

A shirtless Vaughn was seated at one of the machines, his expression full of intent and his tanned skin glistening with sweat as he used the leather pad to curl his muscular legs.

I wasn't sure how long I watched transfixed until I remembered the reason I was there. He'd hung on me, and *then* he sent me to voicemail when I called him back.

"Vaughn." I waited for him to stop and turn, to face me despite his unwillingness to.

I got nothing, not even a twinge.

I could barely hear myself think and realized the music was too loud. Vaughn had turned the volume up as if he were trying to drown me out. Spotting his phone sitting near a set of Bluetooth speakers behind me, I crossed over to it with the intent of cutting the music. Remembering how he'd ignored me, my lips tightened as I set his phone on the cement floor instead. I made sure he was still unaware of my presence before lifting one of the weights on the rack next to me. Letting my anger roll through me, I released my fingers one by one until the weight slipped from my hand.

Oops.

The music cut immediately when the entire phone splintered into tiny pieces.

Vaughn was up in no time, and the moment he turned to find me standing there, his eyes widened. I took a step back when his shock cleared, and anger filled his eyes. He was across the room in five long strides and gripping my arms so tight I was sure he'd leave bruises. I didn't care. This pain would never equate to the bruises he constantly left on my heart. Words uttered by my great aunt and long forgotten came to mind.

You think you've stolen his heart, but if all you feel is pain when you carry it around, then, honey, that's not what you have in your pocket.

"What are you doing here?" Vaughn demanded, his words sounding like a growl. "Are you insane? If my father catches you here—for fuck's sake. If he had *been* here…"

"So what?" I wiggled, trying to free myself from his hold. "I'm not afraid of your father."

Vaughn's fingers tightened around my arm, making me wince and keeping me still. "You should be." He then let me go, but he didn't allow me any space to breathe and being the silly thing that I am, I was having a hard time not becoming intoxicated by his scent. He was soaked in sweat, but he might as well have been wrapped in flowers the way my body was reacting to him. I couldn't get enough.

Why was I mad at him again?

Oh…right.

"I'm not ashamed of who I am, Vaughn." The vulnerability and fear in my tone couldn't be helped when I spoke again. "Are you?"

Vaughn looked confused for a moment before remembering the lie he'd told me about his father being racist. "Never," he said so fiercely that I believed him.

"Then what's the problem? So I won't get invited to any Rees family reunions. *Fine by me.*" I wouldn't be the first girlfriend not accepted by their boyfriend's family, and I wouldn't be the last. Also, screw them for putting me in the position where I had to bargain for a boyfriend.

Vaughn's lips twisted in amusement, and then he gave me a look that said to cut it out, but I wasn't feeling very obedient at the moment. "It's not that simple." He blew out a breath and shoved his fingers through his hair because he could see in my eyes that I wasn't backing down. I'd been rolling over for almost a year. I was so done with it that it wasn't even funny.

"Yes, *it is.* Why do you care so much about what your father thinks? Is it because you're afraid he'll cut you off or something?"

He seemed insulted, but what else was I supposed to think? "Money is the last thing I care about," he retorted before his lips curled in disgust.

"You drive a Lamborghini."

"That was to fuck over my dad."

His dismissive tone and the conversation I overheard between him, Ever, and their lackeys that first day of junior year, the day I met Four, made me believe him.

"He bought you that car so you'd work for him." Vaughn frowned, and I could tell he was trying to figure out when I'd learned that little tidbit and how. "Four and I overheard Adam Turner ask if your father still wanted you to work for him," I explained, referring to his old teammate. The next night at the back-to-school bash, Four had cracked another of Vaughn's teammates over the head with a whiskey bottle for calling her mother a whore and holding an auction for Four's…services. Four got sent to reform school after that. Of course, Ever, who hated her at the time, had been behind the whole thing, and when his "step-sister" returned from Europe, she came back with a vengeance.

Vaughn didn't bother confirming nor denying it, so I said, "We've been doing whatever we've been doing for *ten months*. Your father must know about me by now. He must know that we're…friends." The word had never seemed so distasteful before now. What Vaughn and I had was more special than a friendship.

Shoulders slumping, Vaughn rested his forehead against mine even though he was nearly a foot taller. Because of our height difference, he often joked that he'd end up with a hump on his back if he weren't careful. "Maybe. But he doesn't know how much I—" He stopped, and it was all I could do not to scream and beg for him to finish that sentence.

"How much you want to fuck me?" My tone warned him to tread carefully.

Refusing to take the bait, he let me go and looked away. "That too," he mumbled stubbornly.

This road we traveled felt like it had grown just a little bit longer, and I told myself it didn't matter how long the journey took, not as long as Vaughn was with me. So why did it feel as if he were slowly letting go of my hand? Why did it feel as if I were the only one fighting for more? The answer seemed so obvious, and I could no longer deny it.

"Fine."

He had every right to look wary when his gaze met mine a moment later. "Fine?"

Shrugging, I forced myself to appear indifferent when my heart was being ripped in two. "Exactly what I said." His brows dipped even further, but I was already walking away. I felt his hand catch mine before I could get too far, and his gaze was pleading as he held mine. It only took an ounce of strength for him to pull me into his arms.

"Promise me you won't come back here, not alone and definitely not unannounced. It's not safe." Before I could reply, he kissed my lips, and I let him. Little did he know, it would be the last time.

"I won't come back here," I promised. When he went to kiss me again, I turned my head. "Ever." I took advantage of his shock at the finality of my tone and freed myself before he could recover.

"What did you say?"

"You asked me not to give myself to you unless I could live without more, and I've just decided that I can't." I shook my head, willing my tears away. I'd shed enough for him, and he didn't even know it. "Not when it's you."

I was two steps from being out the door. I was almost free. Realizing it, Vaughn rushed the distance I'd put between us and slammed the door shut. I'd just turned to go when he trapped me inside the gym with him. My lips parted from shock, and then I was frozen in place. Vaughn loomed over me with one hand, keeping the door closed. I'd never felt so small and helpless.

"You're not leaving."

"That's funny," I mocked, a sob stuck in my throat. The dam holding my tears back began splintering down the middle. "You couldn't wait to get rid of me a second ago." I tried to sidestep him, but he turned me to face him, his left hand joining his right until I was caged in. His green eyes glittered when our gazes met, and I willed myself not to fall into them. Not again. *Never* again.

"I'm not done with you."

"But I'm done with you." I rested my head against the door since it was the only space I could put between us. He seemed to read my mind when he stepped closer, taking back the distance I'd gained. I was burning up from the heat of his bare chest so close and wondered if his heart was beating as fast as mine.

Probably not.

It was becoming clear to me that Vaughn Rees had no heart.

He closed his eyes and didn't open them even after he spoke. "Tyra."

His tone when he uttered my name suggested *he* was the one losing his patience, and that *he* was the one who'd given everything and gotten nothing in return. I could have kneed him in the balls, but I didn't. I couldn't move once I heard the words that fell from his lips next.

"My father threatened to kill me if I didn't give up football." His whisper had stolen the air from my lungs, but he kept speaking as if what he said was perfectly normal. "I kept playing because it was my dream. It was the only thing I had to give my heart and soul to." Finally, he opened his eyes, and what I found in their depths rendered me speechless. "Until you." Without a shred of mercy, Vaughn wrapped his hand around my neck, and then he was pulling me away from the door I'd tried to escape through. "So what makes you think," he continued slowly, "that I'd ever let you walk away from me?" His fingers tightened when I tried to pull away, much like the hold he had on my heart. "I won't. Not now, not ever."

Vaughn must have seen the defiance in my gaze because he loosened his hold enough for me to speak. It took me a second longer to manage it. During that short time, I swore I hated him. "It's," I struggled to speak between pants, "not up...to you."

He looked amused at that. "You're confused and tired," he said, sounding like a condescending pig. "Go home and get some sleep."

"Fuck you."

Releasing me, he opened the gym door and waited for me to walk through. I did, even though my legs threatened to give. "I'll see you in the morning," he said as if the last hundred and twenty seconds hadn't happened.

"If you come near me, I swear to God—"

Grabbing me, he pressed a tender kiss to my lips that contradicted the force he'd used to bend me to his will. "I'll see you in the morning," he repeated. "Now get out." And then he smiled gently before slamming the door in my face.

chapter ten

The Prince

R INGING THE DOORBELL, I STOOD BACK AND CURSED MYSELF FOR not stopping and picking up those flowers Tyra liked. Last night had gotten out of hand. I tossed and turned the entire night over the way I treated her. It was as if I had two personalities, and they were at war with one another. I knew she'd be pissed well before five minutes of ringing the bell passed and no one came to the door. I wasn't sorry for staking my claim, but I regretted the seemingly insurmountable wall it put between us.

Giving up, I rounded the side of the house and peered into the small window built into the two-car garage. Her Honda wasn't parked inside.

I was heading back down the driveway to my car parked on the street when I heard the front door open behind me. Spinning around, I barely held back a groan when I saw Selena standing there instead of Tyra. The only fucking thing she wore was a towel. Her wild hair, so much like Tyra's, was dripping water along with the rest of her.

"Sorry!" Selena yelled when she spotted me. "As you can see, I was in the shower." She smiled, but I couldn't find it in me to return the favor. She'd left me standing out here for over five minutes—plenty of time for her to have put on clothes. I glanced up at the bathroom window overlooking the front lawn, my gut twisting and tightening. "Tyra went to the store for groceries, but she should be back any minute. You can come in and wait if you like." Selena opened the door wider in invitation.

I stood there, contemplating whether it was wise, before deciding I was being paranoid. Even if by some chance Selena was up to no good, I had almost a hundred pounds on her. Sighing deeply, I climbed the stairs and crossed the porch. I had to angle my body so that I didn't touch Selena as I stepped into my former coach's house. When she closed the door, I nearly jumped out of my skin and heard Selena giggle as she followed me into the living room. I needed to get a fucking grip.

"Are you okay?" she asked as she sat next to me on the couch rather than heading upstairs to find some clothes. It wasn't like the sight bothered me, and that was the number one problem. Having a half-naked girl sitting so close next to me wreaked havoc on my baser instincts. My hands were just itching to peel away that towel.

"Fine."

"So did you and my sister have a fight? She seemed upset when she came home last night."

"You could say that."

"Well, what did you do?" Offering a sensual smile, she inched closer to me on the couch. "Or rather, what *didn't* she do?"

Shooting to my feet, I started for the stairs. "I have to piss."

It was the only explanation I gave before I hightailed it out of there. If I hadn't, I might have slapped Selena for coming on to me. If she hadn't been Tyra's sister, I might have even bent her over the goddamn couch.

Slipping inside Tyra's room, I took the time to lock the door—because I wasn't a fool—before throwing myself on her bed. The ridiculous number of frilly pillows smothered me while the stuffed animals seemed to stare accusingly. Needing a distraction, I dug my brand-new phone out of my pocket. I thought about what I would say to get Tyra home as fast as possible before shooting off a text.

Be home in ten minutes or say goodbye to Mr. Bear.

Taking a picture of him kissing my junk, I sent it to her for good measure. Unlike a couple of hours ago, when I texted her, she responded immediately. *So her phone does work.*

PIP: Get out of my room and get out of my house.

Grinning, I stroked the soft fur on her favorite stuffed animal as I texted back. Last night, Tyra had claimed she was done with me, and I was determined to make her see how that could never be possible.

It's your father's house, and I think I'll stay.

PIP: I'm on my way, and so are the cops.

I snorted. All those book smarts, and she was still so naïve. Even if she had been telling the truth, the police would take one look at me and apologize for the disturbance. My mother's family owned this town, and though they wanted nothing to do with me because of my father, everyone knew the Blackwood blood ran through my veins. They wouldn't allow the embarrassment of me getting arrested.

It had been years since I'd been in the same room with the Blackwoods. Whenever they saw me, they looked the other way.

Head throbbing, I tossed my phone aside, not bothering to respond, and closed my eyes. Five minutes later, I heard the front door slam below and footsteps pound up the stairs. The knob turned, and then Tyra released a frustrated growl when she realized her bedroom door was locked.

"Vaughn, open this door!" she yelled while banging on the wood.

"What's the magic word?"

"Are you mental? I'm not begging you!"

I started to think I got off on her being pissed because I added, "Ask me nicely as a good girl would do." I definitely preferred her anger over indifference any day. The latter meant she no longer cared, and I couldn't have that. There were too many people in my life already who had it covered.

"Fine," she huffed. "Stay in there and die of starvation. I truly don't give a shit, Rees."

"You'd never let that happen." I wasn't worried about her calling my bluff, either. I knew Tyra better than she knew herself. I was, however, bored with this game, so I stood from the crowded bed and crossed the small room. "Now tell me you're mine and accept that I can never be yours."

"What the hell does that even mean?" I heard her whisper through the door. When I finally turned the lock and ripped the door open, she wore an incredulous expression as she stared up at me.

"It means you're my girlfriend, but I'm not your fucking boyfriend."

Lips parted, she blinked at me as if I just grew two heads. Sometimes it felt like I had. "In what universe is that fair?"

"In the only one where we have a chance in hell of being together." If the shoe were on the other foot, I'd take whatever I could get because I could never let her go. Obviously, she didn't feel the same. For Tyra, it was all or nothing. What kind of shit was that?

Her gaze narrowed as she seemed to think it over. I didn't know what the hell it meant for me when her shoulders slumped, but a moment later, she made herself clear. "Say I agreed to those terms…" She peered up at me. "Can you honestly say you'd still respect me?"

I started to assure her that I would when my mouth snapped shut.

No. I wouldn't.

It was the same kind of relationship I'd had with every girl that came before her. I allowed them to pretend we had something deep and meaningful as long as I got what I wanted in the end. And when I was done… Hell, I usually pretended not to know them—sometimes while watching two girls that I'd screwed fight over me like dogs for a bone. It seemed cruel, but if my father had gotten wind of it, they'd both be dead.

"Can you?" she pressed, making my frustration rise. We had bigger problems, like the fact that I might already be in love with her, yet she was worried about me fucking respecting her.

"Tyra—"

"Yes or no, Vaughn."

"No."

We stared at each other for a long while, waiting for the other to give in. For a moment, I thought she might, but then Tyra did something I didn't think was possible. She stepped aside, making way for me to leave. I didn't understand the strange feeling in my chest. It felt as if my heart had crumbled at my feet. My steps were slow as I made my way toward the stairs, giving her time to change her mind.

She didn't.

I made it all the way down, locked eyes with Selena, and my jaw tightened at her salacious smile. She'd heard every word.

I considered turning around and warning Tyra about her slutty sister, but my anger and the need to make Tyra hurt propelled me through the front door instead. As the summer sun beat down on me, I decided that Tyra was no longer my concern.

I should have been relieved about that.

"Son, you seem distracted," my father observed as I sat across from him in his office. It had been a day, and Tyra hadn't come crawling back yet. That had to be a record. "Is everything okay?"

I almost laughed in my father's face at the idea of him caring. Maybe he'd even break out his knuckledusters until the pain in my body numbed the pain in my heart.

No, everything isn't o-fucking-kay, Pop. I'm pissed. I'm pissed about the fact that Tyra had given up and pissed about the fact that you so clearly haven't.

"Fine."

"Good," he said, not bothering to pry since he didn't give a shit. "I have important business in Colombia that must be taken care of immediately."

Good riddance.

"Fingers crossed your plane doesn't crash on the way," I responded dryly.

He paused at that but then continued as if I hadn't spoken. "As Father," he said, referring to the moniker he inherited when he ascended, "you know that I am not allowed to take such liberties and risks by showing my face. The strength of Thirteen depends on it." I'd been drowning out the sound of his voice until he made his next announcement. "You'll go in my place."

I did laugh then, long and hard while my father simply stared at me. I wiped the tears that had slipped from my eyes, but it hadn't been all from humor. "What makes you think that?" I finally asked when my laughter died.

My father took the time to pick some invisible lint from the breast pocket of his suit before speaking. "Because your future, your *real* future, is inevitable. It's time you accept that, son."

"What will you do if I don't?"

"If you prove to be no use to me, we'll cross that bridge when we get there."

"You mean, you'll toss me off of it."

He chuckled heartily at that as if I'd told a joke. "More or less."

The next morning, I boarded a small, private plane to Colombia, and although I was empty-handed, I wasn't alone. I was accompanied by four grim-faced men, three of whom I immediately recognized as Siko, Eddie, and Mr. Palmer. The latter was nearing his fifties and, as he liked to put it, "getting too old for this shit." He was my father's closest confidant, although he treated Mr. Palmer like a secretary more than anything.

The fourth man was new, or at least he was to me.

Ironically, the stranger seemed to be as interested in me as I was in him. Black hair, black eyes, and even blacker expression, Jeremy Antonov didn't take his gaze from me for a second after the introductions were made. How was it possible that someone I'd never met wanted to murder me this bad? There was no question. It was more evident than the reason why. I tried to guess his age, maybe early to mid-twenties. He was tall, too, at six-four or six-five and muscular, although not as much as me. Somehow, I doubted, though, that I would walk away from a fight with him.

"Aw, don't worry about Rem," Eddie, who looked like a younger Michael Peña, teased after he sat next to me on the leather sofa. He was one of the few men who sat around my father's round table and executed his orders. Up until a few months ago, he and Siko had been serving as my father's spies while trying to herd Nathaniel Fox out of hiding. "And don't take it personally. Bastard's always in a foul mood."

Not that I gave a shit, but I found myself asking anyway, "Did I do something?"

"No." He scratched the stubble under his chin before adding, "At least not yet, anyway." My wariness grew after hearing that. I was already piecing together Jeremy's problem when Eddie spoke again. "Jeremy's impressed a lot of people in a short time. He's got a lot of, uh, special talents. Everyone thinks he's the natural pick when your old man kicks the bucket."

"Except, my father wants me."

Eddie met my gaze, looking serious for the first time since meeting him. "What your father is planning goes against all of Thirteen's rules and could get him killed. The round table, as you like to call it," he whispered with a rueful grin, "has total authority over who succeeds Father. Franklin's reigned the longest and accomplished the most of all Thirteen's leaders. Naturally, he believes that it should remain under his control. For good."

My heart pounded as I recalled the morning nearly a year ago when my father cornered me in my room the first day of senior year and revealed his plans for me. It was the same morning I met Tyra, but I wisely decided not to fixate on that. "He's creating a dynasty."

Eddie nodded in confirmation. "And without you, he'll fail."

Not just me, I wanted to say. My father fully expected me to produce an heir so that he could force the same life on my son. He wanted to crush his hopes and dreams and rot him from the inside out. "So why don't you stop him?" I snapped. I was damn near in a panic at the possibility of that future. "What's in it for you?"

"That's an odd question to ask, considering I just told you this could get your father killed." Eddie eyed me curiously, but I didn't bother making any excuses. There was no love lost between my father and me, and I didn't give a damn who knew it. Sighing, Eddie looked away for a moment as the plane began to taxi down the short runway. "He made me a generous offer, and I've never been one to make waves."

My eyebrow rose at that because it sounded to me like Eddie was a coward in disguise. "And the others?"

"I wouldn't worry about them. Siko and Mr. Palmer are both too afraid and too greedy to ever say no. Everyone except Rem." He looked at me then. "Antonov sits at the table now. If he catches on to what Father plans, Rem can kill him with impunity." Eddie considered his claim for a moment before adding, "As long as he can prove his reasons."

"Sounds like a risky gamble." Or a deadly game of chess.

"It is. Especially now that your father has the rest of us on board."

That left Jeremy Antonov the odd man out and as good as dead if he made a move. Now knowing why he hated me, I found myself meeting his gaze where he sat at the back of the plane and felt my blood run cold at the promise in his smile.

"Don't worry about him," Eddie naïvely assured me. "He's too smart to do anything without proof. Even if he knocked the entire round table off, he'd still have Thirteen to answer to."

I didn't bother responding as I took a huge risk in leaning my head back and closing my eyes to sleep. My father wanted to hand me what rightfully belonged to *Jeremy*. I'd say Antonov had plenty of reason to kill me.

The first black stain on my soul had set, and the blood on my hands could never be washed away. I hadn't been the one to pull the trigger, but I'd done nothing to stop it, either. When my father told me he had business in Colombia, he failed to mention that business included ambushing a man he considered a traitor and killing him.

Even now, I had a hard time keeping the bile rising in my throat from spilling as I watched Siko and Eddie load the crate containing Jacobo Jiménez's remains onto the plane. Amid my dark thoughts, I wondered how they planned to explain the dead body and cocaine to customs. Diego Jiménez, my father's new supplier, had happily looked on as Antonov put a bullet in his older brother's brain. I'd never been more grateful to be an only child.

"Boss's son or not," Jeremy said as he came to stand next to me under the hot Colombian sun. "If you faint, I won't hesitate to leave you kissing the pavement."

"What makes you think I'm going to faint?"

He shrugged, and the simple gesture somehow seemed uncharacteristic of a man I just witnessed kill in cold blood. "Call it a hunch."

The way he spoke, slowly and with a great deal of concentration, didn't escape my notice. I wondered if English was even his first language. Judging by the accent he was trying to conceal with an American one, my guess was Russian. "Twelve hours isn't enough time to have hunches. You don't know me."

"It's plenty when you're not daddy's little bitch boy. And no, I don't know you, but I know what you and your father are up to." He robbed me of having the last word when he swaggered away before I could respond.

Moments later, I felt a slap on my back as I watched Antonov board the plane and found Siko—blonde, in his thirties, and completely crazy—watching him as well. "He's not all talk, you know. Whatever he said to you, I'd believe it if I were you."

"Yeah, thanks."

Jeremy hadn't actually threatened me, but I guess a man like him didn't need to. The icing on the cake was Antonov didn't seem to be afraid of my father or the repercussions of being openly hostile to his heir. I didn't know yet if that was a good or bad thing.

Someone more ruthless than I would have recognized a potential ally. How easy would it be for me to provide Jeremy the proof he needed and rid myself of my father once and for all? Knowing that it meant getting my father killed kept me silent. I may not have any affection for Franklin Rees, but I was no cold-blooded killer.

Thinking about Jacobo Jiménez, a man whose life I stood by and watched be taken, I boarded the plane, but home was the last place I wanted to be. I didn't know yet that it wouldn't matter where I ended up. The rot was already spreading, devouring everything I was and hoped to be, and after today, I'd never be the same.

chapter eleven

The Pawn

WHEN THE DAY CAME TO MAKE THE THREE-HOUR TRIP TO some never-heard-of town near the Poconos, I was a ball of nerves. I'd thrown up my breakfast at the thought of seeing Vaughn. It had been nearly a week since he stormed out of my father's house. I didn't know what to expect. I told myself that I wouldn't be intimidated or upset by his presence, but that was before the hours and minutes leading up to our little road trip ticked down to zero.

"So tell me again why we're going to some little dirt patch to watch people drive through mud?"

Tomorrow was Four's second pro-am race, and up until now, I'd been excited. "It's called motocross, and it's pretty cool," I re-iterated for the third time since I invited her to come along, "they race off-road on these bikes that—"

"Whatever," Selena interrupted as she studied herself in her little compact mirror. "Seems boring."

"It's not, but even if it was, it's important to Four, so it's important to me." *Also, you didn't have to come.* I chose to keep that thought to myself.

"I know she's your best friend but…why? It's not like you two have anything in common."

Despite it being dangerous, I took my eyes off the road to gage whether Selena was serious or not. I couldn't really tell since her oversized sunglasses shielded her gaze from me. "How would you know? We've only known each other for a couple of weeks. Less actually."

"Because I'm your sister. We share the same blood. Besides, we're not only the same on the inside, but we're the same on the outside, too. You don't think that matters to them and everyone else?"

My stomach twisted and turned as I picked apart her words. As much as I wanted to brush them off and pretend they never happened, I knew I couldn't. "What do you mean?"

"I mean, they're white, Tyra, and you're not."

I slammed on the brakes despite being in the middle of the tree-lined road leading to Four and Ever's. "Shut up!" I yelled, my lips parted in mock horror. "You mean they've been white this *entire time?*"

I watched her lips purse as she sat with her arms crossed. "You don't have to be a bitch, little sis. I'm just trying to open your eyes and help you see that you're just a token to them."

Stunned into silence, I collapsed against my seat, forgetting about the fact that I'd stopped in the middle of a road.

"You don't even know them." My argument would have been more meaningful had my voice been stronger. Disappointment ripped through me. It wasn't because I believed her words held even an ounce of truth. It was because I began to wonder if a relationship with Selena was truly possible. The people she'd judged so harshly after a mere meeting, I'd spent the last year getting to know. I never once had reason to doubt them the way I did my own sister right now.

"No, but I have twenty-one years of being discriminated against to tell me all I need to know."

"So that's it then? You just lump the entire race together? What if they did that to you and me?"

Removing her sunglasses, she met my gaze. "What makes you think they haven't?"

I shook my head as I stared out of the front windshield. My

father had once claimed that many people of color were also prejudiced and felt justified in being so. Until now, I didn't think that was possible—just as two wrongs didn't make a right, fighting hate with hate never once created love.

Sighing, I slowly pressed on the gas until we picked up speed. I refused to let Selena's skewed views bully me out of the best friends I'll ever have, and I didn't care if they were white, black, or purple.

But I also wouldn't give up my only sister so easily, either. Not when I'd only just found her.

I couldn't change Vaughn's mind about us being together, but I had all summer to try to change Selena's. Not fully knowing her story and how she came to these conclusions, I refused to be as quick to judge her as she had my friends. By seeking me out, Selena had given me another precious piece of the mother I never knew. Realizing this, I gripped the steering wheel tighter, determined not to take my sister or this gift for granted.

"Hey, hold on a second."

Selena's plea had me pausing when I started to climb into the Mercedes Sprinter Ever's father had generously rented for the occasion. The black passenger van wasn't the sexiest, but it was better than having to take separate cars. Unlike last time, everyone was here, even Wren and Lou. I'd yet to lay eyes on Vaughn, who was already seated inside. I tried desperately not to stare too hard at the outline of his body through the tinted windows. It was quickly becoming a losing battle.

Wren was busy tossing our bags in the back while Jamie and Ever loaded Four's bike on the trailer hitched to the van. Four, Bee, and Lou must have still been inside the house because I hadn't seen them, either.

Sighing, I let Selena pull me to the side out of earshot.

"You probably don't think much of me right now," she began as she tucked her straightened hair behind her ear while staring at the ground, "but I wanted to apologize for earlier. I shouldn't have said that."

Still feeling a little vulnerable, I crossed my arms over my chest. "Why did you?"

"I don't know…jealous, maybe?"

I frowned at that. "Why?"

"Because I'm your sister, and they know you better than I do?"

"That's not their fault," I scolded. "It's not yours or mine, either. Our parents lied to us, and when my father comes back, we'll get to the bottom of it."

"I know." Selena stared at the ground, her shoulders bowing in shame. "And I'm sorry I implied that you and Four have nothing in common. As much as I might not want to, I can see why you like her. She seems sweet and genuine—not to mention a total badass." She gestured toward Four's bike that Jamie and Ever were still fighting to secure.

"She is, and you'll like all of them if you give them a chance. I don't know what you've been through, and I know that you're older, but I'm here now, and I'd never let anyone hurt you."

She smiled at that before pulling me into a hug. "Ditto, baby sis."

Arms linked, we headed back to the van, all smiles.

"You know you girls could pass for twins?" Jamie observed. He was now leaning against the side of the van near the sliding door, loudly smacking on what I was sure was nicotine gum. I guess he'd quit smoking again. "I've never fucked twins," he purred, surprising me. I didn't think there was anything Jamie hadn't done. "Not at the same time, at least."

"Well, that's a shame," Selena said before sticking her hands in the back pocket of her shorts. It made her chest, which was a little bigger than mine, stick out. "Maybe we could rectify that for you someday."

Jamie's eyebrows shot up at Selena's offer. It was obvious he hadn't been expecting that since Selena knew he was with Bee. "Flattered, kitten, but I'm spoken for."

As Jamie wisely walked away, unease spread through me. My sister hadn't cared that Jamie had a girlfriend, someone I now considered a friend. "What was that?" I snapped as soon as Jamie was out of earshot. I wondered if he was heading to tell Bee about Selena coming on to him. And if he wasn't, should I?

"What was what?"

"Why were you flirting with him when you know he has a girlfriend?"

"So what? He flirted first," she pointed out.

"He wasn't really flirting," I tried to explain. "He's just... Jamie. He doesn't have a filter and likes to mess with people."

Selena looked completely unapologetic as she tossed her long hair over her shoulder. "Well, Tyra, tell me something. How was I supposed to know that?"

Feeling like my head was about to explode, I stormed up the van steps without responding. Selena was proving to be a handful, making me feel like the older and more mature sister. I was at my wit's end, and it had only been a week.

It wasn't until I nearly tripped over a pair of long legs that I remembered Vaughn. Mortification filled my already boiling pot of emotions when I met his green gaze. He had to have heard everything, but I didn't care about that as much as the emptiness in his eyes. Why did it look like he hadn't slept in days?

"Excuse me." My voice was meek, doing nothing to break the thick tension or ease the awkwardness between us. We'd fought before, but we'd never broken up. Or whatever it was called when you weren't a couple, to begin with.

Rather than remove his legs from blocking my path, he rose from the bench he'd been lying prone on and claimed the entire back row for himself. Feeling the need to be close to him even though I couldn't offer him comfort, I chose the row in front of him. I was only slightly annoyed when Selena plopped down next to me as if nothing had ever happened.

Vaughn was lying down again, and thankfully, his eyes were closed because I couldn't keep mine off of him. Something was wrong, and I didn't need the past year I spent getting close to him to know that. Had he really taken me calling things off that hard?

I knew he was upset, but…

I took a deep breath and told myself not to feel guilty. I did what any woman would when she accepted that she was being strung along. It took me a while to find my way out of the fog. Now I saw vividly the version of Vaughn that had been there all along.

Everyone—Four's blue-eyed, black Lab included—started loading into the van, and when Four spotted me, her brown gaze lit up with excitement. She tried to climb back, but Ever caught her around the waist and deposited her in the passenger seat up the front. He gave her a look not to move before rounding the van and getting into the driver's seat. Jay D happily sat between their seats, his tongue and tail wagging.

Bee and Lou sat in the row in front of me while Jamie and Wren begrudgingly shared the front row. The tension between Wren and Lou hadn't lessened one bit, which explained why Lou chose not to sit with him. I watched her glare at the back of his head before rolling her eyes as if he could see her and turning around to face Selena and me.

"About time you guys got here," she said to me while ignoring Selena. It had only just occurred to me that Lou hadn't taken much interest in my sister. She wasn't rude to her, but… My brows dipped as I wondered if Selena had noticed, too, and that was why she wasn't thrilled with my choice of friends. I made a mental note to corner Lou and to ask her what her deal was later. I knew it wasn't because my sister was black, as Selena had implied, but there had to be a reason Lou wasn't eager to make friends.

Even more surprising was the fact that Lou hadn't already come out with it. Sometimes I couldn't decide who was worse in the no-filter department—Lou or Jamie.

Two peas in a pod indeed.

We were on our way a short time later, and it took no time at all for Jamie to make a dirty joke.

"Have you guys ever watched the videos of the pornstars riding around in a van? They pretty much just look for someone kinky enough to fuck on camera while cruising through town." Jamie looked around, meeting everyone's gaze. "We've already got the talent, and Lou's got her camera. Who wants to go first?"

I locked gazes with Selena, and she rolled her eyes at my smug look. Jamie had just made my point and most predictably.

"Jamie, I'm pretty sure those meetups are prearranged," I argued. It was starting to feel like my duty to challenge Jamie since I was the only one who ever rose to the occasion. Everyone else simply ignored him. "They don't just pick up strangers."

Jamie's eyes widened, and then his grin spread as he energetically pumped his fist. "Yes! Fuck yes! I knew you were a dirty girl, Ty-baby. Whoo!"

It was my turn to roll my eyes because what could I say? I did just admit to watching porn. But really, who didn't?

"Vaughn, are you hearing this?" Jamie naïvely called out. None of them had any clue yet that Vaughn and I had broken things off. "I bet he knows. I bet you guys watch them together while you get each other off." Jamie then waggled his brows suggestively. "Don't you?"

Bee suddenly leaned forward and whispered something in Wren's ear. A moment later, they were switching seats. Wren now sat with Lou, and Bee, thankfully, was there to keep Jamie quiet. Just that quickly, his attention was diverted as he flirted with Bee and forgot about everyone else.

While my friends and sister were distracted, I found myself peeking at Vaughn through my peripheral. He was fast asleep, his chest rising and falling steadily. His expression, however, even while unconscious, was troubled. I wasn't sure when I gave up being subtle, but after a while, I combed my fingers through his hair until his frown slowly cleared. I then rested my cheek on the back of the seat, watching over him as he slept.

The first thing I noticed when I woke up an hour later was that the van was still moving. How could we not be there yet? It felt as if I'd slept for ages. I would have groaned if it hadn't seemed like too much effort. The second thing I noticed was that my bladder was near bursting and the third...

I was now sitting alone.

My eyes were still closed, but I could sense that Selena was no longer next to me. Mainly because her voice, though speaking in a hushed tone, was too far away. Opening my eyes, I blinked in earnest, hoping that the empty seat next to me was just a figment of my imagination. Where else could she have gone? All the other seats were taken. All of them except—

Lifting my head, my suspicions were confirmed when I found her sharing the last row with Vaughn. They even sat close, whispering to each other.

"Selena?" I cringed, hearing my groggy voice while hers had sounded almost sensual and suggestive. I told myself I was imagining things to calm my racing heart.

"Oh, hey, sleepyhead." I didn't return her smile as we stared at one another. I could feel Vaughn's gaze but refused to give him the satisfaction of acknowledging him.

"Why are you sitting back there?"

"Vaughn was looking a little lonely and sad," she cooed as she hugged his arm playfully before letting go. "I thought I'd keep him company and cheer him up. Besides, everyone else had fallen asleep, and I didn't want to wake them."

I turned my head toward the front of the van, and her story was confirmed when I saw the slumped bodies and heard the light snores. The only one still awake was Ever. Our gazes met in the rearview mirror, and my gut twisted painfully when he quickly looked away. Even in the dark, I could see his hands strangling the steering wheel, making my unease grow. Ever had a damn good poker face, but right now, he had a hard time concealing his emotions. What had made him so angry?

Confused, I turned back and regarded my sister, who was still, for some reason, sitting in the back row.

"Okay, I'm awake now. Maybe you should come and sit up here?"

I realized how it might have looked as if I were being petty toward Vaughn, but with each second that passed, my chest grew tighter, and it became harder to breathe. What could they have been discussing so intimately? Had Ever overheard?

Selena shot Vaughn an apologetic look before moving back into the row with me. I took a deep breath before finally, *finally* meeting Vaughn's gaze. The emptiness was still there, but it had only grown since an hour ago. What had happened in the week since I'd last seen him?

A few minutes later, Ever was pulling off the highway, startling everyone when he barely slowed enough. The van took the curve on two wheels, which woke everyone up.

"Dude, what the fuck?" Jamie grumbled. He was always crankiest when he first woke up.

Ever didn't bother to respond as he gunned the van into the nearest parking lot. My stomach growled, seeing that it was an Applebee's. Four was gazing at him worriedly, but he ignored her too as he threw the van into park. "Stay here," he ordered Four. His voice was so thick with anger. He then hopped out, slamming the driver door hard enough that it should have broken glass. A second later, he pounded on the rear window next to Vaughn. "You…get the fuck out of the van." Not giving his best friend a chance to respond, Ever walked away, letting the night swallow him whole.

Everyone then turned their confused gazes on Vaughn. The only one who didn't seem at all surprised was Lou, who had eyes only for Selena. As if he hadn't a care in the world, Vaughn got out and followed Ever into the dark.

"Well, fuck that, I'm hungry," Jamie announced. Leaning over Bee, he slid open the sliding door.

"Ever said to stay here," Lou reminded him.

"He told Four to stay here. He's also not my goddamn daddy." Without further ado, Jamie climbed out before helping Bee down and heading toward the well-lit Applebee's. After a beat, everyone else followed, including Selena, while I sat frozen. My gaze eventually returned to the direction Ever and Vaughn had stalked off in, wondering what the hell had happened while I was asleep.

chapter twelve

The Prince

"ARE YOU OUT OF YOUR MIND?" EVER RAGED. HE SHOVED ME AS soon as I walked up to him. "Are you off your fucking rocker?"

"Chill out, man. Nothing happened."

"Nothing happened? So you're telling me I need to get my hearing checked?" Even when I stood there staring at him, refusing to admit my colossal mistake, he didn't back down. "This is Tyra," he practically begged for me to remember. "*Tyra*. And that girl I heard you kissing is her sister. What the fuck do you think you're doing?"

"It was one kiss," I argued as if it made a difference. "And *she* kissed *me*, or did you miss that part?"

"It's more than e-fucking-nough to make you lose Tyra forever."

"I already lost her." At Ever's confused blink, I added, "She broke…it off," I said, changing gears when I almost admitted to Tyra breaking up with me. We were never in a relationship, which meant it didn't matter who kissed who or why I didn't stop her sister from sticking her tongue down my throat. I hadn't done anything wrong. I started to point this out to Ever when the lie melted like acid on my tongue, rendering me speechless.

I should never have allowed Selena into that backseat with me. Not after seeing her true colors. My anger toward my father had spilled onto Tyra because when you couldn't take your frustrations out on the guilty, the innocent became your casualty.

"I know what you're feeling," Ever conceded, "but a piece of advice? When a girl says it's over, she means try harder. *Unless you kiss her fucking sister.* You pull crap like this on skeezers, gold diggers, and cum buckets. You do not, under any circumstances, do this to the girl who broke your heart. Why do you think you gave it to her in the first place, genius?"

"I'm not in love with Tyra."

"Now you're just insulting my intelligence."

"I'm not, and I *can't* try harder. That's the point, motherfucker. I don't have anything to offer her but a bullet from my father."

"That's your choice," Ever scoffed, pissing me off. "Stop blaming your father when it's your choice to bow to him."

Just then, Jay D appeared out of the dark, bounding up to us and licking my balled fist. I immediately felt myself relax and bent just enough to give him a scratch behind the ears in gratitude. I'd been two seconds from clocking my best friend. A moment later, Four appeared, her gaze flicking between us. "Is everything okay?"

"I told you to wait in the van," Ever said in response.

Shrugging, Four came to stand next to Jay D with her arms crossed defiantly. "I assumed it was a suggestion because I don't take orders."

They became locked in a staring contest that ended with Jay D baring his teeth and growling softly at Ever. Shaking his head, Ever broke the stare.

"I hate that damn dog," he muttered when Four finally walked away. He watched as she made her way across the dark parking lot and didn't look away until she disappeared inside the restaurant.

I frowned at him because who didn't like dogs? "Are you a cat person or something?"

"Fuck no. I just don't like anything I have to share my girl with."

"She had to share you with Bee," I pointed out while holding in my laughter. "The least you can do is be civil to her dog."

"She never had to share me. Not once since the moment she kneed me in the balls over a plate of fucking food."

"You mean her dinner that you ate out of spite? Didn't you also imply that her mother was a whore, fucking for better health benefits?"

He cut his gaze my way before mumbling, "Remind me not to tell you anything ever again." He walked away, and I followed, holding my sides as I tried to keep my laughter in. Ever wouldn't hesitate to turn around and break my jaw, and I wasn't keen on getting arrested for fighting in an Applebee's parking lot.

Just as we neared the van, I spotted Tyra climbing out. She slid the sliding door closed and paused, her arms wrapped around her small frame to shield herself from the cold when she noticed us.

Mumbling to myself, I quickly opened the backdoor and grabbed my letterman jacket that I'd left in the seat. When she tried to pass me as if I didn't fucking exist, I grabbed her and draped the jacket on her shoulders. Our gazes met, and then she took a deep breath as if pained before looking away. Cool as ice, she pushed the jacket off her shoulders and let it fall to the ground. "No, thanks."

Ever and I watched her walk toward the restaurant with variant expressions—his was of shock and amusement while mine was pure fury. *What the fuck was her problem?* She'd been sleeping silently as a baby when Selena kissed me. No way Tyra could have known.

Whistling, Ever stuck his hands in his pockets as he regarded me with only a smidge of sympathy. "You've got major damage control ahead of you, bro."

I grunted my response. Yeah, it seemed so.

Inside the restaurant, we quickly found our friends since the place was deserted and sat down at the large U-shaped booth with its high, leather backing. I ended up being seated next to Tyra, who sat stiffly while doing everything in her power not to even let her elbow rub mine. You'd think I had a contagious disease the way she sat so tightly wound. I was getting ready to call her out on it when the manager came over.

"I'm sorry, miss. We don't allow dogs inside our establishment. It's unsanitary."

Laying on his belly at Ever's feet, Jay D's ear perked as if he understood every word.

"Oh, don't worry," Jamie quipped. "We made sure he wiped his paws before he came in."

"I appreciate that, but I'm afraid I'll have to ask you to remove the dog so as not to disturb our other customers."

Four started to rise dutifully, but when Ever stayed seated, keeping her from leaving the booth, she frowned at him.

"Look around you, Brian," he said, reading the manager's name tag. "We're the only customers you have, and thanks to you, I'm feeling pretty disturbed. The mutt stays, and while you're at it, how about a nice juicy T-bone for his trouble? Medium rare, please."

"I really must insist—"

"If someone comes, I promise we'll remove him," Ever attempted to negotiate. "But since you're closing in less than an hour and we're in the middle of nowhere, I doubt we'll have a problem."

Giving up, the manager reluctantly took our orders, even writing down Ever's order of steak for Jay D.

"Why did you do that?" Four hadn't wasted time showing her displeasure when the manager walked away. Her cheeks were red from embarrassment while her eyes filled with fire. "He was just doing his job. You didn't have to be so rude."

"I know that, princess," Ever mumbled. "And I was just doing mine." He tried to kiss her, but she turned away, so he gripped her chin and made her kiss him anyway.

"Gross," Lou grumbled when they kept right on kissing as if they weren't sitting at a table full of people. "Some of us are trying to enjoy our lukewarm, lemon water." Her button nose wrinkled as she continued to watch them.

Rising, Ever smoothly pulled a starry-eyed Four from the booth, and then they made for the door with Jay D hot on their heels. Everyone left at the table watched them go.

"Oh, my God." Lou groaned, breaking the confused silence first. "I bet they're going to do it in the van." Turning her attention toward Jamie and Bee, she smirked. "Are you sure you guys don't want to join them?"

Bee immediately picked up one of the extra straws and tossed it at Lou. "Give it a rest, Valentine. That is *not* what happened."

Lou snorted before batting her eyes and sipping her tepid water. When she noticed Wren staring at her from across the table, she looked away, her amusement fading. She looked sad now, and I wondered when Wren would finally break down the wall she was slowly building between them.

You're one to talk.

Somehow, my gaze found Selena's who was seated next to Wren on the other side of the booth. She didn't look the least bit guilty about our kiss, and I realized that in the blink of an eye, the wall between Tyra and me had become a mountain to climb.

After Ever tipped the manager generously and Four made him apologize, we were back on the road an hour later. Wren had elected to take over driving while Lou stubbornly reclaimed her seat in the back. Feeling like it was the wise thing to do, I volunteered to keep Wren company and hopped in the front passenger seat. Since it was the middle of the night and everyone seemed to be emotionally exhausted for individual reasons, it didn't take long for them to count sheep. We were only a couple of hours out, but I figured it was for the best. Even snake-in-the-grass Selena had lost her fight with consciousness.

"If you don't mind me asking," I whispered after making sure everyone was deep in their sleep, "what are you waiting for?"

After a couple of minutes passed of Wren not speaking, I almost gave up on learning the answer.

"When I ask her," he finally spoke, "I want to offer her more than just my name."

I scoffed at that. "Lou doesn't care about money." I was living proof that people were always better off without it anyway.

"I'm not talking about money, Fox," he said, referring to his former boss, "wants her dead, and as long as he's alive, he'll never stop." Wren's hands tightened around the steering wheel as he gritted his teeth. "Neither will I."

"So that's why she's rabid one minute and pouting the next? You're out there trying to get yourself killed, man?"

He smirked at that. "I've been on the streets since I was fifteen, and so has she. I know how to handle myself, and she knows that, too. Lou's just stubborn and spoiled. Besides…I'm not hunting him alone."

"What do you mean? Who's helping you?"

Wren's blue eyes darted to the rearview mirror, and I wondered whether he was ensuring himself that Lou was asleep or Ever. "My father."

"Don't you mean 'our' father? We were all there when Ever's pop told him you two were brothers. The question I'd like answered is, why the hell didn't you tell him yourself?"

"Ever doesn't know this yet, but he got a dealt a winning hand. In fact, he dodged a fucking bullet."

"Explain."

Wren took his eyes off the road to study me, his expression one part incredulous and two parts hostile. "What makes you think I owe you an explanation?"

"Because before you came along, I was the closest thing Ever had to a brother besides Jamie."

My reason seemed to be enough for Wren, so he nodded and sighed. "My father is the 'love 'em and leave 'em' type. He did it to Thomas, he did it to my mom, and he did it to Evelyn…"

"And then he did it to you."

It was still jarring finding out that Mr. McNamara played for both teams. I wondered if he'd been afraid to share that part of himself with his son. It would never matter to Ever, but I could understand his father's hesitance. Of course, anything would have been better than Jamie outing his uncle mid-temper tantrum.

"I won't stand by and watch him do that to Ever," Wren vowed.

"Mr. McNamara said Sean wants to meet Ever. How do you plan to stop him?"

"By giving him something he wants more. Our father co-founded Exiled. If we can find Fox and overthrow him—"

"He'll ghost again and be out of your hair forever." At Wren's nod, I admitted to myself that it was a pretty good plan…if not slightly harebrained. "So why don't you just tell Lou this instead of letting her worry?"

Wren grunted at that. "She'll do that anyway, and then she'll try to talk me out of it."

"You think she can?"

I watched what suspiciously looked like a rare grin from Wren. It kind of freaked me out a little. "She has her ways."

Two hours later, I was starting to nod off when Wren punched me in the arm like a dick. "Wake the hell up. We're here."

"Here" was a large lakefront cabin that Ever had rented for the next couple of days. I wasn't sure how since most rentals didn't welcome guests under twenty-five, but I didn't care enough to ask questions. Sleeping in the woods with only the leaves as bedding was better than being back home. I almost hadn't come until I considered the alternative. It had been three days since Colombia, and the smug look my father gave me when I returned still hadn't left my mind.

So I left Blackwood Keep, hoping to run from it.

Wren hopped out, slamming the door behind him, which woke everyone else up. I followed him out into the chilly summer night and started helping him with our bags while Ever looked for the lockbox where the owner left the key. Once we got the doors unlocked and everything unloaded inside, I grabbed a beer from the melted ice water in the cooler and dropped onto the recliner in the corner. I'd chosen it for the unobstructed view it gave me of Tyra.

"There are five bedrooms," Ever announced. He paused, his lips flattening before shooting me a dirty look.

Yup, he's still pissed.

"I guess Tyra and Selena can bunk together," Ever continued.

"Don't you think Tyra will want to stay with Vaughn?" Four pointed out.

Excellent question.

I took advantage of the sudden awkward silence as they all waited for an answer and popped the top on my beer. After I'd loudly slurped my first sip, Tyra met my gaze, and I lifted my beer in salute. Breaking up—off—had been her idea. She could explain it to them herself because I wasn't saying shit.

"Vaughn and I...we're not..."

I thought I'd enjoy watching her struggle to tell them, but instead, it made me feel like shit. It seemed more like I'd hurt her than the other way around.

"My sister decided she could do better," Selena said when Tyra became mute. She then crossed her toned arms over her tits as she met my gaze. "Much better."

You didn't seem to think that when you were slipping me the tongue, bitch.

"That's not exactly true," Tyra said, finally finding her goddamn voice. "It's just that Vaughn and I want different things, and I think we *both* deserve better than to string each other along anymore." I forgot all about her poisonous sister when Tyra's pleading gaze met mine. "Right?"

I didn't realize I'd been crushing the beer can in my hand as Tyra spoke until I felt the cold liquid spill out and onto my lap. Shooting up, I started toward the stairs under the guise of cleaning up, and as I was about to pass Tyra, I stopped. I wanted to smirk when her lips opened and parted like a fish, but smug was the last thing I was feeling.

"You're way off course, pip." I'd whispered it for her ears only, but I knew by the black look in Selena's eyes that she'd heard every word.

Good.

chapter thirteen

The Pawn

WHAT THE HELL HAD VAUGHN MEANT BY THAT?

I told myself that sleeping most of the drive up was the reason it evaded me now. With a sigh, I stood and stretched. After a glance at my sister sleeping soundly on the twin bed next to mine, I slipped from the room. The cabin was quiet and dark. I guessed none of my friends had problems falling asleep. The old wood creaked underneath my bare feet as I blindly made my way to the stairs in the dark. I'd been too emotionally hungover to explore when we arrived, so I had no idea where I was going. My only hope was that no one woke. My prayers went unanswered a moment later when I heard Bee's gentle voice float from one of the bedrooms.

"Who's a good boy?" she cooed. "Who's a good boy?"

Thinking maybe Jay D was bunking with Jamie and Bee since Ever was such a pompous asshole, I waited to hear one of his enthusiastic barks. Instead, what I heard stopped me in my tracks.

"I'm a good boy."

I didn't even want to know what they were up to in there. Of course, the voice had belonged to none other than Jamie's goofy ass. I shook my head as I moved past their room. To each their own, I suppose.

Downstairs, I caught the view of the lake through the sliding glass doors and couldn't help but gravitate toward them. Maybe it was the moonlight causing the water to shimmer. Whatever it was, I felt like I had to be a part of it. As soon as I stepped outside, I realized what had drawn me out here was just my bad luck flaring up again.

Just two feet away, Vaughn leaned against the balcony railing. His head was thrown back in ecstasy as the same moonlight I was admiring made his skin glow. His green and white boxers, the only piece of clothing he wore, was shoved below his ass as he pumped his dick. Even in the dark, I could see the angry veins running the long length of his dick, the piercing glinting in the light, and the pearly drop of fluid threatening to spill onto the deck. It was a sight no woman could look away from. Even one who'd convinced herself she didn't want to be in love with him anymore.

I was spellbound by each slow stroke of his dick. It almost seemed sacrilegious that Vaughn had to pleasure himself. I wanted to fall to my knees like a good girl and tell him how wrong I was to let him go and then prove it by wrapping my lips around him until he came. Instead, I backed away, fearing that I'd do just that. I turned to go at the last moment. Since his eyes were closed, he couldn't have seen me…

But I must have made a sound.

One moment, I was fighting with myself to walk away, and the next, I was being hauled back against my will. I was convinced nothing felt better than Vaughn's dick against my spine or his arm around my waist.

"Going so soon?" he sexily hummed in my ear. "The show was just about to start."

"Vaughn, let me go."

To my surprise, he obliged, but I should have known better. Setting me on my feet, he quickly turned me around. The moment I faced him, Vaughn's hands claimed me once more, holding my hips this time.

"Enjoy the view?"

"If I had, I wouldn't have been running to wash my eyes out."

He scoffed at that while looking slightly pissed. "It's nothing you haven't seen before."

"My view was a lot rosier back then."

"Pip-squeak—"

"Fuck you," I spat before he could finish. I couldn't handle any more of his lies.

With a determined glint in his eye, he backed me onto the picnic table a few feet away and stepped between my legs after forcing them open. Seriously, who kept these on a goddamn balcony anyway? And one sturdy enough to hold the both of us...

"Say yes to me, and I'll do better than that," he promised on a whisper. "I'll fuck *you*."

"Is that your final offer? Losing my virginity on a moldy, old picnic table?" I tried to suppress an eye roll even though I was tempted and failed. "How romantic."

Taking my chin, he made me meet his gaze. "Under the moon, gazing at the stars...with me." His voice almost broke on the last. I didn't even get a chance to question the pain in his eyes when he dropped his head on my shoulder, hiding his face in my neck. "I feel like I'm slipping away, and there's nothing to hold to. Nothing but you. I need you so fucking much, pip."

Feeling his entire body tremble, I found myself wrapping my arms around his neck of my own free will. If he needed me to hold onto him, I would. Nothing else mattered. My own emotions bubbled up, and I found myself demanding answers. "What happened to you?" My frantic tone split the quiet night.

I felt his lips pressing against the small sliver of skin peeking through my T-shirt just before he shook his head. "I can't tell you."

Rather than get upset, I clung to him tighter. "Did someone hurt you?"

He seemed to think about that for a moment before lifting and shaking his head again. "Not on the outside."

"Was it your father?"

His lips tightened, giving me my answer even before he denied me. "I don't want to talk about him." I felt his hands sliding underneath my shirt, reaching for the waistband of my shorts. "I just want to forget," he said before kissing me hard. "Please make me forget."

I couldn't deny him the plea he'd whispered against my lips. At that moment, I would have given anything to take his pain away, so when he started pulling my shorts down, I didn't stop him. I was even willing to risk getting a few splinters in my ass.

"Lift up," he whispered.

I did as he ordered, and then my shorts were gone. I nervously watched as he pushed his boxers down and stepped out of them. Just like that, he was completely naked while I had only my shirt shielding me from prying eyes. As if only just remembering that we weren't here alone, my gaze darted to the still partially opened sliding door. I couldn't see that well inside, but the coast seemed to be clear.

Closing his eyes and throwing his head back in aggravation, Vaughn groaned before padding back inside the cabin.

I watched, trembling with anticipation and fear, as he grabbed a duffel bag with USC's logo on the side. How hadn't I noticed that before? The gears in my mind turned and tumbled as he rifled through it almost desperately before tossing it aside. Next, he grabbed Jamie's bag since everyone had pretty much left theirs. It didn't take him long to find what he was looking for. He then grabbed the knit throw adorning the back of the sectional and stepped back onto the balcony, tossing a box of condoms onto the tabletop.

"You're going to USC?" I asked as if I weren't half-naked and out in the open for anyone to see.

His lips tightened before he responded. "Yeah."

"Why didn't you tell me?" And why didn't he sound excited? The only time Vaughn didn't look like he was two seconds from dozing was when he was on the field...or alone locked away inside of the beach house.

"Because I'm not sure I'm even going."

"Your father?"

He shook his head as his grip tightened around the blanket he was still holding. "Because of you." At my startled look, he said almost impatiently, "I can't stand the thought of being that far away from you, Tyra. Don't you know that by now?"

"But you have to go." I wisely chose to ignore his question. "It's your dream."

"I have to go," he agreed with a nod. "But not because it's my dream."

I knew instantly what he meant, and I swear I never hated anyone as much as I did Franklin Rees. Someone I'd never even met. For all I knew, Vaughn could just be running game. A flawless one at that. One look in his desolate eyes, however, and I knew that he couldn't be. His fears and frustrations that he was trying so hard to hide were very real.

Jaw tight, he stared down into my eyes, willing me to do something. I didn't know what until he spoke. "I guess it doesn't matter now."

"No," I agreed after some time. "I guess it doesn't."

Tonight wouldn't change my decision unless *he* changed his. Feeling like I was falling into trouble, I leaned up to kiss him, hoping he could keep me in the clouds for a little while longer. He hesitated to kiss me back, but when he finally did, I was soaring. It had barely been a week since he last kissed me, and I was already dying. How could I possibly endure the rest of my life without it? Vaughn was the only boy I'd ever kissed, but I was convinced no lips were softer, no one else as skilled, gentle, and greedy all at once.

When we finally came up for air, Vaughn laid the blanket on the table underneath me before removing my T-shirt.

"Lie back."

I was shaking too hard to do as he asked at first, but when I finally did, Vaughn wasted no time rewarding me. Leaning down, he flicked his tongue out, teasing my nipple before closing his lips around it while his hand caressed my knee. I held him there as his hand rose higher on my thigh until I was writhing mess. By the time he moved on to my other nipple, my desperate moans were competing with the sound of his hungry groans. When I felt like I'd reached the edge of the earth, another greedy lick and gentle bite away from coming, he pushed my leg up and out, opening me for him. My next breath stuttered out of me when he moved. His head was suddenly between my legs, and I nearly jumped out of my skin when I felt him kiss me there.

Why was I so nervous? He'd eaten me out before.

"Relax." After kissing my pussy once more, he met my gaze, his green eyes glittering with the command. "You were always meant to be here, Tyra. Like this. For *me*."

My response, which was probably only a jumbled mix of sounds anyway, got caught in my throat when he reached for a condom. I watched him tear it open and slowly sheathe himself with bated breath. Had he always been that big? I couldn't recall.

Noticing my trepidation, the corner of his lips turned up, and if I weren't frozen in place, I would have broken his nose. "Not tonight, pip-squeak," he whispered before kissing me. "I won't fuck you just yet."

I expected to feel relief at his promise, but all I felt was disappointment flowing through me. I never had any doubts that Vaughn was meant to be my first. If only he could let himself be my only.

Hearing something, my heard turned toward the house where the sound had come from. Oblivious, Vaughn began pushing inside me, and the rest of the world ceased to exist.

Even with Vaughn's amazing restraint, I felt full.

My pussy tightened around the tip of his pierced cock, greedily working to pull him deeper. The harsh dip of his brows as he watched himself move in and out of me drew my gaze from the sexy flex of his sculpted abs. He withdrew, and once I lifted onto my elbows, a gasp fell from my lips when I saw the condom coated with my arousal. Vaughn began pushing inside of me once more, our breathing growing heavier, and his lids lowering with every inch he buried. His eyes were slits, and his mouth set in a firm line by the time he withdrew again. I lifted, wanting to kiss the grimness from his lips. At the same time, I felt his fingers digging into my hips. I winced, but he didn't seem to notice as his grip tightened even more.

Something was definitely wrong.

The torment and need on his face were so vivid it set my heart pounding as he transformed before my eyes. I touched his cheek to no avail and no reaction. It was like he was no longer here with me but somewhere else. Someplace that turned his green irises black.

"Vaughn?"

He didn't respond.

"Vaughn?" I repeated a little more urgently.

Pulling back, he flexed his hips to enter me again and—A sharp, pained cry rent the air as he shoved himself inside of me. Right around the time I realized the sound had come from me, I also realized that Vaughn had taken my virginity.

Seemingly realizing it, too, his body stiffened, and then his strong arms closed around me. I wanted to push him away, but the pain was too great. Silly me. I wanted his comfort more.

"Pip?" I couldn't bring myself to speak, so I buried my face in his strong shoulder. "Pip, I'm so fucking sorry," he pleaded. "I didn't mean to—fuck!" he barked when the sob I tried to swallow broke free. Mistaking my physical anguish for mental, he tried to pull away. I dug my nails into his back, keeping him in place. Only when the throbbing between my thighs finally relented did I lift my head to meet his tortured gaze.

"Are you okay?" I asked, making his frown deepen. "You weren't here. Where did you go?"

"Did you seriously just ask me if I was okay after I just—"

He stopped and looked away before I could see his shame. "I can't believe I did that," he mumbled.

"I'm okay," I assured him.

"Yeah, no fucking thanks to me."

I turned his head, and when I lifted my chin, I almost smiled when he swore before giving into me with a kiss that went on until we both ran out of air.

"I'm *okay*," I repeated once I caught my breath. In fact, I was relieved. My virginity had been a barrier—no pun intended—that no longer existed.

What if Selena was right? What if the only way to convince Vaughn that we were fated was to show him what he'd be missing if he walked away? Maybe opening his eyes meant submitting to him completely. I'd given him my mind, my heart, and my soul. The only thing I had left to offer was my body.

Vaughn was already deep inside of me, buried to the hilt in more ways than the obvious. How easy would it be to give in now? I felt reckless and giddy, ready to throw caution to the wind when the sound of the glass door sliding open halted us both.

The very last person I expected to see standing there was my goddamn sister.

Vaughn rushed to cover me as best as he could with the blanket while her sleepy gaze bounced between us, a slow smile spreading her lips.

"Little sister," she cooed as she stepped onto the balcony and closed the door behind her. "I was beginning to think you didn't have it in you." Her focus fell between my legs where Vaughn stood, and her eyebrows rose. "Now I see that you do. Literally."

"How about you give us some fucking privacy?" Vaughn snapped before I could.

Rather than disappear as we both hoped and expected, Selena sauntered over to the table before curling up on the table bench. "I think I'll watch," she announced once she'd made herself comfortable. "I'm wide awake now, and the Wi-Fi is pretty shitty out here." Her gaze raked over us as her excitement grew. "This makes up for that."

"Selena, leave," I finally spoke up.

"Why? What's the point? I'll just watch from inside." Tapping her chin, she pretended to think. "Or maybe I'll shout 'fire' on my way upstairs and wake everyone up." She met my gaze then. "Is that really how you want to remember this night, baby sister?" I watched as her attention shifted to Vaughn. "What about you, stud? You look like you've got a lot on your mind. Would you like to spend the night telling my sister all about it, or would you rather fuck her brains out instead?"

My heart twisted in my chest when something passed silently between them. When the seconds ticked by and Vaughn still didn't make her leave, my confusion only grew. My sister had somehow gained the upper hand, but how? Vaughn and Selena were practically strangers. It was impossible for them to share secrets.

"What's going on?" I asked when the air became charged with violent energy.

Selena was smiling. Vaughn was *not*.

"Pip," I heard Vaughn whisper. There was a note of desperation in his tone, but my attention remained stubbornly locked on my sister. A heartbeat later, I felt his fingers gripping my chin as he forced my gaze away. The moment our eyes connected, he stole my lips. It didn't take him long to get me back under his spell. Selena was a distant memory despite her proximity, and the longer we kissed, the deeper I fell.

I didn't even notice when Vaughn lowered me on my back. My leg was now hooked inside of the crook of his arm, and he never stopped kissing me, even as he began to rock inside of me with gentle, shallow thrusts that made me mindless. It was perfect.

Except for one thing.

I stiffened when I felt fingers that didn't belong to Vaughn caressing my hair.

"Her nipples," my sister whispered. "I want you to suck them."

Confusion and ecstasy battled one another when Vaughn broke our kiss to follow her directive. He offered me so much pleasure that I could barely remember my own name much less that we weren't alone.

Vaughn had only begun laving my other when Selena spoke again. "My selfish little sister teased your cock for months," she cooed as she played with my hair. "She never considered your needs. Instead, she toyed with you." The wood from the picnic table creaked as she leaned over, and I felt Vaughn tense in my arms as he missed a beat. "I know you want to fuck her harder than that," Selena goaded, sounding much closer now—like she was speaking directly in his ear. "Do it. Pound her little pussy until it hurts. Until she *screams.*"

Vaughn released my nipple, and when he turned his head toward my sister, the violence in them startled me. He wanted to hurt my sister badly. Selena didn't so much as blink as she held his gaze.

"Do it."

The muscle in his jaw ticked, and I could tell he wanted to refuse. Feeling like everything was already screwed up, I decided to make the best of this night before it took a turn for the worst.

"Hey." This time it was me forcing his gaze away from Selena, and when he finally looked in my eyes, the turmoil in his own nearly crippled me. "There's no one else here," I whispered to him. I didn't care if Selena heard me or not but judging by her snort, I knew she had. "It's just you and me." After a moment of hesitation, he kissed me, soft and sweet like he knew I needed. Turning my lips toward his ear opposite Selena, I gave him an order of my own. "I want you to fuck me as hard as you can, but only because it's what *I* want."

Lying on my back once more, I watched a wicked grin slowly spread his swollen lips. "Is that, right?" he drawled.

"Yes."

Leaning down, he whispered against my lips. "You want to scream for me?"

"Hell, yes."

He kissed me again, harder this time, before pulling out of me. This time when he filled me, he drove into me so hard my jaw actually dropped from shock as my back bowed. Unrelenting, he slammed into me again before I could even catch my breath.

And then he did it a third time.

By the fourth or fifth shove of his cock, I was convinced I'd spoken too soon. Vaughn Rees was a little more than I could handle. Somehow, it still wasn't enough.

For a while, there was no sound but the crickets and the slap of Vaughn's skin against mine as he fucked the shit out of me. Selena reminded me that she was there when I felt her brush my wild hair from my forehead. The feelings that Vaughn invoked were so intense that for a moment, I was almost grateful that she was there. Almost.

"Where are you going?" he demanded through gritted teeth. My body had begun scooting up the table from the force of Vaughn's hips slamming into me. I hadn't even realized that I was running away from him. Not missing a beat, he yanked me back down to the edge of the table and began peppering my shoulder with gentle kisses. "Want me to stop?"

I looked into his green eyes and forced myself to relax. How could I when he thought of me even he was damn near feral?

"Please don't."

Vaughn wasted no time resuming his rhythm, and when I came, I did indeed scream for him.

chapter fourteen

The Prince

IF PIP-SQUEAK NOTICED ME SWEATING BULLETS THE NEXT MORNING, SHE didn't let on as she nibbled on her toast in my lap. I wondered how much longer I had before the shit hit the fan. Tyra wasn't stupid. She knew something was up, but like me, she was avoiding the storm headed our way. We were alone in the kitchen, cuddled together while watching the sunrise over the lake, and trying not to stare too hard at the picnic table. I imagined many times how popping pip's cherry would go, but I never imagined it being... weird.

The reason sauntered into the kitchen a moment later with a freshly scrubbed face and a treacherous smile. "Morning!"

Neither of us spoke back as Selena poured herself a cup of coffee. Had I known she'd be the first one up, I would have spiked it with something strong enough to eat away at her black heart. Tyra would never forgive me, but what else was new? I was already sailing down that creek with nothing but my dick in my hand.

"Last night was wild, huh?"

"If you say we should do it again sometime, I'm going to waste good coffee boiling your eyeballs—*sis.*"

Selena's lips formed a surprised *O* as she blinked stupidly at her sister. "What the hell is your problem?"

Before Tyra could answer, Bee stumbled into the kitchen, and Selena became engrossed in her phone. I wasn't surprised to find her alone since waking the dead was easier than getting Jamie up before noon. "Morning." Her sleepy gaze traveled the kitchen until it landed on Tyra and me. "You two made up?" she questioned, grinning now. The hopeful look in her eyes warmed me and made me feel like shit all at the same time. Tyra and I had called a truce, but it wouldn't last for long. Not when she found out that I made out with her sister.

I felt pip-squeak tense and knew what her answer would be, so squeezing her hip, I spoke before she could. "Yup. Last night." Tyra was so pissed that she was damn near shaking as she tried to rise from my lap. Leaning forward, I locked my arm around her waist under the guise of reaching for my coffee cup. "Stop wiggling your ass," I whispered when she kept trying to break free. "Unless you want to go upstairs for round two?"

"Fuck you."

"You sure did, pip. Rocked my world, too."

The sound of someone choking and then liquid spilling had me looking up and seeing Bee's wide eyes and flaming cheeks as she hurried to wipe the hot coffee from her chin. She'd heard every word, which meant by the end of the day, everyone else would know, too, that Tyra and I had fucked.

"So," Bee said as she set her coffee mug down. "I guess I'll hit the shower before anyone else wakes up."

I sighed, not bothering to waste my breath, asking her not to blab. Tyra seemed to feel the same way because her only reaction was to stare at her half-eaten toast. Bee made for the exit, and Selena paused mid-selfie to watch her go.

"What's her problem?" she grumbled only to be ignored once again.

Standing from my chair, I abandoned my coffee and Tyra's toast and carried her ninety-pound sack-of-flour ass upstairs to shower. Pretty soon, the entire house was awake, and shortly after that, we were off to the race.

"Fuuuuuck," Jamie grumbled as he glowered behind his shades. "Why are there so many people here?"

We were lounging on the collapsible chairs we brought, watching the scene while Four attended some mandatory meeting before the practice run and finally, the race. I had no idea where everyone else had wandered off to. Trailers and tents littered almost every inch of free space, and over three hundred bystanders crowded the little area that was left—twice as many people as there had been when Four raced in New Jersey.

"Maybe they're really into motocross around here."

Lips curled, Jamie didn't seem willing to accept that explanation, sending some blonde that had been admiring him from afar scampering for the safety of her tent. I made a mental note to bring one next time—the tent, not the blonde—as the sun beat down on me. Even though it was still early, the July heat made the morning brutal. My eyes drifted shut, hoping to block out the sunlight, but the sightless gaze of Jacobo Jiménez staring back at me had them springing open again.

Sitting up, I wiped my palms down my shorts, feeling my hands coated in Jacobo's blood. I wiped until my skin was raw from the friction, but the tainted feeling remained. Why wouldn't it just go the fuck away?

I didn't kill anyone.

I wasn't the murderer my father wanted me to be.

I was never going to take his place.

This sound, an amalgamation of aggravation and desperation, ripped from my throat as I doubled my efforts. A moment later, my hands were ripped away from my lap, and the darkness that had been slowly swallowing me whole dissipated. The same darkness that led to my epic fuck up and Tyra losing her virginity last night. Tatted hands had seized my wrists, and when I tried to free myself, Jamie tightened his hold. He was kneeling in front of me now, his brows bunched so tightly, he looked in danger of losing his piercing.

"You were about to tear a hole in your shorts, man. What the fuck?"

the prince and the pawn | 137

I looked down to see that the material of my cargos had indeed become frayed. My hands were throbbing, and this time, when I pulled them away, Jamie let go, saving me from headbutting his ass. I inspected my palms and blinked at the redness before balling my hands into fists and settling back in my seat. I avoided Jamie's gaze as I pretended to watch the crowd, and he went back to his chair next to me.

"You want to tell me what the fuck that was?" he said after a minute or two.

I'd been waiting, not bothering to hold my breath because I already knew the nosy fucker wouldn't let it go.

"No."

"I know it sounded like a question, but it really wasn't," he retorted.

"And I don't take orders from you or my father, so leave me the fuck alone."

I noticed Jamie stiffen from the corner of my eye before he relaxed with a careless shrug. "Fine. Have it your way." Of course, he relented way too quickly for me to believe. "It's been a while since I've staged an intervention."

"That was three damn months ago," I snapped.

"And my spidey senses are tingling again." I didn't respond, so he took my silence as permission to poke a sleeping bear. "We can talk about this now while it's just the two of us, or we can do it as a group when everyone gets back."

"Fuck you."

"Word on the street," Jamie teased, "is that you got more than enough last night."

I blinked at him.

Two hours. That was all the time it had taken for word to spread in our crew. Bee must have told Jamie, and he definitely told everyone else.

Nice. Real nice.

"Of course, I want all the dirty details—"

"Not going to happen."

"But first," he said as if I hadn't spoken, "I want to know what happened between you and your father."

"No, you don't, Jamie, and that's for your sake and mine."

"Want to bet?" His eyebrow rose, and I should have known he wouldn't be so easily swayed. "You might have all the muscles, but I've got the biggest balls," he said, making me roll my eyes. Jamie never wasted an opportunity to brag about his horse dick. "I'm not afraid of your father."

"That's because you don't know what he's capable of."

Jamie fell silent, but the intensity of his stare told me that this conversation was far from over. "I know he's capable of buying a young girl for his son to turn into some kind of Stepford wife," he whispered.

My heart dropped to the pit of my stomach.

He knew.

He fucking knew my father had been the buyer for Bee.

Fuck. Did she know?

"Bee knows," Jamie said, reading my mind. "She just doesn't want to believe it."

"How?"

"Elliot told her the buyer he had lined up was the father of a friend. He also implied it wasn't Jason's old man. Since I already know my uncle never would, that leaves you."

I couldn't meet his gaze. The lump stuck in my throat was even harder to swallow. "I should have told you," I said, going for the obvious when the right words eluded me. "If I could be honest—"

"That would be nice."

"I was hoping the two of you would never find out."

"You didn't think we'd need some kind of warning? This shit is sick, man. What the fuck?"

"I would have never gone through with it. You fucking know that."

"Somehow, I don't believe it would have been up to you." His shrewd gaze narrowed even more. "What the hell is your father into?"

"I can't tell you."

"You told Ever." The look he gave me warned me not to lie to him when I tried to deny it. "You already lied to me. Don't insult my intelligence, too."

"You were *gone*—an entire fucking ocean away while I got to watch my best friend and your cousin destroy himself over his mother walking out. I didn't have a goddamn choice." Ever hadn't merely accepted the information I offered. He refused to even make a move without knowing exactly how I knew and how long.

"You told him where to find Aunt Evelyn."

Feeling that lump in my throat growing bigger, I nodded. Had I known that Ever would join up with my father's rival to free his mom, I would have kept my mouth shut. I would have felt shitty about it, but not more than if Ever had gotten himself killed.

"I would lecture you right now, but that's not my style."

"I was there in your uncle's office two weeks ago, Buchanan. You would have done the same goddamn thing, and it would have been a lot messier because *that's* your style."

Jamie scratched his chin as he pondered my point. "True."

He was about to say more when he caught sight of Bee heading our way. She was leading the pack with Wren, Lou, Four, and Ever behind her. I scanned the area looking for Tyra, but I didn't see her or Anne Boleyn. Technically, Selena was the older sister, but if the shoe fit…

"When does the party start?" Jamie shouted as soon as they were within hearing distance.

"Twenty minutes," Four answered as she tossed him her helmet to hold. She then caught the bottled water Jamie had dug from the cooler next to him. Uncapping it, she took a sip as I admired her in the black and yellow gear she wore. She looked so fucking badass in her jersey and mesh armor. I snickered, despite the state I'd been in minutes ago, when I caught my best friend staring at her ass. I was sure that whatever thoughts running wild in Ever's mind right now couldn't become a reality with less than twenty minutes to spare. It would take them that long alone to find somewhere secluded in this crowded, outdoor arena.

"Have you guys seen Tyra?" she asked, making me tense up and frown when her big, brown eyes flitted between Jamie and me.

"I thought she was with you."

"She was, but then Selena had to use the bathroom, so Tyra went with her. Haven't seen them since." Four frowned, but just as quickly, her expression cleared. Something was definitely bothering her, but she was determined not to let it show.

"I told you already," Lou spat. She was the complete opposite of Four, having no problem letting her true feelings show. "Selena is somewhere sacrificing our friend to whatever demon created her."

"Lou, you've known her for two seconds," Bee argued. "You haven't even given her a chance." I tensed even more as I listened because this was starting to sound like an argument they've had before.

"So? I know a snake in the grass when I see one. Besides, everyone told me that *you* were a bitch, but I saw straight through you. Now was I right, or was I wrong?" Refusing to respond, Bee crossed her arms and looked away. "Exactly. Besides, even her phone number is snitching on her," Lou maintained. "Come on...six-six-six-six-nine-six-nine? Do you know what that means?"

"No, but I'm sure you're going to tell us," Bee responded with her lips pursed.

"It means she's Satan's mistress. A devil whore." Lou sounded like the Bible thumpers she claimed she hated.

"You're being ridiculous," Four chimed in, making it two against one.

Lou didn't seem bothered by those odds as she rolled her eyes.

"News flash, Four. Tyra's not just your best friend anymore. She's mine, too."

Four smirked at that. "I thought Jamie was your best friend?"

"I'm her fucking best friend!" Wren shouted from inside the Sprinter. He'd wisely climbed inside once the arguing between the girls started.

"You get to see me naked," Lou reminded him. Silence from the van followed. I guess Wren had been placated. "Anyway, I don't trust her. Doesn't anyone find it strange that she just shows up out of the blue, claiming to be Tyra's sister?" Lou had put air quotes around the word *sister*. "Coach Bradley is listed, so she could have called. Selena clearly had their address, so she could have written. Anything would have been better than her just showing up and traumatizing our Ty-baby."

Jamie made a face at Lou for poaching his nickname, so Lou flipped him off. "Do you really think it matters?" he argued a moment later. "Either way, Tyra would have been blindsided since her father lied to her."

Lou waved him off. "Well, maybe he had his reasons."

"There's never a reason to lie," Ever said, speaking up for the first time. "No matter how harsh the truth, lies always cut deeper."

A heavy sigh came from the Sprinter that made everyone except Ever wince. Wren keeping the fact that they shared a father was still very much a sore subject between the two—partially because they both refused to talk about it.

"You're one to talk," Lou snapped, defending her man. "Have you told Four about the tracking app you put on her phone?" At the guilty shift of Ever's gaze, Lou became even more smug, if that were possible. "Didn't think so. I saw it last week when I showed her how to set up Instagram."

"And you waited until now to tell me?" Four shrieked.

Unapologetic, Lou studied her nails. "I had my reasons."

"Which were?"

"There was no one else around."

With fire in her eyes, Four rounded on Ever before shoving her hand in his pocket and digging out her phone. Once it was free, she slammed the iPhone into his chest. "Delete it."

Shaking his head, Ever accepted her phone before smoothly slipping it back into his pocket. "No."

Big surprise there.

Four's hands balled into fists just as someone called for the riders over the loudspeaker, making everyone collectively release their breath. None of us put it past Four to draw blood if she had to. Without a word, she turned away from Ever and accepted the helmet Jamie held out for her before storming off.

"Thanks a lot, brat," Ever spat before rushing after Four.

Lou cheekily saluted his retreating back just as the missing sisters appeared.

Note to self: get pip's phone and *delete that damn app.*

"What happened?" Tyra inquired. "What's wrong with Four?" She was too busy watching Ever shove through the crowd to get to Four to notice me staring her down. Where the hell had she been?

"Lou opened her mouth, and the entire universe imploded," Bee informed her.

"So nothing out of the ordinary," Tyra responded with a shake of her head. She was smiling until her gaze met mine. I watched as she bit her lip and wondered what she had to be nervous about. Or maybe my guilt was just making me paranoid. "What happened to your shorts?" Her gaze had fallen to my lap.

"Oh, nothing," Jamie responded before I could. "He was going for the ripped jeans look, but they don't really work with cargos, right, man?" Jamie clapped me on my back, and if his girl hadn't sat in his lap that very moment, I would have decked him. Bee narrowed her eyes at me like she'd read my mind, so I smirked.

"Come on," I said when I noticed everyone heading toward the track. "We need to get closer." I stood and stretched, ignoring Selena eyeing me as I took Tyra's hand and led her away from that poisonous bitch. As we moved through the crowd, I wondered what betraying Tyra made me since there had been two of us in that back seat. I couldn't put all the blame on her sister now, could I?

The track turned out to be a bigger challenge in size and obstacles than the one in Jersey. The heels were steeper, the jumps higher, and the turns seemed to be sharper. For miles, there was nothing but dirt as everyone gathered around the rope they used to keep bystanders off the track.

I glanced down at Tyra and got caught up in the wonder etched on her face. "A lot bigger than a junkyard, huh?"

"And not nearly as smelly," she observed.

Leaning down, I whispered in her ear. "Sadly, I won't be tempted to spank you when it's all over, either." The night Four raced for Mickey in an abandoned junkyard and had almost gotten Tyra and herself killed had been the moment I realized how badly I was screwed. I'd almost wrung Tyra's goddamn neck for scaring me the way that she had, which could only mean one thing—I cared about more than just getting under her clothes.

"Give it time," Tyra flirted back, surprising me at the same time. "I've got a few tricks up my sleeve."

My dick began responding to the promise in her eyes when her sister spoke, dumping a bucket of cold water over us both.

"So, how much money does Four get if she wins?" Selena asked.

"Not much, if any," Tyra answered.

Selena turned her nose up at that. "Then what's the point?"

Tyra paused to take a deep breath before answering. "She's not racing for cash," she explained somewhat impatiently. "She's racing for the points she needs to get her professional license."

"Well, I hope she's good. I heard that motocross riders don't make a ton of money." I stood there wondering when the fuck she became an expert. "Not without endorsements."

"It doesn't really matter how much Four makes as long as she's doing what she loves."

"Hm…I guess." Selena then rolled her eyes at her sister before refocusing on her phone.

Having been on the receiving end of Tyra's fury once or twice, I quickly grabbed pip-squeak and wrapped my arms around her waist when she froze at her sister's words.

"You're here for Four," I reminded her when she didn't seem willing to let it go. "Don't spoil it by fighting with your sister."

It took her a few seconds more to finally relax in my arms, but I kept her in place just in case. Besides, if she gave me a woody again, I damn well didn't want everyone seeing so…win-win.

A few minutes later, the race started, and for a while, all of our problems were forgotten.

chapter fifteen

The Pawn

"THIRD PLACE!" JAMIE CHEERED DESPITE FOUR'S SCOWL. NO ONE knew if it was because Four had technically lost or because she'd discovered Ever had been tracking her phone without her knowledge. Whatever the reason, at least her boyfriend was wise enough to give her a wide berth. I almost felt sorry for him when he kept glancing at her through the rearview mirror of the van.

After the race, we'd immediately loaded up, eager to celebrate. Four had come in third out of thirty, getting her twenty-two points closer to her license. If she won her next race, she'd finally have the sixty she needed. Of course, no pressure or anything.

Back at the cabin, Jamie immediately got busy on the hot tub while Vaughn grabbed the beers, and Bee searched for Jamie's iPod and speakers. Four and Ever had disappeared upstairs while the rest of us migrated into the living room.

"So, Wren," my sister said, drawing Lou's attention when Selena sat a little too close to him on the sofa. "I couldn't help noticing the tattoo on your nape. It's pretty cool. What does it mean?"

"It's pretty self-explanatory, really." Lou hadn't even given Wren a whiff of a chance to respond. "There's one way to interpret '*I am not led.*'"

"Sure, but the X makes it so edgy," Selena said, her gaze growing excited as she puffed out her chest in that low-cut top. "How'd you come up with that?"

"He didn't, I did," Lou lied while speaking for Wren again. "He also has a gun, and I know how to use it."

Selena seemed startled by Lou's sudden hostility, but she recovered quickly, a condescending smile on her lips. "Oh, I get it. You're one of *those* girls."

"And what would that be?"

Of course, Selena rose to the challenge. "The insecure type who's afraid of a little competition."

"I'm not afraid of competition because I see no competition. However, I am afraid of hepatitis, herpes, HPV, HIV, and whatever incurable STDs are crawling inside that biological hazard you call a vagina."

Lou stood from the recliner, intent on having the last word. Never bothering to stop on her way toward the stairs, she passed the couch where Selena and Wren sat and held out her hand. Without even a moment's hesitation, Wren grasped it before following her upstairs to the room they shared.

I waited until I heard the door close behind them before I met my sister's gaze.

"Give them a chance, huh? It doesn't seem like she's willing to return the favor," Selena spat.

"You were flirting with her boyfriend. What did you expect?"

"I asked him a simple question. How was that flirting?"

I frowned at that because I realized she was right. If it had been anyone else, I wouldn't have thought anything of it. Guilt rushed through me as I wondered if I was judging my own sister too harshly, too soon.

I didn't respond as I stood, and as I made my way toward the stairs, I glanced at the kitchen where Vaughn had disappeared and wondered how long it took someone to grab a few beers. Once upstairs, I crossed the landing to one of the bedrooms and knocked. I was left standing there a little longer than necessary before the door finally opened. I found myself staring into eyes so blue they were almost electrifying—a far cry from the usual cool gray of Wren's irises.

"I need to speak to Lou."

He stood back, allowing me inside before disappearing into their en suite to offer us privacy. Lou was sitting crossed-legged on the bed, her hair mussed, and lips swollen. I'd definitely interrupted something.

"What's up?" she asked a little too casually after what had just occurred downstairs.

I crossed my arms over my chest as I stared her down. "I want to know what your problem is with my sister."

"Oh, that," she said as if it was of little consequence. "I don't like her."

"Why? What did she do to you?"

"Nothing. It's what she's doing to you or what she's trying to do. I don't know," she said, sounding like a paranoid lunatic while throwing up her hands in frustration. "I can't explain it, Ty-baby. All I can say is, I have a gut, and I trust it."

I found myself lowering onto the edge of the bed and trying not to think about what Wren and Lou might have done on it. "What do you think she's trying to do?"

Lou stared at me for a long time before lying straight through her teeth. See, I have a gut, too. It's just that, unlike Lou, I doubted mine from time to time. "I wish I knew."

I inhaled deeply before releasing it slowly. "Lou, do you care about me?"

She grumbled before responding because she hated being mushy. "Sure."

"This is my *sister*," I stressed. "I don't want to her lose her when I've only just found her. Promise me you'll try to be civil. For me?"

I added a pout at the black look she gave me.

"I guess I can try," she agreed after some time. I didn't doubt that she was unhappy about it. A second later, we heard a snort come from behind the closed door of the bathroom. Obviously, Wren wasn't as gullible as me. He was also eavesdropping.

"Thank you."

Lou leaned over to wrap her arms around my neck, so I hugged her back. When I tried to pull away, however, she tightened her hold, keeping me in place. "I really do care about you," she whispered far too low for Wren to overhear. "And I wasn't bluffing about Wren's gun. If she screws you, I'll help you hide the body." Kissing my cheek, she let me go and winked.

The laugh that escaped me as I stood and made for the door sounded nervous to my own ears. I couldn't tell if she were serious or not. Squaring my shoulders, I decided it didn't matter. Despite my determination to make a relationship with my sister work, I couldn't help but feel better about my decision, knowing I had friends like Lou to catch me if I fell.

And what a hard fall it would be.

Our weekend at the cabin came to an end, and our return to Blackwood Keep also meant my return to work. It's barely been a week, and I already wished that Terry had suspended me for the entire summer. Especially when I had a sexy quarterback to keep me busy. It seemed Vaughn was determined to do that anyway.

A moan slipped through my lips as I gripped the brick wall in front of me, not caring that it was ruining my fresh manicure.

"Break's almost over," Vaughn teased as he gripped my hips. "I'd come on my cock if I were you, pip."

A whimper escaped me as my eyes flew to the big metal door a few feet away. I wondered how long I'd be suspended if Terry were to step outside this very moment. Although, when he found me with my pants around my ankles and the town prince balls deep inside of me, I was sure he'd flat out fire me this time.

It was my own fault for responding to Vaughn's text to meet him outside. He'd been waiting for me behind the coffee shop where I stupidly allowed him to bend me over for my first quickie. The damn dumpster was only ten feet away, but none of that mattered when he kissed me. *Stupid girl.*

The sound of our skin slapping filled the small alley as Vaughn shoved into me from behind. The only things keeping me up at this point were his hands since my legs had long grown weak.

"But I've already come twice," I whined, even though I was eager to do it again. "Just come already."

"What's my favorite number?" he asked me as his hand left my hip and his fingers found my clit. "What's my favorite fucking number?"

"Three."

"That's how many times you're going to come for me before I even *think* about letting you go." He slowed his pace just enough to thrust deep, and a choked cry ripped from my throat when I felt his piercing tease a spot deep inside of me. Pulling me up until my back was against his chest, he began strumming my clit until I finally came for him a third time. With one hand over my mouth to keep my cries muffled and the other gripping my neck, he pounded me with a savageness that made it hard to believe I was a virgin only five days ago.

His breathing turned ragged as he neared his release, and I swore there was no sweeter sound than the soft moan that slipped from his lips when he finally spilled inside the condom.

He held me captive for long moments after as we tried to catch our breath. I then stood still as he bent and pulled my uniform pants up. He took the time to zip and close me up before slipping his basketball shorts back over his hips. When he turned me around and pulled me close rather than let me go, I let him do that, too.

"Please forgive me," he begged after he kissed my lips.

"For what?"

"You're late," he whispered as he squeezed me tighter, almost desperately. "But I still can't seem to let you go."

I couldn't ignore the bags under his eyes, making me wonder about the last time he'd slept a full night—or the bleakness within them. Vaughn had always been broody, but this was different. Something had broken inside of him. He was clinging to the pieces, hoping to be put back together again, but whatever demons he'd been fighting had grown too strong.

"Then I'll stay with you," I promised him.

And I would.

I'd be whatever he needed—his angel of mercy, his light out of the darkness. I'd corrupt my soul to save his if I had to. Terry or anyone else who stood in my way would just have to be my victims.

chapter sixteen

The Pawn

BLACKWOOD KEEP WAS ONE OF THE WEALTHIEST TOWNS IN THE country, attracting celebrities, socialites, and wealthy investment bankers looking to hide from the world in their summer homes and permanent residences. The coastal land had been purchased by Vaughn's ancestor, Peter Blackwood, almost four centuries ago. Today, on the anniversary of that historic day, a parade had been ordered by the mayor to celebrate—the mayor who also happened to be Vaughn's uncle.

I sipped my smoothie, aware of the soreness between my thighs, as I watched the last float pass by. There was already a crew following closely behind, cleaning up the confetti, so to speak. In no time, the affluent town would look good as new. The parade had been a real snooze fest. Not even the retired actress who'd appeared on one of the floats could liven it. They'd been smart to offer free food since not even the wealthy could turn the opportunity down.

"So, what do you want to do next, little sis?"

Selena and I were busy enjoying our last day of freedom before my father came home. So that he wasn't blindsided as I'd been, I called him a couple of days ago to tell him about Selena. To say my father had been furious that I hadn't called sooner was an understatement. He shouted for an hour until he exhausted himself, and I forgot my anger when I realized he was frazzled. Despite their relationship not being what he'd led me to believe, I knew my father loving my mother hadn't been a lie.

"I thought we could get a massage and then maybe—"

My suggestion was abandoned, and our plans were forgotten when I caught sight of a man I recognized but had yet to meet formally. Tall and imposing, he had just stepped from the century-old building across the street that served as Blackwood Keep's Town Hall. His gray hair was thin, his muscles nonexistent, and the scowl he wore looked too natural to be temporary—too deeply embedded to match his son's panty-dropping smile. Although I was too far away to truly tell, I was willing to bet the pinstriped suit he wore cost more than my education. With his hair slicked back, he looked like he was auditioning for a role in *Goodfellas* or maybe *The Godfather*. I couldn't take my eyes away as he checked his watch and then his phone. The very last thing I felt, however, was admiration for the man.

"Tyra?"

I heard my sister calling my name, but I couldn't bring myself to answer. I felt her shaking me, but the poison seeping into my skin was too powerful. This man was the reason Vaughn and I couldn't be together. I watched as Franklin Rees dialed before placing the phone to his ear and speaking.

"Tyra, talk to me," Selena pleaded. "Is everything okay?"

"That's him." Franklin had already hung up after speaking a few terse words. "That's Vaughn's father." Selena paused before looking across the street, her forehead creasing as her brows brunched even tighter. "I told you that Vaughn didn't want to be with me because of football, but that's not true." At least I didn't think it was. We watched as a black SUV rounded the corner and slowed to a stop at the curb. "It's because of him." My voice was barely a whisper when I spoke again. "Vaughn said his father wouldn't accept me because of who I am. Because I'm black."

A bulky, grim-faced man in a black suit hopped from the front passenger seat to open the back door for his boss. Franklin was still standing by the Town Hall entrance, and there were about thirty feet of walkway between the building and the road.

I wanted to run over and confront him before he could get away, but something held me back. If Vaughn weren't willing to stand up to his father, then it would only be in vain, driving an even bigger wedge between us. It wasn't, however, the reason I stayed rooted to the spot. I could feel danger lurking like a dark cloud above.

"Well, we can't let him get away with that now, can we?"

I'd barely processed my sister's words before she grabbed my hand and darted across the street. "Selena, wait!" I pleaded. It wasn't just the oncoming traffic we had to dodge that made my heart race. With each step, we came closer and closer to the man exuding the danger looming ahead. "What are you doing?"

Too late, I realized.

As soon as we stepped on the curb, Franklin's bodyguard rounded on us with his hand inside his jacket. I gulped. My gut told me he wasn't reaching for a Tic Tac. He had a gun tucked away there, and he wouldn't hesitate to use it. The driver was also out of the SUV now, and I felt him closing in on my back. Franklin, whose pace remained unhurried as he reached the car, seemed amused. I knew what a sight we must have made. Selena and I barely stood more than five feet high, yet we challenged full-grown armed men. My gaze locked with Franklin's, and then he closed the car door. I could see the curiosity in his eyes as he came to stand before us.

"Gentleman, relax," he ordered as he stepped around his security. "I believe I know this young lady." He pointed at me. "You're my son's little friend." He smiled at me, but it seemed too sharp to be affable.

I wrapped my arms around my waist when I shivered, feeling like I'd just stepped into the world's deadliest crosshairs.

"She's more than just his friend," Selena spat when I said nothing. "You'd know that if you stepped out of 1865 and joined us in the twenty-first century."

Franklin's eyebrow rose when his attention shifted to my

sister. I wanted to push her behind me to protect her from him, but my entire body remained frozen. "I don't, however, know this young woman," he continued as if Selena hadn't spoken. "What I do know is the year you're referring to. While I was surprised he outgrew his fondness for brunettes, my son's preferences in playmates have never been of interest to me. I'm sorry to disappoint you."

Selena paused at that before recovering quickly and digging a deeper hole for Franklin to bury me in. "My sister is not his playmate. She's his girlfriend. At least she would be if not for you. They love each other."

Franklin seemed genuinely surprised by that, and I wondered whose eyes Vaughn had been pulling the wool over this entire time. His father's or mine.

"Is that right?" Franklin drawled, his focus shifting to me.

Of course, Selena took it upon herself to answer for me. "Yes, and it doesn't matter how you feel about it. Your son's feelings for her will never change."

Silence followed Selena's declaration as Franklin Rees studied me like I was buried treasure after a long voyage. When he finally spoke, his words were directed at Selena, but somehow, they seemed meant for me. "My dear, I really do hope you're right about that."

"Is that him?" Selena was curled up on my bed when she broke the heavy silence.

I rubbed my arms absently as I stared out the window. The goose bumps that appeared on my skin after Vaughn's father wished us a good day were still very much present the next morning. Too many times, I'd picked up the phone to call Vaughn, to warn him of what Selena had done, of what I'd selfishly allowed to happen, but each time, my cowardice won out. Would Vaughn be pissed that I'd essentially forced his hand, or would he be relieved? We'd face challenges knowing his family didn't support us, but nothing worth having was ever easy. I was ready to take them all head-on. For him. For us.

I felt my stomach turn and fought the urge to vomit. My father's return home certainly wasn't helping matters as I watched his red pickup turn into the driveway.

"Yes."

Sighing, I let the curtain covering my bedroom window fall back into place. My feet were heavy as I made my way downstairs. Coach was furious, but so was I. In fact, I was trying so very hard not to hate him, but it was harder than I ever thought it would be.

My bare feet touched the last step, and at the same time, the front door swung open. Average height, hair shaved closely, and a full goatee peppered with gray, my father was a handsome man and undoubtedly a lady killer in his day. Our gazes locked, and whatever he saw in mine had his broad shoulders slumping as his gaze fell to the hardwood floor.

"Tyra—"

"Is it true?" I demanded. Never mind the fact that I hadn't seen him in a month or that he was still standing in the open door with his luggage at his feet and bags under his eyes.

Closing the door, he tried the stern route when he turned and pinned me under his glare. "Why didn't you call me sooner to ask me? Instead, you invited some stranger into my home without my permission and have the audacity to interrogate me under that same roof?"

"Selena's not a stranger, she's my sister, and you knew she existed all along! Why didn't you tell me instead of letting me believe what you and mom had was real?"

He held his hands pressed together and extended them toward me in a pleading gesture. "It was, Tyra. I told you the truth. Your mother and I were in love."

I wanted to believe him, I really did, but there was some

pretty compelling evidence waiting for me upstairs. "Really? Because you also told me you were going to get married before she died giving birth to me. How could that be when she was already married?"

"I don't know what Selena told you, but—"

"You don't have to wonder. She showed me the letter mom wrote to you before she died."

I'd read it so many times I had it committed to memory. In it, my mother had written everything she was feeling, mostly fear, sorrow, and anxiousness for my arrival, but never once did she mention her loving him. The letter had ended rather abruptly, making me wonder if a page was missing, but Selena had sworn that there wasn't. Our mother hadn't even signed her name.

"You can also ask Selena yourself."

My father's expression became absolutely thunderous at my confession. "She's still here?"

He may have told me to ask her to leave, but I couldn't do that. Not when she'd come all this way to find the last piece of family she had left.

"She wants to talk to you."

"I'm sorry, Tyra, but I don't feel the same. You had no right."

"No right?" I sputtered. "You had no right to lie to me! Just like you had no right to ruin a marriage."

"I didn't ruin anything. Your mother wasn't in love with Kevin anymore. She was planning to take Selena and leave, but she—" My father started to say more, but then his attention shifted to something behind me. Even though I knew it could only be one person, I peered over my shoulder and found my sister in tears. She was standing at the landing, her face so much like mine and soaked in sorrow. Before I could go to her and offer her comfort, she was storming down the stairs. I'd barely sidestepped her in time to avoid falling. A moment later, the sound of Selena's palm hitting my father's cheek echoed through the foyer, and then the slam of the front door followed after she fled through it.

By the time I got over my shock, I had heard tires squealing and then an engine racing, telling me that running after Selena would only be in vain. I started toward my father, but he held up his hand. I couldn't bear to see the disappointment in his gaze, so I was relieved when he disappeared inside the kitchen. Ashamed of the mess I'd made and late for work, I slowly made my way back to my bedroom to shower and dress.

Hours after Selena had run out of my father's house in tears, I slyly checked my phone for the thousandth time and found zero notifications waiting for me once again. I'd even mustered up the courage to reach out to Vaughn, but his call had gone straight to voicemail. I didn't know what to think or what to do on both fronts. Even attempts to talk to my father had been futile. Before I left for work, he'd secluded himself inside his room and hadn't answered the door when I knocked. It had only taken me less than twenty-four hours to alienate everyone important to me.

Well…almost.

I was on barista duty today, and as I was finishing off a latte for a customer, Jamie sauntered in all smiles and wearing a fuck-ing tiara. Of course, Bee was right behind him, trying desperately to remove it, but he kept ducking her hand as they made their way over to the counter. Begrudgingly, I admitted how fucking perfect they were together.

"Ty-baby, we came to spread the word," Jamie greeted when he finally noticed me. "We're partying tonight. You're already a square, so I can't threaten you to be there. I *will* tell you that it's against the rules to say no to the birthday boy. We all know how you love rules, Goody Two."

"And who's the birthday boy?" I teased. Today was Jamie's nineteenth birthday, so naturally, he assumed he had free rein to be even more obnoxious than usual.

Smiling wide, he lifted a party horn I didn't notice him hold-ing and blew into it. "Me, of course." He blew it again, and I cringed when the disturbed patrons glared our way.

I was already on my last leg with Terry after I left during the middle of my shift two weeks ago. Vaughn had taken me to the beach house, where I spent the rest of the day and all night, making sure the only thing he felt was me. And so went the two weeks that followed. I couldn't tell if Vaughn's heightened sex drive was because he'd gone nearly a year without or because he was desperately trying to exorcise whatever demons haunted him. Regardless of the answer, my body had taken a delicious beating.

"Jamie, stop blowing that thing. You're disturbing the other customers."

"Only if you blow me instead." He started to blow the horn again when Bee snatched it and pinned him with her glare. "Force of habit, baby. I'm not used to being a boyfriend."

That much was true. It had only been a month, but I was shocked they'd lasted this long. Just being in the same room with Jameson Buchanan required a lot of patience.

"You won't ever get used to it if you keep testing me," Bee warned. When she looked away, Jamie shot me a cocky look that said, "yeah, right," and I had to agree. Bee was hooked, lined, and Jamie was more than ready to reel her in. She wasn't going anywhere.

"So, anyway," Jamie continued, blatantly dismissing Bee's threat. "We're also celebrating Four winning her race last weekend, and since Vaughn is heading to Cali for training camp next week, I guess we're calling it a send-off, too. But the most important part of tonight," he stressed, "is *me*. It's my day. Don't any of you forget that."

The last couple of weeks had been pretty intense. When Vaughn wasn't trying to knock the lining out of my pussy, he was even more closed off than usual. But some good had occurred, too. Four had qualified for her license, and Vaughn had finally come clean about his plans to play for USC.

I still didn't know why he'd kept it a secret, but I wondered if it had anything to do with his father threatening to kill him. I shuddered. What kind of father did that to his son? Or was the man more monster than father?

"So, where is this party occurring?"

"The beach house," Jamie answered as if it were obvious. Maybe it would have been if Vaughn hadn't gone MIA on me again.

"The beach house?" I echoed, frowning. "You've spoken to Vaughn?"

Jamie shrugged in response like it was no big deal while Bee bit her lip nervously when she noticed my ire. "A couple of hours ago. The party was his idea."

Believing I owed it to my sister and father to clean up my mess and try to start over, I'd been planning to blow off tonight despite Jamie's attempt at coercion. I guess that was why plans were never written in stone. At the drop of a dime or swift change of the wind, they altered.

The heels killing my feet and the dress squeezing the air from my body didn't seem to help build my confidence as I pushed inside the beach house later that night. Apocalyptica's "End of Me" was competing with the pounding of my heart as I searched for Vaughn in the crowd. The party was in full swing, yet I was all alone. Four and the others hadn't arrived yet, so I didn't have anyone to distract me from the bad feeling in my gut, the one telling me to turn and run. Maybe Vaughn already knew what I'd done, or perhaps fate would be kind and allow me to come clean on my own. I thought about Selena and what she would do in this situation. She was fearless in ways that I might never be, but maybe just this once I could channel her.

I kept going.

The beach house wasn't anything extravagant, not compared

to the literal castle Vaughn lived in, so there were only so many places to look. The living room turned out to be a dead end—almost literally since the space was so packed, I couldn't get more than a foot inside. The kitchen was also packed to capacity as everyone crowded around the kegs and stray bottles of liquor on the countertops.

Still no Vaughn.

I forced back the urge to stomp my foot in frustration. If there was one thing Vaughn enjoyed imbibing more than me, it was beer. *Where are you?*

My phone vibrated in my hand, and I wasted no time checking the notification. Disappointment and relief flowed through me when I saw that it was a message from Four.

Best (old phone): Parking. B there in 5.

If I weren't so on edge, I would have cheered at her refusal to use the iPhone Ever had gifted her. The controlling asshole still refused to remove the tracking app from her phone. She could have figured it out herself or gotten any of us to show her how, but I think it was important to her that Ever give in and learn the error of his ways.

"Hey." The cloying stench of too much alcohol followed the greeting, and I turned. I didn't even try to mute my sigh or hide my frustration when I found one of Vaughn's old teammates hovering over me. I think his last name was Scott, but I was blanking on his first name since I'd only ever seen his surname printed on the back of his jersey.

"Hi."

"I know you," he slurred. "You're Vaughn's chick, right? Your name's Tina."

"Tyra."

He actually looked offended as he wrinkled his nose. "That's what I said."

"Right. Can I help you?"

"No. Unless…" I barely resisted the urge to hold my nose when he tipped a little closer and flashed his idea of a flirtatious smile. "Vaughn's done with you?"

I silently hoped not, although I wouldn't blame him if he were. I don't regret Franklin knowing about my feelings for his son, but I did regret taking the decision from Vaughn to stand up to his father and admit his own. Even more confusing was Franklin's lack of anger. He seemed to almost relish the thought of his son being in love with me. None of it made sense, including why Vaughn had lied to me.

"He's not." I was proud of the confidence in my tone when I answered though I didn't feel it. "Have you seen him?"

"Sure, I have." He took the time to sip from the beer can he was holding before telling me where to find Vaughn. "He went upstairs with you five minutes ago."

Ignoring what was obviously the rambles of a drunk, I shook my head as I watched him stumble away. How could Vaughn have gone upstairs with me if I was standing right here?

Growling over the precious minutes I wasted talking to Barney Gumble, I headed for the stairs. Some of the party had spilled onto the beach, but I hadn't seen Vaughn on my way in. There was only one place left to look. Despite all the soirees he threw, Vaughn was an introvert at heart and rarely stayed to enjoy his own party. Of course, for the past year, I'd been the only one making sure Vaughn didn't get too lonely. It was possible he'd already drunk too much and was passed out in bed.

On my way up, which was slow going thanks to the revelers crowding it, I dialed Selena's phone. It had been hours since she stormed out this morning, and I was beginning to worry she'd fled back to Texas. My father was missing when I got home after my shift, so I hadn't had the chance to talk to him, either. I didn't blame any of them, Vaughn included, for wanting to avoid me. I hardly recognized myself anymore.

The line began to ring just as I finally reached the landing, and through the background noise, I heard what also sounded like a phone ringing. There were three bedrooms on the second floor, so I figured someone had made use of the two spares. I started toward the master suite that Vaughn kept off-limits to guests just as Selena's voicemail kicked. Gritting my teeth, I stabbed her name again. I felt bad for what had happened, but I was also done with being ignored.

The ringing began again but not just in my ear. My heart dropped to my stomach as I stared at the door of the master suite in front of me. It had to be a coincidence. Hanging up, I listened as the ringing on the other side stopped. My breaths came faster now, and anxiety warmed my skin as my thumb hovered over my sister's name. I couldn't find the courage to dial again— not when a moan loud enough for me to hear over the music downstairs escaped through the closed bedroom door. I felt robbed of everything I held dear. Empty. So, so empty.

He went upstairs with you five minutes ago.

Knowing I would never truly believe it unless I saw for myself, I forced my trembling hand to grip the doorknob.

And then I pushed inside.

The room that had been covered in darkness was now bathed in the light from the hallway. It allowed me to see the two figures clearly, despite the tears stinging my eyes and flowing freely now.

Vaughn's teammate hadn't been mistaken.

My legs threatened to collapse from under me while my feet begged for me to flee. Impossible. My heart had been a snow-topped mountain, and this was the avalanche coming to bury me. I couldn't look away any more than I could go back in time before I opened the door to the end of me. My soul had been crushed, the tethered bond slashed.

The head that had been tilted back in ecstasy, pleasure my sister eagerly gave, lowered. Slowly, his green eyes opened. All I saw in them was the reflection of my own sorrow. His gaze was an empty mirror. There was no remorse, no guilt, no surprise.

Vaughn simply closed his eyes again as if I weren't standing there.

"What the hell?"

To my complete humiliation, I recognized the voice. I felt my friends standing behind me in the doorway, witnessing everything. I couldn't bear the thought of facing them, but I couldn't stay here, either. Turning on my heel, I pushed past them. No one resisted or tried to stop me. I think they were all too shocked by what they saw to react. I was grateful for it allowed me the head start I'd need moments later.

chapter seventeen

The Prince

"H ey." I FLICKED SELENA'S FOREHEAD TO GET HER ATTENTION when she continued gnawing on my dick long after we were alone. My friends had taken off after Tyra, which meant the torture could finally end.

Have you ever been sucked off by a horny shark?

Would not recommend.

When she finally released my dick and met my gaze, I pushed her away, making her fall on her trifling ass. Who the hell sucks dick with their eyes closed anyway? "We're done here."

"But you didn't come," she flirted, reaching for me again.

"Do you really care?" I challenged as I quickly tucked myself back inside my sweats. "She saw us. She's broken. Mission accomplished."

Standing, Selena placed her hands on her hips with a conspiratorial smile. "What do you mean?"

"I mean, you got the pound of flesh you came here for, now pack up, and get the fuck out of my town."

"Hmmm…I kind of like it here. I think I'll stay."

Over my dead body. Or yours. "Do you really think Tyra's going to go for that after what we just did?"

"Why wouldn't she?" When she shrugged her shoulders, I knew she thought she'd get away with it. "I'm her sister. She'll forgive me eventually. It's not like you two were serious or anything."

I paused, mentally calculating how long I'd go to prison if I strangled her to death. "That's not what you had to say twenty-four hours ago when you couldn't keep your fucking mouth shut."

"Huh?"

"Nothing." I shoved past her on my way out of the room, and when I hit the stairs, it was hard as fuck keeping my pace casual and my expression impassive as I made my way down. Getting through the thick crowd was even harder, but finally, I made it outside in time to see my friends rushing toward the parked cars in search of Tyra. They'd be pissed, that much was inevitable, and I was not looking forward to the hell they'd bring down on my head when the dust cleared.

I wasn't sure what led me underneath the house, but when I found her there, hugging one of the stilts, my resolve almost broke for the first time since she caught me with my pants down.

Almost.

"I'm sorry you had to see that," I said when she didn't turn around. Tyra knew I was there, but she avoided facing me as if it would delay the inevitable.

"But you're not—" Her voice broke, and I forced my feet not to move. "You're not sorry you did it?"

"No." It was amazing how our tones individually reflected what we were feeling inside—hers in shambles while mine was so incredibly empty.

"And when you said you loved me...are you sorry for that, too?"

I closed my eyes, cursing her for bringing up that night and me for believing I'd meant every word. This would be so much simpler if I weren't so reckless. If I hadn't opened the door and foolishly let her in.

"Yes."

"Why should I believe you?"

I sighed, wanting to walk away right then and there, but the need to see this through kept me rooted to the spot. "I'm bored, Tyra. I don't know how else to put it."

"So, you put it in that bitch instead?"

The part of me that remembered we'd at least been friends once upon a time wanted to assure her that I hadn't fucked her sister—as if that made a difference. Instead, I told myself that it was better if Tyra believed the worst.

"Look at me," I ordered against my better judgment. Always the stubborn pip, Tyra shook her head, refusing. Stepping forward, I gripped her shoulders gently and turned her around. It was now or never. She needed to see that I was completely fucking serious. "I made a mistake."

As if my body were fighting against me, I felt my finger twitch. A moment later, something resembling relief flooded her gaze. I didn't get the chance to question why because Tyra started to melt into my arms. It was all I could do not to take her into them. My fingers dug into her shoulders, the need was so great, but I also realized they were keeping her at bay. I saw her hurt behind my rejection, but it wasn't enough. I needed more. I needed to ensure myself and her that we were done. Irrevocably broken.

Finally, she pushed me away, and I let her. I was relieved to see that her fire still burned, that the most crucial parts of Tyra would survive after she walked away. Otherwise, this would all be in vain. "It took you a year to figure that out?"

I forced myself to shrug, feeling the wind, but nothing was as cold as her icy gaze. Realizing how close I was to our inevitable end, I spoke, driving that final nail into our coffin.

"I was looking for something different, and up until now, you provided that."

"You mean up until I let you—" She looked ready to collapse right then and there. "Until I let you fuck me."

My eyes narrowed at the sorrow in her tone. I might be ending this now, but I didn't regret a single moment. Unlike her.

"Let's not forget," I said, wanting to hurt her for a different reason now, "you begged me not to stop."

"I thought maybe—" She looked away, her guilt and shame overshadowing her pain. "I thought maybe you'd change your mind."

My nostrils flared at her confession. I wanted to shake her for her stupidity. It seemed my father hadn't been the only one with an agenda. "You mean you thought you could manipulate my feelings with sex?" I scoffed at that to hide my own hurt. "While you were a phenomenal fuck, Bradley, no pussy is that good."

"I guess it doesn't matter now."

"Finally, something we can agree on," I heard myself say and none too gently. I was starting to feel like a spectator and not a participant—as if I'd locked away the part of me that wanted to take it all back and threw away the key. "No, it doesn't matter now."

Tyra seemed to stare right through me as I held her gaze, listening to music above us and the waves crashing behind us. I wondered what she was thinking. I reminded myself it didn't matter.

"Just tell me one thing," she pleaded, and it was all I could do not to deny her as a lone tear slipped down her cheek. For some reason, that single tear cut me deeper than all the rest. The determination in her gaze told me I'd won, and it ripped my fucking heart out. "Of all the girls you could have screwed, why did it have to be her? Why did it have to be my sister?"

A thousand truths screamed at me at once, needing to be heard. I ignored them all—except one.

"Because she helped me see who I've been all along. With her, I could finally stop running."

Tyra stilled at what sounded like a confession of love, and then her eyes drifted shut as she inhaled. When she finally opened them, the warmth I'd grown used to seeing in her whiskey gaze was gone. "Good for you. Good for you both. I hope the two of you are very happy burning in hell together."

It was all I could do not to snatch her ass back when she stepped around me. Instead, I stood rooted to the spot, staring at the small footprints she'd left in the sand. Watching Tyra walk away forever was too huge a risk to my willpower. I'd done the impossible and rewritten our stars, and I knew she would never forgive me for it.

Feeling my hands shake, I took a deep breath and balled them into fists before checking my watch. *Ten minutes.* Finding my car, I abandoned my party and sped all the way home. When I walked through the iron doors, my father was there to greet me with a small army of men prepared to do his bidding if I'd been even a second late.

"Is it done?"

"It's done."

"Good." Reaching inside his suit jacket, my father removed a small, blue box. He'd found it in my room yesterday after he'd gone looking for proof of Selena's claim. It was the same blue box containing Wren's engagement ring. The ring my father assumed I'd intended for Tyra.

It was all the proof he needed that he'd found his perfect pawn.

"You won't be needing this anymore," he said as he handed it over. "So consider this a show of mercy. Son or not, it's the only one you'll get from me." As soon I took it from him, he looked over his shoulder. A man I'd only met once and already loathed appeared. "You remember Jeremy Antonov. My most promising protégé." The malice I detected in my father's tone was due to what Antonov really represented. Not the preservation of Thirteen, but the ruin of my father's coveted dynasty. "Jeremy here is going to make sure you keep your word."

PART TWO

Lies

chapter eighteen

The Pawn

Five months later

HAVE YOU EVER NOTICED HOW THE STILLNESS OF A ROOM COULD make your thoughts feel a little less private? It was as if suddenly you were thinking through a megaphone, and the people around you could hear every word. It was all I could do not to look up and search for that knowing gaze in the crowd, the one who knew the sin that had been festering in my mind for the last five months.

Murder.

Specifically, how to get away with it. I wished Harvard had taken a page from Shonda Rhimes and offered that course instead of the humdrum philosophies of frail men long dead. Reading one of the questions on my final Ethics exam for the third time, I inhaled deeply when the fluttering in my stomach continued as it had for the past hour.

Not now. Please stop. Please, please, please stop.

Glancing at the clock above the professor's desk, my heart quickened as a bead of sweat rolled down my temple. Filling in *A*, whether it was the right answer or not, I moved on.

"Hey, are you okay?" The bespectacled guy seated next to me leaned over and whispered again. "Are you…should I call someone?"

"I'm fine." I kept my eyes on my test even though I knew it

was rude. He was just trying to be nice, but the last thing—*the very last thing*—I needed was to be caught by the proctors and accused of cheating. Not when I was already failing.

Okay, technically, a C minus wasn't failing, but it might as well be when you're used to getting perfect grades.

Shrugging, the guy went back to his test while I gripped my pencil. Feeling it crack under pressure, I wondered if I'd really been broken this easily, too.

Harvard had promised to be challenging enough. Toss in a broken heart, however, and it was more than hard. It was fucking brutal. And my GPA…if I didn't score at least a ninety on all of my exams, I was toast. My scholarship would be pulled, and I'd have no way to pay for school.

Among other things.

Tossing my broken pencil aside, I picked up my spare. I then spent the next hour tapping my foot and probably irritating my classmates, thanks to my bladder threatening to burst. I'd been sure to go before the test started, but it hadn't been enough. I almost whimpered. I still had twenty questions I couldn't remember the answers to and an hour left.

I wasn't sure if my sudden need to cry was just hormones or the fact that medical school was slipping further and further from my grasp. Gritting my teeth, I told myself to get a grip. I wasn't letting that asshole destroy me a second time.

As soon as I filled in the last question, I shot to my feet, ignoring the startled gazes as I rushed up the short aisle toward the front of the room and handed over my Scantron sheet. Thankfully, the nearest bathroom was only a few feet away. Bursting inside, I barely made it inside one of the stalls and thanked my lucky stars for wearing sweats today. Not that any of my jeans were an option anymore. Once my bladder was relieved, I made my way out of Emerson Hall and descended the steps.

Pausing on the sidewalk, a cold wind blew, making me shiver as I casually let my gaze pass over the area. I was half expecting

the prince and the pawn | 173

to see a silver BMW parked somewhere on the street. The make and color seemed to be a popular style in the Boston/Cambridge area. I always seemed to spot one wherever I went. One time, I'd gotten paranoid enough to call campus security because I started seeing one with the same license plate over and over. I felt a little stupid when they calmly pointed out how the car might have belonged to another student. Oddly enough, I hadn't seen it again, and all of the silver beamers I'd spotted since all had different plates.

Sighing, I begin the trek to Ivy Yard while wishing I had my own car. I'd left my Honda back home since the public transportation was ten times more convenient. Five measly minutes, and I was out of breath by the time I pushed through the doors of Apley Court. Becoming taxed easily was my new reality. At least for a little while longer. The judgmental stares and pitying glances I received weren't new, either, but I doubt those would ever change.

Fuck them.

The dorm I'd been assigned to used to be home to some famous poet who, rumor had it, hid his work in the walls. Jamie and Bee had paid me a surprise visit for Halloween, and Bee spent the entire time staring at the walls when I told her. Jamie spent it gazing at her ass, so it had worked out marvelously for me and the oversized kangaroo costume I'd worn. Since today was the last day of final exams and Christmas was just a few days away, Apley Court was a ghost town. Most of the residents who'd avoided me like the plague these last couple of months had already migrated back home for winter break, and I was grateful. I kept my fingers crossed as I slowly climbed the stairs that my roommate had already fled campus, too.

Nope. No such luck.

I barely suppressed a groan when I stepped inside and found her zipping her suitcase closed. Mary Marshall was a law major— or at least she planned to be. She definitely had the personality for it with her inquisitive nature and tendency to give strangers the third degree. She was also high-strung and a chatterbox, but at least she kept her side of the room clean. If only she could figure out how to stay on it. Personal space was not something the freckle-faced redhead understood.

Hearing me enter, she looked up, offering me a cheerful smile that I managed to return before turning toward the walk-in closet I'd lucked out on and dragging my suitcase out.

"I'm so excited to see my mama and daddy and little brothers," she immediately began. I closed my eyes, hoping to block out the sound of her voice. Mary was a Georgia native, and her southern accent only reminded me that I hadn't spoken to my best friend in more than two months—despite her frequent calls and texts. "I've never gone this long without seeing them before."

Mary kept speaking despite my lack of response, and the more she talked, the more I began to contemplate calling my dad and telling him that I wasn't coming home for winter break. I couldn't do it. I couldn't go back to Blackwood Keep and face all that I'd left behind and the people I pushed away. All because of *him*.

Vaughn.

What if he also went home for winter break? How could anyone expect me to breathe the same air as him after what he'd done and *who* he'd done? Already feeling like I was suffocating slowly, my breaths became short and rapid.

"Are you okay?" my roommate paused long enough to ask. She rushed over to me, concern in her wide-eyed gaze. "Is it—"

"I'm fine."

Like my classmate, she immediately backed off, and I started grabbing shit. I didn't care what as I threw them inside of my open suitcase.

"Do you need help?" she asked as if I were a fucking invalid. "My cab is already on the way, but I can—"

"I said I'm fine." *Jeez, relax your tits, Bradley. She's just trying to help.* Except, I'd already learned the hard way what letting people in got me. Sighing, I forced my tone to sound more pleasant. "But thank you, Mary. You go," I insisted. "I'll be okay."

She stood there watching me for a few seconds longer before grabbing the handle of her suitcase. "Okay!" Her tone was cheerful again, though, for the first time, it sounded forced. "Try not to have too…much…fun…" She faltered, her gaze dipping briefly, and then her cheeks turned tomato red before she made a break for the door.

I sighed.

Thirty minutes later, I got a text from my dad telling me he'd arrived. Grabbing my suitcase, I locked up and stubbornly dragged it downstairs despite his offer to come up and help. I didn't know if anyone was left in the dorm. I couldn't risk anyone witnessing my father go ballistic when he finally saw me for the first time since August.

Here goes nothing.

A mere two days after my arrival, Four had shown up unannounced. My father turned her away at my bidding, but he hadn't approved of me taking the coward's way. Considering the circumstances, however, he had no choice but to relent. I knew when I watched from my bedroom window as she roared off on her Café Racer that I wouldn't be able to hide forever. I missed her so much my heart ached, but it was also because the spring semester wouldn't begin for another three weeks. That gave her plenty of time to corner me, and I knew she wouldn't give up. If you looked up *stubborn* in the dictionary, you'd find Four with her middle finger up.

To delay the inevitable, I didn't leave the house. Not even to check the mailbox or to celebrate the new year. I'd spent the entire two weeks since my return to Blackwood Keep—or, more accurately, the outskirts since my father's salary wasn't high enough—holed up in my room. I wasn't sure how much more of this I could take before cabin fever got the best of me. For some reason, I'd already cleaned and rearranged my bedroom from top to bottom three times and was fighting the urge to do it again. I needed it perfect and could only assume it was out of boredom as I slowly tore my hair out.

It was barely dawn when I gingerly walked into the kitchen and found my father staring into his coffee cup for the third morning in a row. Brynwood Academy was still closed for winter break, so it had been just the two of us. Our reunion had gone about how I expected only a thousand times worse. My father hadn't been able to look at me, so I wasn't surprised when he didn't acknowledge my presence. He didn't stir when I tossed his cold coffee in the sink and poured him a fresh cup. I wasn't sure what stage of grief he was in for his little girl right now, but I had a feeling we were a long way from acceptance.

Not even I had gotten that far, and I'd known for months.

With the school's approval, I'd stayed on campus for Thanksgiving, and now my father, who was disappointed at the time, knew why. He'd screamed as much at me during the long drive home.

I'd stayed silent the entire way, letting him have his anger because I understood it and refraining from offering excuses when he demanded answers. I had none. And when the tears came, and I heard my father cry for the very first time, I broke, too. Suddenly, I was back inside my dorm bathroom, confused, terrified, and holding a little white stick again.

What had I done?

"Tyra."

My head shot up, and my heart started pounding, seeing my father's red-rimmed eyes watching me. His gaze didn't waver, and neither did mine even when I recognized his disappointment.

"Yes, Daddy?"

"We need to talk about this," he decided, waving toward my oversized Harvard sweatshirt and what was hidden underneath.

My next breath shuddered out of me, and then I felt a cramp preventing me from taking another. It was all the same. Talking was the last thing I wanted, but I nodded anyway. I wasn't naïve enough to think I had a choice in the matter. Besides, I couldn't find it in me to be defiant when I'd ruined everything. I'd spat on my dreams and crushed my father's hope. I'd never been so cruel or careless.

"What do you want to talk about?"

"I want to know who did this to you."

I immediately turned away from him, ignoring the dull ache in my lower back that had kept me up half the night to pull the milk, butter, and eggs from the fridge. I couldn't remember the last time I had the luxury of an appetite but making pancakes sounded like a good distraction. Pulling the mixing bowl from one of the cabinets, I faced my father again. "I can't tell you that, Daddy."

"Why the hell not?" he roared, making me flinch.

I wanted to tell him that if anyone got to kill Vaughn, it had damn well better be me. I cracked an egg on the rim of the bowl and pretended that it was his skull. I wasn't sure when the majority of my fantasies became so morbid, but I found that I didn't mind them so much. They kept me warm at night during the rare and shameful times I actually longed for Vaughn. "Because it doesn't matter."

"The hell it doesn't, young lady. He needs to be held accountable!"

"I don't want him to be." It seemed remorse had taken a back seat as some of my defiance returned. "I don't want him anywhere near me."

"Well, here's some news for you," my father scolded as he stabbed the countertop with his finger, "you don't just have yourself to consider anymore."

Guilt made me look away, but then I gripped the counter-top and winced as another sharp pain, this one lasting longer, ripped through my stomach. *What the hell?*

"Yes, I do," I pushed through gritted teeth. My father was too wrapped in his despair to notice mine. The pain shooting through my abdomen didn't seem to be going away. In fact, it was happening more frequently and lasting longer. Just then, my phone chimed on the countertop, notifying me of an incoming email.

Coach blinked at my announcement before recovering quickly. "And how do you figure that?"

"Because," I slowly answered while panting, "there's someone out there better suited for this. Someone who *wants* this."

While my father was shocked into silence, I seized the opportunity to check my phone. It was an email from the Theodore Lidle Foundation. Feeling my hands shake, I plucked my phone from the counter and abandoned the pancake batter. I was slightly bent over, and each step felt impossible as I slowly made my way toward the stairs. My mind was in two places, and I couldn't decide which crisis to focus on. Thinking it would distract me from the pain, I shifted my mind toward the email.

It couldn't be good news if they were emailing me.

My heart began pounding faster in anticipation of the bad news while my breaths grew shorter. By the time I finally made it upstairs, I was clutching my belly. Another cramp hit me that nearly doubled me over. My gaze widened in alarm as the pressure in my pelvis increased, and the world seemed to spin. I'd read about this happening but never thought it would be this intense. The Harvard clinic doctors had even made them sound harmless.

Something's not right.

Passing my bedroom for the bathroom down the hall, I stumbled inside, and just as I reached for my leggings, I felt fluid gushing down my thighs. My lips parted in horror. Unwilling to accept it, for months I'd distanced myself from reality to the point that I'd been almost cruel. My callousness was the reason for my surprise when the wail that ripped from my chest a moment later wasn't from physical pain but an emotional one.

It was much too early.

chapter nineteen

The Prince

THE SNOW MELTED, AND INCH BY INCH, IT REVEALED THE WORLD I'D left behind buried underneath. I didn't recognize any of it, not after being away for so long. My nostrils flared as I inhaled the fresh, frigid air and wondered if it had always been this heavy. Even though I wasn't kept in a dungeon or anything quite so dramatic, my eyes had trouble adjusting when I stepped through the iron doors.

Freedom.

It didn't matter how harshly the sun stung or that each step strangely felt like learning to walk again.

I had freedom.

I only wondered why. I'd been told that it was never wise to look a gift horse in the mouth, but I couldn't help questioning the reason my father had let me out of my cage. He wasn't a benevolent man; he was a calculating man. He'd implied as much, mere moments ago, the conversation and its meaning still heavy on my mind.

Walking through the doors of my father's office, I found him waiting for me with a drink in hand that he offered to me as soon as I stood in front of him.

"What is this?" I asked once the doors closed behind me. Jeremy was left outside, and I took pleasure in knowing how much that must have annoyed him. Antonov hadn't been thrilled about being reduced to

a glorified babysitter and made his feelings known, so I slept with one eye open. Or not all.

"A toast."

Swallowing my pride, I accepted the glass. Even though I'd rather suck my own dick than share a drink with my father, I needed it. Feeling the alcohol burn its way down my throat, I snatched the crystal decanter from the sideboard and helped myself to more before asking the question foremost in my mind. "For?"

"Jeremy tells me you've been drinking more," he observed as if this was a goddamn AA meeting. I needed therapy, all right, and my father was the reason.

"Did he also mention I shit twice a day, too?"

"Careful, boy. I still have eyes and ears everywhere."

Recognizing the threat that had kept me under his heel for months, I took a deep breath and forced the anger from my tone. "What are we toasting?"

"Your recent accomplishments."

"I have none. I've been here. What is this really about?"

"Exactly as I said, son." Sensing the dread pooling in my gut as the wheels in my head turned desperately, he continued, "All will be revealed in due time." With a dismissive wave of his hand, he started for his desk. "For now, you're free to go."

The part of me that wanted to stay and grill my father for answers lost to the part that didn't give a shit and wanted out. I had my hand on the doorknob, ready to flee when he spoke.

"Oh, and, son?" I froze against my better judgment. "I wouldn't wander too far if I were you."

Peering over my shoulder, I expected to see the warning in his eyes, but all I found was smug satisfaction and a smile.

And now here I was, standing on the front lawn, my precious baby already idling a few feet away. Tearing my gaze from the Aventador blending into the snowy background, I looked around my father's property. Even the armed guards he'd posted to keep me inside were gone. I took a deep breath when the churning in my stomach intensified to no avail. This all felt like a trap and one I freely fell into.

Though Ever had likely returned to Cornell, I found myself at the Manor anyway. Since it was a Saturday and Valentine's Day had just passed, I had hope. Even back when Ever convinced himself that he despised her, my best friend could never stay away from Four. Not for long anyway.

"Where the hell have you been?"

I wasn't quick enough to block the blow and grimaced as pain shot through my arm. For such a little thing, she could pack a fucking punch. "I see you still haven't found any manners," I griped as I rubbed my arm. There wasn't as much muscle there as before, even though I'd had nothing but time. My brute strength would be one less weapon for my father to use.

"The fact that you're alive is the only reason I'm even speaking to you," Lou snapped, putting me in my place. She then slapped me with her ponytail when she pivoted on her heel, and I watched her storm back to the couch where Ever, Four, and Wren sat gaping in shock. I was relieved to see that none of them had changed, either. At least, not from what my roving eyes could see. Their feelings for me might tell a different story. Mrs. Greene had been the one to answer the door when I arrived, and after welcoming me warmly, she led me to my friends.

"Dude, is that really you?" Jamie shouted through the phone.

Lou had wasted no time FaceTiming him and shoving the screen in my face with a "Look who crawled out of his scum hole."

Nice.

"In the bruised, fucking flesh," I responded with a pointed glare at Lou. Giving me her profile, she stared at her nails in that way she did when she really didn't give a damn. I turned my attention back to the camera and found Bee now staring at me through the screen instead of Jamie. Noticing her tears, I started to feel like a bag of dog shit set on fire.

"Hey, Bee."

My shoulders slumped as I watched her lips tremble. Her only response when she couldn't seem to pull it together was to flip me off before dropping the phone and running off. Jamie picked it up a few seconds later and promised to kick my ass in a couple of weeks before hanging up. Naturally, consoling his girl took priority. Lou then slipped her phone in her pocket and rolled her eyes at me before returning to Wren's side. Guilt shot through me when I remembered his engagement ring. I made a mental note to return it ASAP. I wasn't sure how much of his plans I'd ruined, but I couldn't help noticing Lou's bare ring finger.

All my fault. And that bitch Selena's.

"Would anyone else like to take their shot at maiming me, or should I just go?" I asked when they all continued to stare. This was getting to be uncomfortable as fuck. Maybe I'd overestimated how welcome I'd be after I'd ghosted them. Even while I stood there, seemingly free, my phone was still locked away in my father's safe. He'd even been smart enough to change the code. None of my friends had heard from me, hadn't known whether I was alive or not. I could imagine the worst part was knowing they knew could do nothing about it.

I was still grappling for some way to explain without putting them all in danger when Wren stood. I watched him approach, bracing myself just in case. I'd fought Ever and Jamie plenty, but Wren and I have never had the pleasure. When he hugged me, clapping me on my back, I breathed a sigh of relief. As soon as he let me go, Ever was there, and he embraced me just a little bit longer. He finally let me go only to shove me, and I laughed. Four was still sitting with her arms crossed, and when our gazes connected, she immediately looked away. I'd expected no less. I'd fucked over her best friend and used Tyra's sister to do it. I'd be lucky if Four didn't poison me first chance she got. It didn't seem like her style, though. At least I knew Lou was more direct, which meant I would definitely see it coming.

"What the hell happened to you?" Ever demanded. "We didn't know what to think. Where did you go?"

"Absolutely nowhere," I confessed, letting them know I'd been right under their noses the entire time. "My father thought I needed some time alone to think about what was best for my future."

"You mean he kept you locked up," he retorted, reading between the lines. I didn't respond. My attention had already shifted, my gaze wandering the room. Was she here? "Are you really going to work for him?"

"I don't have a choice," I mumbled, giving up the search and flopping down on the sofa. I wanted to ask about Tyra, but somehow, I refrained. I wasn't in the mood to have my eyes clawed out by Lou or my balls severed by Four for even daring to mention her name.

"What do you mean? You were going to play for USC. What the fuck happened?"

My fists balled at the reminder that someone else was living my dream. Even if my father did me the fucking favor and kicked the bucket tomorrow, I'd never get a chance like that again. My reputation was shot. College ball and the NFL had kissed me goodbye as coldly as I had kissed Tyra. I shook my head, wondering just where the hell I'd gone wrong. She started as a challenge and became a once in a lifetime opportunity. She'd been a shooting star, a goddamn miracle, and I let her slip through my fingers.

"Nothing happened," I snapped before reeling in my anger. After what I'd done, it was the last any of them deserved from me. "It was just time I stopped living a lie." Against my will, I met Four's gaze again, and this time, she looked ready to skin me alive. Her chest rose and fell much faster now as she gripped the sofa underneath her. Any moment now, I expected to see the stuffing pour out when the fabric inevitably gave way.

I winced just as Lou's scathing voice broke the trance. "Next time you feel like seeking some truth," she scolded, "try doing it in a less skeevy way, asshole. You hurt our friend."

My lips parted, but I had no retort, no excuse nor lie to make it all better. Luckily, Wren spoke, saving me from finding one. "Maybe now is not the time for this," he said in a way that brooked no argument.

For once, she listened as her worried gaze shifted to Ever. "We can still call it off," she whispered to him.

Ever didn't respond, so I studied their uneasy expressions and the stiffness of their bodies, recognizing the tension that was there before I ever stepped in the room. "What's going on?"

Surprisingly, it was Four who answered when the rest of them paled. Leaning forward, she pinned me with her brown-eyed gaze. "It's been months since anyone's seen or heard from you," she pointed out sharply enough to sting. "Despite that glaring fact, the police refused to help for some reason." I gulped at that, knowing why. The Blackwoods may have controlled this town, the cops included, but my father controlled them. "Your best friend got desperate and decided to turn elsewhere." Casting a worried glance at her boyfriend, who looked like he was going to be sick, Four sighed and said in a softer tone. "His father is on his way. Ever agreed to meet Sean in exchange for his help."

"What makes you think Ever's father could help?"

Lou was the one to answer this time. "Because the enemy of your enemy is your friend, and if anyone is crazy enough to challenge your father, it's Crow."

I found Wren watching me, his gaze hard and steady. Ever was watching me, too, only his gaze was full of guilt when it should have been fear. By telling them who my father was, he'd put all of them in danger without realizing that I wasn't even worth it.

None of that mattered when I realized what Lou had revealed. "Your father is Crow?" I asked of Ever. "As in the Crow who co-founded Exiled? As in my father's dead rival?"

"He's not dead anymore," Wren answered.

I absently chewed my food as I sat alone in my favorite diner, mulling over what Four had revealed—what Ever had been willing to sacrifice to find me. Luckily, Wren had been willing to do what Ever couldn't out of guilt and called off their father's arrival.

I cursed when I realized my thoughts had led me to strangle my burger until the contents spilled into the little red basket my food had been in. The diner's burgers were the thickest and juiciest I'd ever had, leaving little wonder why the owners set up shop less than half a mile from the local hospital. The burgers were greasy enough to induce a heart attack, yet it tasted like ash in my mouth.

I couldn't stop thinking about Ever almost meeting his father because of me or the fact that Tyra and I had sat in this very booth for our first date. I'd ended up wearing her burger on my face when I teased her for not being able to handle a junior stack. I remembered the grim acceptance that filled her whiskey eyes as she sat there expectantly. Tyra had been waiting for me to throw in the towel and give up the chase, not knowing that she'd revealed her true feelings or that she'd created an addict instead.

"Do you know why people love roses?" I inquired after cleaning her burger off my face. "It's not their soft petals that make them irresistible but their sharp thorns. Instead of warning people away, the thorns tell the beholder that the rose is something worth bleeding for." Throwing the napkin down on the table, I pinned Tyra with my glare. "So give me all you got because I'm not going anywhere."

Cursing the sharp pain in my chest, I turned my attention

toward the window, abandoning memory lane to people-watch instead. Nothing was entertaining enough to distract me, but pretending was better than weeping over my burger like some lovesick sap. The neighborhood was a pretty busy area with the hospital nearby, a slew of specialized doctor's offices surrounding it, a couple of churches, some shops, and a few restaurants. Macchicino, the coffee shop where Tyra used to work, was only a couple of blocks away despite the Starbucks right across the street.

Since it was Saturday, the streets were crowded, and everyone seemed to be in a rush as people hurried off in different directions. I even recognized a couple of people I'd graduated with who already felt like distant strangers. It was funny how only a few months could erase a decade of being crammed into classrooms together and passing each other every day in the halls. Then again, I'd been their quarterback, hoisted onto a pedestal I'd never asked for, virtually untouchable. I guess we'd always been strangers.

Polishing off my triple stack, I started sipping at my shake only to choke and sputter at the small figure darting past my window a moment later. I instantly recognized the curly locks that looked wilder than usual and the rich brown skin I recalled feeling like velvet that now seemed grayish and pale. Shooting from the booth, I questioned my sanity, and if my eyes were playing tricks on me. It couldn't have been her, I reasoned even as I made for the door. It was the middle of February. She was safely tucked away at Harvard. She wouldn't be in Blackwood Keep. She couldn't.

Reason gave way to desperation as I rushed outside. I ignored the shouts of the waitress who'd served my food as I started in the direction the girl had gone.

What if it was Selena?

The realization almost stopped me in my tracks. Almost. Selena's threat to stay in Blackwood Keep could have been real, or she could have gone back to whatever hell she'd risen from. Either way, I had to know.

By the time I hit the end of the block that only led in two directions, the hospital on my right and too many possibilities up ahead, she was gone. Or at least the crowd was too thick for me to spot her. For all I knew, she'd been a mere mirage—a symptom of too much time spent without emotional sustenance. Too much time away from her.

Sighing, I admitted defeat while feeling a little foolish and grateful. If it had been Tyra, I might as well have signed our death certificate. Nothing in this world would have stopped me from approaching her.

Turning around, I started back to the diner only to have the path blocked by my angry waitress and the manager. "Sir, you must pay for your food!"

chapter twenty

The Pawn

OR AS LONG AS I COULD REMEMBER, I'D WANTED TO BE A DOCTOR. It had been my dream to roam the halls of the Susannah Blackwood Medical Center, first as a wide-eyed resident, then confident fellow, and one day, a respected surgeon. I wanted it all—the white lab coat, the stethoscope, the bags under my eyes from working sixty hours a week, and even the mountain of debt if need be. So what if I ate ramen and ravioli and lived in a box for the rest of my life? I was convinced nothing could dissuade me from my dream.

That was until I spent the last six weeks inside these very walls, having my heart ripped out of my chest continuously.

As the elevator doors opened and I rushed onto the third floor, inhaling a lung full of disinfectant, I worried it would be too soon before I saw another hospital again. Mustering a pitiful smile for the cheerful staff and worried families I passed in the hall, I made my way to the wash station. Understanding how vital this step was, I forced myself not to rush through scrubbing my hands properly as I waited for the light above the sink, a clever timer, to turn colors. The moment the glow turned from ominous red to bright green, I was off, rushing for the private room I'd called home these past weeks. The curtains had been drawn for privacy, but the moment the glass door slid open, my gaze connected with my father. Despite the coach's uniform he'd worn proudly for years, he appeared haggard as he waited for me on the sofa that pulled out into a bed.

"I'm sorry I'm late." Crossing the small room, I sat in the specially designed recliner near the sofa. "The interview ran longer than I thought it would."

Coach waved me off as he stood. He was due back at the school any moment now, but he didn't seem to care as he stared at the small bed encased in hard plastic with holes cut in the sides for the doctors and nurses to work through.

"How did it go?" he asked, his voice hoarse as if he hadn't used it in years.

I shook my head, already knowing I didn't get the job. The interview had been a complete disaster. First, I'd shown up fifteen minutes late because I couldn't seem to find the courage to leave the hospital. Today had been the first time since I was wheeled through the doors six weeks ago. The manager had been kind enough to interview me anyway only to discover that I wasn't willing to give up a single day of the week. My anxiety-riddled brain wouldn't allow me to. And if that didn't leave a bad enough impression, I couldn't seem to focus on a single question he'd asked, making him repeat each one twice. My mind and heart, despite my best efforts, had been here.

"Perhaps it's for the best," he whispered when I knew he wanted to lecture me again instead. The room had sound-activated lighting built into the wall that changed colors when the volume became too loud. My father and I had learned that the hard way. "Your place is here."

"And when the hospital hands over the discharge papers?" I argued for the umpteenth time. "What then? Where will I belong then? I can't go back to Harvard."

At least, not without a way to pay for it. The Theodore Lidle Foundation had given me until the end of the semester to improve my grades and keep my scholarship. Since a cruel twist of fate forced me to take the semester off, that was no longer possible. I'd lost everything.

"We'll figure it out," he said as if we hadn't already been

denied the aid I'd need to continue school. My father's salary was too high for need-based aid and too low for the private loans needed to cover my tuition. My only option was to accumulate enough debt to drown and send me to an early grave. Being virtually penniless was something I decided long ago I'd be willing to do, but for some reason, I hesitated.

I stubbornly kept my gaze on the clear, blue sky mocking me through the window rather than seeking out the incubator surrounded by what seemed like countless machines. All of them dedicated to keeping the tiny being sleeping soundly inside alive.

For a while, there was nothing but the beeping of the machines to fill the room.

"Have you—" my father started to speak only to pause. His voice had been thick with emotion as he struggled to find the right words—or perhaps the courage to speak them for fear of heartbreak. I held my breath, knowing what he was about to ask. "Have you thought about what I said? Have you reconsidered?"

I didn't want to, but slowly, I shook my head as I kept my gaze directed out the window. I hated to hurt my father, but he had to understand that I was doing what was best for everyone. My heart had become a withered wasteland. Love no longer bloomed there. "I've already contacted a specialist. We meet next week."

A moment later, my father stood, and without a word, he left the room. Only then did I release the breath I'd been holding. I wasn't sure how long I sat there, but a small sound, not quite a cry, finally drew my gaze from the window. As if on autopilot, I stood, and in two steps, I was standing over the incubator, staring into a set of gray eyes that I knew would change color in the coming months. I couldn't help but wonder if they would be whiskey like mine or jade like his father's. My heart cracked, knowing that I'd never know.

"I know you must hate me," I whispered as he continued to stare through the plastic walls keeping him safe. His movements were more controlled now as he kicked his arms and legs, and although he was still pale, his skin had darkened considerably from the translucent he'd been when he was born. The only thing he wore was a diaper and a blue cap on his tiny head, which covered the wisps of hair I knew were hidden underneath. It was a far cry from all the wires and tubes when he was born. After weeks of watching him fight for every breath, my heart had nearly stopped when his doctor finally removed the ventilator. I must have kept watch for hours, fearing the worst though he didn't seem to mind. Despite his miniature size, he was much bigger than the meager two pounds he weighed when he was born.

"I hate me."

My finger drifted over the glass, drawing countless hearts in lieu of reaching inside and caressing his cheek like I ached to do. It had been the hardest thing, not touching or holding him, even when the doctors had given me the green light.

"I promise you," I whispered as I drew another heart, "I'm going to find you a father who deserves you and a mother who isn't too broken to love you. I'm going to find you a *home.*"

Slowly, my fingers began to trace letters instead of hearts.

R. I. V.

"It's all that I have to give, but it's yours." Ignoring the tear that slipped from my eye, I traced the final letters of his name as the dark, deserted moor inside my chest twisted painfully. "River."

I awoke with a start hours later. My heart was beating out of control, making me wonder if I'd been having a nightmare I couldn't recall now that I was awake. I blinked, and the moment my eyes adjusted, I looked around the dark room. The only light peeked through the swaying curtains from the hallway. I frowned before quickly waving off my paranoia. The hospital prided itself on the NICU's around-the-clock care. A nurse must have stepped in for a moment to check on River.

Sitting up, I listened for sounds beyond the beeping of the machines and the occasional footsteps of a nurse or restless parent passing. Unlike my gut, twisting and turning, the NICU had settled for the night.

Hearing Lou's warning in my head to listen to my instincts, my gaze shifted toward the incubator where River slept. A moment later, I stood from the pull-out sofa before making my way over. Even in the dark, I could see that he was sleeping soundly. Somehow, I still found myself curling into the recliner between the incubator and sofa bed. From there, I kept one watchful eye on the baby and the other on the door for the rest of the night.

"Good morning," I greeted Nurse Honey as everyone called her because she was sweet as pie. I secretly smiled, knowing Jamie would have a field day if he ever met her. It was all I could do not to text him as longing filled my chest. Hell must have frozen over if I actually longed to talk to Jameson Buchanan.

"Morning, sugar. Did you sleep well?" she asked after looking me over.

We both knew I didn't, but what else was new? "Well enough," I mumbled as I checked my phone. Rather than spend my weeks here wringing my hands, I spent much of my time online.

Bee's YouTube channel was my favorite to watch. Her subscriber count had quadrupled after she unknowingly uploaded a makeup tutorial featuring a grainy image of Jamie passing in the background...fully exposed. Her followers started referring to his dick as the Loch Ness monster because of its size and the disbelief that it wasn't photoshopped as a publicity stunt. It didn't stop any of them from hanging around, hoping to get a second glance, though. Recently, to appease her new followers, Bee did a live tutorial called "My Boyfriend Does My Makeup." I spent half an hour watching Jamie flirt with Bee as if they weren't on camera and then him paint her eyes, cheeks, nose, and lips in the colors red, black, and blue. Bee, of course, had been none the wiser until Jamie turned her face toward the camera. With a scowl, he told her followers that it was how anyone getting off to his girl would look after he found them and kicked their ass. He hasn't been allowed back on her channel since.

Seeing no messages waiting, I decided to ask Nurse Honey the question foremost in my mind since she had been the night nurse assigned to his care. "Did River have any trouble last night?"

"Not a bit," she answered as she scrubbed her hands and dried them. "What makes you ask?"

"Just a funny feeling, I guess." And the fact that his chart indicated Nurse Honey had checked on River not even half an hour before I'd woken up. So who had been in our room last night?

"I got those all the time when I had my first child. It's perfectly normal to worry, and I'm sorry to tell you, the feeling never really goes away, not even when your children aren't children anymore. My daughter throws a fit if I try to hold her hand while crossing the street."

"Really? How old is she?"

"Twenty-five."

I barked a laugh, my first in months, but then I clapped my hand over my mouth as my gaze darted to the flashing lights activated by the sound. "Sorry."

"Don't be. In fact, you should do it more often. I'm sure River would love to see his mother smile."

I didn't respond as I chewed on my lower lip thoughtfully. A habit I must have picked up from Four. Ignoring that familiar longing, I watched Nurse Honey lift the door on the side of the incubator. Every morning, they weighed River to monitor his weight gain. He needed to be at least four pounds and graduate from incubator to an open crib before he was allowed to go home—wherever that may be.

I waited with bated breath for her to remove him. He was still so tiny and fragile. Instead, Nurse Honey paused, and I wondered if she could read my thoughts when she stared at me thoughtfully. "Would you like to do the honor?"

Without realizing it, I took a hopeful step forward. "Me?"

Her head tilted to the side as she offered a smile that could only be born of pity. "Of course, dear. We usually encourage the parents to do this part to give them time to hold and bond with their baby."

Panic speared through my chest as I backed up a step. "I-I don't think that's a good idea." Holding him, bonding with him...I couldn't risk that. I would never forgive myself if I didn't keep my promise. River deserved more than me.

Nodding once, she carefully lifted River from the incubator. I quickly calculated his steady growth rate of eight to ten grams per day and held my breath as Nurse Honey set him on the scale nearby. Cranky as ever in the mornings and still sensitive to touch, River fussed and flailed his arms. I knew any moment now he'd fill the room with his hungry cries as the lights built into the wall flashed their warning.

"Three pounds exactly," she noted out loud as she wrote it on her chart. "He's doing so well."

My legs inexplicably shook, so I sank onto the sofa and ignored the warmth flooding my belly as I watched her remove River's pacifier. They'd given it to him to encourage the sucking and swallowing reflexes he'd been born too early to develop. After setting it aside, she returned him to the incubator, and I exhaled my relief only to straighten in my seat when Nurse Honey sat next to me. River was now screaming, most likely from hunger, which made me wonder why she wasn't preparing his feeding tube. As daunting as it sounded, the tube was a step up from the IV line they used when he was first born.

"Is everything okay?"

"Just fine," she quickly assured me. And then with a gentle

smile, she added, "Actually, I'd say everything is perfect. River is showing signs of being ready to be fed normally."

I exhaled though I still felt tense. "So...what happens now?"

"That depends on how you'd like River to be fed."

"What do you mean?"

"Well, you can choose to feed him by bottle or by your breast."

I felt that wildness in my heart again as I ran my suddenly sweaty palms down my burgundy sweatpants bearing Harvard's logo. So many questions and worries flitted through my mind. Was the natural choice to breastfeed him? What would Nurse Honey think if I chose the opposite? I'd accepted the fact that I wasn't ready to be a mother, but that didn't make me feel any less guilty.

"Wouldn't he be safer being fed by a bottle?" I wanted to stand and pace but learned early on how aware River seemed to be of my moods.

"As long as the necessary reflexes have developed properly, either way is perfectly harmless. He'll benefit most from the intimate contact required to feed him now that he's ready to be fed by his mom." Nurse Honey gave me a knowing look, and I realized with a gulp that she meant I'd have to hold him if I didn't want him to starve to death.

"Oh." I almost asked if there was someone else who could do it, but the last shred of respect I had for myself held me back.

"You don't have to decide right now. We'll continue with the tube feedings and nonnutritive sucking for a few more days to ensure he's ready before giving it a shot."

My sigh of relief was audible, causing her to gently pat my hand before standing and grabbing the breast milk I'd pumped and stored in the designated fridge the day before. Deciding that I needed to get a grip, I stood and made my way downstairs to the cafeteria. The food wasn't as bad as I'd expected, but it still sucked. It didn't matter, though, because my appetite was nonexistent. I just needed to escape.

Ten minutes later, I was sitting alone, nibbling on an apple when I felt someone approach. Peeking over my shoulder, I almost groaned, seeing Oliver looming over me with a mop and a smile. He was one of the janitors here and an insatiable flirt. I'd need my fingers and toes to count how many times he'd asked me out on a date.

"Looking good this morning," he greeted when our gazes connected.

Snorting, I looked away. "You say that every morning even though we both know you're full of shit." My skin was dry enough to peel, my eyes were permanently swollen from too much crying, and I couldn't remember the last time I'd brushed my hair or even washed it. And even more tragic, my favorite sweatpants were becoming threadbare from overuse. "What's the matter? Don't think you can get a decent date, so you're willing to settle for the damaged and desolate?"

Shaking his head, Oliver sat across from me as if he weren't in the middle of his shift. He was sweet, funny, and hot as hell with his dark brown skin, black patch of chin hair, and an easy smile. He was only three years older than me, and I could tell, even under the bagginess of his navy-blue uniform, that he had an amazing body. One I was sure he'd gotten working part-time at his father's scrapyard where he told me they recycled and sold car parts.

Still, I felt nothing.

Perhaps, I was doing him a favor. My soul and heart had already been irrevocably mated and shattered just as thoroughly.

"Ah, but that's where you're wrong," he flirted. "You wouldn't protect your heart so fiercely if there wasn't still something worth saving."

I took a huge bite out of my apple to keep from responding. Vaughn had said much of the same during our first date. Back then, I was afraid of being hurt, so I pushed any chance of that happening away. I realize now there was a damn good reason for it.

Stupid.

"So, how's the little guy?" Oliver inquired the moment I finished chewing.

"Still little," I replied around the huge lump in my throat. "But he's strong like his mother."

My gaze dropped to the table as I willed my tears not to come. They didn't listen. I wasn't sure how long I sat there fighting them back before I finally surrendered. Soon, it wasn't the only thing pouring out of me, and I couldn't stop once I started.

"I'm not strong," I whispered. "And I'm not a mother." I looked up then, not caring if Oliver or anyone else saw my tears or the fact that he was startled by the sudden change in my demeanor. "A mother would hold her baby. She wouldn't be afraid to love him. She'd know she could and let no one stand in her way. She'd sing to him when he was afraid and feed him when he was hungry. And she wouldn't *lie*." I shook my head. Was it a warning to turn back now before I said more or an admission of the truth? I kept going. "She wouldn't tell her son that she couldn't keep him because it's what's best for him. She'd tell him the truth. She'd tell him she couldn't keep him because she's afraid of seeing his father whenever she looks at him. But then...a mother wouldn't put her broken heart first, would she? She'd break it again and again just to see her son smile. I'm weak, Oliver, and it isn't because my thorns are bent, and my petals have fallen. It's because knowing doesn't make a goddamn difference. *I can't do this.*"

I didn't stick around after I'd shocked Oliver into silence. I was pretty sure I'd finally managed to talk him out of wanting a date. No one in their right mind would want someone as screwed up and selfish as me.

As I slowly followed the path back to NICU, I contemplated

running toward the exit instead. If I abandoned River now, how long would it be before I could stand the sight of myself? I hadn't left his side since he was born, and I could barely manage to look in the mirror now. Hence my disheveled appearance. I was afraid of seeing the old Tyra Bradley and even more terrified of the new Tyra. Neither, as Vaughn had once claimed, was worth bleeding for.

I was still mulling over the steep cost of running away when I stepped onto the third floor and into complete chaos. Some inherent part of me had me rushing for River's room, where I expected to see him sleeping soundly only to find him surrounded by doctors. Time seemed to slow as two of the frantic nurses shifted slightly, allowing me to see my baby's tiny body lying still. So, so still.

River had stopped breathing.

chapter twenty-one

The Prince

"LIKE WHAT YOU SEE?"

Despite the overeager chick riding his cock, Antonov had found the time and willpower to taunt me. Had I not seen the girl's license for myself, I'd question whether she was even legal. She was built like a fucking twelve-year-old and looked like one, too. She also moaned like she was auditioning for a part in a porno rather than interviewing for a position in my father's stable. Shaking my head in disgust, I declined to answer.

Antonov smirked before slapping her bare ass and tossing her aside on the leather sofa next to him. "You're hired," he told her as he stuffed his hard dick back in his pants. Even though she was nineteen, she'd make my father a ton of money from the sick fucks with certain…proclivities.

Feeling like I might fucking puke, I hurried from the parlor room and through the front door of the five-bedroom house my father used for his stable. The black, tailored suit I wore kept me warm as I sucked in the cool air. Even though spring had started a couple of weeks ago, it was still pretty frigid up north. To make matters worse my father's most profitable stable was right here in Blackwood Keep. The clientele, which included my damn uncle, *the fucking mayor*, was pretty exclusive.

Slowing my stride to my car, I watched as Antonov beelined for his vehicle and peeled off before dropping into my own ride. It had been weeks since my father opened my cage, and I still hadn't learned why. Jeremy had been called off as my babysitter except for the jobs my father sent me on, like today. That didn't mean, of course, that he wasn't having me followed, which is why I took extra precautions.

I wasn't exactly eager to sell my soul, but with each menial job that my father gave me, I grew impatient. I'd given up my dream of playing football to traffic drugs and guns and even human fucking beings. I—

No.

I'd given it all up for a much greater cause, and right now, she was somewhere out there, hating my guts. Probably wishing I was dead, too. I wondered at what point over the months I had begun to want the same. Shaking off those thoughts, I slammed my foot on the gas, intending to spend the rest of my day getting shit-faced.

I'd been living at the beach house—my only hope of sanctuary. No one knew that it belonged to me. My mother had placed my name on the deed before she left as if she knew I'd need it. I wondered how she never realized that I needed her and not some goddamn house. Sometimes I thought about flying to Paris to ask her, but I wasn't sure I'd even recognize her. It had been over a decade since my mom left, and I'd only been six years old.

Gripping the steering wheel, I sped down winding roads, taking advantage of the late hour and the lack of other cars on the road until I found myself at my old stomping grounds. I wasn't sure what drove me here, but I didn't bother questioning it as I parked my car, grabbed the bottle of my father's favorite bourbon, and made my way onto Brynwood's empty football field. It was after nine, so I had no worries of being disturbed as I made myself comfortable on the bleachers and stared out onto the field. For years, I'd allowed myself to get caught up in a fantasy. Football was the only thing I'd ever been free to love. The only thing my father hadn't been able to take away from me.

Leaning my head back and closing my eyes, I recalled that

day a year and a half ago when I met what I thought would be just another distraction but had turned out to be my doom instead. I waited, expecting any moment now for the regret I should feel to come.

At some point, I nodded off.

It was a good thing I hadn't chosen to hold my breath as well.

A year and a half ago...

"Son."

Powerful men could command a room and anyone in it with a single word. Cruel men only needed to enter. Unfortunately, and ironically, for my father, I wasn't as easily bent. He'd made sure of that.

Franklin Rees, both powerful and cruel, loomed on the threshold of my bedroom between its double doors. I continued to ignore him as I searched my room for my car keys. Last year, he tried to bribe me with a car for my sixteenth birthday. The sad fact was that he thought it would actually work. Sure, I'd told him so, but for my father to believe it just showed, for all his cunning and calculating ways, how little he knew me.

I threw the last of the shit I needed into my backpack, and only then did I give him my full attention. "I'm late for school."

Today was the first day of my senior year at Brynwood, a private academy with a hefty price tag. Along with the handful of scholarship kids attending, I was given a free ride. The tuition would have only been a drop in the bucket. However, being a Blackwood had its perks, even if being a Rees made me a pariah.

My father cocked his head at my statement, and I gritted my teeth. "Is there someone at your school foolish enough to give you trouble?" He slid hands with too much blood on them into his expensive suit pants. "I'd be happy to pay them a visit and discuss your tardiness if you'd like."

I dropped my bag at my feet and sighed. "Make it quick," I snapped. No one else would have dared, but my father needed me more than I feared him.

Stroking his chin, he gave me a warning look before speaking. "I wanted to congratulate you on making captain. I hear you're Brynwood's new quarterback."

Of course, he wouldn't have had to hear it through the grapevine or even more likely the men he paid to spy on me if I'd bothered to tell him myself. Defiantly, I held my father's gaze and braced myself for what I knew was coming next.

"I suppose this means there will be scouts at your games."

"It's just nice to have someone who cares in the stands." As usual, my father didn't miss a beat or pretend to feel remorse.

"You have your friends," he pointed out dismissively. "Something that can be rectified if you continue to test me."

I quickly bit the inside of my cheek. The little my father allowed me could be taken away with a snap of his fingers. Still, the threat of hurting my friends wasn't enough to give him what he wanted most. My soul as black and unforgiving as his.

"Yes, there will be scouts at the games. Is that a problem?"

My father straightened the cuffs of his suit jacket before responding. "Only if you get any ideas. Football isn't in your future, son. You were born for much greater ambitions. If I believed otherwise, I would have made your mother swallow you instead." I stared at him, refusing to react even when he stepped into the room and my space until we were standing toe to toe. "I seized an empire, and I plan to turn it into a dynasty that begins with you and lasts forever once you bear sons. If you refuse, I'll put you in the ground. Make no mistake about that."

"Noted. Can I go now?"

I snatched my bag from the floor and shouldered it. I should have been pissing my pants, but this wasn't the first time my father threatened my life. I wasn't sure when I stopped being afraid of death, but I knew it pissed my father off to no end. If I wanted to survive this game of chess, I couldn't leave him with weaknesses to exploit.

"Get out of my sight," he ordered.

It was all I could do not to shove past him on my way out. It had been a long time since I was on the receiving end of my father's knuckledusters. There were times when he didn't bother himself with disciplining me and left the task to his men.

After fleeing our mansion that resembled a castle, I sped to school. My white Lamborghini Aventador never failed to turn heads in our small, affluent town even though most of the residents had more money than they knew what to do with. My father usually spent his cash getting his way, and when that didn't work, he used brute force. So far, I'd been the only one his methods failed to work on.

I didn't waste time hopping out once I parked and rushed inside. The halls were emptying quickly, and I only had a couple of minutes to spare. Even though my father didn't care about me maintaining a perfect record, Coach Bradley wasn't as lenient. He had no problem benching my ass even if meant losing every single game. Although I admired the man, I cursed his morals. Unlike my father, he seemed to have his priorities straight.

The bell rang, and door after door slammed shut as I rushed to get to my class. Of course, it had to be on the other side of the fucking school. My foul mood worsened with each desperate step until I was nearly feral. Replaying Coach's warning speech in my head, I broke into a run as I rounded yet another corner. Unfortunately, I was waylaid when I collided with another person and sent them sprawling across the tiled linoleum. I stared down at the dazed kid, wearing bifocals and a fucking pocket protector. He was just a runt. Too bad for him, I wasn't in the mood to feel sorry.

"Watch where the fuck you're going," I snapped as I straightened my tie. Brynwood required its students to wear uniforms.

Today, I'd chosen to wear a red sweater vest to go over my white button-up and navy slacks—our school's colors. I glanced at his companion, some gorgeous fucking chick with brown skin, a hypnotic gaze that reminded me of whiskey, and curly hair sprouting wildly from her scalp. Instantly, I knew she was too good for me. She was a tiny thing, even smaller than the nerd, which I didn't think was possible. Her head barely reached my fucking chest, but the pip-squeak didn't seem to notice that vital fact as she pinned me under her glare. She was wearing a badge that read Student Guide, and I realized the geek still lying on the ground must have been new to the academy. When she continued to stare, waiting for me to apologize, I lifted my brow, daring her to try me before casually stepping over the kid I knocked down. I made it two steps before she spoke. Her soft voice had an edge to it that did something unexpected to me.

"Maybe *you* should open your eyes, and while you're at it, learn some damn manners, Rees."

I kept walking even as I peered over my shoulder. The spitfire had already dismissed me. She was bent over, lips pursed disapprovingly as she helped the kid to his feet as if he were a fucking invalid. I studied her while she was distracted and realized I was drawing a blank though something tugged desperately at my memory. The badge made it clear she wasn't new, so why hadn't I noticed her before?

Whoever she was, we obviously didn't run in the same circles.

Frustrated, I shrugged it off, assuming that I'd glimpsed her before but never looked twice. The next time I ran into her, I wouldn't make the same mistake.

I wondered if that fiery temper of hers would make an appearance when I bent her little ass over and fucked the nerve right out of her. I was Vaughn Rees, star quarterback, and no one, *absolutely no one* talked to me that way. I didn't have to question if she knew who I was. Everyone in Blackwood Keep knew what it meant when I entered the room.

In the meantime, I forced the mystery girl from my thoughts as I headed to class. It didn't escape my notice though that there was an extra pep in my step. It had been a while since I had a challenge. I almost smiled.

Sit tight, baby girl, I'll be fucking you real soon.

Present

I may not be able to feel regret when it came to Tyra Bradley, but *rage* was a different story. After twenty minutes of standing in Brynwood's dark lot with nothing but the crickets and the wind to keep me company, bright headlights washed over me. For a moment, I was frozen, unable to look away from the destruction. My blood was boiling, and I knew if I didn't calm down soon, I'd break my vow.

Stepping from his G-Wagon, my best friend's sleepy eyes widened the moment he noticed the reason for my call. I was just lucky that Ever had been home for spring break. "Vaughn!" he yelled as he rushed over. "Are you okay?" Golden eyes scanned my body frantically, his eyebrows dipping further when he realized that I wasn't hurt. "What the fuck happened?"

I forced a deep breath because if my jaw tightened any further, I'd break a tooth. "*She* happened." I didn't know how or why, but Tyra was here in Blackwood Keep, and the knowledge filled me with adrenaline rather than the panic and dread I expected of my father inevitably finding out. As long as I stayed away from her, she was safe, but the chance of that happening when she so obviously wanted my attention was slim.

Ever's head swung back and forth in disbelief between me and what was now just a heap of metal before silently whispering, "*Fuck.*" Shoulder to shoulder, neither of us spoke for several minutes until Ever eventually broke the silence. "It's not fair," he mumbled with a shake of his head.

I wasn't in the mood for his shit, but since his number, besides the bitch who did this, was the only one I could recall, I decided to amuse him. I wasn't sure anyone else would have come anyway. They'd all taken *her* side. The irony was that none of them had seen or spoken to her either.

"You're the only asshole I know who can hit the jackpot by fucking up."

"How exactly is this winning?" I spat as I gestured toward my totaled Lamborghini. It looked like someone had dropped a goddamn building on it. If I weren't so pissed, I'd be impressed. *How the hell did she do it?* The cheeky bitch had even left a red Christmas bow on the crushed roof along with a four-letter word written in lipstick on the hood.

Liar.

My fists balled at my side while Ever rubbed his chin, studying what was once my car. "Because Jamie made a remark that I thought was ridiculous until I found you stranded out here in the middle of the night."

"And what's that?"

He shrugged before finally meeting my gaze. There was a twinkle in his eye that sent a chill down my spine. "When a good girl is gone, there's no getting her back." Ever laid a placating hand on my shoulder, but I could tell he was biting back a laugh. "If I were you, I'd sleep with one eye open."

I shook off his hand before taking one last look at my baby and turning away. *Yeah, we'll see about that.* One way or another, Tyra was going to get in line, even if it meant facing her to do it.

If I'd known that this was just the beginning, I would have hunted her down much sooner.

chapter twenty-two

The Pawn

"THANKS AGAIN FOR TONIGHT," I WHISPERED EVEN THOUGH WE were, for the most part, alone. "I had a great time."

"It was my pleasure," Oliver whispered back. He cleaned up astonishingly well and had made it impossible, despite my hang-ups, to keep my eyes off him the entire night. Oliver had been a balm on my darkest of days these past weeks and had even become a friend. "To be honest, I was surprised when you finally said yes to a date, but not more than when you suggested what we should do in place of dinner." He winced, and I knew he was reliving our "date." Rubbing the back of his neck, he peered down at me. "Are you sure we won't get into trouble?" he asked for the fifth time. "I don't exactly have half a million dollars lying around."

Brushing off the dust he'd gotten on his button-up, I smiled. It hadn't been hard at all getting Oliver to commit grand theft auto once he saw the car I had in mind. Getting him to destroy it after I had him tow it to his father's recycling center, however, had been the hard part. Contrary to what anyone might think, I hadn't done it for me. Tonight had been for River.

And I refused to believe it meant something that my first sighting of Vaughn, or rather his car, after months of being in Blackwood Keep occurred only after agreeing to a date with Oliver. I'd held my breath the entire time, expecting Vaughn to appear while we waited for Oliver's brother to arrive with the tow truck. It had been a risky move, but everyone who'd ever been wronged hadn't lied. Revenge tasted *good*. I wondered what Vaughn had been doing at Brynwood.

You don't care. "I'm sure."

"So whose car was that anyway?"

"It belonged to River's father."

Oliver stared at me for a few seconds, and I wondered if he could hear my heart racing inside my chest. My only regret was not being there to see Vaughn's face. Imagining it had me pressing my thighs together and my breaths coming a little faster. When Oliver leaned in, mistaking the source of my excitement, I even let him kiss me. His lips touched mine, and I greedily moaned even though there was no spark to set my blood on fire, no feeling like I'd been made whole, that my soul was no longer mine, or that my life had been irrevocably entwined.

I knew it wasn't just a pipe dream.

With one kiss, Vaughn had turned the fantasy of a soulmate into a reality, and then with a single blow job from my sister, he callously destroyed it. As Oliver deepened the connection, I found myself being transported to that first kiss with Vaughn. Not wanting to face it, I pushed Oliver away and, with it, the memory.

"I-I-I'm sorry," he immediately apologized. "Did I hurt you?"

I shook my head when words escaped me. I felt like I'd regressed to that girl who'd gotten her heart broken on the beach eight months ago. "I'm fine. It's just…slow is the only pace I can handle right now." I peeked up at him. "Is that okay?"

He readily nodded, making it even more clear why I could live a thousand years and never deserve him. "I can live with that."

I offered him a shy yet relieved smile, but before I could say more, the door behind me opened, and I groaned. I didn't have to turn to know who was standing there.

"Tyra, it's late, and I have work in the morning." I peered over my shoulder in time to see my dad had shifted his stern expression to Oliver. "Young man, I'm sure you also have somewhere to be."

If fate were kind, the floor would open up and swallow me whole, but fate had a twisted sense of humor.

"Uhh, yeah, sure," Oliver stumbled to agree. "Well, I guess this is good night."

I waved as he headed for the elevators before stepping inside the room. Ignoring my father, who was busy putting on his coat, I immediately headed for the open crib where the incubator used to be. I wasn't at all surprised to find River awake. He'd become a bit of a night owl in the weeks since he stopped breathing and simultaneously ripped out my heart. I *was* surprised to see the deep frown on his face as he waved his fist.

"What's the matter, Riv?"

His only response was to turn his head as if he couldn't stand the sight of me. Puzzled, I checked his pamper while he sucked on his fist and found it dry. Only a couple of weeks from being discharged, he was on a precise feeding schedule to pack on those last few ounces he needed, so I knew he'd been fed less than an hour ago. I started to pick him up, but then Nurse Honey's warning echoed in my mind. It was ironic how much had changed in the last few weeks. I'd gone from running at the prospect of holding my baby to being scolded for holding him too much.

Feeling belligerent, I picked him up anyway. He was mine, and I was his. I could damn well hold him when I pleased.

"Tyra," my father sighed as I made my way to the recliner. "It's late. He needs to be in his crib."

"But something's wrong," I said as I cradled River against my chest. "He's upset."

River's eyebrows were thicker now. Bunched together, I realized that he looked just like his dumbass daddy when he frowned. I held him against my chest and wondered if the hours we'd spent in this chair these past few weeks could really be contributed to his rapid development. River was now considered full-term, but because of the reflux and apnea he experienced a few weeks ago, his doctor had extended our stay until my due date to be safe.

I didn't even want to think about how much the extra couple of weeks in the hospital would cost. I didn't care. As long as River was healthy, nothing else mattered. Not the money, not Harvard, not even the fact that Vaughn had no interest in being a father. Leaning down, I gently touched the tip of our noses. "I'm sorry, River. It looks like it's just us."

A tear slipped from my eye just as he started to cry.

Vaughn was a creature of habit, and the diner a few blocks from the hospital was very much a part of his routine. I knew the risk I was taking by allowing Oliver to bring me here, but I decided that the reward of running into Vaughn was too sweet to pass up. It wasn't enough for him to know that I was the one who'd destroyed his precious car. I also wanted him to see that I hadn't allowed his lies and betrayal to bury me. I was very much alive, and with or without him, River and I would thrive.

Recalling how big the burgers were, I settled for a basket of fries and a coke while Oliver demolished his turkey burger. "So," he said as he pushed the empty food basket away. "Do you think you'll go back to Harvard in the fall?"

My stomach churned as everything I'd eaten threatened to return to the surface. I knew sooner or later I'd have to accept the inevitable and withdraw from school permanently. I'd considered every possibility, every scenario, and even with my father's help, there was just no way, not without my scholarship and not without—My lips tightened as the rot that had taken over my heart threatened to expand again.

Fuck Vaughn Rees.

"I don't think it's in the cards. Even if I hadn't lost my scholarship, I couldn't ask my dad to play the role of a single father all over again while I'm away at school living carefree. I've been selfish long enough."

"I don't think you're selfish," Oliver whispered. "Not every road traveled will be easy. The scrapes and bruises you earn along the way are inevitable. The real test is at the end of your journey. It's when you decide whether to let those wounds fester or allow them to heal."

I thought about what he said as I watched the ice melt in my glass, turning my coke flat. "I'm…trying. To be honest, I think it's going to take some time." An image of my sister with Vaughn's dick down her throat flashed through my mind. "*A lot* of time."

"There's no rush," he promised.

Somehow, I became lost in Oliver's brown eyes. He had the longest lashes, which gave him this wide-eyed innocence. I'd even been bold enough to call him pretty once, and he'd actually blushed, giving me the impression that maybe he was innocent. Dare I say, a virgin? It was a weird change of pace being the wicked one for once. Even more bizarre was the idea that a guy this fine could still be a virgin at twenty-one.

"You say that now," I teased, "but when your balls are blue, you'll be singing a different tune."

"You might be right," he flirted back. "You are pretty fucking sexy. When you're not making babies cry, that is."

I gasped. "When have I ever made a baby cry?"

"Your bitch face is pretty killer. I once saw, with my own two eyes, a newborn burst into tears when you passed."

Gasping, I shoved his shoulder, but he barely moved an inch. "Take that back!"

A devious gleam entered his eyes. "Kiss me, and I will."

Nibbling my lip, I contemplated his offer. Even after eight months, it felt like I was moving too fast. And that's when I decided to take fate into my own hands for once. So what if he wasn't the guy the stars had written for me? I'd rather write my own ending from now on. Leaning forward, I stole his lips, and when Oliver slipped his tongue between my lips, the moan I released this time was for him. I wasn't sure how long we remained locked together, but by the time I finally pulled away, I was damn near sitting in his lap. His erection poked my thigh, and I considered the possibility of letting him take me to his car and finding someplace secluded to park.

"I have to use the bathroom, and then we can go," I whispered against his lips before standing.

Blinking a few times to clear the lust from his eyes, he nodded before reaching for his wallet. That kiss had been pretty fucking great, which explained why I'd practically skipped to the bathroom.

A few minutes later, I was washing my hands when I heard what sounded like a scream.

Springing into action, I fled the bathroom only to stop short at the sight of Oliver sprawled onto the diner floor. I couldn't look away from the blood gushing from his nose, his lips—God, everywhere. He was out cold. Heart racing, I rushed over to him, his name on my lips.

I didn't get very far.

Strong hands wrapped around my ponytail and pulled until my neck felt like it would snap. Expecting to see some masked stranger or just a stranger, my lips parted when my gaze connected with the familiar green eyes glittering above me. And then contrary to the rough way my captor's hands handled me, he laid a gentle kiss on my lips. Vaughn might as well have breathed air into my lungs. I felt alive again like I was flying. Fortunately, I was wiser now. I knew that eventually, I'd crash and burn.

"You wanted my attention, you have it," he promised on a whisper, "and you're going to be sorry that you do."

I was too stunned by his kiss to be afraid. I'd forgotten so many things—how soft his lips were, how talented, and how, with each kiss, it felt like he was signing his name next to mine, sealing our fate on an ironclad contract.

Soulmate.

Fortunately, I didn't get the chance to waltz down memory lane before he shoved me toward the exit. "Walk."

chapter twenty-three

The Prince

'D FUCKED UP, SEALED OUR FATES, AND SIGNED OUR DEATH CERTIFICATES. After witnessing her kiss some prick through the diner window with the promise in her eyes to give him more, I didn't give a fuck. Tomorrow, we would both walk into hell together hand in fucking hand.

"Walk."

I watched Tyra as she stepped over her date and waited to feel some semblance of remorse, not for the asshole I'd left bleeding on the floor, but for the fear making her shoulders tremble. None came. I'd always been a bastard, but I'd never been this cold. I'd been fighting this darkness my entire life, but after losing Tyra, there had been no one left to disappoint. No one to fear hurting.

Getting her out of the diner proved to be easier than I thought. I'd almost gotten her to the car idling across the street when her shock faded, and she remembered to fight back. It was the middle of a weekday, so the roads were mostly deserted. Even if it weren't, there was no one in Blackwood Keep brave or foolish enough to help her. Grabbing her around her waist, I tossed Tyra inside Jeremy's back seat before following her in. Jeremy didn't utter a word or even bother to take his eyes away from his phone. The fucker casually pulled off with a yawn as if we hadn't technically kidnapped someone in broad daylight.

Of course, this hadn't been my plan when I asked him to stop so I could grab a quick bite. I wasn't expecting to find her in the diner on a goddamn date less than twenty-four hours after she destroyed my Lamborghini. I didn't miss the way she stared through the back window, her expression frozen in horror as the diner, hospital, and everything else quickly faded from view. Jealousy had me pulling her into my lap and tightening my grip when she tried to get away. She could worry about her boyfriend later.

"Are you insane? Let me go, Rees!"

"You started this, *Bradley*." In her ear, I whispered, "You can't bow out now when it's starting to get fun for me."

"Fuck you."

"You definitely seemed in the mood," I retorted with a hint of violence. I couldn't get the image of the way she'd dared to look at another man. As if she hadn't once looked at me that way. As if I hadn't sacrificed everything to save her life. Fuck *her* would be the correct sentiment.

Without having to be told, Jeremy drove us to the beach house, and after he parked, I sat there wondering if it was wise to get out. There was no telling what I would do to Tyra once I got her alone.

She fucking kissed him.

She'd been writhing in his lap like she was two seconds from riding his dick right there for all to see. At that moment, I wanted nothing more than to tie cement blocks around her ankles and toss her obstinate ass in the ocean. If I killed her, I'd never see her, touch her, or smell her sweet scent ever again. But then...neither would he.

Opening the car door, I pulled her out and started for the house that had once been our Eden. I didn't bother pleading with Antonov not to tell my father about this. I knew he would if he hadn't already.

Fuck it.

Watching Tyra through that diner window, I realized I had nothing left to lose. Once inside the beach house, and only after closing and locking the door, I set Tyra down only to catch a right hook to the face. I deserved that. When she tried again, I caught her wrist, bending it back and making her whimper in pain.

"This would be considered self-defense," I taunted as I walked her back toward the couch. Pushing her down on it, I climbed on top of her, forcing her to lie flat on her back. "Choking every bit of air from your lungs if you tried that again, might be considered murder." I held her gaze as I smiled. "I'm willing to risk it if you are."

"Vaughn," she said, sounding calmer than I expected. "You have to let me go. I have to get back—"

"Your boyfriend will be well-rested when he wakes up," I snapped before she could finish.

"He's not my boyfriend, and you had no right to do that to him!"

"I had every fucking right unless you want to tell me you destroyed my Lamborghini on your own?" She stilled, and I had my answer. "Didn't think so. You're lucky I didn't break both of his legs."

"For helping me destroy your car or for kissing me?"

"To pay him back for kissing you, I'd have to kill him, pip." Crooking my fingers under her chin, I held her defiant gaze. "And make you watch."

She froze—stunned at my threat or maybe the fact that I wasn't bluffing—before anger took over. "So, what should your punishment be for letting my sister blow you?"

I stared at her for a long while before shaking my head at her cluelessness. Selena had been a pawn and nothing more. Just as Tyra had been my father's. Even if I bit the bullet, *literally*, and told her the truth now, I knew Tyra well enough to know she'd never believe me. She'd taken a chance only to end up feeling like a fool. She wouldn't make that mistake a second time. I could have simply walked away eight months ago, but I had to ensure that she would never forgive me. Not in this lifetime or the next.

Mission accomplished, asshole.

I didn't reveal my true thoughts when I spoke. "The price has already been paid."

Her whiskey gaze roved over me before she snorted and looked away. "You still have all of your limbs. I'd say not well enough."

"I'll be the judge of that."

"Are you kidding me?" she screeched. "You're the one on trial!"

"So which limb would you have me lose?" I asked, my tone lower and deeper now. "My throwing arm? My leg?" Settling between her legs, I pressed my hips against hers. "Or the one you couldn't stop thinking about even while wishing I was dead?"

"You're delusional."

"I'd say you are. You wore this skirt for him, knowing you only get wet for me. I can't compete with that."

Growling, she tried to buck me off as if I didn't have a hundred pounds on her. When that failed, she began wriggling up the couch, uncaring or unaware of the fact that her short skirt was riding up her thighs. In no time, I could see the crotch of her panties and the arousal wetting them. Still, she kept going. I had no intention of fucking her if she wasn't willing, but seeing her like this didn't stop my dick from getting hard. Tyra was nearly free when her skirt cleared her hips, bunching around her waist and displaying the waistband of her panties.

My focus, however, was fixed on the scar right above it.

Five inches long and red.

It couldn't have been more than a few months old.

The questions racing through my mind kept me from noticing much else, such as the fact that Tyra had gotten free and was now lunging for the centerpiece decorating the coffee table. I didn't get the chance to react or demand to know who'd hurt her before she brought the vase full of her favorite flowers crashing down on my head.

I regained consciousness sometime later and found Jeremy Antonov standing over me with his eyebrow perked and amusement shining in his dark gaze. "You won't survive two seconds in this business if a little thing like her can take you out that easily."

Ignoring him, as well as the ringing in my head and ears, I sat up from where I'd been slumped on the couch and looked around the room. My vision hadn't quite cleared, but it didn't matter. I knew she was gone.

"So, you let her go?" I snapped.

He shrugged, his expression and tone matching his disinterest in my love life. "She wasn't my fucking problem."

It didn't escape my notice that he didn't offer me a hand as I slowly rose to my feet, not that I would have taken it. We didn't agree on much, but our mutual dislike was the one thing we had in common, that and our deep-seated hatred for my father.

"Boss wants to see you," he announced once I was on my feet.

I felt my blood turn to ice in my veins, but I didn't bother arguing. Nothing short of killing my father would change anything. It would only end with me being buried next to him—together for all of eternity. I would have snorted if I were still capable of feeling humor.

Following Jeremy to his car, I couldn't help replaying what had gone down between Tyra and me. I never dreamt of being reunited with her, but if I had, I sure as shit wouldn't have imagined it going down like that. I wasn't surprised by her anger, but I expected cold detachment rather than murderous rage. Had I been naïve, or was I missing something?

Remembering what I'd seen before she knocked me out cold, I stopped in my tracks, drawing Jeremy's attention. I could feel him watching me over the hood of his car as my mind raced.

"She had a scar."

"Really? What kind?" The sick fuck actually sounded interested in something for once.

I forced myself to answer. "I don't know." Yanking open the car door, I slid into the passenger seat. Jeremy followed me inside and started the engine. He wasted no time pulling off. "It's healed, but it looked like it was pretty serious. Like someone had cut her open."

"Where was it?"

"Her lower stomach. I thought maybe someone had hurt her, but it was clean. A little too neat to be an accident or done in the heat of the moment."

Jeremy seemed to think about that before pulling out his phone and typing while he drove with one hand. A few seconds later, he was showing me his screen. "Did it look something like that?"

I stared at the screen, my mouth suddenly dry. "Exactly like that. What the hell is that?" I sounded hoarse to my own ears. Without a word, he tapped the picture, zooming back out and showing me the medical article it was attached to. "A cesarean section?" I read out loud.

"More commonly known as a C-section," he calmly informed me.

Meeting his gaze, I swallowed at the knowing look in his eye. A moment later, Antonov's lips quirked as he refocused on the road again. My world had been turned upside down in a matter of seconds, and he was smirking? Before I could rethink it, my fist connected with his jaw, and I watched his head turn as his blood splattered the driver window. It was a sucker punch, but I didn't give a damn. I was pretty sure I loosened a tooth. The only reaction Antonov gave was to meet my gaze with the promise of retribution in them. He'd been barreling all the way home, which meant that whatever my father wanted must have been too important to stop and deal with me.

I sat back and closed my eyes, hoping that Jeremy killed me.

But then...if what he said was true, I couldn't die. Not yet. Not until I figured out how to reach the bottom of this endless well. This cycle of secrets, lies, and betrayal.

220 | B.B. REID

Tyra wouldn't dare have my baby and not tell me. Not because of the danger they'd both unwittingly be in, but because she knew I would never forgive her. It was the perfect way to exact vengeance for my betrayal.

Antonov didn't speak when we finally reached the house, and I didn't offer apologies. I wasn't sorry about a damn thing. I found my father in his study and faltered at the good-natured smile he wore. I immediately crossed over to the sideboard and poured myself a drink. I was still underage, but my father didn't give a shit, and I wouldn't care even if he did.

"You wanted to see me?" With my back still facing him, I fiddled with my phone before slipping it back inside my pocket. My father didn't speak for several moments.

"Did I ever tell you about my ascension?"

God, help me. Not another history lesson.

"No. I don't recall asking."

Or caring.

"Sit down," he ordered me.

Swallowing down the liquor in one gulp, I poured myself another glass before obeying. Before my ass even touched the seat, my father began.

"Did you know I've ruled over Thirteen the longest?" Ignoring my unimpressed shrug, he continued. "Keeping the identity of Father a secret began with my predecessor after too much leadership turnover." At my blank look, he added, "They kept getting assassinated." Leaning back in his chair, he drummed his fingers on the desk as he studied me. "Not even the men who rise and fall in my name every day have a clue who I am. Of course, I can't remain completely anonymous. Nothing would ever get done." I nodded since it seemed to be expected. "It's important to delegate," he continued. "To find men willing to execute your will."

"Your round table."

"Precisely." Removing a cigar from the cherry wood case, he clipped the end and lit up. "Thirteen is mine now, and my dynasty begins with you, so know this now. Surrounding yourself with people you can trust is vital…and nonnegotiable. My predecessor kept thirteen men at his table to honor our founders. Until you, I've only kept four."

"Why so paranoid? Is inspiring loyalty not one of your strengths?"

He took the time to blow a cloud of smoke into the air before responding. "I subscribe to the belief that anyone can be bought, son. The most important lesson my predecessor taught me was to take what I wanted and never apologize for it. I made sure to thank him for his wisdom before I had him killed."

If my father expected a reaction out of me, he didn't get one. I'd made my feelings clear that I didn't care about Thirteen—its past or its future. My presence was contingent on Tyra continuing to breathe.

"Naturally," my father went on, "no one knows about this important moment in Thirteen's history except myself…and the man I ordered to slit his throat."

"Which would be?" I forced myself to ask when my father paused expectantly.

"Nathaniel Fox. To maintain my innocence, I was forced to let him take all the credit for such a power move. Even if in the eyes of Thirteen, he failed by getting caught."

I stiffened at the name. Fox had been the cause of so much pain, and he was still out there—a threat to my friends and my father, and now I knew why.

"Of course, if I'd known what a thorn he'd be in my side, I would have killed him when I had the chance. Nathaniel was only a foot soldier at the time, but he showed promise—enough that he believed me when I offered him a seat at my table once I ascended. All he had to do was kill my predecessor and let an innocent man take the fall—the man who would be sitting in this seat right now instead of me. *He* has reasons to kill me more than anyone. Even you."

"Why should I care?"

"Because up until a few months ago, I thought that man was dead."

My heart thundered in my chest, and it was all I could do not to let it show. Franklin Rees was a bloodhound for weakness.

"Who is the man you're talking about?"

My father's answering smile was razor-sharp. "Son, I think you know."

He didn't give me a chance to deny it before he stood and walked over to his safe. I watched as he punched in the code and opened the door before reaching inside. A moment later, he held my old phone in his grip as he returned to the desk. He didn't know about the one in my pocket—the phone I'd procured without his knowledge. I'd been careful not to use the same number or any of my old email and social media accounts, knowing he was monitoring every single call or message that came in or out. I said nothing, keeping my expression impassive even though my chest ached from my heart pounding as he powered it on.

Had Tyra tried to contact me? What would he do if she had?

I almost swore as I gripped the arms of the chair. My father didn't need much reason to be a monster. I held my breath as he slid it over the wooden surface, and together, we watched as notification after notification filled the screen until the last one, a text message sent from Ever, made my heart stop.

Ever: Get to the hospital! Wren's been shot!

The fact that Ever had texted my old number instead of my new one told me the state he was in right now. Slowly, my gaze rose to meet my father's. I knew well before the bastard winked that he was responsible. He didn't stop me when I shot to my feet, snatching my phone from the desk before I rushed for the door. My father was smart enough to know he'd have to kill me if he wanted to keep me from getting to that hospital.

I just hoped I wasn't too late.

chapter twenty-four

The Pawn

I T HAD BEEN TWO HOURS SINCE I LEFT VAUGHN SLUMPED ON THE couch, and I still couldn't get the image of him collapsing out of my head. Stupidly, I was actually concerned about any permanent damage I might have caused. Replaying his words to me, his many threats, and the look in his eyes as he uttered them, I realized he was already damaged beyond repair. He'd been marred so severely beneath the surface that I hardly recognized him. It didn't matter that his brown hair was just as lush as I remembered or that his vitreous gaze still reminded me of jade. Even his body, though not as muscled as before, was still worthy of a statue in his honor. I hadn't fallen for any of that. I'd tumbled head over heels for *him*—the boy he allowed himself to be for no one else but me.

Despite being eager to get back to my son, worry and guilt had driven me back to that diner only to find Oliver already gone. The wary waitress informed me that he'd been picked up and taken home. I tried calling him to apologize profusely and forever if need be, but he hadn't answered. River still being my top priority, I rushed back to the hospital, where I found him wide awake. I knew it was just a reflex and maybe my guilty conscious talking, but the smile River wore seemed suspiciously mischievous—as if he knew exactly where I'd been and who with.

I wasn't sure I'd ever have the heart to tell him that his father didn't want him. Vaughn hadn't answered any of my phone calls or messages or even the letter I'd grown desperate enough to write him a few weeks ago. In it, I'd poured my heart out, telling him all about River.

He hadn't even asked about his son.

Vaughn had only been concerned with my body and who I dared to share it with. If nothing else, he definitely deserved the headache he'd have whenever he woke up.

River was greedily sucking at his bottle when a voice over the loudspeaker announced a code gray—whatever that meant—and called for a lockdown of the ER.

"Oh, my," one of the day nurses said, excited, and then she wrote on the whiteboard next to River's crib. "It's been a while since we had one of those. I guess I better watch the news tonight."

"What's a code gray?" I asked as I set River's bottle aside and lifted him onto my shoulder to burp him.

"Gunshot victim." Grimly, she added, "It's going to be a long day for a lot of people."

My eyebrows rose at that. At least it wasn't a bomb threat like I initially feared. "Does the hospital really shut down the entire emergency room for one person?"

"If the victim is still alive, it's safer that way, sweetie. Whoever did this might want to finish the job, and then we'll all be in danger." She flounced out the room, and my lips pursed, realizing she was probably headed for all the action.

If I were honest, I'd admit to being curious too though it was likely a huge waste of time. How much would I really get to see if the emergency room was shut down? The victim was probably already in surgery if the doctors deemed it necessary. I said a quick prayer for the poor soul as I waited for River to burp. Of course, he took longer than usual. When he was finally done, I rocked him until his eyes drifted shut and then put him down for his nap.

I wasn't sure how long I watched him sleep, studying his nose, his lips, his golden skin, and the wisps of brown hair peeking from underneath his cap. He was still so small, even though he was twice the size he'd been when he was born. Feeling that familiar ache of guilt and shame, I stepped away. Grabbing the baby monitor that I'd shamelessly purchased, even though River was surrounded by the world's most qualified babysitters, I drifted from his private room. On the way down, I tried calling Oliver again but to no avail. Even though I was disappointed, I didn't blame him if he wanted nothing to do with me ever again. Vaughn had made it clear, though untrue, that there was unfinished business between us.

As I expected, the first floor was in chaos when I stepped off the elevator. There were nurses in scrubs and doctors in lab coats rushing back and forth, some of them in and out of the double doors leading into the emergency room. Some of them covered in blood. My gaze traveled the area, looking for any sign of distraught loved ones waiting nearby. Seeing nothing but curiosity and weariness, I turned back to the emergency room just as the doors burst open.

I sucked in a breath at the sight of a girl who stood at average height with skin paler than usual and waist-long hair as dark as night. I didn't see much else before the doors swung closed, but I didn't need to. I recognized my friend staring blankly through the window of the trauma room, her pretty blue dress darkened with blood. Not caring that I wasn't allowed in, I pushed through the doors, heading straight for Lou. Thankfully, no one stopped me. They were all too busy fighting to save Wren's life to notice me.

"Lou?"

Slowly, her head turned. Her lips were parted, her blue eyes glistening. "It's my fault," she whispered as soon as her unseeing gaze connected with mine. I almost expected her wrath. Grief kept her from remembering she hadn't seen nor heard from me in six months. Lou turned back to the trauma room where Wren was lying deathly still as the doctors and nurses worked on him. "I didn't lock the door."

Speechless and out of my depth, there was nothing I could do but stand next to her and wait. It was the second-longest hour of my life. Nearly losing River had been the first.

Wren would live, but I wasn't sure how much of Lou would survive after almost losing him. I knew just how fractured she was feeling right now. Wren was still unconscious and probably would be for a while, so I steered Lou to the waiting room while they prepped him for visitors.

"I have to check on something," I told her even though I really didn't want to leave her alone. "Are you going to be okay for a few minutes?"

At her weak nod, I exhaled and stood from my crouch in front of her. If she noticed the baby monitor in my hand, she didn't speak a word. I turned and didn't make it further than a step before I came face-to-face with Four and Ever. The grip they had on each other's hands loosened as soon as our gazes met.

"Tyra?" Four said, taking a hopeful step toward me. "Wh—ho—" She didn't get a chance to choose which question to ask me first before she enveloped me. She hugged me so tight I wondered if she'd ever let me go. Considering these past months, I wouldn't be surprised though I'd wonder why she bothered. I've been a shit friend. "I don't care why or how," she whispered to me, making me feel like pig shit baked in the sun for too long. "I'm just glad you're here."

I wasn't sure how long I stood motionless before I pieced some semblance of myself back together. Just enough to hug my best friend. Any other time it would have been super weird, but I didn't care as I inhaled the vanilla and jasmine wafting from Four's hair. She had her very own scent that Ever's possessive and obsessed ass purchased from the soap maker in Cherry, Four's hometown.

"I missed you, too," I finally told her because it was the truth. I felt a gentle tug on my hair, a silent greeting from Ever as he walked around us. Four and I pulled away from each other to watch as Ever lifted a silent Lou from her chair and wrapped her in his arms, and then Lou was holding on tight as if she might crumble any moment. At some point in the year and a half since they'd met, Ever and Lou had bonded like brother and sister despite them fighting constantly. Then again, everyone fought with Lou constantly. Seeing them share their grief like this tugged at heartstrings that I thought destroyed by Vaughn long ago.

Speaking of the devil, Ever kissed Lou's forehead before pulling out his phone. "Someone needs to tell Vaughn to get his ass down here," he griped.

My heart dropped to the pit of my stomach as I watched Ever type. If today proved anything, it was that it was much too soon for Vaughn and me to be in the same room. If ever. Not without killing each other.

I needed an out.

Something that would avoid suspicion or too many questions.

As if my baby knew what I was up to and took it upon himself to thwart my plans, a small cry filled the room. My friends' gazes, including Lou's, immediately flew to the monitor in my hand. By some miracle, I kept my grip on it rather than drop it as if it were a smoking gun. Slowly, their attention drifted back up, and I was their focus as they waited for an explanation. One I wasn't ready to give. Heart pounding, I was already backing away, the elevator doors opening in the nick of time as people poured out. I quickly slipped inside before Ever, Four, or Lou could speak a word or shake free of their shock. I didn't allow myself to breathe until the doors closed again.

That could have gone better.

I had the feeling that it was only going to get worse.

Back in NICU, River was inconsolable as I fought to soothe him, and that was how Four found me—with a screaming, red-faced baby in my arms and me two seconds from bursting into tears myself. The hunt hadn't taken her long at all since there were only two places I could have gone. The maternity ward was on the floor below NICU, so I figured that must have been her first stop. The automatic door to River's room opened, and I silently watched the strained expression on Four's face soften the moment her wide-eyed gaze fell to the wriggling bundle in my arms.

"May I?" she asked, holding out her hands as she inched closer.

I released the breath I'd been holding, not realizing how much I wanted it until the possibility was right in front of me.

"Are you sure?" River hadn't stopped crying, and I was fresh out of ideas. His diaper had been dry, and he kept spitting out the bottle and then the pacifier I tried to give him. I even swaddled him, but he kept on crying. I figured he was just cranky from having one of his many naps interrupted and had trouble falling back to sleep. When Four nodded, I smiled despite my headache. "I'd love that."

Carefully, I handed him over and watched Four smile in awe as River slowly settled down. Of course, he stopped crying when there was a girl to impress. He stared up at her, his mouth forming an *O* and his eyes wide as if he couldn't believe his eyes. If I didn't know better, I'd say River was utterly enchanted with Four. A moment later, he made his scrunchy face, telling me he just shitted himself. I'd wait to break the news to Four once their little moment passed.

"So, is he why you've been avoiding me?" she asked as she and River watched each other. "Avoiding all of us?"

I looked away and then sighed, knowing the subject would come up sooner or later.

"Yes and no." At her puzzled look, I decided to explain as best I could when no explanation could ever make up for how I'd acted. "A part of me was ashamed, and it wasn't just because I'd gotten pregnant at eighteen." My mouth opened and repeatedly closed, the words refusing to come until I forced them out. "I was ashamed because, despite Vaughn fucking my sister, I still wanted to have his baby. I still wanted *him*." Disgusted, I looked away, discreetly wiping away my tears before they could fall. God, I'd been so stupid.

"And the other part?" she quietly demanded.

"Wanted to rebel against living in a world where I could never truly be free of Vaughn." It wasn't just River that I'd planned to give up but my friends, too. It was the only way I knew how to survive my broken heart.

"Since you were so honest, I guess I will be, too," Four said after a long stretch of silence. For the first time since stepping in the room, she pried her gaze away from River, allowing me to see just how much I'd hurt her. "I was so mad at you when you pushed me away. I tried not to be, but I was. It felt like you were punishing me, punishing all of us, for what Vaughn did, I…I started to hate you. I convinced myself that since it was so easy for you to write me off that I could do the same to you." I frowned at that because Four had never stopped reaching for me. Not even for a day. "The next morning, when I woke up in a cold sweat, I didn't just miss you still. I *understood* you." Four returned my hopeful look with a hard one of her own before saying, "If you repeat this to anyone, I'll deny it and never talk to you again. I mean it." When I made the motion of crossing my heart and slitting my own throat, she gave me the tiniest of smiles before shuddering. "That night I…I dreamt that was Ever in that room, not Vaughn. The worst part is that it wasn't even Selena. It was Bee."

My eyes nearly bugged out of my head at her admission. Ever would turn himself into a eunuch before he ever allowed himself to betray Four in that way. He proved as much last year when he defied fate by taking Four to prom instead of Bee. By doing so, he ended his fake-relationship pact with his best friend. "Four, you know—"

She quickly waved me off. "I know. It's not about that. I know it sounds crazy, but I think my subconscious was willing to show me whatever I needed to put myself in your shoes. I wanted to understand you, and now I do." She then offered me a crooked smile. "But you should know, it's besties before testes. You broke the girl code, and I won't forget it any time soon."

I quickly held up a finger before she could continue. "I think the saying is 'chicks before dicks.'"

Four's gaze narrowed playfully. "You haven't answered my calls in six months," she said, reminding me that I've been a total bitch. "It's whatever I say it is."

"Fair enough."

River started to fuss, kicking his legs and wiggling his tiny body just as Four jerked her head back, wrinkling her nose. "Uh… Tyra?"

"Yeah, he totally pooped on you just now."

After showing Four how to change a diaper at her request, we spent the next couple of hours catching up as we waited for River to fall asleep again. Once his eyes drifted closed, we wasted no time hurrying back downstairs to Wren and Lou. I would have taken him with me to meet his aunt and uncles, but he wasn't allowed out of NICU. Not for another two weeks.

I was in the middle of praying that Wren was awake when the elevator's doors opened, and we stepped onto the floor. I didn't make it more than a couple of steps before I found my back slammed against the nearest wall and my next breath impossible. The people passing by gaped in horror as Vaughn held my throat in his hands, his face and neck bearing the scars from the vase I had broken over his head, and his green eyes burned with rage.

"Did you or did you not have my fucking baby?"

chapter twenty-five

The Prince

BEFORE TYRA COULD ANSWER ME, I FELT MYSELF BEING PRIED OFF her, not by hospital security but by my best fucking friend. "Come on, man. Let her go. This isn't you."

On the contrary. Ever had no idea who I was anymore. None of them did. Least of all Tyra. It must be why she continued to test me. "Answer the question," I demanded after I wrestled free of Ever. Tyra's only response was to claw at the skin on my hand, so I tightened my grip. I wasn't even hurting her. Not yet, at least. "Fucking answer me!"

"Sir," one of the doctors called the moment he stepped from the emergency room and saw me. "I'm going to have to ask you to take your hands off that young woman or leave the premises."

I met the older man's gaze, ready to tell Captain-Save-A-Ho to fuck off when I caught the hopeful gleam in Lou's eyes as she stared at him expectantly. Piecing together that he must have been Wren's doctor, I reluctantly let Tyra go. Her dramatic ass sucked in huge gulps of air as tears streamed down her cheeks. Four immediately went to her side as Tyra's angry glare promised retribution. *Bring it the fuck on.*

I was two seconds from tearing this hospital apart to find the kid she'd hidden from me. There was no excuse for it. None. I didn't give a damn how many of her sisters I fucked. I'd already done the math. Tyra was no longer pregnant, which meant she had to have just given birth.

He's still here.

Or she. The sex didn't matter to me. The kid was mine, and so was she.

The doctor was visibly relieved when I turned away from Tyra and stuck my hands in my pockets. He didn't need to know that it was to keep from bashing his skull in. The fact that he'd just saved my friend's life gave him a one-time free pass.

"Wren is stable," he began, making Lou's knees buckle. I wanted to reach for her, but Ever was already there. "We managed to remove the bullet. Luckily, there was no damage to his organs, but he'll be in pain for a few weeks. It'll be manageable as long as he remains on bed rest and takes the medication we prescribe."

I would have snorted at that if it wouldn't have got me gutted by my friends. Wren wasn't the type to lie around, which is likely what had gotten him shot in the first place. *Yeah, good luck with that, Lou.* Then again, if she wanted to keep him in bed, she wouldn't have as hard a time as one might think—if they could manage it.

"So, what happens now?" Four anxiously asked when Lou remained silent.

"We'll monitor him for a few days before sending him home for bed rest."

"Can we see him?" Ever spoke this time.

"Sure, but please," he said, throwing a pointed look in my direction, "keep it peaceful, or I'll ask you all to leave."

I just barely resisted the urge to flip him off. The doctor showed us to Wren's room, and then he was off. As soon as we all crowded inside, Wren's eyes opened. I didn't have to question whether he was in pain. The moment his gaze found Lou's, her composure shattered.

"You didn't need any more scars," she sobbed, referring to the three bullet wounds he already had and the knife to the gut that almost killed him after he freed Evelyn from Fox. "You're already hotter than Ever."

From my peripheral, I caught Ever palming his face as he

slowly shook his head. Leave it to Lou to make light of a heavy situation. As everyone laughed, including a raspy chuckle from Wren, the tension in the room eased somewhat. I was still very much aware of Tyra hovering near the door, though. If she thought she'd slip away without me noticing, she had another thing coming. The moment she moved, I'd be on her ass like white on rice. The thought of her having my kid and not telling me made me want to do unspeakable acts, things that would undoubtedly turn me into my father. But then there was the part of me I kept locked away that wanted to fall to my knees and beg her to take me back.

"Who the hell did this?" Ever demanded.

I was thankful for the distraction when I felt my knees quake as if they'd decided for me. "My father did this."

I felt every single gaze in the room fly over to me. They'd all been looking to Wren for an answer, not once expecting my announcement. I couldn't keep this a secret. Not like I had when my father tried to buy me Bee's hand in marriage. It was too big. Wren had almost died. The first to look away was Ever. The color had leeched from his skin.

"Fuck!" Ever's shout came right before he shot to his feet and shoved his hands through his hair. "Fuck, fuck, fuck!" Apparently, he wasn't finished exploding. Ever seemed perfectly content to leave us all in suspense when he moved to stand and stare out the window. "I should have seen this coming," he mumbled after a while.

Lou's eyes narrowed from her perch on Wren's hospital bed. It barely looked big enough for the two of them, but I doubted even while in pain that Wren minded. "What do you mean you should have seen this coming?"

Wren still looked puzzled as he watched his half brother turn from the window and pace a hole in the floor. Ever ignored Lou, meeting Wren's gaze instead. "That job we did on the house in Long Island. It was a setup. Eddie and Siko were behind it."

Wren didn't reply at first as he seemed to contemplate Ever's confession. "That explains how and why Siko and Eddie rose from the dead to put a bullet in me," he replied, his voice hoarse. The glint in his eyes told me exactly how he felt about being duped and betrayed by men he once thought were his brothers-in-arms. Men he'd likely mourned.

"They were spies for Thirteen the entire time," Ever revealed. "Franklin sent them in to flush out Fox by killing you and Shane."

"Which meant, Franklin knew exactly who Wren was," Lou pieced together. Shooting to her feet, she glared at Ever. "How could you let us move to Blackwood Keep without telling us the danger he'd be in? He's been a sitting fucking duck!"

Ever grimaced as he rubbed the back of his neck. "I fucked up, Lou. I'm sorry. I was a little distracted at the time."

"Really? You were *distracted*? Oh, I wonder why? Could it be because Wren risked everything to save your mom's life, and you couldn't be bothered to do the same for him?"

"Lou," Wren called, but his plea went ignored.

"You've barely spoken two words to him since finding out he was your brother. Wren didn't tell you because he wanted to protect you from that deadbeat you both call a father. He was willing to give up yet another piece of himself to keep *you* in your bubble." Tears glistened in her blue eyes as she continued to read Ever his rights. "You have no idea how lucky you've been. You had a *home,* a father who stuck around, a mother who risked her life just to make you whole, and it still wasn't enough. How long before you push Four away because she won't give your spoiled ass exactly what you want?"

"Louchana!"

This time, she listened, rushing back to Wren's bedside when he grunted in pain from the exertion it took to get her attention. "I'm sorry," she whispered as she ran her fingers through his dark hair. "Your brother's a jerk, and he needed to hear it." Wren didn't respond. He simply grabbed her hand before closing his eyes. He was asleep moments later. Either his pain medicine had kicked in, or he was just that emotionally and physically exhausted. Carefully, Lou curled up by his side, and then she closed her eyes, too.

For several moments, the room was quiet enough to hear a pin drop down the hall before Tyra broke the silence. "Maybe we should give them some privacy," she suggested, speaking for the first time.

No one had the heart to argue when she opened and held the door. Four and Ever were the first out. I caught the door when Tyra watched me expectably. I wasn't about to take my eyes off her for a second. Sensing that, she huffed before stepping out ahead of me.

"Has anyone called his grandmother?" Four inquired once I closed the door behind us.

"She's on a cruise for a couple of more weeks," Ever announced with a sigh. "I'm not sure we should upset her if Wren's not dead. We can break the news when she comes home."

"What about Jamie and Bee?"

Ever nodded. "Jamie's hauling ass. They should be here soon."

Great. Because that was just what everyone needed right now. Jameson's mouth to make shit worse. Hopefully, he wasn't keeping any more secrets up his sleeve. My gaze darted to Tyra, who'd been keeping the biggest of them all. I wanted to wait for a better time, but every fiber down to the tiniest cell was brimming with the need to tear this hospital apart.

My kid was here. She had my kid.

And didn't tell me.

"We need to talk." I'd given up the fight as soon as Ever and Four drifted over to a pair of empty waiting chairs.

"About what?" Her tone was rife with disinterest as she looked everywhere but at me.

Looking both ways to make sure no one was paying

attention, I pushed Tyra into a small, dark alcove near some vending machines. I had her hidden in the shadows and hemmed against the wall before she knew what was happening. Her protest was swallowed by her gasp when I lifted her skirt above her waist without warning, exposing her hot pink panties. My mouth filled with water as I literally salivated. I wanted to slip my hand inside them and didn't give a damn if we were caught. She shouldn't have hidden my fucking kid.

"About this." My voice was a whisper as I fingered the long, thin scar across her lower belly. My fist balled on the wall above her head. As pissed as I was, I couldn't help wishing I'd been there, not just to see my kid born but to hold her fucking hand. What if something had gone wrong? What if they'd needed me? It was her decision not to tell me, but somehow, I still blamed myself for not being there.

"Why are you doing this?" she sobbed, shocking the shit out of me. The guilt and lust vanished, and confusion took its place. "This is cruel, even for you."

I took a step back, watching her eyes fill with tears. "What the hell are you talking about, Tyra?"

"I'm talking about you ignoring me for weeks and now pretending that you want to be a father. I'm not going to let you do this to me, and I'll *kill you* before I let you do this to your son."

My shock allowed her to push me away, and then she quickly escaped the alcove. She didn't even remember to lower her skirt first. She'd made it two steps before noticing the scandalized stares. After yanking her skirt back down, she cursed me in ways I couldn't have imagined all the way to the nearest bathroom where she disappeared inside.

Resting my forehead against the wall, I inhaled deeply.

A son.

I had a son.

The knowledge didn't feel me with the joy I expected.

Ten minutes after learning I had a son, I contemplated proving Tyra's point by walking away from him forever. If my father ever found out about him, he'd never be safe. The only other alternative was a long shot in hell. I could end up dead when staying alive was the only way to ensure my father never got his hands on my kid. His dynasty could suck my dick.

The bathroom door opened, and Tyra finally emerged, her eyes puffy and rimmed red.

I hated myself for making her cry and even more for accepting the fact that I'd have to do it again. And again. And again.

A commotion near the emergency room entrance drew my gaze as a distraught Jamie and Bee rushed inside. I lifted my hand, waving to get their attention. Once they noticed me, I turned back to where Tyra had been to find her gone again.

Fuck.

Shoving to my feet, I ignored the puzzled looks Jamie and Bee gave me as I shoved past them without so much as a "hello" and headed for the elevators. After scanning the floor chart on the wall for the maternity ward, I stabbed the up button. My hands shook as I waited for the elevator to take me to the second floor. Four appeared by my side seconds later though I ignored her. Whatever she had to say, I doubt it was kind, and even though I deserved her wrath and venom, I wasn't in the mood.

"She's on the third floor," she informed me after several seconds passed. I followed her finger to where she pointed on the chart. "In the NICU."

My heart rose to my throat. "What?"

"That's where you'll find them." The look she gave me then was sharp enough to kill. "If you hurt either of them," she whispered, "Lou and I will bury you alive. We've already got a nice, secluded spot picked out." She paused, cocking her head to the side. "Maybe we'll toss in some poisonous snakes, too."

Without another word, she sauntered away just as the elevator doors opened. I wasn't dumb enough not to believe her. For some reason, however, I wasn't afraid of the possibility. Everything I'd done had been to keep Tyra safe. I'd do no less for my son. Stepping inside the elevator, I stabbed the button for the third floor. My hands shook the entire way up.

At nineteen, I was far from ready, but was anyone ever really?

How the hell would I move forward? How would I take care of them? Questions that needed answers.

When the doors opened, and I stepped onto the floor, I felt drawn by a magnet. There was a wash station outside the sliding doors where I followed the directives posted, and then after sanitizing my hands, I entered the NICU. Several cries filled the floor, and I wondered if any of them belonged to my son. The nurse at the reception pointed out the room I was looking for after giving her Tyra's name. Each one of my steps felt heavy as I headed in that direction.

Here goes everything. Every-fucking-thing.

I realized for the first time since letting Tyra go that I still had something to lose. My heart had been hers, but now it belonged to someone else, too. Someone I'd never even met.

The glass door was automated, so it slid open the moment I approached, and I slowly stepped inside. The room was empty save for a couch, a recliner, and machines surrounding a crib.

Tyra was nowhere to be found.

I didn't realize I was walking until I stood over the crib. The moment my gaze connected with the baby inside, my knees threatened to buckle. He started kicking his legs, and what seemed like an excited smile spread his lips.

As if he'd been waiting for me.

I couldn't stop staring as my grip tightened on the railing that kept him safely inside. The need to hold him was great, but, fuck, he was small. So very fragile. I didn't know much about babies, but even for a newborn, he seemed tiny as fuck. I wanted to find Tyra and interrogate her, but I couldn't take my gaze away. I couldn't bring my feet to move. I could have stood here forever.

"He was born three months ago."

The whisper came from behind me. I turned and found Tyra standing inside a door with what looked like a private bathroom behind her. Her whiskey gaze seemed to dim as I scowled at her admission. Tyra hadn't been pregnant the night at the party. I think I would have fucking noticed if she'd been that far along since I'd had my dick in her every goddamn day. I'd been fucking her constantly as if my every breath depended on it. "I was only six months pregnant," she explained at my look. "River could have fit in your palm. Better than any football."

I wanted to rip her a new one for the scorn I heard in her tone at that last part, but I could only focus on one thing.

River...

That was his name.

Had she given my son my last name or hers? I swallowed, too nervous about what I might do to ask. "So, at what point did you think to tell me I had a fucking kid?" I inquired instead.

Squaring her shoulders, she lifted her chin. A moment later, I realized it was to keep from crumbling. "When he almost died."

I froze as fear, disgust, and anger at both of us ripped through me. It was all I could do not to give in to the emotions by putting a fucking hole in the wall. I nearly lost him before I ever even knew I had him.

"And you didn't tell me when you found out you were pregnant because..."

"I wanted to hurt you."

Turning away from her, I watched my son stretch his tiny body and yawn as if he were already bored with the two of us and our bullshit. I didn't blame him. "Congratulations," I muttered as I stared at my son. "You fucking succeeded."

"And I wanted to be free of you."

I stiffened despite her low whisper. "So if he hadn't almost died, you would have never told me?"

"I wasn't planning on either of us being parents. We weren't ready."

More calmly than I would have given myself credit considering her revelation, I spoke. "I suggest you figure it the fuck out because you're not giving up my kid, Bradley."

"I'm keeping him," she snapped. "You can do what you want. You always do."

I didn't bother to respond as I turned toward the crib. Even though I was terrified of hurting him, I couldn't go another second without holding him. Carefully, I lifted River from his crib and felt warmth flood my chest and stomach. Meanwhile, my son stared at me the entire time as if I'd grown two heads. Sometimes, I felt as if I had. More and more, I felt my former self slipping away. I barely recognized the old me who have never considered crushing Tyra's windpipe. What if River's early arrival had been a desperate twist of fate? My son offering me a final chance at salvation?

I didn't fear death, but I was scared shitless of disappointing him.

"If he was born three months ago," I asked as I gently cradled him, "why is he still so small?"

I heard her deep inhale as if she needed to draw strength. "A premature baby develops the same outside the womb as they do inside. River might be three months old, but he's still a newborn. He wasn't even considered full-term until a few days ago." I heard her shift nervously before she added, "My due date wasn't for another couple of weeks."

"What day was he born?"

"January fifth."

I almost swore at how close I'd been to sharing a birthday with my son. Was it corny to wish that we had? I didn't care. When I felt my hands start to shake, I quickly sat down on the sofa. I tracked every move he made and listened to every sound. In no time, I was utterly enthralled and completely fascinated by this little being.

"His last name?" I finally asked, keeping my gaze on River. He started crying the moment I tensed in anticipation. Tyra rushed over, and I let her take him from my arms, feeling helpless and clueless as I watched her soothe him before placing him back inside his crib.

"Rees," she finally answered, her soft lips trembling even as my shoulders sagged with relief. I wondered if she regretted giving my son my last name.

River Rees.

My eyebrows rose at that, but I said nothing. The name she'd chosen was unusual, and I literally bit my tongue until it bled to keep from asking her why. I'd just managed to shake off the urge to know why when I caught sight of Four rounding the corner. Ever, along with a perplexed Jamie and Bee, were right on her heels.

If I could, I would have locked them out—Tyra included— so I could spend some much-needed alone time with my son. Unfortunately, the automatic door slid open, and they all poured in at once.

chapter twenty-six

The Pawn

"HOLY SHIT," JAMIE WHISPERED IN AWE FOR THE thousandth time since meeting River. He still hadn't taken his eyes off the baby even though River had fallen asleep. For a while, he seemed to eat up all of the attention before getting bored and nodding off. "I can't believe one of us has one of these. He's fucking cute as hell." With a twinkle in his eye and a goofy grin, Jamie met my gaze. "Are you sure he's not mine?"

I rolled my eyes while Vaughn growled. *Possessive asshole.* "I'm not sure how much you paid attention in Sex Ed, Jameson, but the possibility would have required us sleeping together."

"And stop cursing around my fucking kid," Vaughn snapped.

Closing my eyes, I rubbed my temples because they were both idiots.

"What's the big deal?" Jamie argued. "He can't even hold his head up much less understand what I'm saying."

Thankfully, one of the nurses arrived at that moment to remind us that visiting hours were over. As happy as I was to be reunited with my friends and for River to meet his aunts and uncles, I was relieved to see them go. If I'd known when I opened my eyes this morning how long this day would be, I would have stayed in bed. So much had happened in twenty-four hours that I'd need at least a week to recover.

"Come back tomorrow?" I invited when they seemed reluctant to leave. I knew they were all silently worried I'd disappear again, and I hated myself for putting that fear in them. Not one of them had been angry or cruel, welcoming me back into their fold as if I'd never left.

Of course, Jamie was the first to accept. "You bet! Maybe then you can both share with us how this *accidentally* happened," he added, using his fingers to make air quotes. I didn't miss the skeptical look he shot Vaughn's way.

For some reason, my gaze followed Jamie's, wondering before waving the paranoid thought away. Vaughn's surprised reaction to River made it more than clear he hadn't planned this.

We said our goodbyes and everyone except for Vaughn filed out of the room.

"How *did* this happen?" Vaughn asked as soon as we were alone. River chose that moment to wake up again and immediately began fussing. After checking his diaper and finding it soaked, I carried him over to the changing table with Vaughn on my heels. "We used a condom. Every fucking time."

"I asked myself the same question whenever my head ended up in a toilet bowl. Apparently, piercings reduce the effectiveness of condoms—by like *a lot.*" I glanced over my shoulder in time to see his puzzled look. I ignored the heat creeping up my neck because I couldn't stop thinking about his dick. *Dumb twat.* "There must have been a hole in the condom."

"I think I would have noticed." His arrogant tone brooked no argument.

"Oh, yeah?" I challenged anyway as I removed River's soiled diaper. I started cleaning him when I spoke again. "Then how do you explain your son?" When Vaughn said nothing, I met his gaze. "The hole must have been small enough for neither of us to notice and big enough for him to slip through."

Our gazes flew to River, and was it me, or did he seem a little smug when his lips spread in what resembled a smile? *Surprise, bitches!* I knew if he could, he'd be laughing right now.

"Maybe you should get on the pill," Vaughn blurted, blowing out air that I felt curl around my nape and work its way down my spine until I shivered. That was how close he was hovering behind me now. Something told me I wouldn't be able to take a single step back without running into his chest first. I could already feel the heat. "Or whatever chicks take so that this doesn't happen again. At least not any time soon."

We both seemed to freeze as soon as he stopped speaking.

"Here's a thought," I mused, recovering from his slip first. "You could remove your piercing. Or better yet, *we don't have sex.*" Grabbing a fresh diaper for River, I muttered, "I like the latter option more."

I felt Vaughn's hands grip my hips as soon as the diaper was on the baby, and then his hard-on pressed into my spine. "It's not a matter of if but *when,* pip-squeak." His whisper sounded suspiciously like a threat even though I knew he wouldn't force me. "Sooner or later, you'll get that itch. You're in for a surprise if you think anyone's scratching it but me."

Recognizing the rabbit hole I'd fallen down once before, I lifted River from the table and kissed his soft cheek before returning him to his crib. Once he was snug as a bug in a rug, I whirled on Vaughn, forcing my lips into a smirk. "It's been a few months since we had sex. What makes you think I haven't already had that itch?"

"Oh, I know you have," he replied while closing the distance between us. "Just like I know you have it right now." Vaughn smiled then, and it was that cocksure smile I both hated and missed so much. "My dick isn't exactly forgettable."

Tucking the hair that slipped from my ponytail behind my ear, I cast my gaze to the floor. The warmth between my legs kept building and building, and it was all I could do not to spread them. "You're right, I...I couldn't forget how good you felt inside of me," I shyly admitted. "I couldn't stop craving the need to let go. I wanted more." The room became charged, and I knew soon, inhibitions would be a thing of the past if we both let go. I was panting by the time Vaughn ate up the distance, so when he caged me in by resting his forearms on the crib railing, I let him. "That's why you should know…"

I heard the unchecked arrogance in his tone when he spoke. "Yes?"

Lucky for me, I knew just the cure. Snapping my gaze from the floor and seeing the lust in his own, I lifted on my toes until our lips nearly touched. "I've had better."

I returned my heels to the floor and watched as he blinked. Then he took a stunned step back as his brain refused to accept my claim. "Come again?"

My lips pulled back in a snarl. "You don't get to fuck my sister and expect my pussy to remain under your lock and key." This time, I was the predator, and he was the prey as I stalked him across the room. Vaughn's eyes were wide with fear as if I truly might eat him alive. "You also don't get to waltz back into my life and start making demands. We don't get to start over as if nothing ever happened. Once a cheater, always a cheater, and I'll *never* forgive you."

Hearing that, he seemed to recover as the shock cleared his green eyes, and rage darkened them. If I were willing, I'd admit to seeing that kernel of hope he held within them vanish. "And once you're mine, you'll never be anyone else's. That I can fucking promise you."

"Wanna bet?"

He made a sound of disbelief. Right in my face, the cocky bastard *scoffed*. "Why would I waste time when we both know I'll be balls deep inside of you the minute you let your guard down? And when that's no longer enough for me, I'm going to steal your heart again without breaking a sweat. Mark my fucking words."

"You mean break it," I corrected him without missing a beat. I refused to acknowledge the sorrow making my body tremble.

I tried to stop it, but it was too great, so I let myself feel it as a reminder. "When sex is no longer enough for you, you're going to break my heart again, not steal it."

He winced. No longer smug, he reached for me, but I dodged his hold. "Pip-squeak, I—"

"Save it."

For a moment, Vaughn looked like he wanted to argue, but then there was defeat in his eyes before he stepped around me. I didn't move to stop him when I heard the automatic door slide open or dare to watch him walk away. Tomorrow would tell if it was just from me or from his son, too.

chapter twenty-seven

The Prince

UNABLE TO FACE MY FATHER JUST YET, I DIDN'T GO HOME WHEN I left the hospital last night. Instead, I'd gone back to the beach house where I tossed and turned all night after cleaning up the glass from the vase Tyra destroyed. I hadn't even felt the cuts and scrapes on my neck and face, but none of them had been major, anyway.

When morning came, I was back at the hospital, but I forced myself to stay away from the third floor for now. I couldn't get the devastation in Tyra's eyes out of my head. It called to the part of me I'd been forced to bury to protect her. And I couldn't even tell her why. I seriously doubted she'd believed me anyway. I played the part of a monster a little too well for it to be anything other than real.

"You look like shit," Wren greeted me as soon as I trudged into his room. Lou was nowhere to be found, and like a coward, I was a little relieved. I was in no mood for even a taste of what Ever had gotten yesterday. I liked my asshole the way it was.

"Indeed, I feel like it, too." I lowered into the chair by his bed with a groan. I'd given up on sleep around the crack of dawn and, for some reason, decided to work out. Every single one of my muscles ached from disuse.

"So I heard about the kid," he said after neither of us had spoken for a while. "Congratulations, asshole."

I shook my head in disbelief. Having a kid at nineteen was not exactly something I aspired to, but now that he was here, I had a hard time feeling any regret. It was a weird fucking space to be in, that's for sure. "Yeah, thanks, man." I couldn't help the prideful grin that spread my lips a moment later. My kid was adorable as fuck even though he scared the shit out of me. I couldn't stop thinking about him and wondered what he was doing at this very moment.

He's a newborn, jackass. He's probably shitting himself or sleeping.

"Just between you and me," Wren said after verifying that we were still alone, "was it really an accident?"

"Seriously? Jamie implied the same thing. The fucking condom broke, bro. Are you mental?" Wren winked before shrugging, and I had a hard time holding back my devious grin when he winced from the movement. "He wasn't planned," I insisted.

"Maybe not by Tyra," he teased.

I found myself smirking, even as I flipped him off. "Fuck you, man."

"You're smart to plead the fifth. I suggest you take it to your grave, or Tyra will dig you an early one."

"Read my lips," I told him slowly. "I did not trap Tyra."

A throat clearing had both of our gazes flying toward the open door where Lou stood with pip-squeak, who was clutching River to her chest.

My brows immediately pulled down. "What the hell do you think you're doing?" Tyra's cold stare shriveled my balls, but she didn't have to know that. Risking them, I shot up from the chair and stalked across the room. "Should he be out of the NICU?"

"I checked with his doctor. He said it was fine as long as he doesn't leave the hospital."

Everything she said had gone in one ear and out the other. "Take him back upstairs."

Ignoring my order, she stepped around me and entered the room. "I thought River might want to meet his uncle," she cooed as she approached Wren's bed. He was already sitting up, a gentle look in his eyes as he accepted the baby from pip. Meanwhile, my blood was boiling as my heart raced. I wasn't sure which one would kill me first. I kept checking for some threat or some sign that River was in distress. Tyra, however, seemed completely relaxed as she watched Wren bond with my son.

"I need to talk to you in private," I practically hissed in Tyra's ear. Over her head, my gaze met Lou's. She mouthed something, and against my will, I read her lips.

I will cut you.

Ignoring her meddling ass, I gripped Tyra's elbow and led her out the room.

"Perhaps instead of fighting about my dick last night, we should have discussed the fact that you didn't make River by yourself," I fussed as soon as we were alone. "You should have called me before you took him out of NICU. We need to make these decisions together."

"I've been calling and sending messages for weeks, and you haven't answered a single one. Why would I bother now?"

"I didn't have my fucking phone," I pushed through gritted teeth. "My father did." I stood perfectly still, ignoring the fact that my dick jumped when she shoved her hand in the pocket of my jeans and pulled out my old phone before holding it up. I couldn't deny that it was damning evidence, making me look like a goddamn liar. "He just gave it back yesterday," I tried to explain. It sounded lame as hell.

"How convenient." Her lips pressed together, and I was one more smart comment away from kissing the anger from them. She never could resist melting for me.

"Look." I huffed before snatching my phone back. It had been twenty-four hours, and I was already pulling my hair over the back and forth. "I screwed your sister, and you didn't tell me you were pregnant. Let's just call it even and move on."

Her gaze narrowed. "Because it's that easy for you."

"Because we have a son to think about," I reminded her. Pip seemed to sober at that. "This isn't going to work unless we can find a way to be civil." I wisely left out the part about us having no choice. I refused to let either of us screw up my son like my parents had done me.

"And what exactly is this?" she asked, waving her hand between us. "I don't want to be with you."

"I'm not that fucking wild about you, either," I lied. For now, it felt like the truth.

"So, what do we do?"

I shrugged when I was feeling anything but nonchalant. "We co-parent."

The disappointment in her eyes seemed to match the turmoil in my gut. I wondered how long I could convince myself that it was enough. It had to be. Even if I told Tyra everything, it could never erase what we've done to each other.

"Okay."

I should have been relieved by her whisper of agreement. The sadness in her eyes was gone, replaced by determination. I felt like I'd just had my heart torn from my chest. I forced myself to speak, to form the words that implied I was content with our new arrangement. "Okay."

Maybe someday I would be, but I highly fucking doubted it.

Tyra took River back upstairs, and Lou had gone with her. Once Wren and I were alone again, I dug into my pocket—the one that didn't hold my phone. I was relieved blabbermouth hadn't checked that one as I removed the small box I'd stowed inside.

"I believe this belongs to you," I told Wren as I held out his engagement ring. "I told you I'd keep it safe."

Wren almost seemed reluctant as he slowly took it from me, his expression solemn. "I thought I'd be able to give this Lou, but now, I'm not so sure." His eyes flashed, and I had the feeling he was remembering getting shot.

"I figured you'd say that. It's the other reason why I'm here," I told him after taking a deep breath. "I have a plan."

His brows dipped as he stared at me. "A plan?"

"This war has never been between Exiled and Thirteen. It's between three men with no honor and too much greed."

Wren seemed to mull that over before shrugging. "What difference does it make? We're caught in the middle regardless."

"Exactly. But we shouldn't have to pay for the sins of our fathers, Wren. We didn't ask for this any more than we asked to be here. Our fathers don't seem to give a shit what their feud does to us as long as they get what they want. We're nothing but collateral damage. Instead of standing by like prey to be picked off, like pawns in their little games, I say we show them what happens when rivals play dirty."

I watched as Wren sat back, his gray eyes slowly turning an electric blue. "I'm listening."

Two days later, when I finally returned to my father's castle on the hill, I found him not in his office as I expected but sitting on the deck. He was soaking in the sun as if he were basking in his glory.

"Son," my father greeted with a surprised raise of his brows. "I'm surprised to see you've returned so soon."

I stood over him with my fists balled, not caring about the threat I posed or the men with their guns aimed at my head. My father was just lucky I wouldn't risk leaving River without *his*. "You knew about my son, didn't you?"

"Of course, I did," he answered without a single flinch. "I know everything that's happening in my town."

I allowed myself to smile. "You didn't know that your enemy was living right underneath your nose for over a year."

He waved his hand dismissively. "An unfortunate mishap I

attribute to my frequent absences and the mediocrity of my spies. Besides, Harlan is not my enemy. I'm told he's no longer Exiled."

"Then why did you have him shot?"

"Because his father is still my enemy."

"Then why not kill Ever, too?" I didn't bother questioning whether my father knew of my best friend's true paternity. Underestimating him is how I'd lost everything.

My father held his hands apart as he smiled. "If I played all of my cards too soon, how will I win the hand?" I watched him take a sip of his bourbon and wondered how easy it would be to poison his supply. I definitely had access. "You should be grateful. If I wanted to kill Wren Harlan, he'd be dead."

I narrowed my gaze. "Then why send men into his home to shoot him?"

"Bait."

It was all the explanation my father offered. Fortunately, I understood, and the realization made my palms sweat. "For Crow or Fox?"

"Both if I'm lucky. It's why my men didn't use your best friend for target practice instead. Ever wasn't incentive enough for Nathaniel to crawl from whatever hole he's hiding in. I could have popped them both, but then Crow would get suspicious and disappear again."

"You really think Fox will show up to finish the job himself?"

"Right now, Harlan's easy enough prey sitting in that hospital wounded, and I'm told that woman of his has enough evidence to put Nathaniel in prison for the rest of his life. I know he'll show."

"And then what? You'll turn Blackwood Keep into a war zone? What about your anonymity? Do you really think you'd be safe hiding out here after that?"

"I've been living in the shadows for too long, son. When Crow and Fox are dead, there will be no one to challenge me."

"You mean no one to hide from."

My father's gaze cut to me, and I almost smirked at the

obvious nerve I hit. Franklin Rees may have been a cunning man, but he would be a sitting duck without the men he paid to protect him. A warrior he was not.

"Careful, boy. Now that you have a son, I no longer need your little slut to keep you in line. The security at Susannah Blackwood is pitifully lax. It will take little effort for me to slip into her room during the night…again." Hearing that my father had gone near Tyra had me dangerously close to gutting him. "I admit I enjoyed more than just watching her sleep. She has the softest skin. I can see why you thought she was worth your career."

I lost it then.

Forgetting about my son, my plans, and my vow to free my friends from my father's grip once and for all, I plowed my fist into my father's withered face. Feeling bone crack and wanting more, I didn't stop. My knuckles were screaming, my hand and shirt covered in blood, and my father slumped in his chair. He was unconscious by the time I was pulled away. I couldn't see or hear anything. I couldn't feel the rough hands holding me hostage. For a while, nothing got through the murderous rage that made me throw my life away. Even as I was forced to my knees with a gun pressed to my skull, I knew I'd do it all over again.

My only regret was not telling Tyra I loved her without fear forcing me to take it all back.

Closing my eyes, I pictured them both, somewhere safe and happy. I almost forgot about the bullet seconds away from ending it all.

A moment later, it finally came.

And then several more as the bodies around me began to drop. I kept my eyes closed, focusing on that image of Tyra and River until the shooting finally stopped. It seemed to last a lifetime. I was just glad I'd emptied my bladder before coming here. Peeking one eye open, I looked around, and when I saw everyone except my father lying bloodied on the ground, I stood and whirled around.

Jeremy casually stepped out from the tree line with a rifle slung over his shoulder as he yawned.

"It fucking took you long enough!" Fear had my voice sounding high-pitched to my own ears.

"Shut the fuck up. I had urgent business," Jeremy replied, his American accent laced with his Russian one. He sauntered the rest of the way across the expansive lawn until he stood beside me.

"More urgent than this?"

Shrugging, he stared down at my unconscious father. "When you gotta go, you gotta go."

I shook my head and wondered how desperate I had to be to ask Jeremy Antonov for help. The dude was a certified sociopath. Who else would have stopped to take a piss while I was on my knees seconds from biting a bullet?

"Help me get him inside."

Jeremy looked like he was going to decline, but the look I gave him had him rolling his eyes. He moved to stand near my father's shoulders, so I bent to grab his legs.

Without warning, however, Jeremy slapped the shit out of my father.

I was surprised when my father actually awoke—disoriented but awake. Jeremy looked at me then, and seeing my bewilderment, he snorted. "You hit like a bitch," he said, referring to a few days ago when I knocked his tooth out. I didn't even want to know what he'd been through to consider that a weak blow. "No way he was out cold enough."

"Whatever," I mumbled as my father groaned.

Jeremy kicked his foot and then growled, "Get up."

My father actually seemed startled, that cool confidence gone as he shakily rose to his feet. Antonov didn't seem at all concerned with the consequences if we failed. I wasn't sure what Jeremy had to lose, but I had a whole fucking lot. For some reason, the thought didn't fill me with dread as it once did.

"You're making a deadly mistake," my father warned when we entered the house.

"Seriously?" Jeremy mocked. "The decades you spent as Thirteen's father is about to end painfully, and the best you can come up with is a fucking cliché?" Antonov peered at the back of my father's head. My gut told me he was thinking about putting a bullet through it.

"We need him," I reminded Antonov as we herded my father toward his office.

"*I* don't, but you do."

I silently swore because he was right. The only way I could convince Antonov to help me was to hand over the recording I took of my father confessing to killing his predecessor and his plans for Thirteen. I thanked my lucky stars that I remembered to record him that day in his office. Learning Wren had been shot had almost made me forget all about it. The recordings were all the evidence Jeremy needed to kill my father with immunity and take his place. I hadn't wanted to hand it over this early, but Antonov had effortlessly outmaneuvered all of the precautions I'd taken to keep him from gaining the upper hand. Now I was reduced to relying on his fragile sense of mercy.

Or so he thought.

"Cut off the head of a snake, and another grows in its place," I told him. "There's no guarantee that head will be yours." Out of the corner of my eye, I noticed Jeremy's jaw clench. I'd finally struck a nerve. "Right now, Crow and Fox are my father's problem, but unless we deal with them too, they'll just become competition."

Antonov was silent as he shoved my father into his desk chair. We then tied him to it. My father had treated that chair like a throne only for it to become his coffin. "And what about you?" Antonov asked once we were done. My father was noticeably silent.

"What about me?"

"Are you competition?"

My heart thundered in my chest, even as I forced myself to remain nonchalant. "Are you looking for an excuse to kill me?"

"I don't need one. Answer the question."

Loud and clear, I could hear the threat woven into his demand. My father seemed smug and not at all fearful of watching his son being killed right before his eyes. I bet he thought my death would get him out of this. How wrong he'd be.

"I don't want this," I assured Jeremy while holding my father's gaze. I felt my lips curl at the lack of remorse in them. My next words were directed at him. "I never did."

I could only assume that Jeremy was appeased since I was still breathing.

"That's a relief and not because I'd have to kill you, which is kind of a disappointment, but because you'd be shit at it."

It was debatable whether Antonov had meant it as a compliment. The doubt didn't stop the black stain eating away at my heart from fading just a little. I felt hope that he was right—hope that I wasn't capable of unleashing horrors on innocents flared in my stomach. I turned and started for the door, not bothering to look back.

"That is a relief," I quietly agreed.

Upstairs in my bedroom, I quickly filled a large duffel bag with clothes and whatever I couldn't bear to leave behind—which, sadly, wasn't much. When I was done, I slowly turned in a circle, staring at the walls and the photos covering almost every inch of space. I contemplated leaving them but knew that I never could. They'd been a balm some days and the sharpest knife cutting deep on others—a gift from my father to keep me shackled. It took some time to take them all down. When I was finished, I stuffed them inside an old folder before shoving it inside my bag.

Downstairs, I found Jeremy waiting for me in the foyer, his eyebrow raised.

"Make sure he's ready."

It was all I bothered to say to him on my way out of the door. I threw my bag in the silver Jag—one of my father's toys—and floored it down the drive. After what my father revealed, I was eager to get back to the hospital, but I forced myself to make one more stop.

The drive to Tigerwood Lane seemed to take forever. My palms turned sweaty as I pulled into the driveway next to Coach Bradley's pickup. I must have sat there for five minutes before I stepped out to face the music.

chapter twenty-eight

The Pawn

VISITING HOURS WERE MINUTES FROM BEING OVER WHEN THE AUTOMATIC door finally slid open, and Vaughn stepped through. I kept my eyes on my Kindle, reading the same sentence for the thirtieth time as I listened to him cross the room. He didn't speak.

It was the hardest thing feigning casual indifference. To pretend I hadn't spent the entire day waiting for him to show. When that failed, I told myself that it had only been for River's sake and that the little white lie was for mine.

When I heard what sounded like a bag hitting the floor, my head shot up. My eyes widened at the bulging duffel lying near Vaughn's feet as he reached inside River's crib. Was he planning to stay? Where would he sleep? His only option was the recliner, which hadn't been designed for a night of comfortable sleep. The sofa bed had room to fit us both but not much more than that. I gulped.

I could ask him to leave, but I'd already denied Vaughn the first three months of his son's life. Months River had been fighting alone because I'd been too selfish and weak.

"Are you okay?" I inquired, breaking the silence first. It was impossible not to notice the fatigue written all over his face. Somehow, he was still heartachingly beautiful. It was a feat I could never pull off even if I had a thousand years.

"Fine." He moved over to the recliner, his stare intense and haunted as he watched River. "I went to see your father today."

I sat up straight at that. "What? Why?"

Vaughn looked at me, and I pressed my hand against my belly as if it would stay the butterflies. "Why do you think? Your father might have already known since you gave River my name, but he needed to hear it from me."

A conversation, I imagined, that did not go well. My father had been under the impression that Vaughn and I had formed an uncomplicated friendship after our many "tutoring" sessions. The wool Vaughn had pulled over my father's eyes had been woven thick, keeping him blind for months. I could still remember the afternoon Vaughn had daringly shown up while I was home alone and refused to leave. Of course, my father had caught us together, and his timing couldn't have been worse. He'd shown up while I'd been busy trying to drown his quarterback with a water hose.

"What's going on here?" my father demanded as his gaze shifted from me and narrowed on his star player. Vaughn was busy trying to blink the water from his eyes. "Rees? What are you doing here?"

"I came to talk to your daughter, Coach."

Vaughn's voice was thick and raspy, and despite the trouble I was in, I smirked. Unfortunately, it was the wrong time for me to be smug because my father's gaze had already returned to me.

"And what is it that you came to talk to her about?"

I tensed, hearing the suspicion in my father's tone. Vaughn's gaze sheepishly fell to the ground as his massive shoulders slumped. My gaze narrowed at the same time he stuck his hands in his pockets. What was this? He was the perfect picture of shy. I wasn't buying it for a second.

"I came to—I came to ask her for help, sir."

"With what, son?"

On the contrary, it seemed that my father was eating it up.

"I was thinking about our talk this afternoon, and I realized you were right. Being the best player on the team doesn't excuse me from making good grades." He chose that moment to look up, his gaze pleading and humble. It was clear my gullible father was buying Vaughn's

bullshit when he laid his hand on the quarterback's shoulder. "Your daughter is the smartest person in our school, sir. I was just hoping she'd tutor me."

"I see. And the reason for the hose?"

My lips parted to answer, but Vaughn beat me to the punch, twisting the truth in his favor.

"It's my fault," he said, his gaze returning to the ground. "I got a little desperate, Coach. I wouldn't take no for an answer."

"He's lying!" I didn't even consider the trouble I'd be in if I told the truth. I wasn't supposed to be at the party where I'd caught Vaughn's eye. Unless...his interest began earlier that day when I told him off at school for being a bully? I shook my head because it seemed so unlikely. Vaughn liked girls who were pliable and easy. Who were...not me.

Fortunately, my claim fell on deaf ears as my father whirled on me, his eyes that weren't as light as mine, ablaze with fury. "Tyra Morgan Bradley, explain yourself!"

"I—" The words became stuck in my throat, not because of my father's anger but because of the grin now spreading across Vaughn's lips. He winked the second he caught my gaze, pissing me off even further. Fine. This game he started was for two. Only I could play it better. "The truth is that he looks awfully like that sex predator we saw on the news the other day. Don't you remember, Daddy? It's uncanny."

My father blinked weary eyes at me. "Enough. I want you to show Rees inside and get him into some dry clothes."

"But—"

"That wasn't a request, Tyra."

And so began Vaughn's embarrassingly easy victory over my heart and soul.

"What did he say?" I asked when I finally found the courage.

Vaughn shrugged as he wiped some of River's drool from his chin. "He was pissed, but he didn't seem surprised. Your father isn't stupid, pip. He trusted you to make smart choices on your own."

Vaughn's lips flattened, and I had the feeling it was out of guilt rather than anger. Despite what he'd done, I didn't put one-hundred percent of the blame on Vaughn. He'd been honest about his intentions from the start. It had been my ego and stubborn heart that chose not to listen.

Of course, I thought with a wry twist of my lips, *it didn't give him the right to fool around with my sister.*

"Hey," I said when his turmoil didn't seem to be passing. He looked at me then, sorrow filling his green gaze, so I flashed him a crooked smile, an olive branch of sorts. "We can't change the past. There's no need to hurt your poor butthole trying."

He quietly mulled that over before offering a reluctant nod. I thought at least my advice would ease the tension, but it only seemed to increase it. "Can I stay?" he asked after a while. My sharp inhale was audible. Sensing my worry, he rushed to add, "I'll sleep on the recliner."

"You'll regret it," I warned him after forcing myself to calm down.

He glanced down at River, but when he met my gaze again, he stared at me for the longest time. "No, I won't."

My reaction, thankfully, was silent this time. A chill worked its way down my spine as my belly tightened and my heart fluttered. I forced myself to smile good-naturedly since Vaughn was always good at reading me. He was especially keen at detecting when I was horny. "Only if River says it's okay."

Our son released a sharp cry, and as he fussed, he turned his head from side to side, making Vaughn wince. I was sure his feelings were a little bruised. "I'm just going to take that as a yes, anyway," Vaughn stubbornly teased him.

"In River's defense, it's probably because you're holding him like a football."

At Vaughn's dumbfounded blink, I tossed aside the blanket that had been wrapped around me, then stood and padded over to them. His gaze dropped, and when it seemed to burn, I remembered that I was only wearing tiny shorts and a thin tank. Despite the hospital feeling like the arctic, I had a habit of over-heating at night, which was why I always wore little to nothing. In fact, I usually wore less, to Vaughn's pleasure, during those nights, I snuck him up to my room after my father had fallen asleep.

"Preemies have a hard time keeping themselves warm." Taking River from him, I told Vaughn to hold out his arms. Swallowing at the veins threading through his forearms, I gently placed River back in his arms. "Hold him close to your chest so that he can feel your heartbeat and share your warmth."

Vaughn did as I directed, and River slowly quieted. "You think I'm warm?" he flirted once River had gone still. Vaughn's head was tilted, and his lips turned up in a smirk.

I rolled my eyes even as my own body temperature rose. "I think basic biology says that you are."

"And what do you say?" he challenged.

Turning back to the sofa, I began pulling out the bed hidden inside. "I say we should steer clear of the subject since nothing good can come of it." I pulled out the sheets and covers I'd brought from home, grateful that Vaughn didn't seem willing to argue.

"Can we talk about what you plan to do when the fall comes?" he asked after I finished making the sofa bed.

I paused from pulling my hair up into a bun. "What do you mean?"

"I mean when school starts up again, and you have to go back to Harvard. What happens to River?"

"I'm not going back to Harvard." The indifference I heard in my tone might as well have been nails on a chalkboard. I cringed. "I lost my scholarship."

Vaughn's fury was immediate.

"How the hell did you do that?" he snapped. If he hadn't been holding River, I would have clawed his eyes out. His blatant disappointment was a kick to my stomach when I was already down. Vaughn had been the wrench in my plans, and I blamed no one but myself. I'd stupidly allowed him in.

"How do you think, Rees?"

I didn't allow him the chance to respond before I hurried inside the mini en suite and slammed the door shut. I wanted to run back out there and scream at him to leave. For River's sake, I sank onto the bathroom floor and hugged my knees instead. Frustration and grief bubbled up inside of me, but it wasn't for Harvard. I didn't want to accept the inevitable truth. The reason I hated Vaughn Rees so deeply. It wasn't because of the wreckage he left of my heart. It was because, despite it all, he still held it in his soulless grip.

All of these months, I'd kidded myself.

I would never be whole again.

Trembling, I wrapped my arms around Vaughn's neck as he moved inside of me slowly.

"Pip," he pleaded, staring into my eyes. Two tears slipped from his own. I never thought I'd see the day Vaughn Rees cried. "I think I'm drowning, pip."

"I'll save you," I vowed. And I would. I'd do whatever it took.

He shook his head before he kissed me, a desperate meeting of our souls as he deepened his strokes. I could feel his piercing teasing a spot deep inside of me. A spot that nearly had my eyes rolling back as I tasted the alcohol on his lips, greedily allowing it to dull my senses more. "That's the last thing I want," he whispered when he came up for air. "Because it's you. You're what's pulling me under." I held him tighter, which seemed to be exactly what he needed. "Promise you won't let go?"

"I promise."

"I love you, pip," he whispered.

"I love you, too."

Admitting it felt as natural as breathing. As natural as the feel of his cum when he released inside of me.

"Pip, wake up."

I groaned, batting at the hand that shook me as I desperately tried to return to the beautiful dream. Only...it hadn't been a dream. It was a wonderful memory.

"Wake the fuck up!"

Gasping, I shot up, clutching the sheets that were soaked in my sweat. Vaughn, who was frowning at me, his gorgeous hair mussed from sleep, stood over me. I must have woken him.

Details of the dream came flooding back to me all at once as my body heated.

"We didn't use a condom." My voice was a whisper of horror. Vaughn's face was contorted from aggravation over having his sleep interrupted.

"What are you talking about?" he demanded impatiently.

"That night at the beach house. We got really drunk, we..." My gaze traveled to the crib. "We didn't use a condom."

Vaughn's only response was to yawn as he stared down at me blankly.

"Well, aren't you going to say something?" I shouted. The lights about the crib flashed, and River gave a short whine. *Shit.*

"Why would I? It's not like we can change the past, right?"

I blinked in shock. What—

He'd thrown my words from earlier back at me.

I never thought for a second that they would anger him, but it was clear they had, and I wondered why. "Vaughn...I didn't say that to hurt you."

"Right. Because I'm so heartless, telling me I don't have a shot in hell with you no matter what I do would have zero effect on me."

My lips parted. *What?*

"That's not—"

"Save it and go back to fucking sleep."

Even at a whisper, Vaughn's tone was harsh. He turned away from me, and I shot up from the sofa bed as he made his way over to the recliner. Vaughn ignored me, closing his eyes to pretend to sleep, even when I stood over him. "How could you twist my words like that?"

"That's what you meant, isn't it?" Before I could tell him no, he continued. "It is. Even if you aren't willing to admit it, deep down, that's what you meant."

"You told me you didn't want to be with me, either."

His eyes opened then as his eyebrow rose in challenge. "Did I?"

"*I'm not that fucking wild about you, either,*" I mocked, echoing his words from a few days ago. I hadn't forgotten them. He slowly stood from the recliner, and I forced myself not to back up a step even when he towered over me.

"I can be pissed at you and still want to kiss the fuck out of you, pip. Don't you know that by now?"

"I—what am I supposed to say to that?"

"Why do you have to say anything at all?" I felt his hand cup my nape, and when he leaned down, I automatically rose to the tips of my toes. The moment his lips touched mine, I could barely remember my own name, much less what we'd done to each other. Each time felt like the first. Even when it was brief, there was no such thing as a casual kiss.

"You...will...always...be...mine," he dictated between kisses. This time when he pulled away, he looked me in my eyes. "Do you understand?" Subtly, I felt his hand tighten on my nape in warning. I wasn't sure if the shudder that made my body tremble was from fear or anticipation.

"We'll see about that." I refused to give in so easily. Or at all.

There was a rumble in his chest, and then he was kissing me again rather than tossing me away. I guess Vaughn wasn't so predictable, after all. It felt like our senior year, and he was chasing me all over again. Something told me this time around, he was playing for keeps, and the thought sent my heart soaring at the same time my hands ached to push him away. His tongue slipped between my lips, and I barely noticed his fingers doing the same beneath the waistband of my shorts. They were so thin and short that I hadn't bothered wearing panties.

"Your pussy better be fucking wet," he threatened against my lips.

Even if by a snowball's chance in hell I hadn't been, his low throaty tone had me gushing between my legs. "See for yourself," I teased at the same time his fingers reached my clit.

Bypassing it completely, he curled two of his fingers before forcing them inside of me and making me cry out from shock as I rose to the tip of my toes. The cruel glint in his green eyes didn't stop my pussy from tightening around his fingers in welcome. He didn't slow down even when another surprised whimper slipped from my lips, one he cut off by closing his hand around my neck.

For a while, there was only the wet sound of his fingers plunging through my arousal. I wanted to tell him how close I was to coming, but his hold around my throat kept me from speaking.

"It's funny," he taunted as he daringly added a third finger. I rotated my hips, wanting to get him deeper. I'd long forgotten that I was supposed to hate him. "I never forgot the feel of your pussy." His lips brushed my ear as if he had a secret to tell me. "How wet it gets, how greedily it squeezes me…how every inch of your pussy molded to the curve of my cock." I whimpered because his words only reminded me that he wasn't inside of me. At least, not the part of him I needed most. "It's exactly how I remember it." His hand tightened until he cut off my air supply. "*Exactly how I left it.*"

Vaughn didn't give me a chance to worry that he'd called me on my shit. I hadn't been with anyone else, and something told me he'd make damn sure that stayed the case.

Releasing me, he dropped to his knees, taking my shorts with him as I gasped for air. Before I could even catch my breath, he had my leg hoisted onto his shoulder, and then his tongue flicked my clit. Vaughn suckled, licked, and even bit me as he fucked me with his fingers and tongue until I came. I clapped my hands over my mouth, keeping my scream inside as I rode Vaughn's face. He didn't seem to mind one bit even when the movement of my hips became jerky and wild.

When the wave eventually passed, I was too weak to stand. Luckily, Vaughn was there to catch me, pulling me onto his lap as we both struggled to catch our breath. I could already see round two in his eyes when I met his gaze. He leaned in, and I was more than willing, rising to meet him halfway, but then short, angry cries had us both freezing.

River had awakened.

Vaughn groaned before setting me aside and rising to his feet. My eyes were already drooping by the time he washed his hands and lifted River from his crib.

"Cockblocker," I swore I heard him mutter. I smiled as I rested my head against the seat of the recliner. In no time, I was asleep, awakening only when I felt myself being lifted. "I wasn't done with you," Vaughn griped as he laid me on the sofa bed.

The room was quiet, so I assumed River was fast asleep. I didn't bother to protest when I felt Vaughn lay beside me. I told myself it was only because I felt guilty about him sleeping on the recliner. In the morning, I'd ask the nursing staff about having an extra bed brought it. It would be a tight fit, but River would be released in just a week and a half. If we couldn't make the next few days work, Vaughn and I would be in for a rude awakening over the next eighteen years.

I expected to feel dread, but all I got was a sleepy yawn as Vaughn curved his hard body behind mine, leaving no space between us. The last thing I felt was his erection in my back and then his arm closing around my waist.

I felt like I was home.

chapter twenty-nine

The Prince

THE NEXT MORNING, I WOKE UP IN BED ALONE.

Or so I thought.

I felt the spot where Tyra had been, and when I came up empty, my eyes slowly opened.

"Good morning, sunshine." I shot up with a scowl at seeing Jamie lying on his side next to me, his head propped in his hand and a wide smile. "You're so beautiful when you sleep, baby."

"Fuck off." I rubbed my eyes before looking around the empty room. *Where the hell was Tyra?*

"If you're looking for your baby mama," Jamie announced as he stood from the bed, "she's downstairs having coffee with some poor sap in a janitor's uniform."

I froze. "What the hell are you talking about?"

"Tyra went on a date while you were up here, getting your beauty sleep."

I was silent, trying to figure out how the hell that could be when I just had her pussy in my mouth. That prick from the diner flashed in my mind. I guess my message hadn't been received. Then again, Tyra could be persuasive. She had me chasing her ass.

"Black, average height, looks like he enjoys pillow talk and long walks on the beach?"

Shoulders trembling, Jamie bit his bottom lip to keep from laughing out loud. "That would be the one."

I felt my nostrils flare as I stood there, contemplating what to do. Obviously, I hadn't scared him off, or maybe Tyra was so determined to piss me off, she didn't care what the hell happened to him.

Seeing tiny movements coming from the crib, I walked over to find River wide awake, his gaze moving all around as if he were looking for his mother, too.

Fuck her. I refused to play this game. She wanted me jealous, she got it, but that didn't mean I had to stoop to her level and act on it.

"If you want my advice," Jamie began before I cut him off.

"I don't."

"Damn, man, you should have told me sooner. I've already started." I rolled my eyes even though my back was turned. "Bee and I had a lot of issues—mountains I thought we'd never climb, but we did." Jamie paused then for dramatic effect. "It's amazing how much two people can accomplish when they sit down and talk their shit out."

"You done, Dr. Phil?"

Of course, it all seemed simple to him. From the outside, without all the facts, one could never truly understand. From the inside, even with all the facts, one could never hope to explain. I looked over my shoulder in time to see Jamie shrug as he stared at his phone.

"Have it your way, poor sap number two. I wake up next to my girl every day."

River began to cry, saving his uncle from a bloody nose. Luckily, Tyra had shown me how to prepare his bottle, so I washed my hands while Jamie babbled nonsense to him, thinking it would actually calm him down. I then grabbed one of the small bottles Tyra had stored in the fridge. Staring at the watery composition that reminded me of skim milk, my chest swelled, knowing Tyra's body had transformed simply for the purpose of feeding my son. Feeling my mouth water and my gut stir for some reason, I set the bottle inside the baby warmer nearby and willed my dick to chill the fuck out.

A moment later, pandemonium ensued.

"Mayday! Mayday!" he screamed dramatically while holding his nose. "I think the little dude just shit himself!" Jamie quickly backed away, his eyes watering. "Fuck…what the hell do you guys feed him?"

Abandoning the bottle, I rushed over, feeling out of my fucking element. I realized this was my first time taking care of River alone, and Jamie sure as shit wasn't helping matters. I lifted River from his crib before carrying him over to the changing table.

Tyra had made it look easy enough.

"The tabs," Jamie reminded me when I just stood there, scratching my head. "Pull the goddamn tabs."

You'd think we were defusing a bomb rather than changing a diaper. I did as Jamie instructed before slowly peeling the diaper away. I almost barfed. It sure as fuck looked like something exploded.

"Dude…he doesn't even look big enough to hold that much poop. What the hell?"

I didn't respond as I balled up the soiled diaper and tossed it inside the designated bin. River was wailing in earnest now, and I felt each cry inside of my chest. I grabbed some wipes and began cleaning him, but when I got to the diaper part, I stalled again. I could call an audible at the drop of a dime and lead an entire team to victory, but I couldn't figure out how to diaper my own kid.

"What is going on here?"

Jamie and I looked behind us to see two nurses standing just inside the door. Seeing the diaper in my hand and my dumbfounded look, they rushed over to the changing table. From there, one of the nurses took over. I watched as she sprinkled powder on his butt, and then she patiently walked me through diapering.

"I take it you're River's father?" she asked once I was finished.

I nodded, though, at that moment, I didn't feel like one.

"Don't stress it too much," she said, reading the look on my face. "You'll get the hang of it eventually." I didn't reply, and they didn't stick around. When the nurses reached the door, I could have sworn I heard one of them mutter, "I told you that baby had milk in his coffee."

Jamie snorted, but I didn't find a damn thing funny. He clapped me on the back and told me to lighten up. I shrugged him off before picking River up from the changing table. Although he wasn't crying anymore, the frown on his face told me he still wasn't content. Handing River over to Jamie, I made quick work of preparing his bottle before taking my son back to feed him.

River was obviously greedy as fuck the way he suckled at the nipple and the hungry sounds he made. I wondered if he'd ever catch up in size to kids his age. It wouldn't matter to me if he one day stood shoulder to shoulder with me or stayed pint-size like his mother. I'd love the hell out of him regardless.

When the bottle was empty, I mimicked Tyra by patting him on the back. My palms turned slick with sweat as I worried that I might be too rough. That was until he gave an anticlimactic, though loud, burp. It was pretty impressive for his size. Not long after that, River was asleep again.

It was impossible to concentrate on anything other than what the hell Tyra thought she was doing with that asshole downstairs. Jamie, on the other hand, had been prattling nonstop for the last thirty minutes, and I'd barely heard a word.

"So, yeah, I found a few bumps on my dick this morning, and I was wondering if you could take a look at it for me. I'd ask Bee, but it's not something you'd want your girl to see, you know?"

I grunted my response. "Wait, what?"

Jamie smiled, his tattooed hand falling from his belt. "Gotcha. You haven't been listening to a fucking word I've said, have you?"

"Of course not." I ran my hand through my hair, feeling my jaw clench. I wanted to go downstairs and rip Tyra away from that asshole. If he had his hands on her, so help me God—

"Let's just go downstairs and see what's up," Jamie suggested, interrupting my murderous thoughts. When I sat back, refusing, he bent over laughing. "We both know you want to, dumb ass."

"Fuck her."

His eyebrows rose. "Did you? I mean other than when you were making Poopy F. Baby over there."

"No."

"That explains why she's looking to get it from someone else. The girl's got needs, too."

I groaned, wondering how much I should reveal about what happened between us last night. Jamie couldn't hold water for shit. "We fucked up and fooled around, but then River woke up, and Tyra fell asleep before I could get him down again. "

"So?"

"She was asleep," I reiterated when Jamie didn't seem moved.

"Was she willing?" I only shrugged in response. "I'm going to take that as a yes," he replied. "If it happens again, put her on her knees. I guarantee she'll wake up once your dick hits her cervix."

His lips twitched when I stared at him blankly.

"Thanks, but no, thanks."

"Whatever, bro. It's your dick's funeral." Jamie then turned and left the room without saying goodbye. A moment later, I was on my feet. I ignored his smirk when I rushed onto the elevator before the doors could close. "Good man," was all he said as the elevator descended.

I didn't know what the hell I would do once I found her, but they both had better pray for an angel of mercy.

chapter thirty

The Pawn

M Y STOMACH TWISTED AND TURNED WITH GUILT EACH TIME MY gaze landed on the yellow bruises marring the janitor turned friend's handsome face. "Oliver, I can't say it enough. I'm really sorry for getting you involved. I didn't intend for this to happen."

Yeah? Well, what were your intentions? Do enlighten us, my conscience seemed to challenge.

Dressed for work, he waved me off for the umpteenth time since we'd sat down. "It's okay. What are a few broken bones if it means getting the prettiest girl to go out with me again?"

Though I wouldn't call meeting for coffee in a hospital cafeteria a date, there was no stopping the heat warming my cheeks. I was just grateful he agreed to meet me. "I don't know about that."

"But you are beautiful," he insisted. "Inside and out." Oliver nodded toward the flowers I'd gotten him as one of my many apologies. "And I have to admit that it explains everything."

"What do you mean?"

"You told me that your son's father was the one to break it off, but he's obviously not over you." He then pointed to his face. "Why else would he do this?"

"Well, that's the other bit of bad news. He kind of knows you helped me destroy his car." I cringed as I watched the color drain from Oliver's skin. "He's not going to press charges or sue," I rushed to say. Even though Vaughn hadn't told me so himself, I knew he wouldn't because it meant getting me in trouble, too. Besides, it wasn't his style. Oliver's brutalized face was more Vaughn's MO.

Still, Oliver rubbed the back of his neck. "I guess I should watch my back, huh?"

I found myself without words. While I could guarantee Oliver wouldn't face jail time or lose everything, I couldn't promise that Vaughn wouldn't come back for seconds just because.

"I understand if you never want to see me again."

"If I'm honest, my head is telling me to stay away…" I felt my shoulders slump before he could even finish. "But my heart is telling me you're worth the trouble."

He flashed a smile that I quickly returned.

"I'll make sure Vaughn won't bother you again. It's over between us, anyway," I muttered though it felt like a lie. And not just because of last night. I wanted to believe Vaughn had assaulted Oliver because of his Lamborghini, but I knew better. Vaughn had hurt him because of me and because he'd needed to repair his ego. He fully expected to find me soaked in tears and wallowing in the destruction he'd left of my heart. I cursed myself because Vaughn had undoubtedly almost gotten what he wanted.

Oliver's gaze lifted as he looked at something over my shoulder. "Are you sure about that?"

I was confused until I felt the presence looming over me and the goose bumps traveling up my arms. Jamie had already rounded the table to stand behind Oliver. I didn't need to turn to know that it was my baby daddy from hell standing behind me.

"This looks cozy," Jamie said, the first as always to speak.

"What it is or isn't is none of your business," I spat. "It's *private*."

"That's funny. Vaughn was just telling me about all the fun you two had in your son's room last night." Jamie sat down next to Oliver and draped his arm over the back of Oliver's chair. "Shall I tell your friend here all about it?"

"Are you serious, Jamie? Stop!" I didn't dare turn and rage at Vaughn for fear that it would only prove my guilt. I was just glad no one could see the blush burning up my skin right now.

Strong hands gripped my shoulders before Jamie could retort.

"Stop?" Vaughn whispered in my ear while his furious gaze was fixed on Oliver. "I'm just getting started." I couldn't decide if the warning for Oliver or me. "Get up." Slowly, his hands moved down to my arms, and I knew his order was for me.

I knew if I didn't obey, Jamie would spill the beans. I saw the warning in his eyes. The first chance I got, I'd make him pay dearly. And then I'd deal with Vaughn.

Rising to my feet, I followed Vaughn to the other side of the cafeteria. Away from prying eyes and ears as well as the exit. Vaughn wasted no time pushing me in front of him and then trapping me against the wall with both of his hands planted on either side of me. My nipples hardened, and I just prayed they didn't start leaking for the umpteenth time this morning. Seriously, having to pump several times a day to keep from looking like a contestant in a wet T-shirt contest was kicking my ass. I found myself short of breath at his close proximity as I thanked the thick material of my nursing bra for small favors. Vaughn was the first to speak, saving me from begging him to fuck me right here and now.

"Have I not made myself clear regarding you and him?"

On the contrary, I'm more confused than ever. Even more so than before he fucked my sister, and I didn't think that was possible. "I don't care how many times you spell it out for me. I'm not bending over for you anymore, emotionally or physically, *Rees.*"

His gaze was full of disgust, even as his eyes narrowed. "So, you're willing to lower your standards and make a fool of yourself just to prove a point to me?"

"God, your ego—"

"Tell me something, *Bradley,*" he interrupted. "After the diner, did he try to contact you?"

"No." I frowned, wondering what Vaughn was getting at. "Why would he after what you did?"

"Because if he cared about you, it wouldn't matter what I did to him. He'd want to know that you were okay. He'd make damn sure I hadn't hurt you and to hell with the consequences." My mouth opened and closed like a fish, but it didn't matter because Vaughn wasn't done. "Instead, he was only concerned with saving his own skin." Vaughn's hand lifted to play with the ends of my curly hair. "I could be hurting you right now," his tone was gentle despite the underlying threat, "but that didn't stop him from getting the hell out of dodge, did it?"

Vaughn's back was turned to the nearly empty cafeteria, so he had no way of knowing if that was true. Against my will, my gaze darted to the table where I'd been sitting. The table was empty except for Jamie, who was now sitting and whistling with his feet propped on the wooden table, and the flowers I gifted Oliver.

"Look at me," Vaughn ordered when my gaze remained fixed on Oliver's vacated chair. The moment I looked into Vaughn's green eyes, I forgot all about Oliver. "You must have lost a few screws if you think I'll stand by and watch you offer *my* pussy to a coward."

"Because I'm only allowed to fuck cheating assholes, is that right?"

"I may be a bastard, but I'm the only man who will ever get close to you. I suggest you get used to me."

I had the feeling he wasn't referring to the sweet, attentive Vaughn I'd left behind but rather this *alpha-hole* standing in front of me. Still, he wasn't the only one who'd changed, and he'd find that out soon enough. "You can't tell me you don't want to be with me and then force me not to date. Your phobia of commitment is the reason we're standing here."

"No. My *son* is the reason we're standing here," he said, jabbing his finger at the hospital floor. "So, get the fuck back upstairs and take care of him."

I forced myself to stay in place even though that was exactly what I wanted to do. "No," I said as I folded my arms. I knew River was fed, dry, and safe. Reluctantly, I admitted it wasn't just because of the wonderful NICU staff, but because Vaughn was already proving to be a great father.

Vaughn took a threatening step forward, leaving no space between us. All I could see were his green eyes and his perfect teeth as his lips pulled back in a snarl. "You either march back up there on your own two feet, or I drag you back by your hair. The choice is yours."

My eyes narrowed and my fists balled, ignorant of the fact that he stood a foot taller than me. "I've moved on, Rees. You got what you wanted, and I learned a valuable lesson. Why are we even fighting about this? Who I date is none of your concern. *River* is your concern."

"Save it." His aggressive tone had me shrinking back against the wall for safety. "You haven't moved on. If you had, you wouldn't be two seconds from getting your ass spanked." As if to prove his point, Vaughn's hand dropped to his waist. "If you're not back upstairs with my son by the time I count to one hundred, the belt comes off."

My jaw dropped because he had to be joking.

To my eternal humiliation and anger, I learned a moment later that he wasn't.

"One."

Needless to say, I heeded Vaughn's warning even though every fiber of my being screamed at me to rebel. I just wasn't sure if it was to show Vaughn that I couldn't be bent or to push him over the edge and force him to deliver his promise.

I didn't need a spine. I needed therapy.

And the part of me that wasn't fantasizing about Vaughn

bending me over his knee hated him for opening my eyes and making me see a different side of Oliver. No, it wasn't his job to play the hero, but I couldn't help feeling disappointed that he hadn't at least tried to defend me. Vaughn was three years his junior, yet my son's father had sent Oliver running with his tail tucked between his legs and all without lifting a finger. Or fist.

Upstairs, I found River sound asleep as I knew he'd be. I didn't mind. Even before I allowed myself to love him, there had been nowhere else I'd rather be.

Not even Harvard.

The spring semester would be ending soon, but I hadn't allowed myself to overthink about school or the fact that I'd have to withdraw. I'd simply cross that bridge when it came. I could always take up nursing when River was old enough. Even though it didn't come close to my dreams of heading my own surgical department one day or maybe even an entire hospital, it was hard and fulfilling work. I had the nurses here to thank for showing me as much.

After an hour of sitting and twiddling my thumbs, I moved around the small room, cleaning and organizing. After picking up the bottoms Vaughn had slept in last night, I grabbed his duffel, ready to stuff them inside when a near-bursting folder caught my attention. I allowed myself only a second to debate whether I should look inside before I flipped it open. What seemed like hundreds of photos came tumbling out.

Every single one of them was of me.

chapter thirty-one

The Prince

DIDN'T BOTHER FOLLOWING TYRA TO MAKE SURE SHE'D GONE BACK UP. She wasn't just book smart, after all. She knew exactly when not to test me.

"Dude," Jamie swore the moment we were alone. His pierced eyebrows were damn near touching his mahogany hairline. "You're lucky. If you still had your Lamborghini, she'd be outside keying it right now."

Nine months ago, I would have snorted at the idea of a good girl like Tyra not toeing the line, but she'd proved me wrong. I had the feeling before we finally reached some understanding that she'd do it again.

"Then it's a good thing I don't." I left the cafeteria and made my way to Wren's room with Jamie hot on my heels. I knew this when I heard him whisper over my shoulder.

"Are you afraid she thinks he's hotter than you?" He chortled in my ear. "Maybe even better in the sack?"

"Fuck off."

"At least I'm fucking," he retorted before veering off after catching sight of Lou perusing the vending machines. I shook my head as I kept going. Sometimes, I cursed the fucking day I agreed to be friends with Jameson Buchanan.

I reached Wren's room and started to push inside when I stopped. Through the cracked door, I heard a familiar voice speak.

"I'm so sorry," my best friend pleaded, making my brows

rise. Ever McNamara was not one who apologized often. He destroyed my first bike doing stunts when we were kids, and I still hadn't gotten an apology out of his ass. "Not just for almost getting you killed but for everything."

"I should have told you," Wren conceded.

"It doesn't matter now." I could almost picture the emphatic shake of Ever's head. I dared not move to see for myself and risk ruining their little moment. Four and Lou would probably kill me, and I was already high on their shit list. "I understand why you didn't. I would have done the same if it meant protecting you."

There was a beat of silence and then, "Nothing has to change. Not if you don't want it to."

Willing the ache away, I pressed a hand to my chest. Wren was giving Ever permission to ignore the blood that tied them. It didn't matter what it would do to him—not as long as Ever was happy. It was hard to believe Wren hated Ever once upon a time.

I didn't realize I was holding my breath until Ever finally spoke. "I always wanted a brother. It sucked being an only child."

Something like relief had me sagging against the wall. I walked away before either of them could say more to give them privacy, but I didn't wander far. Ten minutes later, Ever walked out, and I watched him leave before slipping inside.

"You were right," I greeted Wren as I watched him spoon pudding from a cup. Pretending I hadn't been listening to them proved harder than I thought. "You were bait."

Slowly, he sat down his pudding cup before nodding. "I guess that means your father did us a favor then. There was no other way we could get them all in one place without any of them getting suspicious."

"Are you sure you want to do this?" I asked him.

Setting up his own father? Risking his life? That couldn't

have been an easy choice. I hated my own with every fiber, and I was still having a hard time not backing out. I wondered if that made me weak. Spineless. Jeremy would sure as fuck think so. I could hear him now calling me a pussy.

"First, it was Thirteen, and then it was Exiled. My father spent my entire life choosing them over me. I won't hesitate for a second to do the same for Lou."

I nodded, and for some reason, I felt better about what I'd sacrifice for River and Tyra. And I wasn't just talking about my father. I'd have to live with my decision for the rest of my life. "When are they letting you out of here?"

"A couple of days."

"And if Crow or Fox shows up before then?"

He paused, seemingly mulling it over before shrugging. "Is Franklin secure?" At my nod, Wren turned his head, appearing grim as he stared out the window. "Then we improvise."

I was too afraid to know what he meant by that to ask.

Neither Lou nor Jamie made an appearance, so Wren and I spent an hour going over our plan until it was damn near fail-safe. Of course, when it came to fate, there was no such thing. Only when Wren seemed to be losing energy did I finally leave him.

On my way to the bank of elevators, I noticed Tyra's little boy toy a few feet away, pushing a mop. When our gazes met, he stiffened, his grip tightening on the mop handle as he looked around, ensuring himself that we weren't alone. We hadn't been alone when I kicked his ass the first time, but I wouldn't waste my breath pointing that out. In fact, rather than waltz over to him and issue threats, I stepped onto the elevator. Tyra may not have gotten the message, but Oliver sure as fuck did.

I used the time I spent at the wash station outside the NICU to reflect on what the hell I was doing. I already knew what I wanted. Destroying my father and everything he hoped to build wasn't just for River but for the chance to offer Tyra what I couldn't give her before. Go fucking figure. The biggest obstacle turned out to be convincing her to take the leap with me. I could always shove her ass off the cliff, but that wouldn't be satisfying for either of us.

I didn't want a captive.

I wanted someone who couldn't wait to wake up to me in the morning. I wanted to feel my heart beating inside my chest again. I wanted someone who laughed at my jokes even when they weren't funny, someone to share all of my secrets until we were old and gray and in the grave. I wanted a wife. Unfortunately, I'd waited too long to realize it, and even when I did, I couldn't admit it to the one person who made me want it.

It wouldn't have been possible without Tyra. I would never surrender and allow myself to feel those things for anyone else but her. And if I couldn't convince her of that, I suppose I could settle for her tying her to bed. It wasn't ideal, but it was better than living without her.

Sighing, I dried my hands before stepping into the NICU. I wasn't sure I'd ever grow used to the sound of crying babies. Two seconds and I could already feel my head splitting.

When I stepped inside of River's room, the first thing I noticed was the photos.

Every single one was of Tyra and covering the floor, arranged in chronological order. The girl in question was kneeling before them with a deep frown on her face, not in disbelief of what she was seeing but in concentration. The empty folder I'd place them in had been tossed aside.

Hearing me, she looked up, her pink lips parted. I wasn't sure how long we stared at each other before she spoke. "What is this, Vaughn? Why do you have these?"

Kneeling, I wordlessly started collecting them. The first one I grabbed was a photo of Tyra crossing the street. Her hair had been blowing in the wind, her eyes downcast as if she didn't care whether or not a bus ran her over. The second was a shot of her entering her dorm. The third... I inhaled and exhaled. The third was her sitting alone on a bench, crying her eyes out. I didn't have to question whether each one of those tears had been because of me.

The rest of them were much of the same, and in each one, she'd been sad. Not a single one held a smile, and I knew from the gauntness of her face she'd lost weight despite her being pregnant and not knowing it at the time. I wondered if River's early birth had been because of me. Because I'd reduced Tyra into not caring whether she lived or died.

The irony that I'd given up everything so she could live wasn't lost on me.

"My father had them taken," I finally told her after I'd gathered all of the photos and shoved them back into the folder.

"Why would he do that?"

I almost blinked in surprise. I expected shock, tears, screams, and accusations. Instead, she seemed almost resigned.

"Up until two months ago, I've been his prisoner. He kept me locked up, but he didn't use chains. He hurt me, but he didn't use his men to make me bleed. This..." I waved the folder full of surveillance photos—all of Tyra seemingly safe and sound. With one phone call that could have easily changed. "This was how he tortured me."

"The last one was taken some time after Thanksgiving. Harvard's holiday committee didn't hang Christmas decorations until after everyone was back."

I nodded, remembering how insane it had driven me, not knowing whether Tyra was still alive or not. My father had taken more pleasure in that than anything. "I didn't realize why until I saw you again. Until I knew about River. My father didn't want me to know you were pregnant."

It also explained his toast the day he finally let me free. He'd known about Tyra having my baby and had been waiting for me to lead them both right to him. It was all I could do not to rush home and slit his throat. The plan be damned.

"The silver BMW," she whispered so low I almost didn't catch it. "I'd been noticing a silver BMW everywhere I went for months. At first, I thought it was just a popular style until I realized the license plate was always the same. I reported the car to campus police, but they blew me off. After that, I never saw one with that license plate again."

"He was having you watched."

She gave me a hard look. "You still haven't told me *why*."

I returned her look as I stood. "Because if it weren't for your sister, I'd be at USC playing football right now."

Tyra shot to her feet before planting her hands on her hips. Hips that had birthed my kid. Hips I wanted to hold onto while I bent her over and fucked her from behind. "My sister? What does she have to do with this?"

"She told my father about my feelings for you."

"You didn't *have* any feelings for me. At least, according to you."

Tyra folded her arms over her chest, pushing up her breasts. Luckily, she was too pissed to notice me staring. They were bigger than I remembered. I guess I had my kid to thank.

"Keep telling yourself that, Bradley. It's not going to help you get over me any faster."

River let out a cry before she could let free the barrage of curses I knew where on her tongue. As much as I wanted to console my son, I chose that moment to grab my shit and escape while she was distracted.

chapter thirty-two

The Prince

"TIE HIM TO THE CHAIR." MY TONE WASN'T THE MOST PATIENT, but I'd spent the last couple of days guarding my father in order to avoid Tyra, which meant not seeing my kid. Needless to say, it had made me a little crabby.

"I'm pretty sure I don't work for you, and I didn't come from his shriveled-up nut sack. You tie him up."

I glared at Jeremy, but it made no difference to him as Antonov leaned against the wall of the living room, making himself comfortable. Snatching the coil of rope from one of the end tables, I proceeded to tie my father's feet to the legs of the chair.

"Son, you don't have to do this," my father pleaded. I guess that after a few days of being held captive, he'd finally decided he wasn't too proud to beg.

"Shut the fuck up." I finished tying his right leg and moved onto his left before he spoke again.

"Do you honestly think Antonov won't kill you as soon as you give him what he wants? Look at how he's betrayed me."

Jeremy paused from cleaning his nails with his knife. "I was never loyal to you, bitch."

My father wisely ignored him. "I can protect you."

"You had eighteen years' worth of chances to do just that. I can protect myself now, but thanks."

I was checking the knot I tied to make sure it was secure when I heard Jeremy sigh. "You're not a killer, but you're definitely no

Boy Scout, either. Give me the fucking rope. Even your father could break free of this pitiful-ass knot."

I didn't argue as I stood back, letting Jeremy take over.

"Thirteen will never follow you if you kill me," my father warned Antonov. His voice was no longer pleading, although he hadn't managed to return to his typical cold cruelty. "You might as well dig your own grave next to mine."

"My grave was dug a long time ago, old man. You're just catching up."

Panic flashed in my father's eyes before his lips pulled back in a snarl. "I knew not to trust you. That's why I kept you close."

"Not close enough apparently. I would never have managed to convince the others that you needed to retire if you'd been more careful. To be honest, it wasn't even that hard. You're a joke."

"You're lying."

"Afraid not. You should have taken a lesson from your own history book. I thought Mr. Palmer would be the hardest to convince since he was your glorified secretary. Turns out, you should have treated him better."

"What makes you think they won't do the same to you?"

"They can't if they're all dead."

My heart dropped to my stomach hearing that. Siko, Eddie, Mr. Palmer…the entire round table had been executed. Killing my father's men hadn't been something we'd discussed. I had their deaths on my hands now, too. I shuddered.

"If I could convince them to turn on you, then I obviously can't trust them now, can I?" Jeremy questioned.

For once, my father had no immediate response. Jeremy finished tying him to the chair before stepping from the room to do God knows what. When we brought my father here, he'd sneered in disgust at the loving photos Wren and Lou had filled their home with. A home that was no longer because of him. Once Crow and Fox come up empty in their search for Wren at the hospital, they'd come here where they'd find my father gift wrapped and waiting.

"What exactly is your plan, son? You think my enemies will go quietly into the night once they kill me?"

"I know they won't, which is why you're here."

With Wren's help, I used the bait my father had ruthlessly dangled to set a different trap. If there was anyone Fox wanted dead more than Wren and Lou or that Crow hated enough to override concern for his son, it was Franklin Rees. My father would be the diversion we needed to end this once and for all. All I needed was to get the three of them in the same room for the first time in thirty years and let nature take its course. Fate would decide who was the last man standing and so would begin part two of my plan.

"And once I'm dead? Do you actually think there's anywhere you can run? You're a loose end. Crow and Fox won't make the same mistake I did." He paused, a twisted gleam in his eye. "Neither will Antonov."

"I have no intention of running. Blackwood Keep is my home, my *real* birthright, and I'm going to make it my business to keep it safe from people like you."

My father's lips curled. "If I'd known how weak you'd be, I would have ripped you from your mother's womb when I had the chance."

His cruel words that would have normally left me feeling empty missed their mark. The place inside of me that had been hollow for so long was now overflowing. I wouldn't dwell on the reasons why. Not until I knew they were safe.

Seeing this, my father's sharp smile had me freezing. "Or maybe I should have done you a favor and put that sickly little bastard of yours out of his misery. You should have seen him when he was born," my father continued with a disgusted shake of his head. "Frail and useless like his father."

Before I could react and mete out proper justice, Antonov

appeared, seemingly from thin air. Gripping my father's face in a hold harsh enough to make him cry out, Jeremy rammed his head into the wall behind him. The blow had been hard enough to knock my father out cold. Only then did I feel my hands relax from the fists that had formed.

"Thanks."

As expected, Antonov didn't bother responding as he placed a piece of duct tape from the roll he'd found over my father's mouth. Once he was done, Jeremy turned to face me, his visage black.

"They're here. We need to move."

I quickly ran through everything that could possibly go wrong as I followed Jeremy into the night. Crow and Fox were both in Blackwood Keep, and it was only a matter of time before their paths converged. The best-case scenario was that all three men ended up dead. The worst case was that we did. Me, Antonov, and everyone we cared about. It didn't seem like much of an issue for Jeremy, though.

"They know your friend isn't at the hospital," he announced once he finished picking the lock on the house across the street. According to Lou, the residents were away on vacation for the next few days. Luckily, she hadn't bothered to ask why I'd been curious since she wasn't interested in speaking to me longer than necessary. "They should be here any minute."

Wren had been discharged this morning and had been busy making sure part two went according to plan. We hadn't told anyone else about our plan because too many moving parts meant too many chances for something to go wrong. This wasn't a game of chess where lives lost meant resetting the board and starting over.

Once inside, I followed him upstairs and stood by quietly while Jeremy set up his sniper rifle in the open window. He made quick work of it despite the room and house being dark. We couldn't risk turning on any lights and alerting Crow or Fox. It was well after midnight, and everyone in the neighborhood was out for the count.

I wasn't sure how much time passed, my stomach in knots as we waited for a car I didn't recognize to slowly appear. I knew well before the man cloaked in a dark suit stepped from the car that the show had begun. He scanned the street, his face a cold mask, and his blond hair streaked with gray blowing in the breeze as he ensured himself he was undetected and alone.

"That's Fox," Antonov announced.

I didn't respond as I watched the man round the side of the house, his gun already out. Leaving the door unlocked would have been too obvious, and I imagined a man like Fox would have been sharp enough to be suspicious. Instead, we'd left the tiniest crack in a window. Small enough that it could be waved off as simple carelessness. Barely a minute passed before I heard the sound of another car approaching. I turned my focus from the house, expecting to see another unfamiliar car.

My heart stopped at the army-green SUV, slowly making its way toward the house.

What the hell was he doing here? Spring break had ended two days ago. I watched, feeling helpless as my best friend parked his G-Wagon behind Fox's car. Ever was none the wiser of the danger he was about to enter. It wasn't until he was out of his ride and halfway up the drive that my feet remembered how to move. I made it to the door before I felt myself being grabbed.

"What the hell are you doing?" I roared at Jeremy. I didn't care if anyone heard us or not. The plan was as good as blown as far as I was concerned.

"If you go down there, it's over."

"If I don't go down there, my friend dies."

"I'm okay with that," he easily replied. I could have broken every bone in his body when Jeremy shrugged.

"I'm not." Putting all my considerable strength into freeing my arm, I rammed my elbow into his face, missing his nose by a hair and hitting his cheek. It was enough to dislodge his hold, though, and I was out the bedroom door.

What if I was already too late? What if Ever was already dead?

I hadn't heard any gunshots, but that didn't mean anything. I reached the bottom of the stairs and was almost to the front door when a blow to the back of my skull sent me crashing to my knees. I tried to fight the ringing in my head and the darkness closing in, but a moment later, I was out.

I awoke sometime later, surprised to find that I hadn't been tied up. Groaning, I held my head, knowing this headache wouldn't be clearing anytime soon. I blinked to clear my vision and found Antonov standing by the window, peering out with his brows bunched. It took me a few seconds to remember why he'd knocked me out.

"If my friend is dead, you're next," I told him, meaning every word and to hell with my soul.

Shrugging, Jeremy continued to watch Wren and Lou's house. "He's not dead."

"And how the hell do you know that?"

"No gunshots."

"That doesn't mean shit. Fox could have slit his fucking throat."

Jeremy looked at me, incredulity in his black gaze. "Then why bother bringing a gun?"

"Are you sure you would have heard it? He could have a silencer," I argued though I didn't remember seeing one.

"Maybe." He returned his head toward the window once again. "We don't know if the kid is alive, but I do know you wouldn't be if you had gone over there. If Franklin isn't dead, then Fox must know by now that Crow is coming, which means he needs Ever alive. What he doesn't need is you."

"Suddenly, you care?"

Jeremy barked a laugh that made me bristle. "Fuck no. I care about the plan. If you try to deviate again, I'll remove your head from your shoulders and mail it to your girlfriend and son. We clear?"

"Fuck you." I got to my feet before joining him at the window. "So, what now? I'm not leaving him in there. I don't care about your goddamn threats."

Jeremy nodded toward the street. "Look."

Another car approached for the third time that night, and I knew before he ever emerged that it was Crow this time. A huge part of me was relieved, but a small part wasn't. I knew what it meant for Wren and Ever.

Wren wasn't quite cold enough to lead his father into an ambush, no matter how he felt about the man as a father. He'd left Crow a message telling him our plan and thus giving his father the upper hand, and then he'd given Crow a choice. He could come for Franklin and Fox, seek vengeance and vindication or… he could walk away and be a father instead. Seeing Crow here made it clear the choice he'd made. He'd chosen Exiled and Thirteen over his sons once again.

"If fate is kind, your friend just might live."

I shook my head, realizing there was no such thing as a sure or easy path. Following your heart was the only option. Crow's wrong choice just might lead him to save his son's life. Had he chosen right, to be a father, he would have unknowingly left his youngest son to die.

"I can't just stand here. I need to do something."

"You can," Jeremy said as he bent to peer out of his scope. "You can wait and shut the fuck up."

I let my gaze roam the room as I stood perfectly still until I found what I was looking for. Of course, I'd considered this happening, but it wasn't possible to get my hands on the drugs I'd need without committing a few felonies and getting caught. Once I was sure Jeremy's focus was on the house across the street, I tiptoed over to the nightstand. I only had one shot at this, and I couldn't risk waking the neighbors with an all-out brawl. Curling my fingers around the heavy lamp, I yanked it from the wall. By the time Jeremy caught on, it was too late. I never thought I'd see shock in Jeremy Antonov's eyes. I made sure I put extra power behind the blow. Clutching his head, Jeremy hit the floor a moment later.

No time to waste, I lifted the rope I stashed from my backpack and got to work mimicking the knot he'd used to tie my father. I wouldn't make the same mistake he did of not tying me up. Once he was secure and no longer a threat, I rushed from the room, taking his pistol with me. When I stepped outside, I felt a chill that had nothing to do with the wind. I could very well end up fucking dead, but I was determined to finish what I'd started. I didn't take the front door like Ever or Crow or even the window Fox had crawled through. Fishing the key Wren had loaned me, I entered through the back door. I could hear voices speaking low, each one angry.

"We're all smart men, so we know what's at stake," I heard my father say. A flash of irritation that he wasn't dead yet filled me. Apparently, I'd overestimated Fox's bloodthirst. "It seems we're also at an impasse. Perhaps we can come to some arrangement instead."

"You shot my son." *Crow.* "I'm not interested in negotiating."

"Fine. Have it your way. I only need to convince one of you to spare my life." Fear that my father would somehow weasel his way out of this had me tiptoeing forward. I'd make the kill myself if I had to and deal with the fallout later, whether it be my soul or my life. At least River and Tyra would be safe.

I was almost near the living room when I felt a hand on my shoulder. Panicking, I spun around, aiming without hesitation. I realized, with a sigh of audible relief, that I was pointing a gun at my best friend's head. His golden eyes blinked in surprise.

"What are you doing here?" we both whispered at the same time.

Ever waved his hand impatiently. "I'll explain later. You?"

I nodded toward the living room. "I was waiting for them when I saw you arrive."

His gaze flitted from me to the gun to the living room before he spoke, his voice a harsh whisper. "What the hell were you planning to do when they got here, and when were you going to tell me about this?"

"Nothing, and I wasn't. Not until it was over." I paused, swallowing hard. "Your father is in there."

Ever's golden eyes flared with anger. I'd worry over whether he would ever forgive me for sending his father to slaughter later. "I know. I hid when I heard Fox and Franklin talking, and then I saw Crow come in."

I shook my head in awe. My best friend definitely had nine fucking lives. "I thought you were in trouble. How the hell did you escape their notice?"

"What makes you think he escaped our notice?"

I spun on my heel, seeing Fox and Crow standing before me. My father must have still been tied up thankfully.

"Put down the gun, son, and join us."

Even though Fox had been speaking to me, his gun was trained on Ever. Turning his head toward his partner turned rival, I realized he'd just gained the upper hand. "You, too," he told Sean.

Fuck.

When I'd sifted through all the ways my plan could go to shit, being the sole cause hadn't been one of them.

Fuck, fuck, fuck!

I dropped my gun, and Sean did the same when Fox grabbed Ever, pressing the Glock to his skull. A moment later, we were all huddled in the living room. I ignored the smug look my father tossed me even though he was the only one tied up and truly defenseless. Knocking out and tying up Jeremy Antonov had seemed like a good idea at the time, but now I wasn't so sure.

"You must be Danny Boy," Fox greeted Ever, using the pseudonym Ever had used when he infiltrated Exiled two years ago. "I'd say it's a pleasure to meet you finally, but that's only because I get to put a bullet in you." Fox kept his gun trained on Ever, the only thing keeping Crow and me at bay, as he surveyed the room.

His gaze finally landed on me.

"A fox is never the prey. As impressive as this set up is, you should have considered that before you sprung your trap. I am, however, willing to acknowledge your noble effort. Unfortunately, it's going to get you killed." His attention shifted to my father. "Unless...you're willing to bargain?"

My father spat on the floor.

I rolled my eyes because I figured as much. There was no love lost between my father and me.

"Well, then," Fox said with amusement in his gaze. "I guess you die first since I have no need for you." He lifted his gun, pointing it right at my heart.

I closed my eyes, thinking only of River and Tyra so as not to give away the colossal mistake Fox had just made. A moment later, I felt two quick vibrations in my pocket.

It was the signal from Wren I'd been waiting for.

Even though Fox's gun was no longer trained on Ever, Crow was too far away to reach his son in time. Besides, nothing was faster than a bullet.

I took a deep breath, said a quick prayer, and then I ducked.

Before I could even draw my next breath, the sound of the window behind me shattering followed and then the wet crunch of a bullet piercing a skull. I didn't see whose, but I had a pretty good idea. Slowly, I opened my eyes.

My legs protested, threatening to collapse right from under me as I stood. I couldn't take my gaze away from the dead body and unseeing eyes. Blood and brain matter splattered the wall, and a little had gotten on Ever, but he was too stunned to notice.

Nathaniel Fox was dead.

"Son."

I finally looked away from the carnage, but it wasn't my father who had spoken. No, it had been Crow who spoke as he took a hesitant step toward his youngest son. Other than the cleft chin hidden under Crow's beard and the dark hair they shared, the two looked nothing alike.

"In a moment, you're going to hear sirens," I told Crow, making him pause in his tracks. His blue-gray eyes seemed to pierce straight through me. "They're here for you both, but they don't have to be." His gaze followed mine to where my father was still tied to the chair, his face void of color as he stared at his dead rival. "You can still walk away."

Crow walking away would mean that my father would live, and then Tyra and River would never be safe. It was a chance I never thought I'd see myself taking, but there was no clear right or wrong answer.

Crow looked at Ever, longing in gaze, and Ever stared right back, giving nothing away. Ever was too stubborn to make the choice easy for Crow. No, the father would have to decide on his own.

Crow shocked us both when he detoured toward the door without looking back. Unfortunately, my father had chosen that moment to break free of his stunned silence.

"You're a fool," he spat at Crow. "I own this town and every cop in it. They won't touch me. They can't. I'll find you and make you watch your boys scream and die in agony."

Crow had reached the threshold of the living room, pausing when my father uttered his threat. Ever and I both seemed to hold our breath as we waited. Crow seemed to mull it over before resuming his strides. A moment later, all that was left was the sound of the front door opening and softly closing behind him.

I stood there, wondering what to do. Should I take Tyra and

296 | B.B. REID

River and run as far and fast as I could? Ever seemed to be contemplating the same before he stepped over Fox and laid a hand on my shoulder. "Are you okay?"

"Are you?" I challenged.

Neither of us answered.

A low chuckle drew our gazes to my father. "I'm going to enjoy making you beg, boy."

I suddenly felt the wind howling outside on my nape. It whistled as it blew through the hole in the window. My gaze then traveled to Fox's gun that had skidded across the floor, less than a foot from my father's feet. Feeling the hunch burning in my gut, I crossed the room, enjoying the way my father's eyes widened in fear as I approached.

To his surprise and mine, I simply untied him.

"Don't think you can convince me to show you mercy," he spat once he was free. I didn't respond as I put some distance between us, steering clear of the window. I kept my expression impassive even when Ever began looking at me like I was crazy. The front door opened and closed, and a moment later, Wren and Jeremy appeared.

Antonov, of course, was pissed. Not only had I gotten the drop on him, but the plan had failed. "Why the hell is he still alive?" he snarled.

No one got the chance to answer.

My father, as I predicted, had lunged for Fox's gun. I held his gaze as he held me at gunpoint. I wouldn't give him the pleasure of bargaining or begging. "After I kill you and your friends, I'll be sure to pay a visit to your son."

"How about you tell Fox I said hèllo instead?"

The confusion in my father's eyes was only momentary.

Glass shattered.

Skull fractured.

Blood and brains spattered.

My bastard father was finally dead. Everyone's gaze followed mine to the broken window, where there were now two identical holes. The wind outside whistled louder now. The sound of sirens drowned it out a moment later. Even though Fox and Franklin were both dead, I realized just how fucked my plan had gone. Ever, Wren, Antonov, and I were now standing over two dead bodies and no explanation. The sirens were too close to get away in time.

"Shit," Ever breathed, the first to speak and verbalize just how fucked we were.

My shoulders sagged as I looked at Wren and Antonov. They were both still thinking of a way out of this.

Wren turned to Ever. I knew what he thought before he even spoke. He was willing to take the fall for his younger brother. "I'll stay behind. Go while you still can." I wasn't expecting him to face me next. "You, too." I was already turning him down when he spoke again. "Think of River."

My lips slammed shut, but my feet refused to move. This had all been my idea. If anyone took the fall, it would be me.

Wren looked at Antonov. "I don't give a shit what you do."

"Likewise," Jeremy returned.

"Let's just all go," Ever suggested. "It's our word against theirs." He nodded toward Franklin and Fox. I bit my lip to keep from pointing out that defense only worked when the opposition was *still alive*. We all had their blood on our hands, clothes, and shoes, and since there was no sign of forced entry or a struggle, it was an open and shut case.

The squad cars had swarmed the neighborhood before we could agree, so as one, we each headed for the front door. By the time we poured out into the night, the police were already out of their cars, guns pointed.

But it wasn't at us.

Slowly making his way down the driveway across the street, was Crow. His arms were raised, and the sniper rifle used to kill Franklin and Fox was firmly clutched in his hand.

chapter thirty-three

The Pawn

AFTER THREE MONTHS OF BEING HOSPITALIZED, RIVER WAS FINALLY going home.

I tried and failed not to dwell on the fact that I hadn't seen his father in over a week. Not since I found the photos, and he left without offering much of an explanation. Franklin Rees using those photos of me to torture his son had only sparked more questions than answers.

My friends had also been too busy to stop by. I figured Jamie and Bee had finally headed back to Philly while Ever went back to Cornell. Yesterday, my father, our only visitor in two days, had come bearing a brand-new car seat for River. As nervous as I was about no longer having the NICU staff for support, if I never saw another hospital again, it would be too soon. It was frustrating since I still harbored dreams of being a doctor. I'd gotten an email today from Harvard, reminding me of the course section for the fall semester coming up. Never mind that I'd had them picked out from the moment I received Harvard's acceptance letter last year. I never once imagined it not coming to fruition, though.

As if reading my thoughts, River made a noise from his crib. I smiled down at him dressed in a blue onesie. The words on the front read My Favorite Uncle's Wingman.

A gift from Jamie, of course.

Once River was bundled in his car seat, despite the warm weather, and the discharge papers were signed, I left the hospital with my son for the very first time. I promised Coach that we'd be ready by three. Five minutes past the hour, my father was a no-show. Oddly, the last person I expected to arrive in front of the hospital entrance was River's father.

And he was driving a minivan.

Despite the tension when his gaze met mine, seeing him climb from the van...I burst out laughing. "Tell me you did not buy that because of River."

Vaughn's brows dipped as he watched me laugh at his expense. River's expression matched his father's, but I couldn't stop. Oh, God. It was just too much.

"What? Aren't kids required to ride in these things?"

I swiped the tear that escaped from the corner of my eye. "It's the law that kids under a certain height, age, and weight ride in the back secured by a car seat and safety belt. They don't require the back seat to be inside of a tank." *And a hideous one at that.*

What was so comical, however, was seeing Vaughn drive it. The minivan was a far cry from his panty-dropping Lamborghini. Not that I'd ever risk putting my child in what was essentially a toy car.

Vaughn's shoulder sagged with palpable relief. "Oh, thank God." He then looked at me, his gaze sheepish. "Are you ready?"

My jaw dropped when his cheeks heated. Vaughn Rees was actually embarrassed.

I immediately sobered.

"I'm sorry. I shouldn't have laughed." Against my better judgment, I laid my hand on his arm. The muscles bunched when he tensed from my touch, so I dropped my hand. "It was a wonderful gesture. Really."

He nodded before picking up River's car seat. He then kissed his son's cheek, mumbling something that sounded like "I missed you" before carrying him to the van. Silently, I hoped there was some sort of flexible return policy on that thing. I wrinkled my nose at muted gray paint. Even brand new, it was like Vaughn purposely picked the ugliest one he could find.

"I should call my father," I announced once we were all inside and strapped in. Instead of riding in the front, I'd chosen to ride in the back with the baby. "He was supposed to pick us up." I left out the reason being that River and I hadn't seen Vaughn in over a week.

"Don't bother. He told me what time you were expecting him. I told him I wanted to be the one to bring you guys home."

"Oh…thanks."

Vaughn didn't respond, and the ride was mostly silent after that. Music played, but he kept the volume low even though he usually liked it loud enough to be earsplitting. River began crying, so I spent the next fifteen minutes trying to console him. There wasn't much I could do without removing him from the seat. My attention had been fixed on River the entire time, so when the van slowed, I realized much too late that Vaughn hadn't taken us to my father's house.

We were at the beach house.

"What are we doing here?"

Vaughn pretended he didn't hear me when he hopped out and pulled open the sliding door on River's side before removing him. "Come on."

Of course, he'd give me an order rather than an explanation.

We entered through the kitchen, and I wasn't sure what I was expecting, but I found the house oddly silent. Even the waves from the beach seemed to be whispering. Vaughn led us through the kitchen and into the living room, where I found every single piece of furniture missing, and my friends waiting.

"Welcome home!"

Of course, River, who had only just stopped crying, started up again. I barely noticed their apologetic cringes as I looked around in awe. The living room hadn't been left bare. Instead, the furniture had been replaced with decorations to welcome River home.

Blue, green, and silver balloons covered the floor and even floated like centerpieces in each of the four corners. It was the only constant in the room.

The left side of the room had been decorated in what was clearly a nautical theme. Hung between the windows was a large ship wheel and the words *Ahoy, Captain River!* The small table covered by a navy and white striped cloth held refreshments, which included a three-layered cake in the center that was actually shaped like a ship. The life ring hanging in front read Welcome Home, and there was a banner strung across made of little red anchors.

The right side of the room had been turned into a tiny farm. A cardboard red and white barn along with a green tractor had been erected. There were even real bales of hay in front of yet another short table, but this one held wrapped gifts and cardboard cutouts of sheep, pigs, chickens, cows, and even a dog.

The third and longest wall resembled a football field. A green rug with yard lines, two field goal posts, and footballs at each end adorned the floor. A realistic scoreboard hung from the wall that read #TeamRiverRees on top. White wooden chairs, the only seating in the room, had been placed against the wall below it. Each one had jerseys of varying adult sizes with River's name hanging from the back, and I knew they were meant to be party favors for our friends.

The fourth and final wall was the shortest since it had been cut out to make an entryway to the kitchen. It was the most confusing of all the themes but not because of the top hats, bow ties, and mustaches decorating the wall. But because of the empty table covered by a black tablecloth.

"So, what exactly is the theme?" I asked to keep from crying. This was more than I expected, more than I deserved. My friends were the best, and I'd been ready to give them all up over my broken heart. I knew now that a piece of it had remained all along and intact—because of them.

302 | B.B. REID

Vaughn looked sheepish as he scratched the back of his neck. "We had creative differences."

"But which one do you like best?" Jamie asked as he swaggered over holding a cane and wearing a black tux, top hat, mustache, and round spectacles with the words *Oh, baby* on the top of the rim. His mahogany hair had even been slicked back with gel and oil. It was apparent which theme had been his. Bee was dressed identically, even going so far as wearing the mustache. The two of them made an intriguing yet perfect combination.

"Give it a rest, Jameson," Lou said as she came to stand beside him. I wasn't at all surprised to she was dressed like Olive Oil, making me immediately search the room for Wren. My eyes nearly fell out of my head when I saw him wearing a black collared shirt, red ribbon tied around his throat, light blue chinos, and a white sailor cap. It was impossible not to shed a few tears after seeing the broody, ex-gangbanger wearing a costume. "Yours doesn't even make sense. His name is *River*. Obviously, going full nautical made the most sense."

"Yeah, you're right," Ever deadpanned as he joined our circle. "It's obvious as fuck."

I almost choked when I realized he was dressed in a rooster costume. I couldn't help gaping at the former king of Brynwood, who'd made a reputation for being unapproachable. Four wasn't far behind him, and of course, she wore a white feathered skirt with a white long-sleeve bodysuit, yellow chucks, and a red cone on her head. They were all dressed in costume despite it being the middle of April.

"As opposed to the unoriginal farm animal theme?" Lou sassed back.

"It's classic."

"It's cliché."

I turned to peer up at Vaughn, who was ignoring them all as he unbuckled River from his car seat. "So, I suppose the football theme was your idea?"

Vaughn glanced at me before shrugging, his lips turning up in a crooked smile. River stopped crying the moment Vaughn lifted him, and I pursed my lips, hoping this wasn't the beginning of him demanding to be held all the time.

Without explanation, Vaughn disappeared upstairs with River. I was ready to follow him out of curiosity when my father walked up to me and pulled me aside. I hadn't even realized he was here. Ever's parents, Evelyn and Thomas, were there as well though they stood on opposite sides of the room. Evelyn was currently engaged in a conversation with Winny, Wren's grandmother.

"Vaughn did good," my father said with a nod as he looked around.

I blinked stupidly. I hadn't even considered the possibility of this being Vaughn's idea. My stubbornness had made a baby shower impossible, but this more than made up for that. Staring at the mountain of wrapped gifts waiting on Four and Ever's table, I realized once again how unprepared I was for motherhood. I hadn't even considered all of the things River would need once he was home. Sweat beaded my brow and upper lip as I ran through the list in my head. It was never-ending.

Right now, all I had was the small supply of diapers and wipes the hospital had sent home with me, a couple of baby bottles, and my breast milk.

"I just want you to know that this doesn't change anything," my father told me, drawing my attention back to him and out of the turmoil wreaking havoc in my head. "I'm still proud of you."

I felt my legs quake hearing that.

"Thanks, Coach." I had to clear my throat of the raspiness before speaking again. "That means a lot." It was a simple response despite the emotions running wild inside of me.

"So when the fall comes, I want you back at school, Tyra. Don't worry about River," he quickly added when my lips parted in protest. "I'll take care of my grandson."

"Dad, it's not just River. I don't have the money."

"I have some savings," he announced, making me blink. I knew my father's salary. No matter how much money he had stashed, it couldn't have been enough to pay for three more years of out-of-state tuition at a private ivy league. "It's enough to cover you for the rest of your time at Harvard."

My stomach dipped but not with relief.

I knew without him elaborating that he meant his retirement fund. The one he'd been working for his entire life. He had intended to withdraw every single cent for me, the daughter who'd already disappointed him once by getting knocked up at eighteen and losing her scholarship.

I couldn't and wouldn't let him do that.

"We don't have to decide this now," I pleaded. I had no intention of taking his money, but immediately blowing off such a loving gesture as if he'd offered me a stick of gum seemed callous. "We've got time."

It was the truth, at least. I still had the entire summer to figure things out.

Before my father could argue, music started playing, and I felt relief flow through me for the distraction. I felt like throwing up, and it wasn't because the song playing was fucking "Baby Shark."

"Jamie, can't you play something else?" Four complained.

"No, I can't, doo doo doo doo doo doo," he sang.

And so the party began.

It lasted the rest of the afternoon and into the evening despite there not being alcohol. I scratched my head at that because it wasn't like there were other children present. Vaughn had reappeared at some point without our son, and I forced myself to stay put despite my need to check on River myself. I admitted that if not my heart, I trusted Vaughn to take care of our son.

Wren's grandmother was the first to bow out, Evelyn and Thomas were second, and my father was the last at a quarter past nine.

"For fuck's sake, I never thought they'd leave," Jamie said once the door closed behind my father. He sauntered over to the mysterious empty table, lifted the black cloth, and began setting out the beer and booze he'd stashed underneath. In no time, Jamie had the table looking like a minibar. He then switched the music over but kept the volume low before pouring everyone a shot. When he got to me, I shook my head. "Oh, come on, Ty-baby," he whined. "I saw all that titty milk you stashed in the fridge. By the time you need to pump again, it will be out of your system."

Only Jamie would make a valid point while being obnoxiously crude.

I took the shot from him, making him whoop. Vaughn frowned at me, but for once, I didn't care about the rules. Obviously, I wouldn't get wasted with my newborn sleeping upstairs. He could relax.

Too many shots later, Jamie made a liar out of me.

I wasn't falling over or wearing a lampshade, but I was pretty fucking close. When was the last time I let go? Could it have been when Vaughn last had his dick in me? Even when he'd gone down on me a week ago, I'd still been afraid. Letting go meant letting my guard down, and everyone in this room knew where that would lead.

Around two a.m., when River woke up for the third time that night, our friends finally called it quits. None of them had given me a chance to ask for a ride home. I shrugged it off. My mind was too imbibed with booze to worry about the consequences. At least now I could help Vaughn clean up before heading home. He'd gone above and beyond. It was the least I could do.

I located the trash bags and started dumping shit inside without paying much attention to what I was throwing away. Perhaps, I'd overestimated how bombed I was, or maybe I was just that eager to pass out.

"Why don't we leave this for the morning?" Vaughn suggested, taking away the stuffed animal and the trash bag I almost tossed it in. He'd been upstairs putting River back to sleep. "Come on." He jerked his head toward the stairs, and I followed him for some reason.

Halfway up, I snorted. "I'm going to be a terrible mom, you know." Vaughn peered over his shoulder, expecting an explanation for my randomness. "I didn't even remember to get all the things River would need once he came home." Stopping, I plopped down on the third step from the landing. "God, what am I going to do?" I moaned before peering into the darkness below as if it held the answers. Vaughn was so silent I'd forgotten he was there until he lifted me. I didn't speak until he carried me into the master bedroom. "Why are we in here?"

"Because you need to sleep."

"So, why are you in here?" Despite the third degree, I didn't fight him when he wrestled my jeans down my legs and removed my shirt. It was the least sexy he'd ever undressed me, and yet I was blushing anyway.

"To make sure that you do."

I didn't argue when he pulled back the covers, indicating I get in. I just stared at the sheets, trying to remember why my feet wouldn't move and why the thought of sleeping in this bed, *Vaughn's* bed, made me want to throw up. Yawning, I gave up a moment later, stumbling and fumbling as I crawled inside and pulled the covers up to my chin.

"Where's River?" I asked, even as my eyes were already drifting closed.

If Vaughn answered, I didn't hear it.

The next morning, I found a glass of water and aspirin waiting for me on the nightstand. Sitting up with a groan, I swallowed the pills and downed the entire glass, but even that proved to be exhausting. I then looked around the room, my blood turning

the prince and the pawn | 307

to ice in my veins when I realized where I was and whose bed I
was in. I wasn't sure how long I glowered at the spot on the floor
where Selena had knelt before tossing back the covers. I gasped
as soon as the cool air touched my bare skin.

I was only wearing my bra and panties.

The clothes that I'd worn from the hospital were hanging
over a chair in the corner. I rushed over to them before shoving
them on. I knew by the lack of soreness between my thighs and
the marks Vaughn always left on my skin that drinking too much
had been the only mistake I'd made last night. It didn't help my
mood, though. Nothing short of getting out of this house would
do.

Downstairs, I found River and Vaughn already awake and
watching cartoons. Well...Vaughn was. The living room had
been cleared of all signs of the party. Vaughn had obviously been
up for a while.

"Hey," I greeted, albeit a bit sourly. "What time is it?"

"Ten after noon," he announced, making my heart beat a
little faster. I'd slept for ten hours. Vaughn didn't seem startled
by me sneaking up on him. In fact, he hadn't bothered to take his
eyes off the TV. I kicked myself for sleeping so late. Thankfully,
River didn't look like he'd suffered.

"Why didn't you wake me?"

He shrugged. "What for?"

"So I could take care of River?"

Losing his patience, he finally turned his head away from
Blue's Clues. "As you can see, I've done that."

Running my fingers through my hair, I told myself to get a
grip as shame filled me. I wasn't upset because of River, and yet
I was making it about him. He looked perfectly content, lying in
his father's arms. It was Vaughn and my sister that had caused the
slow slip of my sanity. How could he put me in that bed and in
that room after what he'd done with her in there? How could he
think I'd be okay reliving it?

308 | B.B. REID

Rather than ask, I forced myself to take my own advice about not changing the past and let it go. "I'm sorry. Thank you for looking after River."

Vaughn looked down his nose at me, telling me I'd somehow put my foot in my mouth again. "You don't need to thank me for taking care of my son."

"Fine. Thank you for letting me sleep in. Now that I'm awake, though, we should get going." I paused, chewing on my lip. "Can you give us a ride home?"

Vaughn stood from the couch, but the relief I felt was short-lived. "You are home." He started for the stairs with River, and by the time he reached them, I shook free of my shock.

"What do you mean?" I squeaked as I trailed him upstairs. I hated that my voice didn't sound stronger. "We can't stay here."

Vaughn entered one of the spare bedrooms, and I followed. What I found inside—the walls painted to look like raging waves—took my breath away, and I forgot all about the bomb Vaughn dropped in my lap.

He'd turned the spare bedroom into a nursery.

Everything River would need was right inside this room. There was a crib, a changing table fully stocked, and even a rocking chair in the corner. Vaughn crossed the room and placed River inside the gray crib before ushering me out and shutting the door. I wanted to open it again and admire it some more. It was perfect. I almost felt guilty for wanting to take River away.

"Why can't you stay?"

As patiently as I could, I explained why that would be a huge mistake. Nothing good could come of it. "Because that's something parents do when they're together, which you and I are not. We're barely civil, Vaughn."

"It's not a big deal. I can sleep in the third bedroom."

"And where do I sleep?" I challenged.

"The master bedroom is bigger and closer to River. You'll be comfortable in there."

"You mean the one where I caught you and my sister together?"

Vaughn's lips snapped shut at the reminder. I could tell he hadn't even thought of that. It was almost like my sister had ceased to exist to him. Stupidly, the thought filled my belly with warmth.

"Then I'll take the master," he continued to bargain. "You can take the spare."

"But that's what you're not getting!" I exploded. I couldn't just feel the sob clogging my throat. I could hear it trying to break free. "I don't want to be here. I don't want to be trapped inside of these walls and reminded of what you did!" I'd needed alcohol last night just to bear it.

For some reason, I kept that part to myself. It had all been for River even though he'd slept the entire party. Secretly, I admitted that I hadn't wanted to put my feelings before my friends and family yet again. Not after all the trouble they'd gone through for River and me.

So I drowned myself in alcohol to hide the drowning I felt inside.

Vaughn glowered down at me for a long time. If he felt remorse for the fumble he'd made, he didn't show it. Nostrils flaring, he finally spoke. "Then do what you want, but River stays here."

I didn't follow him when he pushed past me for the stairs.

I snagged the keys to the hideous minivan the moment Vaughn dropped his guard. Some detectives had shown up to speak to him, and although I wanted to know the reason why, I realized this would be my only chance at freedom.

Technically, he wasn't holding me hostage, but he also knew I wasn't going anywhere without River. It was a clever move. To keep me captive without breaking the law.

I had the baby buckled in and was speeding away by the time Vaughn had caught on. From the rearview mirror, I watched him stare at us, driving away until he disappeared from view. Judging by his scowl, I knew he'd make me pay. He could try, but I wasn't about to let him trap me in a beautiful glass house on a beach like I was Julia fucking Roberts.

I found myself driving aimlessly around Blackwood Keep. My father's house and our friends were the first places he'd look. It wasn't like I planned to go on the lam or anything. I just needed a peaceful place to think.

Somehow, I ended up at Macchicino's of all places. River and I snagged one of the last empty tables, and with pen in hand, I inhaled the scent of coffee beans as I stared hopelessly at job applications. Filling them out felt like giving up, a betrayal of the dream I'd worked hard for, but what choice did I have? I couldn't let my dad drain his savings, and with my GPA, I had no hope of getting another scholarship, not one that could cover my entire tuition. I had to accept the fact that I wasn't going back to Harvard.

Twenty minutes passed before I felt someone standing over me. Heart in my throat, I looked up, expecting to see my son's father. Maybe my old job hadn't been the best place to hide. I felt relief when I looked into the eyes of a stranger instead. The first words I thought of when I described her in my head was tall and lithe. She reminded me of Bee except for the dark hair cropped short and the extra years this woman had on her.

"I'm sorry to disturb you, but is this seat taken? All of the other tables were full." I checked on River, who was sound asleep, before waving my hand toward the empty seat. "Thanks," she whispered as she sat across from me. I watched her gaze drift to River, and then her smile brightened. "Cute kid."

"Appreciate it." I then went back to staring at the job applications.

"I just had one myself," she announced even though I didn't ask. "Well...if you consider two years ago recent. They grow up so fast. She'll be three this November."

I nodded because it seemed like the polite thing to do. Unfortunately, she was one of those people who couldn't take a hint.

"You must have just had him. How old is your little guy?"

I felt my stomach dip. This had been the question I'd been dreading. I debated not responding, but I didn't want to be a bitch to someone just making conversation. As unwanted as it may be. "Three months." I looked up from the applications in time to see her surprise. I could read the indecision of whether to remark on his size or not in her eyes and decided to put her out of her misery. "He was born prematurely."

"Oh..." She grappled for an appropriate response. "Well then, I'm happy for you both."

"Thanks. It was all him," I admitted despite her being a stranger. "He's a fighter."

"So, what's his name if you don't mind me asking?"

I mind, but it hasn't stopped you before. I forced myself to respond. "River."

"Oh, how cute! How did you come up with that?"

My stomach twisted again. "I think I saw it in a baby book," I lied.

"Well, it's a great choice. He's going to be a lady killer, I can tell. Maybe River and my daughter can have a playdate sometime. Her name is Alison."

I laughed at that, but it wasn't forced. "I think River is a long way from making dates."

"Well, you never know." She reached into her purse and quickly pulled out a pad and pen. "Here's my number if you change your mind." She wrote down her number and then her name, and I snorted when I saw that it was Charlie. It was obviously short for something, but I didn't ask. When she slid the paper over, I politely took it and stuck it inside of River's diaper bag. It had his name on it and everything, a gift from his uncle Ever.

Charlie then peered at the applications in front of me. "You're looking for a job?" She then gave me a frustrated look—one that said she found it impossible to pry without being rude. "You barely look older than sixteen. I-I thought you might be in college or something."

"I was, but it's not really an option anymore."

"Oh." She flashed me a look of pity that made me want to stick my pen in her eye. "Is his father not around?"

"He is." I once again decided to put her out of her misery when she simply stared at me, waiting to hear what was stopping me from going back to school. "Let's just say Harvard is expensive and leave it at that."

She sat back in her chair, her lips round in awe. "Harvard... wow. That's pretty impressive. So what were you studying?"

"Well, I haven't declared a major yet, but I plan to study medicine." I looked at River. "I can always give nursing a try later."

"Sweetie, I have nothing against nursing. My mother was one, and no one worked harder, but this is *Harvard* we're talking about. You have to go back."

"I can't go back," I snapped, forgetting all about being polite. Then again, it wasn't polite for a stranger to judge my decisions. With or without the facts. "Even if I worked sixteen jobs this summer, there's no way I can make that much money in time."

She pursed her red-painted lips, and then I froze when her gaze slowly raked my form. I had already grabbed the handle of River's car seat and was about to leave when she spoke. "What if I told you I had a job that could guarantee you'll make the money in time?"

I felt my ass touching the seat again despite my

reservations. "I'd ask you what kind of job could possibly pay that much."

Her expression was curious as she seemed to contemplate something. "Do me a favor…promise not to freak out when I ask you this next thing."

I kept my expression impassive, not willing to give an inch. "That depends on what you ask."

Charlie's smile was nonthreatening, but I was still on edge, especially when she spoke. "It's just one little thing. Stand up and slowly turn for me."

chapter thirty-four

The Prince

DIDN'T CHASE AFTER TYRA AS SHE PROBABLY EXPECTED, MOSTLY because she'd left me without a car and a note.

Seems to me like we both need some time alone to think.

The joke, she'd find, was on her. The only thing I could think about was getting my hands around her throat and how much time I'd spend in prison if I choked the life out of River's mother. He was what kept me from pouncing on her when she waltzed through the door hours later. Neither of us spoke as I followed her upstairs and into the bathroom. I silently sat on the toilet as she carefully washed the day from River in his tiny bathtub.

The moment she closed the door to his room after he was dry, fed, and asleep, I had her hair in my hands and was pushing her against the wall.

"Don't you ever do that again."

"Do what?" she challenged, pretending to be unfazed. Fortunately, I knew her better than she knew herself. I also knew that she was terrified, and her pussy was probably wet, too. "Take my child with me when I leave the house?"

"You know what the fuck I mean. You should have told me where you were taking him."

"Were you really concerned about him, or were you just pissed that I left?"

"I'd say it was fifty-fifty."

Actually, it was ninety-ten. Ninety percent pissed and ten

percent concerned for them both. Jeremy had ensured that no one would retaliate over my father's death, but Fox was still a big question mark. He had a son and daughter, Royal and Scarlett—twins, who were only a year or two younger. Wren, who had delivered the news to Royal about Fox's death himself, had assured me that it was no love lost, but that didn't help me sleep better at night. It didn't stop me from wanting to keep River and Tyra close. Sometimes all that mattered was the principle.

"Well, we're back now." Tyra's flippant tone and that twinkle in her gaze boiled my blood. She knew it would piss me the fuck off. "Have you used the time to think?"

"I thought about a lot of things," I said as I trapped her more firmly against the wall. I pressed my hips against hers, leaving no space at all between us. "Mostly, I thought about what I might do if you continue to test me."

"I'm not—"

God, help me. I kissed her before she could finish that sentence. Tyra had no idea how much my father had changed me. I'd do everything in my power not to give her a demonstration. Secretly, I admitted that I was scared shitless of losing her for good. The way she moaned as she kissed me back told me I hadn't just yet despite what she claimed.

I tore my lips from hers, eager to devour every inch as they moved down her neck. I wanted to sink my teeth into her as I licked the spot where her pulse pounded. Somehow, after corrupting her so completely, she still tasted ripe for picking. Lifting her up before she could come to her senses, I dove my hands inside her leggings, kneading that perky ass she loved to torture me with. Tyra lived inside of her head and touching her was one of the few ways I could get her out of it.

Unlike Tyra, her T-shirt was a fragile thing. With a snip of my knife and barely a tug, it tore right off her torso. I barely noticed the weird bra she was wearing before I removed it. As quickly as I chucked it, it was a distant memory. I nearly swallowed my tongue, seeing how swollen her nipples were. This was some next level shit. I had my lips around one of her puckered nips before I could even form another thought. Tyra made a sound that was drowned out by my own groan the moment I tasted something sweet and creamy on my tongue. I suckled eagerly, only vaguely realizing that it must have been her breast milk. Before I knew what was happening, I began gorging myself.

"Vaughn…" I gripped her hips in warning when I felt her hands in my hair, tugging. I couldn't stop. Not until she was drained of every drop. "Vaughn, baby, the other one," she damn near begged.

I lifted my head enough to see that the other was now leaking too as if I'd tapped an endless well. With a growl that sounded savage to my own ears, I drew that neglected nipple between my lips and drank.

"Yes!" I heard her cry. She moved her hips, grinding her pussy against my stomach, and I could feel the damp evidence of her arousal through her leggings.

Fuck me.

This was not something I ever thought I'd do, but I was too far gone to question it. I suckled at her breasts until she tapped out, claiming she was sore. Stepping away from the wall, I hurried down the hall. I might have been dumb as shit last night, putting her in my bed to sleep, but this time, with so much at stake, I was thinking as clearly as I could with her tongue down my throat.

I burst into the spare bedroom, nearly tripping over my own feet before wisely deciding to set her down. As we fought to catch our breath, Tyra gazed up at me as if she might pounce at any moment. With the sternest expression I could muster with my dick this hard, I broke the lust-filled silence.

"Don't you dare look at me like your pussy is on a platter unless you're ready to sit on my dick."

My tone might have been harsh, but I didn't give a fuck. I'd had months of Tyra teasing me. Enough to last a lifetime.

She planted her hands on her hips as she closed the distance between us. "You're the one who brought me in here."

I knew what she was doing. She was provoking me into making the first move so that in the morning, she could blame me for her mistakes. *Not going to happen.* "To fuck, not cuddle, so what will it be?"

She shook her head though I wasn't sure why she was surprised. "You're an asshole."

"Yet, your horny ass is still standing here." Reaching behind my neck, I grabbed my T-shirt, pulling it over my head. My sweatpants were next to go while she just stood there watching me. I knew she wanted to say yes, but her pride wasn't making it easy. Neither would I. When she woke up in the morning, well fucked, I wanted her to know that it was because she'd chosen not to resist. "You can always go back to hating me in the morning."

I dropped my boxers before stepping around her and climbing onto the bed. Pretending my balls weren't damn near blue, I watched her with my arm tucked underneath my head as casually as if she were a show on TV. A moment later, she huffed and stormed from my room, and I released a quiet laugh before closing my eyes. If she thought I'd chase after her, she was dead wrong.

I had only just dozed off when I shot up in surprise.

My head wildly turned back and forth as I choked and sputtered. It felt like someone had dunked me headfirst in the ocean outside. Shivering, I blinked, desperately trying to clear the salt water dripping from my eyelashes. Meanwhile, Tyra was standing at the foot of the bed, clutching an empty bucket she'd found.

She placed her finger to her lips. "I wouldn't scream if I were you. You'll wake the baby."

"Why the fuck would I scream?"

Eyes wide, she nodded at the bed. I looked down and found a pair of black, beady eyes staring at me from the peak of a hard shell surrounded by ten legs. The sharp claws at the front clicked in warning just before the fucking crab shot forward.

"What the fuck!" Jumping from the bed, I barely escaped getting my dick trapped between those pincers. I stared in disbelief seeing two more of those things crawling around in the sheets. "Are you out of your mind!"

It wasn't really a question, but the faint cry down the hall kept her from giving me an answer. The crazy bitch turned on her heel and left to see to our son while I hurriedly pulled on the sweats I'd discarded. I then tried and failed to grab those mean fuckers. I ended up using the soaked sheets as a sack to carry the crabs downstairs and out to the beach, where they reburied themselves under the sand and tide.

For a long while after, I simply stood under the moonlight, watching the waves crash as I tried to figure out how the hell Tyra and I had gotten to this place and whether we were too far gone to ever turn back. I wouldn't be surprised if next time it were poisonous snakes that she slipped in my bed. I knew I deserved every ounce of her wrath, but it made me no less pissed the hell off.

The only sound when I returned to the house was the shower running in the master bedroom, but I headed to River's room anyway despite Tyra not being there. After confirming for myself that River was fast asleep, I made my way down the hall.

For some reason, Tyra had felt secure enough not to lock the door behind her, but I ignored my surprise as I pushed inside the master bedroom. She hadn't been in long enough for the steam to hide my view of her through the glass walls of the shower. Leaning against the jamb of the bathroom door, I licked my lips at the tempting contrast of the soap against her brown skin before stepping inside and closing the door behind me. For what I had planned, I couldn't chance River waking up again. Since my sweats were all I wore, I was naked in no time. By the time Tyra became aware of my presence, it was already too late. Her eyes were wide as she watched me step into the shower, her hands frozen around the loofah.

"Let me guess. You thought I'd let you get away with your

little stunt." Closing my hand around her wrist, I brought the hand clutching the loofah to my chest. "Clean up your mess." Every second I felt the sand between my toes and smelled the salt on my skin, I grew more irritated.

Tyra blinked at me before forcing her expression into an impassive one. "It was only crabs. I'm sure you've had them before."

Ignoring her dig, I forced her closer to me. "Wash it off."

Lips pursed, her hand began to travel up and down and across my chest until my skin was covered in suds. She used some kind of apricot shit for body wash, but the fruity smell was the last thing I cared about right now. I didn't let my gaze stray as she washed my abs and smirked when she took her time. Her movements were almost reverent.

"Turn around so I can wash your back," she whispered.

My eyebrows rose. "Aren't you forgetting something?"

"No..." Her gaze quickly darted to the side before returning to me. "What?"

"My dick. The one you almost got sliced in half."

Scoffing, she rolled her eyes. "Don't be dramatic, Rees."

"Dramatic was going out into the middle of the night and digging up crabs because I wouldn't give you what you wanted. My dick, Tyra."

Her lips were parted, her gaze unsure. She wanted to talk herself out of this but had a hard time finding the words. A moment later, she dropped the loofah. Her soapy hands wrapped around my dick as she used them instead to clean me off. "Is this what you wanted?" she whispered, her tone husky as she stroked me. Her whiskey eyes had glazed over, a visual sign of her surrender.

My breathing turned heavy when I felt her thumb toying with my piercing. I almost begged her right then. For what, I didn't know. It sure as shit didn't matter. I needed everything she had to give. I was very close to exploding, so I knocked her hand away. "What I want is you on your knees."

"I'm not begging you to fuck me, Vaughn."

"Coy doesn't suit you." I leaned down enough to skim my lips over her ear. "I want you to clean me off, and I want you to use your lips." My hands were already on her shoulders, and it didn't take much pressure to get her on her knees.

"You're an asshole."

"Is that why you look so eager?" Gripping my dick, I skimmed my piercing across her bottom lip. "It's time you put that mouth of yours to good use."

As predicted, Tyra opened said mouth to flay me alive.

She barely uttered a syllable before I slipped between her lips. Her eyes, once they cleared of shock, promised death—but that sharp tongue of hers... I braced my hand against the shower wall, feeling my legs turn to jelly. After a while, she was no longer content to toy with the silver barbell. Half my dick was down her throat. And the hungry sounds she made...

I watched, my jaw dropping with each second, as her head bobbed, and the delicate hand she used to jerk me kept me from going too deep. It was a smart move. If I had my way, my balls would be tickling her tonsils by now. Soon, Tyra's chin became wet with more than just the water streaming down as, what started as her cleaning me, turned messy.

And when her free hand sneakily slipped between her legs, my resolve broke.

Tyra whimpered, clearly not done playing with me, before I lifted her. If she was coming anywhere, it was going to be on my dick. She happily wrapped her legs around my waist, and I found her entrance. She was so fucking ready, and I couldn't wait. Before either of us could come to our senses, I slid into her unprotected pussy and swallowed her cry so that it didn't wake our son. "You know exactly what I want," I whispered as I pushed every inch inside of her. She was tight, but she took me. She had no fucking choice. "But for now, this will do."

Bracing Tyra against the wall, I pumped my hips, giving her what she'd been willing to maim me for.

Nothing else mattered.

The water turned cold, but neither of us noticed as we kept on fucking. Her nails in my back, digging deeper, and each thrust of my cock growing more desperate. Soon after, I felt her pussy gripping me as she came with a curse. "Fuck!"

I knew it was for more than just her climax. She did indeed make one epic mistake because no way was I letting her go now.

Feeling myself tipping over that edge and remembering I wore no condom, I pulled out just in time, coming in my hand instead.

The next morning, when my hand drifted over the side of the bed where Tyra had been and found it cold, I realized I was alone. Sitting up, I listened for her, but the house was quiet as a mouse. My irritation was skyrocketing, already knowing she was gone, as I reached out for my phone.

I paused, seeing twenty dollars and a note waiting for me on the nightstand. Ignoring my phone and the money, I picked up the note and squinted at the words.

Last night was great. Buy yourself something nice.
xoxo Tyra

I quickly flipped her cheeky little note over because she had to be joking.

Just kidding! Had a job interview this morning. Caught a ride from Four to pick up my car. P.S. River's been fed and changed.

I grabbed my phone to call her anyway, but then my son's cry kept me from dialing. I headed to the nursery, and the moment he saw me standing over his crib, he cranked up the volume, crying even louder. I quickly changed his diaper before dressing him for the day. Immediately after, I began grabbing stuff to pack into his diaper bag. No way I'd be able to stay in this house without pacing a hole in the floor. Maybe I'd crack a few beers with Wren instead despite it being nine in the morning.

Last night had been an amalgamation of many things, and I wasn't sure if they'd all been good or bad. This crossroads we were at just kept getting darker, making it harder to see the right path ahead. I grabbed River's diaper bag and started to fill it when I paused at the folded sheet of paper inside. Setting aside the items I was holding, I plucked the note from the bag and unfolded it. There was only a name and number written inside, but it was enough to make my blood boil. What if her "interview" was really a date?

I crumbled the note in my fist.

Storming from the room, I located my old phone and opened the tracking app I never got around to deleting. If I hadn't made myself perfectly clear before, I'd make sure Tyra understood every word I uttered this time around.

chapter thirty-five

The Pawn

"YOU COME HIGHLY RECOMMENDED. CHARLIE'S ONE OF OUR top girls here, and if she says to give you a shot, I'm not inclined to argue. When can you start?"

I never imagined a job offer making my gut pool with dread rather than relief. It wasn't something I ever saw myself doing in a million years, but I also never predicted these circumstances, either.

"How about tonight?"

Neil, the club manager, didn't seem surprised by my eagerness. Many of the girls who'd passed through those doors had likely been in similar straits. I couldn't imagine anyone doing it for a good time. It was all about the easy money.

My new boss nodded as he shifted around some papers. "Tonight's good. It's a weekday, and we'll need to train you, so don't expect too much action on the first night."

"I'm good with slow."

The manager's gaze raked me in that assessing way Charlie's had before he shrugged. "Then enjoy it while it lasts, kid. You'll be a favorite in no time."

I slowly rose from my chair, ignoring the urge to tell him that I'd reconsidered. Rather than warning him about how wrong I was for this job, I heard myself thanking him for the opportunity. He simply waved me out the door, and I quickly obliged him. As I made my way toward the exit, I wisely kept my gaze off the huge platform in the center.

I could do this.

For River, I could do this.

I didn't want to think about whether it would be enough to pay for River's medical expenses as well as Harvard. Maybe Vaughn could help, but it wouldn't be fair of me to put it all on him even if he could afford it.

I was in my car and a few miles down the road when I passed a familiar looking van. I glanced in my rearview in time to see the back lights as the driver slammed on brakes. A second later, it made a U-turn in the street and was barreling after me. Knowing it could only be my son's father stalking me, I sighed and pulled over on the side of the road. Getting out, I met him halfway, trying not to snicker at the sight of him climbing from the minivan. I was the first to speak.

"Is River okay?"

"Who the hell is Charlie?"

I was frowning until he held up the paper with *Charlene's* name and number. I didn't bother telling him that Charlie was a nickname, though. Instead, I folded my arms. "Why?"

His brows dipped even further if that was possible. "Why what?"

"Why do you need to know?"

"Because I thought I made it clear that you weren't seeing other guys."

"But you can see other women? Is that the double standard you're trying to force on me? How did you even find me?"

"That's for me to know."

"Yeah? Well, so is Charlie." I spun on my heel and started for my car. Vaughn, knowing he couldn't stop me from walking away or dating if I pleased, didn't stop me. I wasn't about to let him bully me into being with him when he couldn't even be man enough to admit that it was what he wanted. I mean, when was that ever acceptable?

Smart enough not to let Vaughn get me alone, I decided I

needed some girl time. Vaughn, wouldn't you know, followed me like a class-A stalker the entire way there. I guess it was his way of making sure that I didn't meet with my imaginary beau.

The soreness he left between my legs seemed to intensify because while Vaughn displayed jealousy in the past, he'd never been so openly blatant about it. Last night had been amazing and all the things I remembered it being but *more*.

And that, unfortunately, was the issue.

I was hooked for him to line and sink me all over again.

I shook my head as I drove through the gates of the Manor with Vaughn on my bumper. If my son hadn't been in the car, I would have slammed on my brakes to teach him another lesson. After parking, I waited for Vaughn to unbuckle and remove River from his car seat.

Missing my baby and wanting to snuggle and kiss him, I reached out to take him, but Vaughn turned his shoulder away, making my jaw drop. I watch as he continued walking toward the front door, and then they both entered the house.

Asshole!

When I stepped inside, I grumbled, seeing he had no problem relinquishing our son to Mrs. Greene—who, as usual, had been there to greet whoever came through the door.

"You two must be very proud," she gushed as she held River.

"I am," Vaughn murmured. He was gazing down at the baby with so much pride in his eyes.

"Yes, *we* are."

Vaughn shifted his irritated gaze over to me, and I returned his glare. I didn't give a shit how pissed or jealous he was. He wasn't the one who went through labor and now bore the scar.

"You two stop that," Mrs. Greene scolded. "You lost the right to act like children when you made one." She held her hand out for River's diaper bag, and Vaughn handed it over. She then told us where to find our friends before disappearing with River.

I frowned.

Although I liked Mrs. Greene a lot, I wasn't sure I knew her well enough to leave her alone with my kid. I started to follow her when Vaughn seized my hand and pulled me in the opposite direction.

"He's fine."

"She's a housekeeper, not a nanny and not *our* nanny."

Vaughn sighed but didn't let me go. We found Lou and Four but no sign of Ever or Wren. I figured Ever must have finally gone back to school. I didn't want to think about how much work he'd missed. I sighed as longing filled my chest. I hadn't appreciated the stress that came with college when I had it. It seemed so carefree compared to my life now.

"Oh, hell, no!" Lou fussed when we walked into the room together. "You're both still alive? How is that possible?" She actually looked disappointed when her gaze met mine. "I was expecting the call to help you bury him any day now. What the hell, Bradley?" The longer she stared, the narrower her gaze got. "You fucked him, didn't you?"

"How would you know that? Better yet, why is that your business?" Vaughn asked her.

Lou and Four gave each other knowing looks before their gazes pointedly fell to our joined hands. I hadn't even remembered Vaughn holding my hand. It felt so natural. I pulled free of him before moving over to the couch.

"So tell us everything," Lou demanded as if Vaughn weren't standing five feet away.

Rolling his eyes, he stalked from the room. He'd probably realized he didn't stand a chance on his own. Especially since I spent the next hour telling Four and Lou everything that happened between River's homecoming party and now, leaving out the part of us having sex. I wasn't yet ready to admit that even to myself.

"I don't know…" I stubbornly kept silent as I watched Lou tap her chin. "There seem to be some elements of that story missing," she insisted. "Perhaps a few hours and a couple of screaming orgasms?"

"Okay, we had sex."

"I knew it!" Lou shot up from her seat before whirling on Four. "Pay up, bitch." Four looked at me, disappointment in her brown gaze before forking over the cash she'd obviously bet Lou. "Don't forget you owe Bee, too," Lou announced, making my jaw drop.

"Are you guys serious?"

"Yeah, totally." There was zero remorse in Lou's tone when she spoke. "Four here was the only one who thought you'd resist temptation."

I sat back and folded my arms because what could I say? "Guys...what should I do?" I asked once Lou finished counting her money.

Four was the one who spoke when Lou just stared. "What do you mean?"

"About Vaughn and me?" Neither of them seemed surprised by my question—even Four, who thought I'd hold out on forgiving Vaughn a little while longer. I wasn't sure I had just yet, but I was finding it harder and harder to say no to him.

"Do you want to be with him?" There was no judgment in Four's gaze though she'd barely spoken two words to Vaughn since I caught him with my sister.

"No."

Lou tapped Four on her arm with the back of her hand. "Ask her again, and maybe this time, she'll tell the truth."

I felt myself growing annoyed, not with my friends, but with myself. "He fooled around with my sister, Lou. I'll never forget that."

"No one is saying you have to. Look, I don't condone cheating for any reason, but at least Vaughn's were noble if not misguided by like *ten thousand* miles."

"Noble?" I frowned at that. "What are you talking about?"

How could anyone think that what Vaughn did was even remotely okay?

Lou's eyes widened in shock, and for once, she had nothing to say as she tucked her lips inside of her mouth.

"Nice going," Four snapped. She then turned to me. "Have you and Vaughn not talked about what happened?"

"Sort of."

"And did he tell you why he and Selena…"

I took a deep breath, and it shuddered out of me. "Yeah. He told me the night of the party that he was bored."

"And since then?"

I shrugged. "We've argued, but really, what is there to talk about?"

"Sweet baby Jesus." Lou rolled her eyes toward the ceiling. Apparently, she'd found her voice again. "I don't know who's dumber, but maybe you both deserve to be alone."

"Lou!" Four barked.

Lou blinked in surprise before covering her mouth. "Oh, shit? Did I say that out loud?"

"Yup." Surprisingly, I hadn't taken offense. Lou was that friend everyone needed. She always told the truth even when you didn't want to hear it.

Taking my hands, Lou got this vulnerable look in her eyes that no one, except Wren, got to see very often. "We can't tell you what's in your heart. We can only tell you to follow it, but before you can do that, you need all the facts. Talk to Vaughn and get them. If you have to tie him down and torture it out of him, so be it."

"Are you saying there's another reason Vaughn messed with Selena? How do you know that?" I demanded before she could respond to my first question.

Lou shrugged, looking smug. "We figured that out right around the time he kidnapped and killed his father. I figured if he'd go through all of that trouble just to be with you, he has to love you, and a man in love doesn't desire other women."

Heart stopping in my chest, I pulled my hands from hers before shooting to my feet. Four had her face in her hand as she shook her head, so she was no help. "I'm sorry…*what?*"

I found Vaughn in the kitchen, where he was devouring a turkey sandwich. Lou had refused to talk after dropping one too many bombs, and Four had advised me to find Vaughn. So I did.

"Your father's dead?"

Vaughn's head swiveled toward the entrance where I stood. He seemed to be debating what to say before nodding and turning back to his sandwich. "He died a week ago."

Even knowing the less than stellar relationship he had with his father, I was still startled by his composure. Figuring he was giving into some macho need to hold his emotions back, I walked over to him and wrapped my arms around his muscled torso. I felt his abs contract, the only reaction he gave. "I'm so sorry. When is the funeral? I'll go with you if you like."

"There's not going to be a funeral."

"What do you mean?"

"I had him cremated and dumped his ashes three days ago."

I let him go and stepped back. Vaughn turned his head, watching me carefully. There was no grief in his green gaze. Suddenly, I remembered Lou's words. She'd spoken them minutes ago, yet I'd already forgotten them. *"We figured that out right around the time he kidnapped and killed his father."*

"You?" I had to grip the island for support. My legs felt like they'd give out at any moment now. "How? Why?"

"Does it matter?"

"It does if you're going to prison. What about River?"

"I did it *for* River," he snapped. Tossing his sandwich down, he stood and yanked me into him. "And you."

I shook my head as guilt turned my stomach and heart until

I was overwhelmed—guilt over unknowingly causing a man his life and woe for Vaughn feeling like he had to go to those lengths to be with me. "I didn't ask you to—"

"That's the thing you need to understand. You'll never have to ask me to protect you."

"Protect me from *what?*"

Vaughn's gaze flashed with impatience. I didn't fight him as he led me through the family room that had been deserted into the breakfast room and through a door out onto the veranda. We were away from prying eyes and ears. "My father isn't racist," he announced. "He's far worse, and I don't say that lightly."

"What could be worse?"

His hand lifted and brushed the tear I hadn't realized had fallen away. I couldn't help but be sad for Vaughn. "Hating you because I love you." Vaughn took his hand away, and I almost snatched it back. "He would have taken the one thing that kept me whole and then used me to wreak that same havoc on the world." I stayed where I was when he moved toward the stone railing. Something told me he needed the distance to share what I could only imagine was his shame. "My father couldn't kill me, so he spent my entire life searching for the perfect pawn. Someone I cared about enough to make me come to heel. Sometimes I wondered if my mother left me and moved to Paris, not to save herself, but so that he couldn't have it. Even if she'd been here, I wouldn't have been allowed to care for her."

"Your mother's alive? You never talk about her. I thought that maybe she…"

"That she's dead?" He shook his head as he stared at the green lawn below us. "She's alive, but she might as well be a stranger. I haven't seen or heard from her since I was six."

I gulped at that. With his father dead, Vaughn was as good as an orphan—unless he decided to reach out to her. I already knew his pride wouldn't allow him to, so I hoped that, eventually, when she heard of his father's death, she'd be strong enough to reach out to him.

"Your father wanted you to work for him…what was it that he wanted you to do?"

Vaughn studied me for a long while, debating how much he should reveal or if he should reveal anything at all. His father was gone, and he still didn't feel safe. Was it a sin to hate the dead? If so, I'd burn for sure. "Have you heard of Thirteen?"

Warily, I nodded. I wasn't sure where this was going. Surely, Vaughn's father—I couldn't finish the thought for fear of knowing the answer even when the man was dead. Everyone feared Thirteen, even people like me who'd been lucky enough never to encounter that kind of danger. Or so I thought.

"He was their leader."

I pressed a hand to my stomach, feeling it twist and turn. It was so much worse than I imagined. "He wanted you to murder people?"

"And sell guns and drugs and…people."

"People?"

Slowly, Vaughn nodded. "Thirteen is responsible for nearly ten percent of the trafficking in and out of the United States— women, men, children. It doesn't matter to them."

"Did you do any of this?" When he simply stared at me, I had my answer. Children? What if it had been River? My legs almost collapsed from under me. Sensing this, he closed the distance between us and held on to me.

"I wish I could make excuses and say that I didn't have a choice, but the truth is I did choose, and I chose to keep you safe. I was willing to do whatever it took to make that happen." Instead of pulling away, I clung to him tighter. I was glad Franklin Rees was dead because I just might have killed him myself. "And when River was born," he continued, "I knew bowing to my father wouldn't be enough. One of the expectations he'd made clear to me was that I would have sons to take over when I fell. He was going to do to

River what he did to me, and I couldn't let that happen. I no longer had a soul to protect, but I had you and River. It was more than enough." His eyes moved back and forth as he searched my gaze for resentment and disgust. "But if it makes you feel any better, I didn't pull the trigger. I didn't actually murder my father. I simply commandeered fate and made it work for me for a while."

After hearing what he revealed, I didn't care about what he did. I only cared about what it might do to him. How long would this casual nonchalance over his father's murder last? I hoped it wasn't forever. I hoped that his soul wasn't gone as he'd claimed. To feel, even if it was pain and sorrow, meant to possess that vital part still.

When we were silent for a while, I drew a deep breath, afraid to ask this next question. "And Selena?"

He swallowed, and I knew that whatever he was about to say wouldn't be easy for me to hear. "I suppose I should start from the beginning." I frowned at the bead of sweat that slipped from his hairline and down his achingly gorgeous face. Whatever he was about to say, my reaction and the consequences scared him shitless. More than his father threatening to end everything that Vaughn dared to love. "Your sister and I kissed…" He took a deep breath that shuddered out of him a moment later. "Before that night you caught us together."

My arms dropped, and I took a step away from him. He let me. Sorrow and guilt ravaged his face, but he let me go anyway, knew that he wouldn't be able to make me stay. "What?"

"That night we drove to the Poconos, Selena kissed me in the van. I have no excuse for what happened, pip. None. But—"

"But what?" I demanded. What could he possibly say that would make me understand? His father hadn't threatened him then, so what did he have to betray me?"

"You asked me if I'd done things for Thirteen. After you ended things between us, my father sent me to Colombia to track down his supplier who'd double-crossed him."

My gut twisted painfully before Vaughn could finish. Oh, God. He hadn't, had he? *Please no.*

"He sent me and a few others to kill him."

"Vaughn…"

"I watched that man take a bullet to the brain and did nothing. We even brought his body back to the States like a trophy."

My mind raced as Vaughn spoke, remembering every detail of that weekend, including the haunted look in Vaughn's eyes. I'd mistaken him for being upset over me ending things. For a moment, I wondered if I hadn't, would he have gone? Just as quickly, I realized it wouldn't have mattered. Vaughn wouldn't have had a choice either way. I'd never regretted giving myself to him that night, but I'd never been so grateful either. I'd kept him tethered to that part of himself his father wanted to destroy. Only time would tell if it had been in vain. If his father, though dead, had won anyway.

"What does this have to do with my sister kissing you?"

"I let her, Tyra. For a split second, I let her take what she wanted because I wanted to hurt you." He blew out air and swore at what I was sure was devastation written on my face. "You have every right to hate me. I do. I knew then that I was losing the battle with my father, and I hated myself. I was exactly who he claimed all along. After Colombia, I didn't know how much longer I could fight. I was so tired, pip. I thought if I stopped resisting the inevitable, if I surrendered, then maybe I could feel a *smidgen* of the peace I felt when I was with you. The only thing holding me back was your feelings for me. As long as I still had a chance with you, I could never give in. I thought I wanted to hurt you for letting me go, but really, I wanted to destroy me."

Wordlessly, I wrapped my arms around myself despite the warm spring air. It did nothing to staunch the frost creeping over my heart once again. Vaughn daringly wrapped himself around me.

"I'm so fucking sorry," he pleaded.

"Tell me about the party," was all I said in return. Vaughn might have thawed the ice around my heart, but the muscle was still numb. Time indeed was what it would take, but how much was required remained to be seen. Like him, I was tired of fighting the inevitable too. The reality that maybe Vaughn and I weren't fated after all.

"My father ordered me to get rid of you permanently, or he would." A chill ran down my spine, and as if sensing it, Vaughn ran his fingers down my back soothingly. "I wasn't strong enough to walk away from you. Not without crawling back." He held me tighter, and I did the same. "So I took a page from my father's book and used her to get what I needed." He peered down at me, sorrow and regret making his green gaze brighter. "I needed to take away any chance in hell of you ever forgiving me." I could see the fear in his eyes and hear the question on his lips before he spoke again. "Did I succeed?"

My lips parted, but no words came. I couldn't figure out which direction my heart was tugging me in. Everything was so damned jumbled. Finally, I answered him, telling him the truth. "I'm not sure yet."

His arms slackened in defeat, and I pulled away from him— pulled away before he could feel that lurch in my chest. The one that choked the air from my lungs and demanded I take back the words or perish. My own soul had turned on me.

Still, I walked away.

The beach house was quiet when I snuck inside. Of course, at three a.m., it would be. Tonight had been my first day on the job, and it was amazing that I didn't screw up. There had been no distraction big enough to keep me from replaying Vaughn's confession. And right before we left the Manor, Lou stirred the pot when she handed over a framed portrait almost as big as I was. In it, Vaughn was gazing down at me though I hadn't noticed. The picture had been taken last summer just before everything went to shit. Lou's explanation had only partly eased the tension.

"By my calculations, River was cooking in your stomach, and you didn't know it, so technically, *it's a family portrait."*

"Gee, thanks, Lou."

My dry response had been the only thing holding back my tears at the time. Apparently, Ever had gone over to Wren's house the night Vaughn's father died to retrieve it at Lou's request. Needless to say, we hung it over River's crib as soon as we got home. It required a place of honor since Ever had almost lost his life over it. He'd also met his biological father for the first time, but no one was sure yet whether Ever considered that a bright side.

I was almost to the stairs when light flooded the living room, making me jump out of my skin.

"Where have you been?"

Vaughn was sitting in an armchair—all of the furniture had been returned to the room after the party—with River resting in his arms. He must have woken up, making his father aware of my absence. *Shit, shit, shit!* How quickly I'd forgotten. Newborns don't sleep the entire night through. I swear it seemed as if River woke up more often than he did at the hospital and wondered if that would change once he got used to the change of scenery.

"I would have told you if you hadn't been in the middle of a jealous rage. I got the job." Despite my irritation, I hesitated, and it took all of my concentration not to stumble over the rest. "I was working."

He didn't seem impressed. "Where?"

Even though I anticipated the question, I still had trouble answering. "At a club."

"Don't play games with me, Tyra. What's this club called?"

"Recognize that I'm just declining to tell you because it's none of your business. We are not in a relationship." When he simply stared at me, I set down my duffel bag, and when his eyes shot to it, I quickly diverted his attention. "Look, I've had some time to think—"

"You mean since this morning?"

Ignoring his sarcasm, I continued. "Yes." Surprisingly, the truth tumbled out easier than I had expected it to. "I forgive you, Vaughn, I really do. How could I not after what you did for River?"

Vaughn blinked in surprise, and then relief replaced his anger. "And you," he reminded.

I paused before relenting with a nod. "And me."

His gaze narrowed as he sensed the *but* coming. "So then, what's the problem? Why won't you tell me where you were?" We both knew it wasn't the question he really wanted to ask.

"The problem is I-I can't trust you." He started to argue, but I held up my hand, cutting him off. My head knew that he'd only been using Selena, but my heart was a different story. I just didn't think that I was strong enough to trust Vaughn with it again. Not now that I knew how far he was willing to go. There were boundaries I didn't believe anyone should cross for any reason. "I know, okay? I know that it couldn't have been easy for you, but it doesn't change that you did it. I want more than anything to promise you that I will only need some time, but what if I never get over it? What if I just string you along until your heart is just as withered and broken as mine? I can't do that to you. After everything you've been through, all you've done for River and me, you don't deserve that. I'm not just asking you to let me go but to free yourself as well." I moved over to the recliner until I knelt in front of him, one hand on each of his strong knees. "Vaughn, think about it," I pleaded. "You spent your entire life not allowing yourself to feel for anyone because of your father. Now that he's dead, you can. What if…" I bit my lip because the very thought of it made bile rise in my throat. But I couldn't ignore it even if it caused me pain.

"What if what?"

As we stared at each other, River sleeping peacefully in his father's arms, unaware of the turmoil surrounding him, I forced myself to swallow past the resistance keeping the words at bay.

"What if I'm not the girl you were meant to be with? How do you know there isn't someone better out there?"

chapter thirty-six

The Prince

"CONGRATULATIONS, MAN. NOW THAT I'M NO LONGER ON the market, I knew she'd say yes." Jamie then held up his beer, and Ever, Wren, and I did the same. "Cheers."

We were standing in my kitchen, congratulating Wren on getting engaged. He'd finally popped the question, and no one was surprised when Lou accepted despite the rough months they'd had.

"So when is the wedding?" Ever asked Wren. The two brothers had finally kissed and made up and not just because Four and Lou made them.

"We're not going to have one."

"Aw, man." Jamie groaned. "You're eloping?" He didn't bother hiding his disappointment and disgust.

Wren shrugged. "No. We're going down to the courthouse."

"Yeah, that's not going to work for me."

"It's what Lou wants, and I'm not going to say no to getting it over with. I just want the girl, not the frills and pomp."

"K." Jamie then began tapping away on his phone while Wren finished his beer. Ever and I exchanged a look, knowing Jameson all too well. Wren and Lou were getting a wedding, whether they wanted one or not. "So, what should we do to celebrate?"

I paused from sipping at my beer. "I thought we were doing it?"

the prince and the pawn | 339

Jamie raised a brow as he looked around the island. "Beers and Cheez-It? Are you kidding me? It's Wren's stag night."

"Well, what would you suggest?"

Jamie pocketed his phone with a twinkle in his eye. "Let's go to The Suite of Dreams."

"What the hell is that?"

"It's a club that opened up just outside of town. I heard they have all types of chicks in there. Tall, short, skinny, curvy, good girls, bad girls, good girls who want to be bad." For some reason, he eyed me when he said that last part. I seriously hoped this wasn't some scheme to hook me up with a stripper.

"I'll have to pass. Sorry."

"What the fuck? Why? So you can sit up all night waiting for Tyra to take you back? Have some dignity, man."

"You're one to talk. Who was it that pined and whined over Bee because you thought she preferred Ever? Besides, my kid's upstairs sleeping, numbnuts. Tyra's working."

"So I'll call Four to watch him. No big deal."

Ever scowled as he stared Jamie down. "Why can't you call your own girl to babysit?"

"Because I need her naked and horny when I get home, not exhausted and covered in spit-up."

I scrubbed my hand down my face, wondering if it was too late to get a new set of friends. "Look, just go without me."

"Negative. I already texted Four. She's on her way."

If possible, Ever's scowl deepened, but he said nothing. To save myself the headache, I decided not to fight the inevitable and headed upstairs. On a whim, I donned one of the suits my father had tailored for me, thinking that maybe tonight I'd take Tyra up on her advice. It had been two weeks, and she didn't seem any closer to changing her mind. In fact, she appeared firmer in her idiotic belief that I could ever love anyone other than her, so I went with the flow.

Fuck it.

After checking on River, I returned downstairs just as the doorbell rang. Jamie whistled when he saw me, winking and blowing me a kiss.

"Just get the damn door," I snapped.

Laughing, he obliged. "What the—aww, come on!" he whined when he saw Bee standing there next to Four and Lou.

Bee smirked as she shouldered past him, stepping into the house.

Four eyed us before crossing her arms. "You guys wouldn't happen to be going to a strip club, would you?"

"No." We'd all spoken at once.

"Where's River?" she asked with a shake of her head.

"He's in the nursery. He should be good for another hour or two." I then launched into a full list of instructions. Wren, Jamie, and Ever practically had to pull me out of the house after I spent ten minutes giving the girls the rundown with no sign of being done.

"Jesus, you're not going to war," Jamie muttered after they successfully got me into his Jeep. My stomach was in knots over leaving River for the first time since coming home.

"I know that."

"So, where's Tyra working anyway?"

"I don't know." And I didn't. I forced myself to delete the tracking app after she practically pushed me into another girl's arms. She had it in her head that there might be someone more forgiving, someone out there better for me than her. I shook my head.

"What do you mean you don't know?" Jamie continued to interrogate. "She didn't tell you?"

"I asked, but no, she wouldn't tell me. She only mentioned that it was a club."

"What kind of club?" Wren inquired.

I shrugged. "Don't know."

Everyone in the Jeep fell silent, and I knew they were all

trying to figure out what the hell had gotten into me. I wondered the same. The drive wasn't long. Despite the distance from the beach house, it took about thirty minutes with Jamie's wild driving. I looked around the parking lot as Jamie pulled up to valet and saw nothing but foreign and luxury cars. The red Jeep Sahara stood out like a sore thumb despite Jamie being worth billions. Jamie whooped and pounded the roof of his car before hopping out. He practically ran over to where two bouncers and some short, bespectacled guy stood with a clipboard near the entrance.

Wren, Ever, and I exchanged a look. Anyone who knew Jamie well knew to be suspicious when he was excited.

The club was huge, and I could tell from the outside and even with the blinding bright lights of a neon sign that it had more than one level.

"Mr. Buchanan, what an honor," Mr. Clipboard greeted. "It's been a while since we've seen you. We certainly missed your enthusiasm for our girls."

Ever looked over at his cousin—the two not being blood-related after all didn't change the fact that they were family. "You 'heard,' huh? Been here much?"

"A few times," Jamie muttered. He avoided our gazes while sticking his hands in his pockets.

"Up until a year ago, we saw Mr. Buchanan almost every weekend! He really had a thing for our leggy blondes."

"Can it, Dan, and stop calling me Mr. Buchanan."

"Right away, Mr. Buchanan." Dan reached out, shaking my hand, then Ever's and Wren's. "I'm Dan."

Once the introductions were made, Dan nodded to the bouncer on his left. He had muscles that put mine to shame, not that I ever aspired to be that big. It wasn't like I needed them now anyway. Even if by some miracle USC did take me back, I could never move across the country and leave River. The bouncer gripped a gold knob and pushed open one of the tall, royal-blue doors.

It was dark inside, but Jamie seemed to know exactly where he was going as he led us up a flight of stairs with dim lighting built along the side. Once we reached the landing, my gaze traveled the spacious floor. The crowd was thick considering the late Friday night, and almost every one of the tufted gold ottomans that could easily seat six was filled.

There was a bar, but Wren, having turned twenty-one last August, was the only one old enough to drink—not that he would. Even with Fox dead and Royal promising not to retaliate, he remained wary of the world. The bouncers hadn't even checked him for the gun I knew was tucked inside his suit jacket.

Strategically positioned to form a triangle were three round stages, each with a girl dancing around a pole. Extending from the back of the club was a catwalk of sorts, but instead of showing off their clothes, the girls shed them. And there were men—some eager, some bored—watching them in the chairs lining the sides and curved front of the platform. I hadn't really paid more than a passing glance to any of them as I felt myself yawning and checking the time. River would be awake now and screaming for his bottle.

"Don't you dare call them," Jamie warned.

"Who?"

"The girls. River's fine, but you're not." Jamie clapped me on the shoulder. "Let's have some fun, brother." A girl who was actually dressed in a pencil skirt and blouse introduced herself before leading us across the club. Finding myself agreeing with Jamie, I followed my friends up another set of stairs, this one shorter. This level was like a loft, but instead of one section, there were three, each designed to look like a bedroom suite. Rather than ordinary bedroom furniture, however, there was a small round platform with two high-backed armchairs on each side and a short catwalk extending from the platform and disappearing behind the curtains.

"I hope this will be to your liking, gentlemen."

As soon as we nodded, she walked away, and we took our seats. Drinks appeared a moment later despite Ever, Jamie, and me being underage. I didn't question it and lifted the glass of bourbon. "So tell me," I shouted to Jamie over the music. "What is the point of being here if none of you can get lap dances?"

Before he could answer, a girl strutted through the blue curtains. She wasn't wearing much—a gold G-string and the matching top. I forced myself to watch the leggy stripper in a strawberry blonde wig as she seductively danced her way down the short catwalk. She had her top off before she even reached the round stage where she swayed and climbed and flipped to four songs—it was the longest twenty minutes of my life.

And then came another blonde.

The second dancer's hair was darker, and her legs weren't as long, but she reminded me of someone with her brown eyes. Noticing the provocative motorcycle uniform and Ever's tight expression, I realized what Jamie was up to. He'd obviously called ahead and set this up. When the two girls started to dance with their bodies pressed close, and the taller dancer began to undress the chick in the biker getup, I choked on my drink. Ever looked two seconds from punching Jamie, who couldn't be more amused by his own antics.

I wasn't even surprised when the girls finally disappeared, and out came a brunette in a long, white veil, matching lingerie and a garter around her ankle. She descended the short steps of the stage to give Wren a lap dance per Jamie's request, but the look Wren gave her had the dancer scurrying back up to the stage. Her movements were jerky during the first song thanks to Wren scaring the shit out of her, but by the second song, she'd seemingly forgotten all about it.

Lou would probably carve Wren's eyes out just for looking, so a lap dance was definitely out of the question. The dancer disappeared after three songs, and I realized we hadn't tipped any of them.

"Don't worry. It's covered," Jamie announced, reading my mind.

I ignored him as I eyed the curtain. After ten minutes passed without a Tyra look-alike appearing, I exhaled. I felt my friends watching me, but I didn't even give a shit if they knew how relieved I was. I probably *would* punch Jamie. Getting tossed out on my ass wasn't even close to being a concern.

Dan appeared along with some girls carrying a two-tiered cake with sparklers and Congratulations, Wren! written on the frosting as if it were his birthday. "Since you won't take a lap dance, how about several?" Jamie said before waggling his brows.

Suddenly, more girls appeared, surrounding Wren's chair before he knew what was happening. He'd been too busy scowling at the cake. None of the girls got too close, but there was nothing Wren could do as they waved their tits and stripped their clothing in front of him. I just hoped Jamie wasn't dumb enough to still be around when it was over.

The song ended, and the girls disappeared. Wren sat perfectly still, watching Jamie and Dan as they whispered back and forth. I wouldn't be surprised if Wren were planning just how slowly he wanted to kill Jamie. Dan began nodding enthusiastically before pulling his radio and speaking into it. I almost groaned when the music started up again. I wasn't sure what the hell I was thinking coming here. No way I could get over Tyra.

As if I conjured her up—or at least someone who looked a hell of a lot like her—a tiny thing with brown skin, wild curls, and dressed in nothing but a football jersey and thigh-high patent-leather boots, crawled from behind the curtains. My heart felt like it was in my throat. I couldn't take my eyes off her. She reached the pole in the center of the catwalk and used it to seductively regain her feet. Her head was still down as she kept going, making her way to the center stage. I didn't even recognize the song playing, but I was convinced it had been made for her rhythm alone.

By the time she reached the stage, I was enthralled though I didn't want to be. I couldn't stop watching the way her hips moved. My hands flexed, wanting to grab them. I subtly shifted when my pants tightened, but it was no use. I was good and hard.

And that was when she finally lifted her head.

The first thing I noticed was the fullness of her red lips and the two black streaks painted underneath her eyes. I would have snorted if not for the dim light somewhere high up, revealing those whiskey eyes. The section was dark, but I might as well have had night vision. I was caught between rage and disbelief as I realized who the girl was slowly undoing the strings keeping the jersey around her. Tyra was staring at the curtains behind us as if the thought of making eye contact was too much to bear. She had yet to recognize the men she was dancing for. The jersey covering her fell to the stage, and then she was left in nothing but a thong and her boots.

"Jamie, are you kidding me? What the fuck?" Ever spat in a low tone.

It didn't matter, though.

Tyra had heard him.

Her gaze shot toward the sound of Ever's voice, and her jaw dropped as mortification filled her eyes. She then looked at Jamie sitting next to him and then Wren and then me. My body tensed as she took a step back and then another. By the time she realized how close she was to the edge, it was too late. She'd fallen right off the stage.

The sound of her body hitting the floor was enough to make everything and everyone in the section come to a screeching halt. I was the first one there as we all shot out of our seats. Tyra was grimacing and holding the back of her head as she struggled to sit up. I gripped her arms, helping her, and as soon as she was on her feet, Wren offered her his suit jacket. She gratefully took it just as Dan, a couple of bouncers, and what

I could only assume was the manager rushed over. I let her go, only so she could put the jacket on.

"My name is Neil. I'm the manager. What's going on here?" he demanded. "What happened?"

"She fell," Ever informed him.

Neil whirled on Tyra, anger in his gaze rather than concern. "I see. My apologies for the disturbance, gentlemen." He then crooked a finger at Tyra as if she were a child or a dog. "Tyra, I'd like to see you in my office. Immediately."

I gripped Tyra's arm, keeping her from taking a single step when she tried to follow after him. "What for?" I challenged. "It was an accident, and we're to blame."

"Oh?"

"We startled her on account of the fact that we know her. It's not her fault."

"Regardless," Neil shot back, clearly not giving a shit. "She is expected to remain professional at all times. Tyra, in my office, please."

I let her go when Tyra began to wrestle her arm free. She'd been hurt enough tonight. With her head down, she followed her boss through the club, and I watched them until they disappeared in his office. The moment the door cleared, I whirled on Jamie so I could knock his teeth down his throat.

"You knew."

"Well, obviously, I didn't know *that* was going to happen. And honestly, how the fuck didn't you know that she worked here? That's your girl—"

"As you pointed out, not three hours ago, she's not my girl and never will be."

It was his turn to dismiss me. "You need to nip this shit in the bud. You can't let her work here."

"Tyra can do whatever she wants." I turned and headed for the stairs before turning back out of curiosity. "How did you even find out?"

"Dan sent me a photo of their new girl a week ago. He was trying to win my business back."

If he sent that to Jamie, then it was likely he'd sent it to others, too. Jamie's claim that I needed to end Tyra's employment here was starting to sound better and better. Still, I headed for the exit, anyway. I donned that cape once before and look where the hell it got me.

chapter thirty-seven

The Pawn

NEIL FINED ME FOR THE TUMBLE I'D TAKEN OFF THE STAGE, NO matter how hard I begged him not to. I tried to think of a way my first stage dance could have gone worse but nothing, *nothing* topped stripping in front of my friends as well as the father of my child. Nothing.

I shoved on my hoodie, grabbed my duffel, and slammed my locker closed with a growl. Keeping my head down, I pretended not to hear the snickering of the other dancers. Surprise, surprise, I was surrounded by catty bitches. Their kind seemed to follow me wherever I went. Charlie was the only one of my new coworkers who'd proved bearable. I was on my way toward the exit, forcing myself to stop when she waved me down.

"Don't be too hard on yourself, kid. You did good, and you wouldn't be the first girl to fall off the stage. At least it wasn't because you were too drunk or high." I nodded, and then she reached inside her Chanel pouch. She then handed over a thick wad of bills. "Take it."

As tempting as it was, I shook my head, declining. "I can't do that. That's yours."

"Actually, it's yours," she informed me. "This is your tip." My eyes bulged because how the hell could I have made that much from one dance? There had to be at least a few hundred in her hand. "I convinced Neil not to fine you, but you're going to have to work double hours tomorrow. It's Saturday, our best night, so it will be worth the punishment."

I eagerly took the money, resisting the urge to count it right then and there. How much closer was I to Harvard? To leaving this all behind?

"Thanks, Charlie, and I'm sorry again."

"Don't sweat it."

Charlie wished me a good night before sending me off into the night. I still had a couple of hours left of my shift, but the club didn't want the liability if I had a head injury. As I made my way to my car, I checked my head for lumps.

"You should go to the emergency room. You might have a concussion."

I stopped in my tracks, my head shooting up and finding Vaughn leaning against the hood of my car. "What are you doing here?" I looked around for Jamie, Ever, and Wren but didn't see them. Why had Vaughn stayed?

"I wanted to make sure you got home safely."

"I suppose that means you also need a ride now." To my surprise, he held out his hand. "What?" I asked when he said nothing. He only waited expectantly.

"Give me the keys."

I held them tighter. "Why?"

"Because we don't know if you have a concussion, and I'm not leaving my son an orphan. Give me the keys."

I started to argue, but then I realized the last thing I felt like doing was driving, so I held them out. I hopped in on the passenger side and held my giggle back when he tried to get into the driver's side but ended up bumping his knee on the wheel and cursing my short legs.

Grumbling, he moved the seat back before trying again. "How the hell can you possibly drive with your chest on the steering wheel?"

I shrugged. "I suppose the same way you can with your ass in the trunk."

He stared at me, lips turning to the side as he adjusted the seat. When that gaze became less cold and more heated, I looked away. He got in, and we were off. Every time I tried to doze off, he'd shake me awake. He did it enough times that I was ready to punch him in the throat when the car finally stopped.

I realized too late that he had driven us to the hospital.

"It's Friday night. Do you realize how long this could take? I don't have a concussion. Let's just go home." I quickly cleared my throat. "I meant back to your place."

Vaughn didn't look happy about me changing direction, but he didn't comment on it. "Come on." He got out, but I didn't follow him. Instead, I sat back with my arms crossed. I just wanted to see my little love butt and go to sleep.

Unfazed, as if he expected me to be stubborn, Vaughn rounded the hood of the car. I tried to lock the door, but I was too late. He got the door open, so I started screaming instead.

"Help! This crazy Neanderthal won't take me back to his cave!" I slapped his hands when he tried to unbuckle my seat belt. When he finally succeeded, I quickly crawled into the back seat.

"Goddamn it, pip-squeak!" He yanked the backdoor open before crawling inside and slamming it behind him. It took him a few seconds to notice that I wasn't trying to escape. "Wha—"

I didn't let him finish that sentence before grabbing his face and kissing him. I felt his body tense before he realized what was happening and taking over as I knew he would. Call me crazy, but it worked for me. I craved his domination even when I cursed it.

I had his suit jacket off and was tearing at his tie and the buttons on his shirt before he could even slip me the tongue. "Please fuck me, Vaughn. Right now."

"Is bipolar one of your new personality traits?" He'd whispered it against my lips as he continued kissing me. Despite his question, he was already ripping at my clothes.

I wasn't sure what had gotten into me. I just knew I needed to erase tonight, to erase the feel of all those men peering at me and caressing my skin when the bouncers weren't looking. I knew the only one capable of that was Vaughn.

And then there was the other reason.

The fact that I simply needed him.

It had been two weeks since I sealed the fate of our relationship. Parents to River   that was what I had reduced us to. Two weeks of establishing a routine, sharing a space, and passing each other in the hall, never looking too long at one another for fear of what might come tumbling out. But then tonight, when he saw me dancing for him and his friends, and I saw the promise in his eyes to punish me, I knew we weren't through. Not by a long shot. A part of me wished he would make me pay. To offer me that solace, the knowledge that he'd never give up fighting for me.

As if reading my mind, Vaughn sat back once I was naked. I wasn't worried about being seen in the dark and the nearly empty parking garage. I felt him gripping my arm and yanking me forward until I tumbled over his lap. For a moment, I stared at the back door in shock before peering over my shoulder at him. Vaughn wasn't looking at me, though. He was staring at my ass. "What are you doing?"

"Did you really think I'd find you in that club and not make you think twice about going back?" Before I could answer him, he finally met my gaze. "This might hurt a little."

I didn't get the chance to ask him what he meant before I felt the sting of his palm hitting my backside. I turned my head as I cried out. My nails gripped the fabric of my seats, threatening to tear holes in them. I couldn't think about that, though. All I could think about was what Vaughn was doing to me.

His fingers gripped my hair, and then he turned my head around, forcing my gaze to meet his. "Eyes on me. Watch me punish you."

"Vaughn—"

He spanked me again before I could finish my plea. This time, he soothed the ache with his palm as he stared into my eyes.

"What kind of a man do you take me for, Tyra?"

I slowly shook my head because I genuinely didn't know. Somehow, I still loved him. I never thought I'd live to see the day where that wasn't enough. I couldn't trust him, my broken heart wouldn't allow me to, but I could have this—with him.

I felt his palm on my ass again and again until I was a crying, blubbering mess. Vaughn soothed the ache each time only to spank me harder. I could already feel his erection pressing into my stomach, so I moved my hips, hoping to divert his needs elsewhere.

His hand paused in midair. He'd been admiring his handiwork when his gaze flew to mine. "That's not going to work," he whispered.

"Isn't it?" My sore throat had my voice sounding husky.

I watched his jaw harden, and then he was lifting me and tossing me on the other side of the car as if his dick wasn't making an obscene bulge in the front of his pants. Chest heaving, I licked my lips. "Vaughn—"

He was already turning toward the door. "Put your clothes back on and get out of the car."

"Vaughn!" Hearing my plea in his name, he glanced over his shoulder. The moment our gazes connected, he swore.

"Fucking spoiled brat." Hand moving to his belt, he unbuckled it before shoving his pants down his thighs and freeing his cock. "Get over here."

Eagerly, I climbed onto his lap. I didn't even think about the fact that he wore no condom as I slowly lowered myself onto him. I paused midway, my lips parting as I panted. I'd forgotten how unforgiving he filled me in this position. I started moving up and down, only taking what I could handle and ignoring the fact that I needed more when I felt his hands close around my hips. I only had a moment to brace before he shoved inside of me with a growl, opening me all the way for him. Still needing to punish me, he didn't give me time to get used to him.

For a while, there was nothing but the wet sound of him plunging in and out me, the sound of our skin slapping, and my pained cries.

My ass was on fucking fire.

Every time he forced me down, my skin smarted.

"It hurts," I whined.

"Mm-hmm, I know," he purred. "You stop, I stop."

I shook my head at his warning because it was the last thing I wanted. So like a big girl, I endured. I ignored the feel of my abused ass hitting his thighs for the pleasure of his pierced cock filling me over and over. The moment I felt my nipples leaking, Vaughn was there, gorging himself on more than just my pussy. It was the best fucking feeling in the world, even when my nipples became sore. Everything hurt at this point, but it was a beautiful sort of pain. One I'd endure over and over just to feel Vaughn all over.

"I'm going to come," he announced, and it took me a moment to recognize the warning. He wasn't protected, and neither was I. "Fuck, I'm close. Tyra…"

This time, it was my turn to shut him up as I crushed my lips against his and continued to bounce on his cock. My little car was rocking, giving no doubt to what we were doing to anyone who passed. I didn't care about that, either.

"Come inside of me." I squeezed my walls around him with the command. Maybe I did have a head injury after all. "Come right now. I want to feel you leaking on my thighs while we wait to see the doctor. Please, Vaughn, I need it."

His only response was a grunt, and then I felt the splash of his warm cum. Completely spent, Vaughn laid his head back on the seat while I gripped his shoulder with one hand, his knee with the other, and rode him like I was a jockey and he the prized stallion.

When I came soon after, I could have sworn I saw the bursting stars behind my eyelids align.

Soulmate.

Sweating, out of breath, and legs feeling like they'd collapse any moment, I strutted off the stage the next night and headed for the locker room. The doctor had cleared me to return to work, much to Vaughn's displeasure. I'd snuck out a few hours ago to avoid another argument like the one we had after we returned to the beach house. It was as if our time in the car had never happened. Luckily, we'd been smart enough to do it outside where River couldn't hear his parents screaming at each other.

"Why do you even need to go back there?"

"Because I need money! Have you even thought about how much River's hospital bill will be? Insurance will only cover so much."

Storming over to the minivan, he removed an envelope from the glove compartment before damn near shoving it in my hands. I took my time opening it to piss him off before staring at what was clearly the bill for River's stay in NICU. The number was even higher than I thought it would be but even more shocking was the zero-dollar balance and the word PAID highlighted in green. It almost seemed like a taunt rather than a miracle.

"You paid it?"

"Of fucking course, I did. Did you really think I wouldn't?"

"I-I'll pay you back my half." It was the only thing I could think to say. I was that stunned. The amount on that bill hadn't been small. "You've just got to give me some time."

"I didn't ask for your money, did I? I've got plenty of it."

"That doesn't matter. It's my fault he was even in there in the first place. I—" A sob kept the rest of the words from coming. "I need to make it right."

"You are. Right now. By being his mother."

My shoulders slumped because I couldn't hide the huge burden Vaughn had lifted from them. "Thank you."

"You're welcome. Don't go back."

Guilt and frustration bubbled up inside of me as I stood there saying nothing. After what Vaughn had done for me, I hated to say no. "I have to," *I finally told him.* "I still need to pay for school. My dad will use his retirement savings if I don't find a way. He'll take a huge hit in penalties alone. I can't let that happen."

"What if I paid for it?"

I took a step back. "Why would you do that? How would you do that?" *I had to imagine he'd used up most of his money paying River's hospital bill unless…his father left him money. I wasn't sure I wanted to take anything from that man.*

"Because it's not even close to what my father owes me. Or you," he said, confirming my suspicions.

"Thanks, but no thanks. Even if I could, I wouldn't want to take anything he owned."

"It never belonged to him," Vaughn retorted. *"Franklin Rees doesn't exist.* Edward Ridge *died a long time ago. The house, the bank accounts, the assets, all of it have been in my name the whole time. I thought I was at his mercy, under his thumb, but this entire time he'd been under mine."*

"That's great news, but Vaughn, I can't…I'm sorry." Even as I felt his cum drying on my thighs, I added, *"I'll only feel guilty taking your money, knowing it won't change anything between us. I'm not your responsibility."*

Vaughn stared at me for a long while before turning on his heel and silently walking away.

The locker room was empty when I stepped inside. Since it was a Saturday, all the girls were out there working, knowing they wouldn't see money like this all week. The weekends were the real cash cow, and even I, with all my reservations, was eager to get back out there. My toes were barking in the acrylic heels as I made my way to the locker in the far back corner. It was silent as a mouse, which was why I was surprised to see that I wasn't alone after all. I forgot how to breathe long before the girl leaning against my locker and wearing a pink wig cut into a bob looked up. She was the last person I ever expected to see.

"Selena?"

"Hey, little sis." Looking none the worse for wear, she smiled, and I hated her even more for looking exactly like me. "I missed you."

"I can't say the same, and I'm not even sorry. What the hell are you doing here?"

"I was just about to ask you that very question." I could see the amusement written all over her as she crossed her arms. "What happened to Harvard?"

"Nothing. I'm going back in the fall." Warmth bloomed in my chest because it felt like the truth. I told myself that this was just like high school when I was determined to get straight As. "A girl's just doing what she has to."

"My, my, how far we've come. I'm proud of you. You're not so naïve anymore, are you, little sis?"

No. I wasn't. I'd tried so hard to hold on to Selena because of the blood we shared and all along she'd been out for mine. Closing my eyes, I inhaled deeply to calm the bitter emotions roiling in my gut. Family hadn't mattered to her as much as it had to me. Nothing she said or did would make me forget that. Slowly, my eyes opened as I felt my shoulders square.

"You have no idea, and if you don't get the hell out of my sight, you're going to."

The laugh Selena released was condescending. "Little Ty-ty, don't tell me you're still upset about that whole Vaughn thing. He was just a fling for both of us. What's the big deal?"

"Except he wasn't just a fling. I loved him, and he loved me." And despite the betrayal twisting my gut seeing Selena standing here, I knew in my heart that he still did. Vaughn risked his life, taking out his father when bowing down would have been simpler. Safer.

"Is that what he told you?" Selena mocked. "Well, if he did, why did he fool around with me?" When I didn't respond, her smugness grew. "If it's any consolation, I did you a favor. Besides, we'll never stop being family. Meanwhile, Vaughn is old news. Let's just put him behind us and be sisters again. I hear I'm an auntie now."

I allowed my gaze to soften and the tension to leave my body. Seeing this, Selena stepped forward, ready to hug me. Quicker than I'd ever moved before, I grabbed Selena by her hideous pink wig and used my hold to slam the side of her head into the locker. "Stay away from me, stay away from Vaughn, and if you even think about going near my son, I'll fucking kill you."

Letting her go, Selena crumpled to the floor. Ripping open my locker, I paid her no mind as she crawled away. Only when I heard the outer door slam did I rest my head against the shelf inside my locker. She was probably off to tell Neil what I'd done, which meant I'd be fired before the end of the night. Neil had made his rule about fighting clear.

The regret I should have felt never came.

Hurting Selena had been worth it, but my lack of remorse was mostly because I no longer cared if I lost this job. I couldn't stop replaying the sheer devastation in Vaughn's eyes when he walked away last night.

chapter thirty-eight

The Prince

FOR MOST OF THE NIGHT, I KEPT TYRA IN MY SIGHTS, FOLLOWING HER around the floor as she offered lap dance after lap dance. The entire time, I sat there watching her like a chump. One punch and I would have ended them all and her employment here, but I couldn't bring myself to do it. A part of me welcomed this torture, felt like I deserved it, and the other knew there was nothing I could do. I could haul her ass out of there, but she'd only be back the next night. So instead, I made sure I was present for each shift. My friends were racking up all the favors I owed them for giving up their nights to babysit, but I didn't give a shit about that. I couldn't leave Tyra unprotected. I didn't trust the jerkoffs that worked here anymore than the patrons. Neil's treatment of Tyra that night a week ago had proved my paranoia. So here I sat, using the hours I spent torturing myself to think of a way to gain Tyra's trust. I already knew I had her heart.

I'd just finished waving off another hopeful dancer when I caught sight of a familiar face. Not familiar in the sense of the similar features the sisters shared, but familiar because that face literally haunted my fucking dreams. I'd hoped she had gone back to wherever she'd come from, but her threat to stick around hadn't been a bluff, after all.

"Fancy seeing you here," Selena greeted as she took a seat next to me uninvited. She then wasted no time pushing out her chest. There was nothing more annoying than a girl who assumed being hot made her irresistible. I had x-ray fucking vision and could see right through that coquettish smile, right down to her black heart.

"What the fuck are you still doing in my town? I thought I made myself clear."

"Technically, this isn't your town," she retorted with a bash of her lashes. "And I have more right to be in The Suite of Dreams than you do." It was then I noticed that she had little to nothing on, just heels, a thong, and some pasties. I didn't allow myself to get too caught up in the details.

Selena worked here? Why hadn't Tyra told me?

To be fair, we'd barely spoken two words since the night she rode me in the back seat of her car. It was safe to say that *she* fucked *me* versus the other way around. It was partly the reason I was sitting here crying into the whiskey I'd conned out of a waitress.

"I'm guessing my little sister didn't tell you."

"No."

"I'm not surprised. She wasn't exactly happy to see me, either." Turning her head, Selena allowed me to see the small bruise on her forehead that hadn't completely faded.

Nicely done, pip.

"So, what's the deal with you and my sister?"

"None of your business. Leave." My gaze frantically traveled the club, hoping Tyra hadn't reappeared yet. She'd gone to the back fifteen minutes ago for what I was assuming was her break.

"Relax," Selena cooed as she laid her hand on my chest. "She'll be out in a moment. Besides, you're going to want to hear what I have to say first."

"And what's that?" I forced myself to ask.

"You were right about me."

I simply stared at her, well aware of her hand moving in slow, soothing motions across my chest. It was having the opposite effect of what she intended, but I'd be damned if I touched her long enough to remove her hand. Look where the fuck it had gotten me.

"I came to Blackwood Keep to ruin my sister's life. Unfortunately, she didn't have much of one. I've got to say, you were the most interesting thing about her. The jock falling for the nerd." Selena rolled her eyes. "How poetic."

"Get to the point."

"The point is that all my life, I hated my sister for being born. Because of Tyra, our mom died, and I got stuck with my spineless father. Once I didn't need him anymore, I decided to come here and pay my dear little sister back for ruining my life." Selena shrugged as if her reasons were simple or sane. "Is that so wrong?"

Was that a serious question? "Do you honestly believe that Tyra is to blame for your mom dying?"

"Yeah, I do. Why else would I be here? Haven't you ever heard that fair exchange is no robbery?"

Crazy bitch. "I have, but usually, only sane people utter those words."

"Regardless of what you think of me, I'd like you to return the favor."

"What favor?"

"To use you like you used me." I simply stared at her, refusing to give anything away. "Come on," she said, laughing as she swayed into me. "You begged me for a blow job, but then you could barely stay hard when I've been deep throating guys since I was sixteen. Not to mention the perfect timing of Tyra catching us. I barely got your pants unzipped before she was walking in on us. Tyra may be blind, but I'm not. You wanted her to break up with you."

I sighed with impatience, but judging by the gleam in Selena's eyes, she mistook it for defeat. Especially when I asked, "What do you want, Selena?"

"I want you to do the same thing again, but for good."

"That's going to be pretty hard to do since we're not together."

"But you have a kid together. You're living together, too."

I didn't even want to know how she knew that. All that mattered was that Selena had to go. "What exactly do you expect me to do?"

"Walk away from them. Go play football, become a star, and forget they ever existed. I want my sister to suffer."

"You clearly don't know your sister if you think I'm what's keeping her together. She was strong before me, and she'll be strong without me."

"Oh, yeah? Then why did she lose her scholarship? Could it have been because of a broken heart?" Thankfully, she explained without me having to ask. "There's no such thing as a secret around here. Charlie told me everything once I told her I was Tyra's sister. She's a chatterbox that one."

"It doesn't matter because it's not going to happen. You're a sick, lonely, bitter bitch, and you're going to rot from the inside out."

"Maybe, but not before I take my sister with me."

Shaking my head, I started to rise when she laid her hand on my thigh. It was a flirtatious move, one I knew was meant for an audience. I started to search the club again when Selena gripped my chin, forcing my attention back on her.

"You're going to get up and leave with me, and you're going to make it look damn good. I might even want to continue what we started in that van and at the beach house."

"Or what?"

"Or I'll send this video of Tyra to the Dean of Harvard." She showed me her phone.

I swore when I saw the clear footage of Tyra removing her clothes on stage, and I wondered how Selena got it when recording and taking pictures weren't allowed in here. My next thought was how Tyra had shed all of her basic principles to achieve her dreams. How it had almost been ripped away from her and how it was happening again, only this time for good. I couldn't let that happen.

"As soon as we're outside, delete that fucking video," I warned her.

Her lips spread, bright and victorious. It was about how one would imagine a snake smiling. I shuddered. "Let's just see how the night goes."

She stood, and even as scantily dressed as she was, she started for the exit. My feet were heavy as I followed her, and I didn't allow myself to look to the stage where I knew Tyra now stood, watching us go.

That night, I could have cut the tension with a knife when I returned home. Incidentally, I'd also slept with one eye open just in case Tyra cut *me* with a knife. The next morning, I found her and most of River's stuff gone. She'd up and left me in the wee hours of the morning and took my kid with her without a single word. How fucking cold was that?

I didn't call her. I didn't go after her, either. At least, not yet. I knew there would be no getting through to her.

So I waited.

Impatiently, but I bid my time until the right moment. Three days later, that moment had come. I sat alone at a table by the window in Macchicino's, watching the door when she finally walked through it. She had sunglasses on, but I could tell she was pissed long before she removed them and stormed over to the table.

"Thank you for coming."

"You said you wanted to discuss River," she replied, making the only reason she'd come clear. I should have been ashamed for using my son under false pretenses, but I didn't know how else to fight for them. My family. "You've got two minutes."

My eyebrows rose, but I swallowed my retort and said instead, "To start, I wanted you to know that I'm keeping the minivan."

"What for? Minivans are for large families not—" Her lips pressed together when she remembered that she hated me. "I mean, why did you bring me down here to tell me that?"

"I didn't. I brought you down here to tell you that you're wrong."

"Wrong about what?"

"I didn't touch your sister, pip."

She cocked her head to the side, her gaze colder than I'd ever seen it. "The first time or the second?"

I wished at that moment that I could say both. "I know you saw me leave with her at the club."

"Yeah, so? You're single." Looking away, she absently fingered the sugar packets waiting on the table as she whispered her next lie. "You can do whatever you want."

"Then why did you take my kid and leave?"

She shrugged. "Because we didn't belong there anyway."

"Bullshit. It's exactly where you belonged, pip-squeak."

"Well then, how about because I didn't want to be there when you eventually brought her home with you."

"I'd never do that."

"There's a lot of things I thought you'd never do, but you surprised me at every turn. What's next?"

"Marrying you? Having lots of babies to fill that ugly ass van one day?"

She leaned forward, a challenge in her eyes. "Never."

"Then why were you begging for me to come inside you not even two weeks ago?" A throat clearing had us both looking at the table next to us and the reproachful gaze of the older man sitting there. When Tyra looked at me, I was sure she was going to kill me.

"Let me take a wild guess and say that you didn't call me down here to talk about River?"

"Other than the fact that I want him and you back under my roof, not really."

She started to stand, but I quickly caught her hand. "I promise you, Tyra. I didn't sleep with Selena. She tried, but…"

"But what?"

"I couldn't make the same mistake again."

I exhaled when Tyra relaxed in her chair with a frown, so I let her hand go. "What are you talking about?"

"Selena had a video of you dancing at the club. She was going to send it to the Dean, and God knows who else if I didn't sleep with her and walk away from you."

"So if you're telling me you didn't, then that means—"

I shook my head before she could finish. "I took care of it."

"How exactly did you take care of it?"

I ran my sweaty palms down my jeans. I still hadn't gotten up the nerve to tell her that her sister was a psychopath. I couldn't get the comments she'd made at the club about her father out of my head. "Did she ever tell you how her father died?"

Slowly, Tyra shook her head.

"Selena killed him. Or at least the police think she did. She was out on bond when she skipped town. For some reason, they didn't think the crazy bitch was a flight risk. She's been hiding out here ever since. Selena sought you out because she blamed you for killing her mom. Quite frankly, I'm pretty sure she's insane."

"How do you know all of this?"

"Because after I knocked her out and locked her in my trunk, I did some research." Digging into my back pocket, I pulled out the folded slip of pale, pink paper. "I also found this."

Recognition erased the wariness in Tyra's eyes as she took it from me. Her lips were parted as she slowly unfolded it. The final page of her mother's letter to her father. The one Selena had claimed never existed. I already knew what it said, along with the rest of the letter.

I know by now that you must have grabbed your keys and coat and plotted the quickest route to get to me...to us. I want you to know that there's no need. I might have broken my vows to Sam, but the promise I made to you is the only one that ever mattered. I'm leaving him, Cedric. I'm coming home to you, and I'm bringing our baby girl, both of my girls, with me. I love you. No matter the trial and doubts we've faced, that has always been true. And will never change.

Forever yours,
Monica
...loves Cedric

Tyra's hands were shaking uncontrollably by the time she'd finished. Her mother's affair with her father, the lies Selena sowed, had broken apart everything Tyra believed in love. Even if I couldn't win her heart back, I hoped to give her this last healing kernel before she walked away for good.

"Thank you," she said when the tears clogging her throat finally cleared.

"You're welcome."

"So...what happens now? We can't just let Selena literally get away with murder."

Taking a quick glance at the clock on the wall, I nodded toward the window. As if on cue, Selena appeared on the other side of the street. Tyra wasn't the only one I'd asked to meet me.

"You called her here?" Tyra spat. She was already standing before I could respond. This time, I let her go, but I was right on her heels as she stepped outside into the warm spring air.

It didn't take long for Selena to notice us, wariness in her gaze when she saw us together. Still, she kept coming, that cocky boldness returning to her eyes with each step. She never made it past the line dividing the street before two squad cards appeared, blocking her path and any chance to escape. They were out of the car, guns raised, screaming at her to put her hands up.

The mayor appeared and spoke to the arresting officer before making his way over to me. "I appreciate you notifying me of her presence, nephew. I've collaborated with the chief, and we'll have her extradited soon enough."

"Thanks." It was all I could muster for the man. My mother's family hadn't been any kinder to me than my father had. For years, they stood by and let my father abuse me out of fear of standing up to him. Neither of them had thought to protect anyone other than themselves. Taking a page from my father's book, I pointed this out to him, and fear of me tarnishing their good name had my uncle using his influence to arrange Selena's arrest quickly. I'd already deleted the video of Tyra from her phone and cloud drive.

My uncle scurried away, and while Tyra was distracted, I used the opportunity to pull her back into the coffee shop. I sat next to her this time to keep her from running away though neither of us spoke as we watched the cops do their job. Selena was still hurling obscenities even after she'd been put in the back of a squad car and had the door slammed in her face.

Once they drove away, Tyra's head turned, her whiskey eyes glistening. I said a quick prayer that I hadn't hurt her more. "You did this?"

Grimly, I nodded. She didn't speak, and I was ready to admit defeat when she threw her arms around me.

"You really didn't sleep with her?"

I pulled away before gripping her shoulders. My hands shook when they touched her, and I wondered if it was what made her body tremble or if it was the same raw emotions flowing uncontrollably through me. "I love you too much to hurt you ever again. Please, *please* believe me and come home."

Chewing her lip, she stared at me so long I thought my heart would stop from the agony of wondering if maybe we were too far gone to ever be again. And as if she were life itself, she revived me with three words.

"I believe you." The moment my mind processed the words,

I leaned down to kiss her to keep from crying out like a bitch, but she stopped me with a finger pressed to my lips. "I just have one request."

"Name it." I didn't give a damn how eager I sounded.

Glancing out the window toward the minivan, she turned back to me with her nose wrinkled. "Can we at least trade it for a pretty red one?"

I laughed a little harder than I should, but if the other patrons only knew what this girl did to me...it had taken me too damn long to realize it myself. Now that I had, all bets were off.

"Deal."

chapter thirty-nine

The Pawn

I HUFFED FOR A THIRD TIME. EVEN THOUGH THIS WAS GOING TO BE ONE of the most memorable days of our lives, I was miserable. It turned out the thong that had been oh so necessary for this dress was two sizes too small. My ass hadn't quite rebounded to its original size after giving birth, but until now, I hadn't minded. And neither did Vaughn. Maybe it was the sand stuck between my toes or my so-called waterproof mascara burning my eyes.

"Maybe if you stopped crying, your makeup wouldn't be ruined," I heard whispered in my ear.

I peered over my shoulder to where Vaughn was standing behind me, waiting for our cue. "I can't help it," I blubbered, hiccupping and sniffling at the same time. "She was so beautiful. You should have seen her. It's all just so beautiful," I sobbed.

I couldn't pull it together if I tried.

"If she looked even half as gorgeous as you do right now, I'm sure I'll be amazed," he gamed.

I blushed despite rolling my eyes. Vaughn looked even more intimidatingly beautiful in his black tux.

Jamie, who'd put this all together in a month, began to play some soft melody on his guitar, and I started my slow walk down the sandy aisle. The bouquet of white flowers I clutched in my trembling hands shook as I stared despite my blurry vision at the waves crashing ahead. The sun was slowly lowering, so the sky glowed as blue gave way to the gold and orange of sunset. I could feel the silk material of my blue gown swishing about my feet and was grateful we hadn't been required to wear heels.

I gave a shaky yet reassuring smile to the male pretending not to be nervous as he waited under the arch that looked like a giant wreath of white silk and gold lanterns. Once Vaughn and I were in position, facing one another with a few feet separating us, Bee followed. Jamie, clad in a tux as well, couldn't take his eyes from her even as he played. Four and Ever were next to walk the aisle. Heart-stuttering moments later, the handful of guests rose from the elegant, white folding chairs.

I discreetly wiped away my leaking mascara and blinked away the tears so that I could see clearly. This wasn't a moment I wanted to miss. Lou appeared, and she was just as breathtaking as I remembered her not five minutes ago. She looked like a princess in the white, ball gown with her dark hair pinned up. I wasn't the only one who couldn't take my eyes away. Wren, who had been stoic—the only emotion he ever allowed anyone but Lou to see— melted before everyone's eyes. The Hendersons, Lou's former foster family who'd flown from Texas to be here. Miles and Leo, who'd run the streets with her whenever she ditched her foster home. How Jamie had tracked them down, I didn't know. He'd do well to manage his family's billion-dollar business one day since he was a wizard at getting what he wanted. Kendra was in attendance as well, and everyone had held their breath, hoping Lou wouldn't claw her eyes out. She'd seemingly gotten over Kendra's history with Wren. Of course, Winny, Wren's grandmother, had come and even Thomas and Evelyn. There'd been a seat left for Sean, even though he couldn't be there, and it was still up for debate whether Wren would have wanted him to be. He was currently awaiting trial for the murder of Fox and Franklin after taking the fall. Thomas hadn't hesitated to get him the best lawyers to work on his defense, but it was too soon to say whether the outcome would be good

And then there were the mysterious vampire twins.

Royal and Scarlett Fox.

I'd only met them briefly before, and my first thought was how eerily similar they reminded me of the undead. Especially Scarlett. I'd never seen anyone so pale or with hair as dark as hers. It was as if someone had taken the night and poured it onto the strands. And her lips had me wondering if it was how she'd gotten her name or if she really did drink blood in her free time Jamie called her Snow White ever since. Scarlett had barely muttered two words or even moved for that matter, so naturally, she hadn't reacted to the name.

Royal was her twin in every way except he wasn't as pale, and his lips were more of a dark pink than blood red. Wren and Vaughn had invited them to Blackwood Keep a few days ago, but not just for the wedding Jamie had forced on Wren and Lou but to negotiate a truce between Exiled and Thirteen. Jeremy had been the only wild card, but surprisingly, he'd agreed. Jeremy didn't seem like the type to lead with the wrong head, but I couldn't help wondering if the interest he'd shown in Scarlett was the reason why. I only wished I understood what he'd muttered in Russian when I tried to peer into his mind.

"She's beautiful, isn't she?" I dared to ask as I came to stand beside Jeremy. He'd been watching the twins walk away after they agreed to a "temporary" ceasefire. Vaughn would probably throw a fit if he found me this close to his frenemy, but I was too curious. He had this aura that yes, was dark and dangerous, but magnetic as well.

"YA ne smotryu na neye. YA smotryu na nego."

With an expert flick of his fingers, Jamie played Lou's cue to begin moving down the aisle, so I pushed the memory away and focused on the present...and the future. Somehow, my gaze found the will to shift away from the vision Lou created, and I found Vaughn watching me. After a knowing tip of his lips, he winked—a promise that our day would come. I inhaled, feeling the butterflies in my stomach take flight. I couldn't wait.

Needless to say, I'd quit dancing at the Suite of Dreams. Come the fall, I would be heading back to Harvard to finish my *sophomore* year. Since I'd taken so many AP courses in high school, I'd been on track to graduate an entire year early, but now it looked like I'd be graduating only one semester but still early.

With Vaughn footing the bill.

He'd been relentless, so I gave in on the condition that he didn't give up on his dreams, either. USC might have been a colossal bust, but Vaughn was too talented not to have his pick of the litter. After doing my research, I convinced him as ruthlessly as he had done me that if he acted now, he could still complete his college eligibility in time to qualify for the draft. He was adamant, however, about not straying far from River and me. It limited his options for the well-funded and preferable division one teams, but...at least he still had a chance. I still shivered, remembering his promise to me that day.

"But you won't get as much publicity at a lower division," I argued.

"Then I'll make them notice me. I'm not leaving my family."

Lou reached Wren underneath the arch, and I watched, willing myself not to cry when they faced each other. Lou had refused to wear a veil, so nothing was hindering them from staring into each other's eyes with all the love and hope they shared.

The officiant began, and I forced myself to listen to him drone. When it was time for the vows, Wren went first, shocking everyone—saying vows required flaying yourself open and allowing nothing to stay hidden. It wasn't exactly in the top million of the things he considered a good time.

"Fuck, Lou," he began, despite the officiant standing next to him. I knew right then that Wren hadn't prepared a word of what he said next. He blew out air as his eyes began to glisten. Wren Harland—former Exiled lieutenant and king of the stoic—was crying. "This is the last place I ever thought I'd be standing. When

I found you in that snowstorm, I thought you'd be my end, not the beginning. I carried you like a burden on my shoulders for a long time, not knowing I held you in my heart instead. I accepted you as the penance I accepted for what I'd done because I was too blind to see that you were a gift. I had no idea just what you had in store for me. You were the knight to slay the darkness, my light and salvation. Stubborn and willful to the end, you kept me alive so we could be here right now, and for that, I am indebted to you. If my heart is worthy and yours is willing, please let me spend every breath I have left repaying it."

My mouth dropped as I gaped. I then felt the well inside my chest, filling up fast—a force to be reckoned and too determined to stop.

Holy fuck, this is going to burn.

I didn't care so much this time as I let the tears and mascara fall freely.

epilogue

The Prince

Seven years later
Boston

M Y EYES DRIFTED OPEN, AND I IMMEDIATELY ROLLED OVER. After checking the time, I groaned, not at the early hour, but because I knew that soon, I'd be boarding a flight for the first game of the season. Taking Tyra's advice not to give up on my dreams, four years ago, I signed with the Boston Breakers as their new quarterback after playing for the University of Massachusetts right here in Boston. Every decision, every move I made had been on the condition that I stayed close to home, and I didn't mean Blackwood Keep or the beautiful condo I'd found in the suburbs.

Entering the en suite, I took a quick shower, dressed, and grabbed the bag my wife had packed for me before heading downstairs. I listened to the telltale sounds of my son eating his breakfast before school and pictured the mess he'd make for his mother to clean up. Just as I knew I'd find her, Tyra was darting around the kitchen dressed in charcoal slacks and a black blouse, packing River's lunch while making herself breakfast at the same time. It was anyone's guess when she'd find the time to eat again. She was two months into her five-year surgical residency at Massachusetts General, and of course, she had to be top of her class.

Dropping my bag and finally catching her attention, her

stress seemed to fade away when she looked at me. It made me even more reluctant to go and guilty for leaving her to do this alone despite the fact that it was only for a few days. Even with River being in school, football season was always a rough time for us with my frequent absences and her long hours.

Palming my son's head in greeting and feeling his soft, brown curls under my palm, I moved to stand before my wife. "Good morning."

"Morning."

Tyra and I let the world pause long enough to share a kiss that deepened by the second. Our lives might be chaotic as fuck, but we still had this and more.

"We need to talk about this situation of ours when I get back."

"What situation?"

"About needing help with River. We need to hire someone."

Picking up her coffee mug, she stared at me over the rim with an amused twinkle in her eye. "We did discuss it, remember? And then we tried to find someone, but somehow, you find something wrong with each person we interviewed."

I waved her off as I headed for the fridge, where I knew I'd find my morning smoothie already waiting for me. *Goddamn it, I love this woman.*

"I don't care what you say," I said as I removed the tumbler. "That guy looked like a—" Glancing at River, who always seemed to hear more than he let on, I spelled out the word, "P-E-D-O-P-H-I-L-E."

"Mm-hmm. And the nice lady with all the amazing references? She was more than qualified."

"If she was so qualified and amazing, why did all the others let her go?"

Tyra shook her head, a wry smile twisting her lips. "You're impossible."

Coming to stand behind her, I fingered the diamond ring I'd

put on her finger four years ago. "And you promised to put up with it forever." I leaned down, and she lifted to meet me halfway before I pulled back. "So, the joke's on you."

Hitting my chest, she shoved me back, making me laugh.

River turned his head from the TV, letting me see his hazel eyes, a perfect combination of my jade and Tyra's whiskey, before deciding his parents weren't as entertaining as his favorite cartoon. River was like a damn zombie when the TV was on, but when it wasn't, he was a hurricane. He seemed to take an interest in sports whenever we went a few rounds in the backyard, but he was also wicked smart like his mother. A little *too* smart if you asked me. Some of the shit that came out of his mouth astounded me. The only peace we seemed to have was when the TV was on. Despite his miniature size when he was born, he was easily the tallest in his class, surpassing all of our hopes and expectations. None of it would have mattered, but I was grateful for this boon. Our son wouldn't spend the rest of his life paying for our mistakes.

"I've always meant to ask," I said even though it had been seven years. "Why River?"

Tyra looked up in surprise before biting her lip and turning around in my arms to stare at our son. "Because he was proof that no matter which way the water flowed, it would always lead me back to you. You were the definite course."

I sucked in a breath. Tyra had known, even when she resisted, that she'd be mine again, and I'd be hers. The doorbell rang, saving me from responding. No way could I have managed any more than the chaste kiss I placed on her head before stepping back and noticing the wrapped gift on the counter. I'd almost forgotten that today was my best friend's twenty-seventh birthday. Tonight, Tyra and River would be heading to Blackwood Keep for the surprise party that Four was throwing him. Warmth bloomed in my chest at the thought of home as I moved for the front door. Four and Ever had been the only one of us who hadn't left the place behind. The distance between us wasn't significant, but it felt as if we'd been spread to the four corners of the world.

With all of our busy schedules, it had been almost three years since I'd seen any of them. It went without saying that I missed them.

I began to consider how deep in shit I'd be in if I blew off the first game of the season, even though I was the goddamn quarterback, to be with my friends when I yanked open the front door. A woman was standing there in a white trench coat and large rose-tinted sunglasses that covered her eyes. Her hair was pulled back in a neat bun, and behind her, a Bentley and driver waited. In a word, she looked…pricey.

"Can I help you?" I said a little impatiently when she continued to stand there and stare. It wasn't unusual for a sports fanatic to find out where their favorite athlete lived, but this woman didn't look like a fan. No, she looked nervous as hell even though she'd been the stranger to ring my doorbell.

Tyra had grown curious by now, and I felt her presence hovering just as the woman's shaking, gloved hands rose, and she slowly removed her sunglasses. Any fear I had of too many years passing for me to recognize the woman who gave birth before abandoning me vanished. I knew before she could find the words to explain who she was.

"Mom?"

"For twenty years, I've thought of this moment and what I would say. Nothing seems quite adequate."

I just stood there, finding it even harder to form words. My father had been dead for seven years, and I hadn't heard a peep. I'd already written her off, written off the possibility that she would even want me.

Tyra moved to stand beside me, and with one hand on my arm, soothing the warring emotions inside, she shook my mother's hand with the other. "I'm Tyra Rees. Why don't you come in? It's so nice to meet you."

My mother's gaze flitted to me and then back to Tyra before nodding hesitantly.

"Tyra, what are you—"

"If you could give us a moment," she asked of my mother, who quickly disappeared off to God knows where. She was in for the shock of her life when she saw that I had a son of my own, one I would never abandon. Tyra reached up as if hearing my thoughts and held my face between both hands. "I know that you are scared shitless and angry as hell right now, but I'm here with you, and we'll get through this together. Do you believe me?"

I stared at my wife for the longest while. Tyra had given me seven years of bliss and not one moment of doubt, not one moment where I questioned if I'd made the right choice in not letting her slip through my fingers a second time.

"I believe you." Remembering how to use my limbs again, I wrapped my arms around her. "I also love you." My head was no longer heavy with the weight of the crown I'd been born with. Instead, my heart had been filled with a far greater honor—a husband and a father. I wouldn't fall or fail them now.

"I love you more."

"Good. Because, if this shit with my mother goes south, I'm not helping you clean up your mess." Hefting her onto my shoulder, I slapped her ass for good measure, making her shriek and giggle before I slammed the front door closed.

The rest of the world could wait.

Turn the page for an extended epilogue.

Jamie

"W HAT'S SHAKIN', CHIEF?"

Bernie, the building's doorman, who I'd gotten to know pretty well since Bee and I moved into the penthouse two years ago, smiled at my greeting. I'd only been CEO of NaMara for six months, having spent two years under my uncle's wing, training for the role after earning my MBA. Once Uncle Thomas felt I was ready, he stepped down and took with his wife with him to Ireland, where he was currently enjoying retirement. Repairing their marriage had taken some time, but without the lies and guilt between them, they were happier than ever.

"Nothing but my knees if your friend doesn't bring it home on Sunday," Bernie replied, reminding me of Vaughn's game this weekend. I wasn't much of a sports fan, but I made sure to watch him whenever I could. "I bet two hundred on the game."

"Well then, you're definitely screwed. You should have bet more."

I clapped him on the back before heading inside. I was eager to see Barbette, who'd been out of town on business. Bee's YouTube channel had been just the start, and it wasn't just because I'd actually flashed my dick to her subscribers. The inspiration women initially sought her out for turned into empowerment, and before I knew it, I found it harder and harder to keep her all to myself. Not without burdening my conscience and not to mention, I was proud as fuck of her.

I entered the elevator and took the long ride up to the top floor. I was more eager than ever for the summer—for many reasons.

The doors slid open, and I stepped inside. Bee's luggage was waiting by the entrance, making me giddy as fuck.

"Barbette!" I removed my suit jacket and then loosened my tie as I moved deeper into the apartment. "Get your ass out here, woman. Daddy's home."

I waited a moment and then two before she appeared, her blue eyes ablaze. "Do you mind? I almost got your son down to sleep. Now he's wide awake, thanks to you."

Closing the distance, I kissed her like a man who hadn't seen his wife in three days should. Pulling away for air, I whispered against her lips, "You and I both know he wasn't counting a single sheep until he saw me."

I plucked our six-month-old baby from her arms, and he started bouncing, all happy as fuck, as soon as I got him in my hands.

"You missed Daddy, Lyric?"

I stared into his brown eyes as he made random noises and drooled all over himself. It was safe to say that I made some cute as fuck babies. He even had my mahogany hair. I ruffled it as I carried him to the nursery. It was anyone's guess where Selma, our nanny, had disappeared to. Bee followed me and watched with her arms crossed and a smirk as I struggled to get Lyric's hyper ass down to sleep. I loved him, but he could be such a cockblocker sometimes. I was eager to celebrate the news Bee had purposely waited until she was boarding our private jet to share.

"Come here," I ordered as soon as Lyric finally shut his goddamn eyes. I pulled her down the hall to our bedroom before closing the door. "How are you feeling?"

"Good," she said, blushing like we were still eighteen and too stubborn to admit that we were in love. "It's still early."

I rested my hand on her stomach where baby number two was cooking. I made a mental note to contact the builder and request they make the nursery in our home bigger. Lyric was still young, so I didn't see any need to separate the two of them just yet—extra time for them to bond. Perhaps, I'd tell the contractor in person tomorrow since tonight we were heading to Blackwood Keep for Ever's birthday party. How long had it been since I'd seen my cousin? I shook the thoughts from my head, focusing on the beautiful woman in front of me now instead.

"Thank you for this."

"You're welcome. I didn't think I would be, but I'm pretty excited myself. I hope it's a girl."

"Nah," I told her as I reluctantly took my hand away and started opening the buttons on her blouse. "It's a boy, and he's a junior for sure."

Bee stared up at me as if I had shit on my face. "Jameson John Jr.? Are you kidding me?"

I grinned down at her. "You promised me I could name this one."

"But it sounds so backwoods!"

I kissed her, and she melted in my arms like butter. I didn't give a damn what anyone thought. That was my kid, which automatically made him epic. I removed her jeans, panties, and bra before pulling her over to our king-size bed. Laying her on the plush comforter, I stared down at her as I slowly removed my clothes.

"Two down, eight to go," I told her.

She stopped me when I tried to climb on top of her. "Jamie, we are not having ten kids. I don't care how rich you are or how many nannies you hire."

Leaning down, I kissed her nose because she was so darn cute when she was mad. "I'm sure we can come to some kind of arrangement. How about nine?"

"Three."

"Eight."

She sighed as I settled between her legs. "Five. Final offer."

"Deal," I said quickly, making her eye me skeptically.

"That was your real number all along, wasn't it?"

I lifted her leg into the crook of my arm before sliding inside of her. "Maybe." She growled, but then it was cut short when I hit the spot deep inside of her. "Fuck, I missed you, Bee."

"Oh, yeah? Well, show me how much, and stop fucking me like I'm fragile."

I immediately stopped moving as I stared down at her, feigning offense. "It's called making love."

She dug the heels of her pumps into my ass, the only item of her clothing I hadn't removed, propelling me faster.

All right then.

An hour later, we were showered and dressed and kissing our son good night before heading out into the New York night.

"You look beautiful, baby." I kissed the side of her neck as I held the door of the limo that was waiting to drive us to Blackwood Keep open for her. "And I can't wait to make more babies and grow old and gray with you."

Bee kissed my lips before pulling back to peer at me. "Are you just sucking up so I'll agree to the name Jameson John Jr.?"

I laughed because there was no such thing as getting anything past my wife. "You got me." Leaning forward, I whispered in her ear. "But you should know…I'd rather go down than suck up."

Blushing, she stepped away from me before peeking over her shoulder with heat in her eyes. "Well then, you better get started, Mr. Buchanan."

"Right away, Mrs. Buchanan."

Eagerly, I followed Bee into the car, pressing the button for the partition before the limo even took off.

Lou

Sunset Bay

"LICENSE AND REGISTRATION, PLEASE."

Peering up from the open window, I forced myself to smile and act normal despite the load of trouble I was undoubtedly in. Sunset Bay, where Wren and I had found our forever home, was a small town. Nothing ever got by anyone. Especially my husband. I had still been adjusting to small-town life when Wren relocated us here shortly after our home in Blackwood Keep became a crime scene. It had been a hard choice, moving away from our friends, but we were all comforted by the fact that there were only a couple of hours separating us. Less depending on traffic. For a while, we'd stayed with Winny, twiddling our thumbs until Wren and I had a long, *long* talk. And somehow, during that discussion, we both figured out what to do with the rest of our lives. The first step, since we were both high-school dropouts, had been getting our GED.

"Officer, is something wrong?"

"License and registration," he ordered more firmly. Grumbling, I reached into my glove compartment before handing both over. He didn't even bother looking at them as he pinned me under his glare. "Do you know how fast you were going?"

"I don't know, but I'm sure you're going to tell me."

Anger and something akin to retribution flared in the man's blue eyes. "Sixty-five."

"Is that bad?"

"It is when the posted speed limit is thirty miles per hour, ma'am."

"Oh…" I pretended to think it over before snapping my fingers. "Shoot, you know what probably happened? The pedometer on this old thing has been a little trippy," I said as I patted Paula's steering wheel. "She's well past her prime, but my husband loves her." I pouted then. "Probably more than me."

The man's lips twitched as his brown hair blew in the wind. "I'm sure that's not even a little true."

"Oh, for sure, he does. He waxes her twice a day even if we don't take her out."

"So, this car belongs to your husband?"

"Maybe."

The cop perked a brow as he leaned his forearm on the roof of the car. Inhaling his scent, my panties flooded with arousal, and I prayed I didn't ruin my pencil skirt. Driving all the way back home was out of the question. "You don't know how fast you were going, and you don't know who the car belongs to, but I bet you know that he'll be pissed as *fuck* if he finds out you're speeding around town in his ride."

I folded my forearms on the open window and fluttered my lashes. "But I don't think he'll be upset, officer."

"Is that right?"

"Yes…because my husband doesn't have to find out." Daring to reach my hand out, I ran a finger down his chest, feeling his muscles and heat underneath the white button-up. "I'm sure we can come to some kind of arrangement. The back seat is pretty spacious. My husband and I tested it out a few times ourselves."

"I'm sure we can," he said with a smile, "and it's Lieutenant."

"That's impressive," I returned with a smile of my own. Letting my hand trail over his belt buckle and his badge, and then the smooth material of his dress pants, I massaged the bulge growing there. I couldn't wait to feel it inside of me. "But not as impressive as this."

"What will your husband think of you rubbing my dick?"

"He doesn't have to know about this, either, *Lieutenant*."

Surprisingly, he gripped my wrist, stopping me from unzipping his pants and pulling him out. I was ready to suck him off through the window somehow if I had to. "Are you sure you have time now, or is there somewhere you have to be?"

"Shit!" I jerked my hand back inside, remembering that I'd been speeding because I was running late for my first day of work. "Sorry, but I'm going to have to take a rain check."

He silently handed over my license and registration before bending down to kiss me deeply. The rest of the world and the fact that I was late faded away once more. "No more speeding," he ordered before pecking me once more. "I mean it."

I placed the side of my hand to my hairline in a mock salute. "Yes, sir!"

Wren immediately stilled. "Louchana."

"Okay, I won't speed anymore," I whined.

"I know you won't because I'm following you," Wren announced, already backing away from the Impala.

"Is that really necessary, officer?"

"It's Lieutenant," he shot back, reminding me of his recent promotion.

"What's the difference? All you pigs look alike to me!"

Shooting a rare and gorgeous smile, Wren simply shook his head as he stalked for the all-black Charger. When he first graduated from the academy, I went from jumping his bones whenever he was in uniform—holy hell, he looked damn good—to giving him a hard time.

I was so proud of the steps Wren had taken not just to turn over a new leaf but to right the wrongs of his past. Wanting him to feel that same pride I felt, I turned a few leaves myself though it had taken me a whole lot longer. I'd only just recently obtained my master's degree in social work, and today was my first day on the job. Did I mention that I was already late as hell?

Still, I sat there for a few moments more, watching Wren climb into his ride. He pulled up beside me and lowered his passenger window, probably wondering why I hadn't already taken off yet.

"Race you there?" I joked, making him scowl. "Kidding! See you at home?"

My husband nodded his head toward the road ahead, ordering me to get a move on. True to his word, Wren followed me while I drove with one hand resting on my belly. I smiled to myself, impatiently waiting for this day to be over so that I could finally tell Wren the good news. He'd been my best friend turned lover and now husband.

I had no doubt he'd make a wonderful father.

Four

Blackwood Keep

INHALED DEEPLY ONCE AGAIN AS I WATCHED THE WOMAN OUTSIDE planting flowers. The small garden surrounding her was beautiful—a hobby, no doubt, that required passion as well as patience. Rosalyn and I were both surprised by her green thumb. It had done her so much good. To focus on something other than finding love in all the wrong places. She'd even come to a few of my races. The biggest thing, however, was when she'd contacted my father, telling him all about me. The months that followed had been trying. I was still getting to know my father and my younger half brother, but the distance made it somewhat difficult.

I took another deep breath before forcing myself to step through the sliding door. I'd been so confident about this next step I was about to take that I'd made Ever keep his plans to visit his father in prison. He'd been visiting Sean ever since his father was sentenced to fifteen years for manslaughter. Though harsh, Ever and Wren's testimony that he had been defending them had kept Sean from facing the rest of his life in prison for murder. He was even up for parole in a few months as long as he kept on his good behavior. After slowly repairing their relationship with their son, Thomas and Evelyn had run away together to Ireland to work on their marriage.

Hearing me approach, Rosalyn looked up, a soft smile covering her face when she saw me. It had been years, and it still felt like getting hit by lightning. I was buzzing with warmth and just a little bit frazzled. She quickly set down the hoe she'd been using to make a new hole for the flower pot next to her and stood.

"Four, it's good to see you."

A few small steps, and she was hugging me. I inhaled the

floral scent of her hair and wondered if it had always smelled this good.

"Hey," I greeted when she finally pulled away. "I hope I'm not interrupting?"

My hands began to shake as I itched to call Ever. I couldn't do this. At least, not alone. I needed him.

"Nonsense." Noticing my nervousness, she gently pulled me over to the patio table and chairs she'd set out among her plants. "Lemonade?" She gestured toward the pitcher that still had condensation dripping down its sides.

"I'm fine. Thanks." My mouth was dry, and I could definitely use some, but I was terrified I'd only throw it up. Running my hands down my bare legs since I was wearing a yellow sundress, I forced the words out of my mouth. "I actually came to talk to you about something. Something important."

"Oh?" Rosalyn looked as startled as I felt.

Before either of us could say anymore, the glass door leading to the patio opened, and Ever appeared, still dressed for work at the high-end architect firm he now managed. The sigh of relief I released was audible, but I didn't care. He was here.

"You okay?" he asked me after he'd strolled over and kissed me.

"Better now. What about your father?"

Ever smiled at that. "I'm sure he'll understand. He can hear about our news next week."

Right…today was Ever's birthday, and tonight was his party. At least, that was what we'd told all of our friends when we invited them. They'd been hounding us to marry, and tonight, we were finally announcing our engagement.

Neither of us missed the uncomfortable expression on Rosalyn's face. It was gone as quickly as it had come, but we didn't bother explaining that I'd meant Sean, not Thomas. Even though she'd moved on from Thomas, breaking up their relationship to work on his marriage, I could imagine seeing Ever and I together felt like being flayed raw all over again. After all, if it hadn't been for Rosalyn and Thomas, Ever and I would have never met.

Ever took the seat next to me and turning back to Rosalyn, I forced a smile. *"We,"* I began, rephrasing, "would like to ask you something."

Just as I felt like I was going to be sick again, I felt Ever's hand on my protruding belly and our daughter growing inside. I looked at him, and he smiled his encouragement. I was so afraid. Afraid that I was asking too much and afraid of what it might do to her. I didn't want to be responsible for Rosalyn's first relapse in years. We were so close, for the first time, to a real mother and daughter relationship. I didn't want to mess that up, but I knew of no other way to finally bridge the gap between us. Something more concrete than a mere olive branch. A foundation.

"Four," Rosalyn said, sensing my trepidation and taking my trembling hand. "I've given you no reason to believe me, but...I want you to know that it's going to be okay. I'm here, and I won't fall apart on you ever again."

Ever's hand drifted down to my thigh, giving it an encouraging squeeze. There was so much love and strength packed into such a simple gesture. It was like he'd released all of the pent-up air trapped inside of my lungs. I held my mother's gaze and felt my shaking body settle, seeing the assurance there.

"We wanted to ask if you'd name our baby?"

And they all lived happily ever after...

The crew huddled together outside the hospital room, eagerly waiting for Bee to give birth. It was the last child any of them would ever have. Well into their thirties, their careers, and their family life, the friends were all pretty damn sure they were done reproducing.

Tyra and Vaughn stood together next to River, who was holding Raven, his sleeping baby sister, in his arms. After fifteen years of living in Boston, Tyra and Vaughn had finally moved their family back to Blackwood Keep. Tyra, after completing her fellowship, was offered a position as a heart surgeon at the Susannah Blackwood Medical Center. Vaughn, on the other hand, decided to hang up his cleats and, with his mother's help, was now thinking of ways to commandeer Blackwood Keep from his corrupt family.

Wren and Lou were still living in Sunset Bay and now had two kids of their own, Luke and Lucy. Unfortunately, Lou had insisted that both of their names sound like hers.

Four and Ever were still living in Blackwood Keep. They'd made the Manor, as Four still called it, their home. It had been a gift from Thomas, who was still retired in Ireland with Evelyn... and Sean. None of the friends knew why Four and Ever decided on having only one child, but no one could deny that their daughter was well-loved. Erica was a perfect combination of the two in every way. Four no longer raced and instead built a track in Blackwood Keep for anyone looking to follow their dreams or have a good time. Ever now headed his own architectural firm.

Jamie often hired Ever's firm for the hotels and resorts he was still putting up all around the globe. Bee now had her own makeup and lingerie line. How she did it with Jameson and their four boys running her ragged no one could quite pinpoint, but they were all proud and happy for her. As predicted, their brood was all spaced a year apart with the exception of their fifth, who'd eluded them for years. Jamie and Bee also moved back to Blackwood Keep before the birth of their second child. Unfortunately, they did name him Jameson John Jr. Lyric was the oldest with their twins, Saint and Justus, being the youngest—until today. So confident in their fifth child being a boy, as well, Jamie had foregone learning the sex and had been walking around with his chest poked out, more insufferable than usual, for the entire pregnancy.

A cry drifted into the hall from the hospital room, washing away the exhaustion from all of the friends and the families they had made. They'd been waiting for hours.

"Congratulations on your new bundle of joy, Mr. Buchanan."

"What the—yo, doc, where's his dick?" Jamie yelped.

Bee's voice, though laden with exhaustion, also held traces of humor and triumph. "Baby, I'd like you to meet Summer. Your *daughter*."

acknowledgments

Three years. That's how long I've been writing these characters so not only does it hurt to say goodbye, but I've accumulated quite a few people to thank. I'll start with the team who made this book bearable to read. Rogena and Colleen, can you believe I made my deadline this time? It must be snowing in hell. Thank you for your editing powers and finding the rhyme and reason to my madness. Amanda, you've been battling some tough issues this past year and still you managed to make my dreams come true with the covers and anything else I needed. Thank you for being a friend and shit-talking with me when I needed it. Stacey, you're amazing as always. Every time I hold one of my paperbacks in my hands, I'm in awe of you. You're the best in the business and anyone who says differently can fight me. Thank you for being patient with me. I seem to only know what I need *after* I've sent the book to you. I'd like to thank Tijuana, Sunny, and Sarah for just being there when I need you. I don't ever have to think twice before flooding your inbox with voice messages and corny jokes. Janese, thank you for coming through at the last minute. Jamie, thank you for keeping Reiderville together whenever I'm off writing. I hope you both find some peace soon. And thank you to Reiderville for constantly giving me the courage to write more books. I'd be nothing without you. Last but not least, I'd like to thank my family and friends for being my tempered glass—not easily broken.

contact the author

Follow me on Facebook
www.facebook.com/authorbbreid

Join Reiderville on Facebook
www.facebook.com/groups/reiderville

Follow me on Twitter
www.twitter.com/_BBREID

Follow me on Instagram
www.instagram.com/_bbreid

Subscribe to my newsletter
www.bbreid.com/news

Visit my website
www.bbreid.com

Text REIDER to 474747 for new release alerts
(US only)

about

B.B. REID

B.B. Reid is the author of several novels including the hit enemies-to-lovers, *Fear Me*. She grew up the only daughter and middle child in a small town in North Carolina. After graduating with a Bachelors in Finance, she started her career at an investment research firm while continuing to serve in the National Guard. She currently resides in Charlotte with her moody cat and enjoys collecting Chuck Taylors and binge-eating chocolate.